DESECRATION

*Also by Tim LaHaye
and Jerry B. Jenkins
in Large Print:*

Left Behind
Tribulation Force
Nicolae
Soul Harvest
Apollyon
Assassins
The Indwelling
The Mark

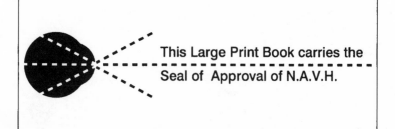

This Large Print Book carries the
Seal of Approval of N.A.V.H.

Antichrist Takes the Throne

DESECRATION

TIM LaHaye

JERRY B. JENKINS

Thorndike Press • Waterville, Maine

Published in 2002 by arrangement with Tyndale House Publishers, Inc.

Thorndike Press Large Print Basic Series.

The tree indicium is a trademark of Thorndike Press.

The text of this Large Print edition is unabridged. Other aspects of the book may vary from the original edition.

Set in 16 pt. Plantin by Elena Picard.

Printed in the United States on permanent paper.

Library of Congress Cataloging-in-Publication Data

LaHaye, Tim F.
  Desecration : Antichrist takes the throne / Tim LaHaye, Jerry B. Jenkins.
    p. cm.
  ISBN 0-7862-3861-5 (lg. print : hc : alk. paper)
  1. Steele, Rayford (Fictitious character) — Fiction.
2. Rapture (Christian eschatology) — Fiction.
3. Antichrist — Fiction. 4. Israel — Fiction. 5. Large type books. I. Jenkins, Jerry B. II. Title.
PS3562.A315 D47 2002
813'.54—dc21   2001056504

To Murf, Timmy Mac, and Mary,
with gratitude

Special thanks
to David Allen
for expert technical consultation

Forty-Two Months into the Tribulation; Twenty-Five Days into the Great Tribulation

The Believers

Rayford Steele, mid-forties; former 747 captain for Pan-Continental; lost wife and son in the Rapture; former pilot for Global Community Potentate Nicolae Carpathia; original member of the Tribulation Force; international fugitive; on assignment at Mizpe Ramon in the Negev Desert, center for Operation Eagle

Cameron ("Buck") Williams, early thirties; former senior writer for *Global Weekly*; former publisher of *Global Community Weekly* for Carpathia; original member of the Trib Force; editor of cybermagazine *The Truth*; fugitive; incognito at the King David Hotel, Jerusalem

Chloe Steele Williams, early twenties; former student, Stanford University; lost mother and brother in the Rapture; daughter of Rayford; wife of Buck; mother of fifteen-month-old Kenny Bruce; CEO of International Commodity Co-op, an underground network of believers; original Trib Force member; fugitive in exile, Strong Building, Chicago

Tsion Ben-Judah, late forties; former rabbinical scholar and Israeli statesman; revealed belief in Jesus as the Messiah on international TV — wife and two teenagers subsequently murdered; escaped to U.S.; spiritual leader and teacher of the Trib Force; cyberaudience of more than a billion daily; fugitive in exile, Strong Building, Chicago

Dr. Chaim Rosenzweig, late sixties; Nobel Prize–winning Israeli botanist and statesman; former *Global Weekly* Newsmaker of the Year; murderer of Carpathia; incognito, the King David Hotel, Jerusalem

Leah Rose, late thirties; former head nurse, Arthur Young Memorial Hospital, Palatine, Illinois; on Trib Force assignment en route to Mizpe Ramon

Hattie Durham, early thirties; former Pan-Continental flight attendant; former personal assistant to Carpathia; on Trib Force assignment in Israel

Al B. (aka "Albie"), late forties; native of Al Basrah, north of Kuwait; pilot; former international black marketer; assisting Rayford at Mizpe Ramon

David Hassid, mid-twenties; high-level director for the GC; presumed dead in plane crash; actually en route to Mizpe Ramon

Mac McCullum, late fifties; pilot for Carpathia; presumed dead in plane crash; actually en route to Mizpe Ramon

Abdullah Smith, early thirties; former Jordanian fighter pilot; first officer, Phoenix 216; presumed dead in plane crash; actually en route to Mizpe Ramon

Hannah Palemoon, late twenties; GC nurse; presumed dead in plane crash; actually en route to Mizpe Ramon

Ming Toy, early twenties; widow; former guard at the Belgium Facility for Female Rehabilitation (Buffer); AWOL from the GC; Strong Building, Chicago

Chang Wong, seventeen; Ming Toy's brother; new employee, Global Community Headquarters, New Babylon

Lukas ("Laslos") Miklos, mid-fifties; lignite-mining magnate; lost wife, pastor, and pastor's wife to Nicolae Carpathia's guillotines; in hiding, Greece, United Carpathian States

Gustaf Zuckermandel Jr. (aka "Zeke" or "Z"), early twenties; document forger and disguise specialist; lost father to guillotine; fugitive in exile, Strong Building, Chicago

Steve Plank (aka Pinkerton Stephens), fiftyish, former editor of *Global Weekly*; former public relations director for Carpathia; assumed dead in wrath of the Lamb earthquake; undercover with GC Peacekeeping forces

Unknown male, fifteen; escaped loyalty mark center in Ptolemaïs, Greece, with Albie's and Buck's help; whereabouts unknown

Unknown female, sixteen; escaped loyalty mark center in Ptolemaïs, Greece, with Albie's and Buck's help; whereabouts unknown

10

Nicolae Jetty Carpathia, mid-thirties; former president of Romania; former secretary-general, United Nations; self-appointed Global Community potentate; assassinated in Jerusalem; resurrected at GC palace complex, New Babylon; visiting Jerusalem

Leon Fortunato, early fifties; former supreme commander and Carpathia's right hand; now Most High Reverend Father of Carpathianism, proclaiming the potentate as the risen god; in Jerusalem with Carpathia

Prologue

From **The Mark**

"We can all keep our fingers crossed," Mac said. "I've seen those Quasis do amazing things based solely on what the flight management system onboard computer tells it to do. But this is a long flight on its own, and I've asked it to do some interesting stuff, barring turbulence."

"Cross our fingers?" Hannah said. "Only God can make this work. You're the expert, Captain McCullum, but if this thing goes down anywhere but deep in the Mediterranean, it won't take long for someone to discover no one was aboard."

This plane was not free-falling toward the Mediterranean. No, this multimillion-Nick marvel of modern technology was accelerating, her burner cans hot, the vapor shimmering in a long trail. The strange attitude and angle sent the craft careening toward the shore approximately three-quarters of a mile south of the crowd.

The Quasi and ostensibly her two-man crew and two passengers slammed the beach perfectly perpendicular at near the speed of sound. The first impression of the shocked-to-silence crowd had to be the same as Buck's. The screaming jet engines still resonated even after the plane disintegrated, hidden in a billowing globe of angry black-and-orange flames. An eerie silence swept in, followed less than half a second later by the nauseating sound of the impact, a thundering explosion accompanied by the roar and hiss of the raging fire.

Buck hurried to his car and phoned Rayford. "The ship is down on the shore. No one could have survived it. On my way back to the voice that will cry in the wilderness."

Buck was struck by an unusual emotion as he merged into traffic that crawled toward the ancient city. It was as if he had seen his comrades go down in that plane. He knew it was empty, yet there had been such a dramatic finality to the ruse. He wished he knew whether it was the end of something or the beginning of something. Could he hope the GC was too busy to thoroughly investigate the site? Fat chance.

All Buck knew was that what he had endured in three and a half years was a walk in the park compared to what was coming. The entire drive back he spent in silent prayer for every loved one and Trib Force member. Buck had little doubt that the indwelt Antichrist would not hesitate to use his every resource to quash the rebellion scheduled to rise against him the next day.

Buck had never been fearful, never one to back down in the face of mortal danger. But Nicolae Carpathia was evil personified, and the next day Buck would be in the line of fire when the battle of the ages between good and evil for the very souls of men and women would burst from the heavens, and all hell would break loose on earth.

Then I heard a loud voice from the temple saying to the seven angels, "Go and pour out the bowls of the wrath of God on the earth."

So the first went and poured out his bowl upon the earth, and a foul and loathsome sore came upon the men who had the mark of the beast and those who worshiped his image.

Revelation 16:1–2

One

Rayford Steele slept fitfully and awoke tangled in a prickly woolen blanket, knees drawn to his chest and fists balled under his chin. He bolted from the cot and peered out of his tiny makeshift quarters near Mizpe Ramon in the Negev Desert.

The sun cast an eerie, orange glow, but it would soon grow harsh and yellow, shimmering off rock and sand. The thermometer would exceed 100 degrees Fahrenheit by noon — another typical day in the United Carpathian States.

Engaged in the riskiest endeavor of his life, Rayford had cast his lot with God and the miracle of technology. There was no hiding a jury-rigged airstrip on the desert

15

floor — not from the stratospheric cameras of the Global Community. Ridiculously vulnerable, Rayford and his ragtag team of flying rebels — having arrived by the dozens from around the globe — were at the mercy of the most audacious ruse imaginable.

His comrade in the enemy's lair had planted evidence in the Global Community database that the massive effort at Mizpe Ramon was an exercise of the GC's. As long as GC Security and Intelligence personnel bought the great "lie in the sky," Rayford and his extended Tribulation Force would continue what he called Operation Eagle. The name was inspired by the prophecy in Revelation 12:14: "The woman was given two wings of a great eagle, that she might fly into the wilderness to her place, where she is nourished for a time and times and half a time, from the presence of the serpent."

Dr. Tsion Ben-Judah, spiritual mentor of the Tribulation Force, taught that the "woman" represented God's chosen people; the "two wings," land and air; "her place," Petra — the city of stone; "a time," one year — thus "a time and times and half a time" to be three and a half years; and the "serpent," Antichrist.

The Tribulation Force believed that Antichrist and his minions were about to attack Israeli Christ-followers and that, when they fled, Rayford and his recruited fellow believers would serve as agents of rescue.

He dressed in a khaki shirt and shorts and went looking for Albie, his second-in-command. The helpers, rallied via the Internet by Rayford's daughter, Chloe, from the safe house in Chicago, had only recently finished the landing strip. They had alternated shifts; some were instructed in flight plans by the same personnel who had checked them in and verified the mark of the believer on their foreheads, while others ran heavy equipment or toiled as laborers.

"Here, Chief," Albie said, as Rayford took in the row after row of helicopters, jets, and even the occasional prop plane lining the far side of the strip. "First mission accomplished."

The small, dark, former black marketer, nicknamed after his home city of Al Basrah, wore his bogus GC deputy commander uniform and had in tow a large young man who, Rayford was not surprised to learn, was from California.

"George Sebastian," the tall, thick blond said, extending a powerful hand.

"Rayf—"

"Oh, I know who you are, sir," George

17

said. "Pretty sure everybody here does."

"Let's hope nobody outside here does," Rayford said. "So you're Albie's choice for chopper lead."

"Well, he, uh, asked that I refer to him as Commander Elbaz, but yes, sir."

"What do we like about him?" Rayford asked Albie.

"Experienced. Smart. Knows how to handle a bird."

"Fine by me. Wish I had time to socialize, George, but —"

"If you have just another minute, Captain Steele . . ."

Rayford glanced at his watch. "Walk with us, George."

They headed to the south end of the new airstrip, Rayford's eyes and ears alert for unfriendly skies. "I'll make it quick, sir. It's just that I like to tell people how it happened with me."

"It?"

"You know, sir."

Rayford loved these stories, but there was a time and place for everything, and this was neither.

"Nothing dramatic, Captain. Had a chopper instructor, Jeremy Murphy, who always told me Jesus was coming to take Christians to heaven. 'Course, I thought he was a nutcase, and I even got him in trouble for proselytizing on the job. But he wouldn't quit. He was a good instructor, but I didn't want a thing to do with the other stuff. I was loving life — newly married, you know."

"Sure."

"He invited me to church and everything. I never went. Then the big day happens. Millions missing everywhere. Smart as I'm supposed to be, I actually tried calling him to see if my session was called off that day 'cause of all the chaos and everything. Later that night somebody found his clothes on a chair in front of his TV."

Rayford stopped and studied George. He would have enjoyed hearing more, but the clock was ticking. "Didn't take you long after that, did it?"

George shook his head. "I went cold. I felt so lucky I hadn't been killed. I prayed, I mean right then, that I would remember the name of his church. And I did, but hardly anybody was there. Anyway, I found somebody who knew what was going on, they reminded me what Murphy had been telling me, and they prayed with me. I've been a believer ever since. My wife too."

"My story's almost the same," Rayford said, "and maybe one of these days I'll have time to tell you. But —"

19

"Sir," the young man said, "I need another second."

"I don't want to be rude, son, but —"

"You need to hear him out, Cap," Albie said.

Rayford sighed.

George pointed to the other end of the airstrip. "I brought samples of the cargo that's followin' me, soon as the strip can handle a transport."

"Cargo?"

"Weapons."

"Not in the market."

"These are free, sir."

"Still —"

"Our base trained for combat," George said. "When Carpathia told the nations to destroy 90 percent of their weapons and send the other 10 percent to him, you can imagine how that went over."

"The U.S. was the largest contributor," Rayford said.

"But I'll bet we also held on to more."

"What've you got?"

"Probably more than you need. Want to see the samples?"

David Hassid sat in the front passenger seat of the rented van with his solar-powered laptop. Leah Rose was driving. Behind her, Hannah Palemoon sat next to Mac McCullum, while Abdullah Smith lay on his back across the third seat. They had spent the night hidden behind a rock outcropping a mile and a half off the main road, midway between Resurrection Airport in Amman, Jordan, and Mizpe Ramon. The last thing they wanted was to lead the GC to Operation Eagle.

David found on the Net that he, Hannah, Mac, and Abdullah were still presumed dead from the airplane crash in Tel Aviv the day before, but Security and Intelligence personnel were combing the wreckage. "How soon before they realize we're at large?" Hannah said.

Mac shook his head. "I hope they assume we'd a been vaporized in a deal like that. Pray they find small bits of shoes or somethin' they decide is clothing material."

"I can't raise Chang," David said, angrier than he let on.

"I imagine the boy's busy," Mac said.

"Not for this long. He knows I need to be sure he's all right."

"Worryin' gets us nowhere," Mac said. "Look at Smitty."

David turned in his seat. Abdullah slept soundly. Hannah and Leah had hit it off and were planning a mobile first-aid center at the airstrip. "We all fly back to the States when the operation is over," Leah said.

"Not me," David said, and he felt the eyes of the others. "I'm going to Petra before anybody else even gets there. That place is going to need a tech center, and Chang and I have already put a satellite in geosynchronous orbit above it."

His phone chirped, and he dug it from his belt. "Hey," he heard. "You know where I am, because I'm on schedule."

"You don't need to talk in code, Buck. Nothing's more secure than these phones."

"Force of habit. Listen, somebody missed their rendezvous."

"Just say who, Buck. If we were going to be compromised, it's happened already."

"Hattie."

"She was with Leah in Tel Aviv. Then she was supposed to —"

"I know, David," Buck said. "She was to check in with me at dawn today in Jerusalem."

"The old man's there and okay?"

"Scared to death, but yeah."

"Tell him we're with him."

"No offense, David, but he knows that, and Hattie is a much bigger problem."

"She's got her alias, right?"

"David! Can we assume the obvious and

deal with the problem? She's supposed to be here, but I haven't heard from her. I can't go looking for her. Just let everybody know that if they hear from her, she needs to call me."

"She crucial to your assignment?"

"No," Buck said, "but if we don't know where she is, we're going to feel exposed."

"The GC lists her deceased, just like us."

"That could be what they want us to think they believe."

"Hang on," David said, turning to Leah. "What was Hattie supposed to do after you two split up?"

"Disguise herself as an Israeli, blend into the crowd in Tel Aviv, go to Jerusalem, check in with Buck, and watch for signs that Carpathia's people recognized either Buck or Dr. Rosenzweig."

"Then?"

"Lie low in Jerusalem until everything blew up there, then head back to Tel Aviv. Someone from the operation was going to pick her up and fly her back to Chicago while all the attention was on Jerusalem and the escape."

David turned back to the phone. "Maybe she got spooked in Tel Aviv and never got to Jerusalem."

"She needs to let me know that, David. I've got to hold Chaim's hand for a while here, so inform everybody, will you?"

A few minutes after midnight, Chicago time, Dr. Tsion Ben-Judah knelt before his huge curved desk at the Strong Building and prayed for Chaim. The former rabbi's confidence in his old mentor's ability to play a modern-day Moses was only as strong as Chaim's own. And while Rosenzweig had proved a quick and thorough study, he had left the United North American States still clearly resisting the mantle.

Tsion's reverie was interrupted by the low tone on his computer that could be triggered by only a handful of people around the world who knew the code to summon him. He struggled to his feet and peered at the screen. "Dr. Ben-Judah, I hope you're there," came the message from Chang Wong, the teenager David had left in his place at Global Community headquarters in New Babylon. "I am despairing for my life."

Tsion groaned and pulled his chair into place. He sat and pounded the keys. "I am here, my young brother. I know you must feel very much alone, but do not despair. The Lord is with you. He will give his angels charge over you. You have much to do as the point man for all the various activities of the

Tribulation Force around the world. Yes, it is probably too much to ask of one so young, in years and in the faith, but we all must do what we have to. Tell me how I can encourage and help you so you can return to the task."

"I want to kill myself."

"Chang! Unless you have purposely jeopardized our mission, you need feel no such remorse. If you have made a mistake, reveal it so we can all adapt. But you have satellites to manipulate and monitor. You have records to keep in order, in case the enemy checks the various aliases and operations. We are nearly at zero hour, so do not lose heart. You can do this."

Chang's message came back: "I am in my room at the palace with everything set up the way Mr. Hassid and I designed. My machinations are filtered through a scrambler so complex that it would not be able to unravel itself. I could end my life right now and not affect the Tribulation Force."

"Stop this talk, Chang! We need you. You must stay in position and adjust the databases depending upon what we encounter. Now, quickly, please, what is the problem?"

"The problem is the mirror, Dr. Ben-Judah! I thought I could do this! I thought the mark that was forced on me would be an advantage. But it mocks me, and I hate it! I want to take a razor blade and slice it from my head, then slit my wrists and let God decide my fate."

"God has decided, my friend. You have the seal of God upon you, according to our trusted brothers. You did not *accept* the mark of Antichrist, nor will you worship him."

"But I have been studying your own writings, Doctor! The mark of the beast brings damnation, and the Bible says we can't have both marks!"

"It says we cannot *take* both."

"But the heroes, the martyrs, the brave ones accepted death for the sake of the truth! You said a true believer would be given the grace and courage to stand for his faith in the face of the blade."

"Did you not resist? God is no liar. I have told people that they cannot lose the mark of the seal of God and that they need not worry they will lose heart because of their human weakness, but that God will grant them peace and courage to accept their fate."

"That proves I am lost! I did not have that peace and courage! I resisted, yes, but I did not speak out for God. I cried like a baby. My father says I pleaded fear of the needle.

When it became clear they were really going to do this, I *wanted* to die for my faith! I planned to resist till the end, though I knew my father would then find out about my sister and expose her too. Right up until the time they stuck me, I was prepared to say no, to say that I was a believer in Christ."

Tsion slumped in his chair. Could it be true? Was it possible God had not given Chang the power to resist unto death? And if not, was he not truly a believer? "Do me this favor," he tapped in slowly. "Do not do anything rash for twenty-four hours. We need you, and there must be an answer. I do not want to gloss over it, for I confess it puzzles me too. Will you stay at the task and fight your temptation until I get back to you?"

Tsion stared at the screen for several minutes, worried he was already too late.

Rayford's breath caught when he saw what George Sebastian had apparently already shown Albie. "We're not soldiers," he said. "We're flyers."

"With these you can be soldiers too," George said. "But it's your call."

"I wish it were *my* call," Albie said. "If Carpathia's troops are not our mortal enemies . . ."

George handed Rayford a weapon more than four feet long that weighed at least thirty-five pounds and had a built-in bipod. Rayford could barely heft it horizontally. "Carry it nose up," George said.

"I won't be carrying it at all," Rayford said. "What in the world kind of ammo does this thing take?"

"Fifty-caliber, Captain," George said, digging out a clip of four six-inch bullets. "They weigh more than five ounces each, but get this, they have a range of four miles."

"C'mon!"

"I wouldn't lie to ya. A round leaves the chamber at three thousand feet a second, but it takes a full seven seconds to hit a target two miles away, considering deceleration, wind, all that."

"You couldn't hope for any kind of accuracy —"

"It's on record that a guy put five rounds within three inches of each other from a thousand yards. At two hundred yards you can put one of these through an inch of rolled steel."

"The recoil must be —"

"Enormous. And the sound? Without an earplug you could damage your hearing. Wanna try one?"

"Not on your life. I can't imagine a use for

these monstrosities, and I sure wouldn't want to produce a sound that would alert the GC before the fun starts."

George pressed his lips together and shook his head. "Should have checked with you first. I've got a hundred of 'em on the way with all the ammo you'd need, some with incendiary tips."

"Dare I ask?"

"A primer inside makes the casing separate if it hits soft material."

"Like flesh?"

George nodded.

Rayford shook his head. "My flyers would never be able to manage these from the air, and that's top priority."

Albie said, "We'll store them. You never know."

"Wanna see the other?" George said.

"Not if it's anything like these," Rayford said.

"It's not." George carefully set the fifty-caliber back into the cargo hold. "These are designed to use from planes or ground vehicles," he said, producing a lightweight rifle and tossing it to Rayford. "No projectiles."

"Then what — ?"

"It's a DEW, a directed energy weapon. From a little under half a mile you can shoot a concentrated beam of waves that penetrates clothing and heats any moisture on the skin to 130 degrees in a couple of seconds."

"What does it do to a man's innards?"

"Not a thing. Nonlethal."

Rayford handed it back. "Impressive," he said. "And we appreciate it. My problem is, I don't have combat troops, and even if I did, we'd be no match for the GC."

George shrugged. "They'll be here if you need 'em."

Had the day's prospects not been so dire and Buck not so worried about Hattie's whereabouts, he might have chuckled at the sight of Dr. Rosenzweig. The old man opened his door to Buck's knock at the King David Hotel wearing baggy boxer shorts, a sleeveless T-shirt, and the sandals he was to wear with the brown robe. "Cameron, my friend, forgive me; come in, come in."

Buck was used to Rosenzweig's normal appearance: wiry, clean shaven, slight, in his late sixties, pale for an Israeli, and with hazel eyes and wisps of wild white hair reminiscent of pictures of Albert Einstein. Normally the decorated statesman and Nobel Prize winner wore wire-rimmed glasses, bulky sweaters, baggy trousers, and comfortable shoes.

Buck found it hard to get used to his old friend with burnt amber skin, very short dark hair, a bushy beard and mustache, deep brown contact lenses, and a protruding chin caused by a tiny appliance in his back teeth. "Zeke sure did a job on you," Buck said, aware that surviving a horrific plane crash had also left its effects on Chaim.

Dr. Rosenzweig retreated to a chair near where he had laid out his Bible and two commentaries, which he had hidden in his luggage for the flight from the United North American States. A half glass of water sat next to him on a lamp table. His roomy, hooded, monklike robe lay on the bed.

"Why not dress, brother?"

The old man sighed. "I am not ready for the uniform yet, Cameron. I am not ready for the task," Chaim said, his speech altered not only by the appliance but also from damage to his jaw.

Buck checked the closet and found a hotel robe. "Put this on for now," he said. "We've got a couple of hours."

Dr. Rosenzweig seemed grateful to be helped into the terry-cloth garment, but it was white and a one-size-fits-all. The contrast between it and his new skin color, and the hem bunching up on the floor when he sat again, made him look no less comical.

Chaim lowered his head, then looked at the hotel name on the breast pocket. "King David," he said. "Do you not think we should have 'Patriarch Moses' sewn onto the brown one?"

Buck smiled. He could not imagine the pressure on his friend. "God will be with you, Doctor," he said.

Suddenly Rosenzweig shuddered and slid to the floor. He turned and knelt, his elbows on the chair. "Oh, God, oh, God," Chaim prayed, then quickly tore off his sandals, casting them aside.

Buck himself was driven to his knees with emotion so deep he believed he could not speak. Just before he closed his eyes he noticed the rising sun reach between the curtains and bathe the room. He too slipped off his shoes, then buried his face in his hands, flat on the floor.

Chaim's voice was weak. "Who am I that I should go and bring the children of Israel out?"

Buck, despite the heat of the day, found himself chilled and trembling. He was overwhelmed with the conviction that he should answer Chaim, but who was he to speak for God? He had drunk in the teaching of Dr. Ben-Judah and overheard his counsel to

Chaim on the calling of Moses. But he had not realized that the dialogue had been burned into his brain.

Silence hung in the room. Buck allowed himself to peek for an instant before squeezing his eyes shut again. The room was so bright that the orange stayed in his vision the way Chaim's question lingered in the air. The man wept aloud.

"God will certainly be with you," Buck whispered, and Chaim stopped crying. Buck added, "And this shall be a sign to you that God has sent you: When you have brought the people out, you shall serve him."

The old man said, "Indeed, when I come to the remnant of Israel and say to them, 'The God of your fathers has sent me to you,' and they say to me, 'What is his name?' what shall I say to them?"

Buck pressed his fingers against his temples. "As God said to Moses," he said, " 'I Am Who I Am.' Thus you shall say to the children of Israel, 'I Am has sent me to you. The Lord God of your fathers, the God of Abraham, the God of Isaac, and the God of Jacob, has sent me to you.' This is God's name forever, and this is his memorial to all generations. 'The Lord God of your fathers has seen what has been done to you and will bring you up out of the affliction to a land of safety and refuge.' They will heed your voice; and you shall come to the king of this world and you shall say to him, 'The Lord God has met with me; and now, please, let us journey into the wilderness, that we may sacrifice to the Lord our God.' But the king will not let you go, so God will stretch out his hand and strike those who would oppose you."

"But suppose they will not believe me or listen to my voice?" Chaim said, so faintly that Buck could barely hear him. "Suppose they say, 'The Lord has not appeared to you'?"

Buck rolled onto his back and sat up, suddenly frustrated and impatient with Chaim. He stared at the old man kneeling there, and Buck's head was abuzz, his eyes full of the color permeating the room. Buck had not felt so close to God since he had witnessed Dr. Ben-Judah's conversing with Eli and Moishe at the Wailing Wall. "Reach out your hand and take the water," he said, suddenly feeling authoritative.

Chaim turned to stare at him. "Cameron, I did not know you knew Hebrew."

Buck knew enough not to argue, though he knew no Hebrew and was thinking and forming his words in English. "The water," he said.

Chaim held his stare, then turned and grasped the glass. The water turned to blood, and Chaim set it down so quickly that it sloshed onto the back of his hand.

Buck said, "This is so that they may believe the Lord God has appeared to you. Now take the water again."

Chaim timidly reached for the glass, and when he touched it, the blood became water, even on his hand.

"Now turn your hand toward God's servant," Buck said. Chaim set the water down again and gestured questioningly toward Buck. And Buck was paralyzed, unable even to move his lips.

"Cameron, are you all right?"

Buck could not respond, light-headed from having stopped breathing. He tried to signal Chaim with his eyes, but the man looked terrified. Chaim pulled his hand back to his chest, as if afraid of its power, and Buck dropped, gasping, his palms on the floor. When he had caught his breath, he said, "Then it will be, if they do not believe you, nor heed the message of the first sign, that they may believe the message of the latter sign."

"Cameron! I am sorry! I —"

But Buck continued, "And it shall be, if they do not believe even these two signs, or listen to your voice, that you shall take water from the river and pour it on the dry land. And the water which you take from the river will become blood on the dry land."

Buck sat back on his haunches, hands on his thighs, exhausted.

Chaim said, "But I am not eloquent, even now since God has spoken to me. I am slow of speech and slow of tongue."

"Who has made man's mouth?" Buck said. "Or who makes the mute, the deaf, the seeing, or the blind? Has not the Lord? Now therefore, go, and he will be with your mouth and teach you what you shall say."

Chaim turned away again and knelt at the chair. "O my Lord," he cried out, "is there no other you can send?"

Buck knew the story. But there was no Aaron. Tsion was at the safe house, not having felt led to help in person. The only other member of the Trib Force with Jewish blood, though he had grown up in Poland, was David Hassid, and he had his own special skills and assignment. Anyway, there was no time to disguise him. If David suddenly appeared in public, he would expose the others who were assumed dead in the plane crash — at least for now.

Buck waited for God to give him an answer for Chaim, but nothing came.

Two

Just before 9 a.m. and about an hour east of Mizpe Ramon, David told Leah to pull over. "I'm sorry, everyone," he said, "but I just got something from Tsion you need to hear, and I have to get a message to Chang. It's too hard with this thing bouncing in my lap."

"Better hide the van," Mac said. "We're pretty conspicuous."

Leah checked her mirrors, switched into four-wheel drive, and aimed toward the sand. Abdullah sat up, fastened his seat belt, and said, "You would think it was the end of the world."

"Hilarious," Mac said.

Leah stopped a couple of miles off the road in the shadow of a small crag and two scraggly trees. David set his machine on the seat and stood outside, leaning in. The others stretched, then gathered to hear him read Tsion's copy of his back-and-forth with Chang.

"That does not sound so good," Abdullah said. "What to do?"

"I'd take a tone with that boy," Mac said.

"Just what I was thinking," David said. "Somebody update Rayford while I'm working here."

"Got it covered," Mac said, flipping open his phone.

David wrote:

You've got time to interrupt Dr. Ben-Judah but not to check in with your immediate superior? You think this is a game, Chang? What happened to the smart-aleck know-it-all who was going to handle all this in his sleep? Nobody begrudges you your second thoughts and spiritual angst, but you had better come to grips with the fact that you accepted this assignment.

Bottom line, Chang, is that you don't have time for this right now. Too many people are counting on you, and the very success of a life-and-death operation is in your hands. Doing harm to yourself because you can't figure out why God might have let something happen would be the most royally selfish act you could conjure up.

Now as soon as I transmit this, I want a reply from you that you're still on the job. If it is not forthcoming, I'll be forced to initiate the codes that destroy your setup and all the stuff I built there and explained to you. You know we can't risk your doing yourself in and leaving evidence that something was amiss. We need to know Suhail Akbar's plans on investigating the crash site. You need to hack into Sandra's files and be sure we're up-to-date on Carpathia's schedule. And if he holds meetings anywhere you can tap into, you've got to direct that transmission to Chicago, to Mizpe Ramon, and to me. Where's the 216, who's flying it, and is Carpathia using it for meetings?

Hear me, Chang. Something you wrote to Dr. Ben-Judah reminded me of something you said to me about this whole dual mark thing. I know you didn't take it on purpose, though you wanted me to think you got used to it right away and see, as you called it, the "upside." But it's not so easy, is it, when we're all so new at this and something doesn't jibe with what God seems to say about it? Dr. Ben-Judah's the expert, and you've got him baffled, so I won't pretend to have an answer for you. But obviously something's not right, and I don't blame you for wanting to find out how God sees you now.

There's no doubt in my mind that nothing can separate you from God and his love, but you're not going to have peace until you know for sure what really happened that morning. Now, again, let me be clear: This is not your top priority. Most important for you is to complete the tasks I listed above and make sure we're all safe and still undetected. Last we knew, Carpathia was to make his public appearance in Jerusalem at 11:00 a.m. Carpathian time.

But once you're sure everything is under control and that we are all up to speed, try the coordinates I list below. It's a long shot, but I programmed in a string that might allow access to surveillance equipment I did not install. It's possible there's a record, video or audio or both, of what went on that day. The problem is that Building D was a maintenance facility that the brass rarely, if ever, visited. I didn't bother planting bugs there, but for all I know, something was already in place.

You told me in person, and Dr. Ben-

Judah a little while ago, that you were trying to get out of taking the mark and were even prepared to tell the truth right up to the time they "stuck" you. I took that to mean up to the time you were given the mark. Maybe that *is* what you meant, but that's not the way most people refer to the application of the tattoo and the embedding of the chip. I don't know. Maybe I'm reaching. But maybe something else was going on. You never told me what happened from the time you got to the basement of Building D until you got to my office. Do you remember? And if not, why not?

So, first, tell me you're there and doing your job. Give us everything we need. Then see what you can find for Building D. Answer back as soon as you've read this.

David transmitted the message, then let Mac read it before they headed off for Mizpe Ramon. Mac nodded. "How much time do you give him?"

David shrugged. "Not much, but I don't want to nuke the system because he's on a bathroom break either."

Within minutes of their return to the road, David had a reply from Chang: "Following orders. And, Mr. Hassid, I thought the mark was administered in the basement of the palace. Blueprints show Building D several hundred yards from here. I have no memory of having been there. And by being 'stuck,' I meant the anesthetic they gave me prior to the procedure. I thought that was done in the palace too."

Rayford was encouraged to hear how close the Quasi Two quartet and Leah were to Mizpe Ramon. He told Mac about the weapons George Sebastian was having flown in.

"Smitty will want to see those," Mac said. "He was a combat man before he flew fighters, you know."

Rayford hadn't known, and he could hear Abdullah in the background, demanding to know what they were talking about.

"Just keep a rein on that camel there, desert boy," Mac said.

"You watch it, Texas-cowboy boy. I will learn some slurs about you and torment your ancestors."

"Just a minute, Ray," Mac said. "Smitty, you mean my descendants. My ancestors are dead."

"So much the better. I will make them turn over in their tombs."

"Albie's a gun guy too," Rayford said.

"But I've had my fill. Anyway, I need both him and Abdullah in the air."

He was glad to hear of Leah and Hannah's plans, but he fell silent at the news that David wanted to precede everyone to Petra. In the background he heard Hassid say, "I wanted to tell him that myself, Mac."

But as Rayford turned it over in his mind, David's setting up Petra for Chaim and the Israeli believers made sense. He asked Mac what anyone knew about Carpathia's latest plans. Mac brought him up-to-date on the troubles with Chang.

"I need to know as soon as possible," Rayford said. "The parade or whatever you want to call it, the desecration, and the attack could all happen this week."

Buck carried his Corporal Jack Jensen GC Peacekeeper ID, but he wore civilian clothes and counted on his own new hair and eye color, not to mention his severely scarred face, to throw off anyone who might otherwise recognize him. He and Chaim left the King David by car at 9:30 and picked their way through heavy traffic to within walking distance of the Old City. Chaim's robe was gathered at the waist by a braid of rope, but the hem brushed the ground and hid his feet, making it appear he was gliding.

The two were soon enveloped by the masses who lined the Via Dolorosa, where Carpathia was expected an hour before noon. Buck was struck by the crowds, despite the waning population around the world. The city still showed residue from the earthquake that had leveled a tenth of it, but nothing stopped the opportunists. On every corner hawkers presented Carpathia memorabilia, including real and plastic fronds to toss before him as he would make what was becoming known as his triumphal entry.

Apparently, Nicolae Carpathia the pacifist was no more. Convoys of tanks, military trucks, fighters and bombers on flatbed trucks, and even missiles slowly rolled through the streets. Buck knew they wouldn't fit within the Old City without choking the tiny thoroughfares, but they were pervasive everywhere else.

Buck kept an eye out for Hattie and a hand on his phone, but he had long since despaired of a reasonable explanation for her disappearance. He tried not to think the worst, but reaching him or anyone else in the Trib Force should have been easy for her.

Chaim trudged along beside him, hunched, hands deep in the folds of his brown robe, his nearly bald head hidden by the hood. He had uttered not a word since the hotel-room experience. He had merely traded the King David terry cloth for the burlap-looking but soft flannel robe and slipped into his sandals.

It seemed the city was short of Peace-keepers, local or international. Many shop-windows were boarded up, and anything and everything served as a taxi, even dilapidated private vehicles. At the occasional open appliance store, TVs blared from the windows as onlookers gathered and gaped. Buck put a hand on Chaim's shoulder and nodded toward such a place. They joined the crowd to watch a replay of the crash of the Quasi Two, coverage of rubber-gloved technicians picking through the wreckage, and the somber statements from Potentate Carpathia, Most High Reverend Father Leon Fortunato, Supreme Commander Walter Moon and, finally, Security and Intelligence Director Suhail Akbar.

"Unfortunately," the latter said, "while the investigation continues, we have been unable to confirm the evidence of any human remains. It is, of course, possible that four loyal patriots of the Global Community were vaporized upon impact in this tragedy. Medical personnel tell us they would have died without pain. Once we have confirmed the deaths, prayers will go to the risen potentate on behalf of their eternal souls, and we will extend our sympathies to their families and loved ones."

The news anchor intoned that further investigation revealed pilot error on the part of Captain Mac McCullum and that a New Babylon–based loadmaster had warned the crew of a cargo weight-and-balance problem and had begged them not to take off.

Buck knew he should dread what was coming, but having felt the presence of God at the King David, he was filled with courage. He didn't know how he and Chaim were going to avoid detection or what might happen once Carpathia had initiated his awful deed. He only wished he detected some evidence that Chaim had derived the same confidence from what had happened while they were on their knees.

David and the others in the van listened to Suhail Akbar's conclusions on the radio as Leah followed careful directions and pulled to within sight of the landing strip outside Mizpe Ramon. David was moved by the shock and sadness in the voice of Tiffany, his assistant, as she was interviewed about him. He wished he could tell her he was all right, but he feared some might already suspect that.

He embraced Rayford, shook hands with Albie, and introduced Hannah all around. As the rest were briefed on plans wholly dependent on the unpredictable Carpathia, David was pointed to Rayford's quarters, where he cleared a table and set up his computer to monitor Chang Wong's success at keeping up with the potentate.

The young man had succeeded in getting the latest copy of Carpathia's itinerary. It showed a meeting including NC, LF, WM, SA, and LH on the FX at 1000 hours. "I know that's now," Chang reported, "but I'm lost after the initials for the four we know. Help?"

"I don't know LH either," David wrote back, "but come on, smart boy. Go phonetic and assume FX is the Phoenix and patch me in there."

"I've got the Akbar press conference downloaded. You want that first?"

"Priorities, man! The press conference was broadcast internationally."

David rustled through his bag for earphones and was slipping them on just as Chang made the connection to the Phoenix. He felt the ambience of the idle plane, and Chang transmitted an inset screen listing

GC replacements for David, Mac, and Abdullah. "A. Figueroa for you," Chang wrote. "Know him? Apparently they're not replacing Nurse Palemoon. Still no idea who LH is."

"No need to prolong this meeting with Hut." That was clearly Carpathia. "Get on with it."

"Right away, Excellency," Moon said. "Leon, uh, Reverend Fortunato would like to update you on the image and the animal."

"I just saw him. Where is he?"

"The head, sir. Feeling some discomfort."

"What is the problem?"

"I don't know."

"He was sitting right here a moment ago, Walter."

"Squirming."

"About what?"

"I'm sorry, sir. I —"

"Well, find out, would you? And get Akbar and Hut in here now."

David heard Moon on a walkie-talkie, directing someone to "let Akbar and Hut board. And have the purser check on Reverend Fortunato."

"Come back?"

"Fortunato. First-class can."

Carpathia roared with laughter in the background. "An apt description, Mr. Moon!"

"I didn't mean that, sir. I was just —"

"Can we get on with this, Walter? Should Fortunato not find his way back here, what is he going to tell me about the image and the animal?"

"He didn't tell me, Lordship, but he seemed very excited."

"Until he went to the bathroom in discomfort."

"Exactly."

After a few seconds of silence, Carpathia barked, "Walter, tell Suhail if he does not have his new man aboard in thirty seconds —"

"Supreme Potentate Carpathia, sir, Security and Intelligence Director Suhail Akbar of Pakistan and Global Community Morale Monitor Chief Loren Hut of Canada."

Akbar said, "Forgive the delay, Potentate, but —"

"Sit, both of you. Director Akbar, where did you find this tall specimen and why is he not still a rodeo cowboy in Calgary?"

David noticed that Carpathia had pronounced the city with emphasis on the second syllable, just like the locals.

"I enjoy ropin' dissidents more," the young man said.

Carpathia laughed. "I was not speaking to you, Chief Hut, but —"

"Sorry."

"— you saved yourself with that answer. Got everything you need?"

"Yes, sir."

"Yes, *Potentate*," Carpathia corrected. "*Sir* will not cut it when addressing your risen —"

"Absolutely, Excellency, Lordship, Potentate. I was told. I just misspoke there."

"You would *mock* me?"

"No, sir! Potentate!"

"I asked you a question."

"I would not mock —"

"Whether you have what you need, imbecile! Honestly, Director Akbar, this is the best we could do?"

"He is quite accomplished and decorated, Excellency, and merely too intimidated in your presence to exhibit the loyalty he's known for."

"Indeed?"

"Yes, sir, Potentate. I'm loyal to you and always have been."

"And you worship me?"

"Whenever I can."

Carpathia chuckled. "Is every Morale Monitor armed, Hut?"

"Here in Israel, yes, they are. And everywhere else, they will be by the end of next week."

"Why the delay?"

"The sheer numbers. But we have the

weapons. It's just a matter of getting 'em to everyone."

"Your top priority is here, Hut. You understand that."

"Absolutely."

"And then it is to arm every one of your troops."

"Yes."

"What is the male-female ratio among the monitors?"

"About sixty-forty males, Excellency."

"About?"

"It's almost exactly fifty-eight to forty-two."

"Excellent. Leon! You're back!"

"Forgive me, Lordship."

"Sit, please. Meet —"

"I'd rather stand, if you don't mind, Excellency. And I have met Mr. Hut. Impressive young man."

"Yes, well, I am glad you find him so. I will decide for myself by the end of next week when I learn whether he has accomplished his task. And I will be interested to know how he handles incorrigibles here."

"In Israel, sir, Potentate?" Hut said.

"That is what 'here' would mean, yes."

"I just can't imagine anybody givin' you a problem here, but if they do —"

David heard Carpathia suck in a breath.

"Yes!" he hissed. "Tell me, Hut, what you have in store for people who would be so impudent as to oppose me here in the Holy City."

"They would be immediately apprehended and incarcerated!"

"Wrong!" Carpathia shouted. "Wrong answer! Akbar, I swear, if you do not —"

David could hear Akbar whispering urgently. Then an earnest Loren Hut: "I would have them killed, Potentate. On the spot. Or I would kill them myself!"

"And how would you do this?"

"Probably shoot them."

"Where?"

"In the street. In public. In front of everybody."

"I mean, where on their body?"

"Their body?"

"Where would you shoot them?" Carpathia was speaking quickly now, his delivery liquid, as if savoring the mere thought.

"In the heart or in the head, Potentate, for a sure kill."

"Yes! No! You have how many rounds in your personal side arm?"

"Me? I'm carryin' a semiautomatic handgun with a nine-round clip."

"Use it all!"

"All?"

"Start with the hands. First one, and when they grab it, the other. As they scream and dance and turn and try to flee, shoot first one foot, then the other."

"I see."

"Do you? As they lie howling and others abandon them in fear, you still have five rounds, do you not?"

"Yes." Hut sounded terrified.

"Both knees, each shoulder. Particularly painful. Make them change their mind, Hut. Make them say they love me and that they are sorry they opposed me. And you know what to do with the final round."

"Heart?"

"A cliché! No creativity!" David heard the leather seat squeak and imagined Carpathia shifting to act this out. "You put the hot muzzle of the weapon to their forehead, right where their mark should be. And you ask if they are prepared to pledge their loyalty. And even if they scream to the heavens that they have seen the light, you give them their own mark. It will be the only round they do not hear or feel. And then what?"

"And then?"

"What do you do, Hut? With a dead victim at your feet, nine rounds in or through the body, surely you do not leave the carcass in the street."

"No, I'd have him hauled off."

"To the guillotine!"

"Sir? Potentate?"

"The price of disloyalty is the head, Hut!"

"But they are —"

"Already dead, of course. But the world is clear on the choice and the consequence, friend. Dead or not, a disloyal citizen sacrifices his head."

"All right."

"Did you know, Hut, that when a live victim is beheaded, the heart can continue to beat for more than half an hour?"

Apparently Hut was stunned to silence.

"It is true. That is a medical fact. Well, we would not be able to test it with a victim you riddled with bullets, would we?"

"No."

"But one day we will get the chance. I look forward to it. Do you?"

"No."

"You do not? I hope you are not too timid for your job, son."

"I'm not. I'll shoot your bad guys and chop their heads off, but I don't need to check the other victims to see if their —"

"Do you not? I do! This is life and death, Hut! Nothing is purer! I have come to give life! But to the one who chooses to place his loyalty elsewhere? Well, he has chosen death. What could be so stark, so clear, so black-and-white?"

"I understand, Potentate."

"Do you?"

"I think so."

"You will."

"Yes."

"Now go. Big week ahead. Be prepared."

David, chilled and disgusted, scribbled himself a note. It would be just like Carpathia to milk this for days.

He heard Carpathia tell Moon to see Akbar and Hut out and to leave him alone with Fortunato. "Excuse us for a moment, would you?" he said to others apparently attending to them in the cabin. After a beat, "Leon, do you not agree that fear is a form of worship?"

"In your case, certainly, Excellency. The fear of our god is the beginning of wisdom."

"I like that. Biblical, is it not?"

"Yes, Lordship."

"Sit, Leon, please!"

"I'd like to, but — well, all right."

Leon let out a tiny cry as he settled.

"What is it, my friend? Food disagreeing with you?"

"No, excuse me, but —"

Carpathia snickered. "A true friend feels

free to scratch himself in front of his risen potentate."

"I am so sorry, Excellency."

"Think nothing of it. You are in such discomfort because your hip itches?"

"I'm afraid it's more than that, sir. But I'd rather not —"

"Bring me up-to-date on your assignments, then."

"The animal is in place."

"You may feel free to call it what it is, Leon."

"The pig."

"Oh, I hear it is much more than a pig. A hog! A sow! A huge, ugly, snorting, smelly beast."

"Yes, sir."

"I cannot wait to see it."

"Anytime you wish."

"Well, I am due aboard her not long from now, am I not?"

"Yes, sir. But you would have slipped off."

"Would have?"

"I had a saddle made for you, Excellency."

"Leon! You do not say! A saddle for a pig?"

"And the biggest pig I've ever seen."

"I should hope so! How did you do it?"

"People are happy to serve you, Potentate."

"It must be wide."

"I worry you will feel as if you are doing the splits."

"You look as if *you* would like to, Leon. Stand if you must. There you go! And yes! Scratch if you must!"

"I'm so sorry, Excellency."

"Why, you are wriggling like a schoolboy at his first dance!"

"Forgive me, I'd better head back to the —"

"Go then, by all means. What is it? A bite? An itch can be terribly annoying."

"I wish that's all it was, Excellency. It's quite painful too. When I scratch it, it hurts worse. I am miserable."

"You must have been bitten."

"Perhaps. Excuse me."

"Go!"

"I wanted to tell you about the image."

"And I want to hear it, but I cannot stand to see you in such agony."

"I will return before you must leave and tell you about it."

David sat shaking his head. How he wished he could see what was going on. But the theater of the mind was that much better anyway. Carpathia called someone to fetch Walter Moon, and then he had Moon "bring me that costume."

Moon told him the caravan to Pilate's court would be leaving inside ten minutes. "Did Reverend Fortunato run down the sites for you?"

"No. He seems to be in considerable discomfort."

"Still? Well, we go from Pilate's court to the street. A ways down we have Viv Ivins in place to meet with you as a stand-in for your mother." David heard the rustle of paper — a map, he assumed. "Here's where we have a young woman come out and wipe your face; then two stops later you exhort the women of Jerusalem. And then, after Golgotha, you see Viv again, playing your mother. Then it's on to the Garden Tomb."

Someone seemed to be making a sound through his teeth, and David couldn't imagine Moon doing that in front of Carpathia. Finally Nicolae said, "All right, cut out half of these. This part, and that one with Viv, and this, and the one with the young woman and the speech to the women, this one, and the last one with Viv."

"May I ask —"

"The point is reenacting, Walter. Half of these never happened."

"We don't know that. They're tradi—"

"They never happened. Believe me. I know."

"You'll want to change clothes now?"

58

"As soon as Leon is finished in the — ah, Leon! Feeling better?"

"Sadly, no."

"So what is it?"

"I'd rather not talk about this with you, sir."

"Nonsense! So is it a bite?"

"I don't think so, sir. But it's large and painful and infected."

"And it is right there?"

"Yes." Leon sounded miserable.

"Poor man! A sore on your left —"

"Yes. On my, uh — on my behind."

Carpathia seemed to be stifling a giggle. "You must tell me about the image."

"On the way, sir. I was hoping you'd notice."

"Notice?"

"My mark."

"Let me see! On your hand! Striking! Two-one-six! Excellent. Thank you, my friend. Does it hurt?"

"I wouldn't know. Because of the, uh —"

"Yes, well . . ."

"Anyway, I'll show you the chosen image. It's life-size and gold and beautiful. And when I had taken the mark of loyalty, I fell before it and worshiped."

"Bless you, Leon. And may you heal quickly."

Three

Hattie knelt in her hotel room in Tel Aviv, thanking God for all she had learned from Tsion Ben-Judah in such a short time. She thanked him for Leah and for Chaim and especially for Buck, whom she had met even before he became a believer. She thanked God for Rayford, who first told her about Christ. She thanked him for Albie who, for some reason, cared so much for her.

As she prayed, she became aware of someone standing in her room. Here she was, one who always checked everywhere before locking herself in. No one else could have been there. Yet the sound of his words made her lower her face to the floor as if in a deep sleep. Suddenly a hand touched her, which made her tremble. And a voice said, "O daughter, you are greatly beloved of God. Understand the words I speak to you, and stand upright, for I have been sent to you."

Hattie had read Dr. Ben-Judah's story of being spoken to in a dream, and she stood, shaking. The voice said, "Do not fear, for from the first day you humbled yourself before your God, your words were heard. I have come because of your words."

"May I know who speaks to me?" Hattie managed.

"I am Michael."

Hattie was too terrified to say anything eloquent. She said, "What are you supposed to tell me?"

He said, "I have come to make you understand what will happen in these latter days." Hattie felt so privileged she couldn't say anything. And Michael added, "O daughter greatly beloved, fear not! Peace be to you; be strong, yes, be strong! Accept not the blasphemy of the evil one and his false prophet. If you are wise, you shall shine like the brightness of the firmament. Those who turn many to righteousness shall shine like the stars forever and ever. Many shall be purified, and made white and refined, but the wicked shall do wickedly; and none of the wicked shall understand, but the wise shall understand."

Hattie sat panting. She took the message to mean she was to speak out against the lies of Antichrist. She prayed that God would give her the courage, because she could only imagine what would happen. She couldn't sleep and asked God if she was deluded. "Why me?" she said. "There are so many older in the faith and better equipped to do such a thing."

Hattie went to her computer and e-mailed Dr. Tsion Ben-Judah, relaying the entire incident. She set the message to be delivered to him after she would have a chance to confront Carpathia the next day, along the Via Dolorosa, she assumed. She concluded,

Perhaps I should have consulted you rather than scheduling this to be sent to you after the fact, but I feel directed to exercise faith and believe God. I look at what I've written and I don't even sound like myself. I know I don't deserve this any more than I deserved God's love and forgiveness.

Maybe this is all silly and will not happen. If I chicken out, it will not have been of God and I will intercept this before it gets to you. But if you receive it, I assume I will not see you until you are in heaven. I love you and all the others, in Christ.

Your sister,
Hattie Durham

Rayford gathered the troops at the airstrip. He introduced the Fatal Four and explained their roles. "Deputy Commander Elbaz," he said, referring to Albie, "will ferry Mr. Hassid to Petra, where he will begin setting up the communications center. Jewish by blood, Mr. Hassid plans to stay with the displaced believers."

A hand went up, an African's. "Is Hassid the one we have to thank for being able to stand here today?"

"Among many," Rayford said. "But it's safe to say that without the GC thinking this is their own operation, we'd be getting strafed right now."

Someone else asked, "How realistic is it that this can last?"

"We're in no-man's-land," Rayford said. "Once the fleeing Israelis are followed here, it will be obvious what we are doing. As you know, the healthy will walk. But it is quite a journey, and the GC should quickly overtake them. We believe God will protect them. The elderly, the toddlers, and the infirm will need rides. You will recognize them by the mark of the believer and probably also by the fear on their faces. Anyone arriving here in any manner should be transported immediately to Petra by helicopter. Some of these birds have huge capacities, so fill 'em up. Petra is about fifty miles southeast of here. You all have the flight plans."

"It sounds like a death flight," someone called out.

"By any human standard, it is," Rayford said. "But we are the wings of the eagle."

"The co-op didn't call for food or clothing," someone said. "How will these people survive?"

"Anyone want to address that?" Rayford said, and several talked over each other, explaining that God would provide manna and water and that clothes would not wear out.

Finally Rayford raised a hand. "One thing we don't know is timing. Carpathia is on schedule to begin down the Via Dolorosa at 1100 hours. That will end at the Garden Tomb. Whether he will speak from there or head for the temple, we don't know. We've heard that the winning image of the potentate has been chosen and moved to the Temple Mount, where people are already gathering to worship it and take the mark of loyalty."

"Of the beast, you mean!"

"Of course. And many want to do that with Carpathia present. When he learns the crowds are waiting for him, he'll want to be there."

"Are your people in place, Captain Steele?"

"As far as we know. The only one we have not heard from is not crucial to the operation, unless she has been compromised."

"When will Carpathia be opposed?"

"Our man may debate him before he enters the temple. Who knows? The crowd may oppose him — at their peril, of course. You must remember, it is not just Jewish and Gentile believers and unbelievers in Jerusalem. There are also Orthodox Jews who do not embrace Jesus as their Messiah but who have never accepted Carpathia as deity either. They could very well oppose him and refuse to take the mark. Then, of course, there are many undecided."

"They'll decide soon, won't they?"

"Likely," Rayford said. "And many will decide the wrong way. Without Christ, they will succumb to fear, especially when they see the consequences of opposing Carpathia. Okay, it's time for transportation troops to head toward Israel. When the time comes, help anyone who needs it."

"And if we are stopped?"

"You're on your own," Rayford said.

"I'm going to tell them I'm on my way to get the mark of loyalty."

"That's lying," someone else shouted.

"I have no problem lying to Carpathia's people!"

"I do!"

Rayford held up a hand again. "Do what God tells you to do," he said. "We're depending on him to protect his chosen people and those who are here to help them."

Buck found a perch overlooking Pilate's court behind several thousand cheering supplicants. The elderly Rosenzweig appeared to gasp for breath without making a sound. Sweat appeared on his forehead, and Buck thought it a credit to Zeke that it did not affect the old man's phony color. This was more than makeup.

Still, Chaim had not spoken since they left the hotel, even when Buck merely asked how he was doing. He only shrugged or nodded. "You'd tell me, wouldn't you, if there was a problem?"

Chaim nodded miserably, looking away.

"God *will* be with you."

He nodded slightly again. But Buck noticed he was trembling. Was it possible they had chosen the wrong Moses? Could Tsion have miscalculated? Tsion himself would have been so much better, having spoken in public for so many years as a rabbi and a scholar. Chaim was brilliant and fluent in his own field, but to expect this ancient, tiny, quaking man with the weak — and perhaps now nonexistent — voice to call down the Antichrist, to rally the very remnant of Israel, to stand against the forces of Satan? Buck wondered if he himself would have been a better choice. Despite Chaim's almost comical getup, he appeared not even to be noticed by the crowd. How could he command an audience?

Buck had worried what he would say or do if GC Peacekeeping forces or Morale Monitors checked for his mark of loyalty. But loudspeaker trucks threaded their way through the streets, announcing that all citizens "are expected to display the mark of loyalty to the risen potentate. Why not take care of this painless and thrilling obligation while His Excellency is here?"

Many in the crowd already had the mark, of course, but others talked among themselves about where the nearest loyalty administration center was. "I'm taking mine at the Temple Mount today," a woman said, and several agreed.

Buck was amazed at the number of men and women who carried toddlers waving real and fake palm branches. Someone passed out sheets with the lyrics to "Hail Carpathia," and when people spontaneously broke into song, others assumed Carpathia had appeared and began a rousing ovation.

Finally Buck spotted a motorcade, led and followed by GC tanks topped with revolving blue and red and orange lights. Between the tanks were three oversized black vehicles. When the convoy stopped, a deafening cheer rose. The first vehicle disgorged local and regional dignitaries, then Most High Reverend Father Leon Fortunato in full clerical regalia. Buck stared as the man straightened his robe, front and back, and slowly continued smoothing it in back. Finally he kept his left hand just below his hip as he walked, clearly trying to hide it but unable to keep from massaging an apparently tender spot.

The second vehicle produced GC brass, including Akbar and Moon, and then, to a renewed burst of applause and waving, Viv Ivins. From more than a hundred yards away, she stood out among the dark-suited men. Her white hair and pale face appeared supported by a column of sky blue, a natty suit tailored to her short, matronly frame. She carried her head high and moved directly to a small lectern and microphone, where she held both hands aloft for silence.

All eyes had been on the third vehicle, its doors still closed, though the driver stood guard at the rear left and Akbar at the rear right, hand on the handle. Buck noticed that while the attention refocused on Viv Ivins, Leon went to work on his backside, riffling his fingers over the area. He couldn't stop, even when Ms. Ivins introduced him as "our spiritual leader of international Carpathianism, the Reverend Fortunato!"

He muted the applause with his free hand, then asked everyone to join him in singing. He began directing with both hands, but Buck wondered if anyone in the crowd missed it when he kept directing with the right hand and scratching with the left.

Hail Carpathia, our lord and risen king;
Hail Carpathia, rules o'er everything.
We'll worship him until we die;
He's our beloved Nicolae.
Hail Carpathia, our lord and risen king.

Buck felt conspicuous not singing, but Chaim seemed not to care what anyone thought. He merely bowed his head and stared at the ground. When Leon urged the people to "sing it once more as we welcome the object of our worship," people clapped and waved as they sang. Buck, ever the wordsmith, changed the lyrics on the spot and sang:

> *Fail, Carpathia, you fake and stupid thing;*
> *Fail, Carpathia, fool of everything.*
> *I'll hassle you until you die;*
> *You're headed for a lake of fire.*
> *Fail, Carpathia, you fake and stupid thing.*

Finally Suhail Akbar opened the car door with a flourish and a deep bow, and Carpathia bounded out alone. The crowds gasped, then roared and applauded at the youthful man wearing gold sandals and an iridescent white robe, cinched at the waist with a silver belt that seemed to glow with its own light source. As bodyguards in sunglasses and black suits, hands clasped before them, formed a half circle behind him, Nicolae stood with eyes closed, face beatifically pointed toward the clouds and palms outstretched as if eager to embrace everyone at once.

Buck stole a glance at Chaim, who merely squinted at Antichrist in the distance, his face a mix of sadness and disgust.

As the vehicles discreetly pulled away, a camouflage canvas-covered military truck slowly rolled to within twenty feet of Carpathia. Buck saw Fortunato kneel and reach under his robe to vigorously scratch his ankle.

Two uniformed GC Peacekeepers lowered a ramp from the truck; then one jumped onto the trailer and the other reached for a dangling rope. One pulling, the other pushing, they brought into view a monstrous pink sow that, despite its enormous bulk, daintily stepped down the ramp and turned slowly to face Carpathia. The animal, which had clearly been drugged, reacted lethargically to the mayhem.

A black leather strap with a flat leather pad and rounded, covered stirrups was fastened around its middle. Carpathia approached and cupped the pig's fleshy face in his hands, looking over his shoulder to the crowd, which was now laughing and whooping in frenzy. One of the Peacekeepers handed him what appeared to be a noose, which Carpathia draped around the sow's neck.

Then, with one hand on the rope and the hem of his own garment — which he hiked up to his knee — and the other steadied by a Peacekeeper, Nicolae placed his left foot in a stirrup and swung his right over the pig's back. He let go of the Peacekeeper's hand and smoothed his robe back down over his legs, held the rope with both hands, and looked again to the crowd for a response. The pig had moved not an inch under Nicolae's weight, and as he yanked on the rope, tightening the knot around its neck, the spindly legs felt for purchase on the pavement and slowly turned to move in the other direction. Nicolae waved as the crowd exulted.

"I don't get it!" a man in front of Buck said, his accent German. "What's he doing?"

"Putting all previous religions in their places, Friedrich!" his wife said, her eyes glued to the scene. "Even Christianity. *Especially* Christianity."

"But what's with the pig?"

"Christianity has Jewish roots," she said, still not looking at him. "What's more offensive to a Jew than an animal he's not allowed to eat?"

The man shrugged, and finally she turned to look at him. "It's hardly subtle."

"That's what *I'm* thinking! You'd think he'd have more class."

"Hey," she said, "you come back from the dead, and you can define class any way you want."

The spectacle was broadcast internationally on radio and television and via the Internet. David followed it on his computer as Albie helicoptered him toward Petra. Carpathia's brazenness shouldn't have surprised him, but with relatives in Israel and childhood memories of the place, the whole pageant gave him a headache. David's scalp itched, but he dared not scratch it. He pressed his palm over the healing area, which reminded him of Hannah's treating him. That, of course, reminded him of what he was doing when he had collapsed — searching for his missing fiancée in the aftermath of Carpathia's resurrection — and he felt the familiar ache for Annie. He would see her again in less than three and a half years, but that made the second half of the Tribulation seem even longer. If he stayed in Petra, it would be that long before he saw Hannah again too.

David envied Buck Williams and his marriage. He couldn't wait to meet Chloe, the brain behind the International Commodity Co-op. Besides creating an underground where believers would be able to buy and sell from each other when they were restricted from world markets, she had almost single-handedly brought together the personnel for Operation Eagle without having met them. In a cooler behind Albie was food enough to last David until the fleeing Israelis joined him. Maybe God would feed David with manna before the others arrived. He hoped bringing food was not evidence of faithlessness.

Chloe Williams had arranged for the shipment of the latest high-tech computer equipment from various parts of the world, and that too was in the cargo hold. David could only guess how long it would take him and Albie to unload. He studied an aerial sketch of the area and wondered where he would set up and where he would live. "This place sure doesn't look like it could house all the believers in Israel."

"It won't," Albie said. "We're estimating a million people will need refuge. Petra will hold about a quarter of that."

"What do you plan to do with the rest?"

"Expand the borders, that's all. The co-op has tents for the others."

"Will they be safe? Outside Petra, I mean?"

Albie shook his head. "There's only so much we know, brother. This is a faith mission."

At a little after three in the morning in Chicago, Tsion lay with his hands behind his head on the cot in his study. He fought sleep as he watched the broadcast on his computer monitor. Hearing voices in the commons area, he padded out to find Chloe, Kenny on her lap, watching television.

"Do you believe this?" he said.

"Dis!" Kenny said, and Chloe shushed him.

She pressed her lips together. "I wish I were there."

"You should be pleased with what God has allowed you to accomplish, Chloe. Every report says things are going like clockwork."

"I know. And I've learned what strangers can do when they have a bond."

Tsion sat on the floor. "The vehicle advance should be underway by now."

"It is," she said. "And it's one of the riskiest parts. We didn't have time to put GC insignias on the vehicles."

"God knows," Tsion said.

"Gott!" Kenny said.

"That's *God* in German, you know," Tsion said.

"I doubt he's bilingual," Chloe said. "But apparently Buck is. Never studied another language and now he's speaking Hebrew without even knowing it."

★ ★ ★

It was clear to Buck that Carpathia had decided not to address the crowds until either the Garden Tomb or the Temple Mount. All along the Via Dolorosa he confused many by skipping traditional sites, and the people sang and chanted and cheered. Chaim seemed to move more and more slowly, and Buck worried about his health.

The drugged pig was even weaker, however, and the milling throngs found it hilarious somehow when her front legs buckled and she dropped to her knees, nearly pitching Carpathia on his head. They laughed and laughed as aides rushed to help Carpathia off the animal. He formed a gun with his thumb and forefinger and pretended to pop the sow where she rested. Then he dragged a finger across his own neck, as if remembering the actual plan for the porker.

Nicolae strode on while the military truck pulled into view and half a dozen Peacekeepers worked on getting the pig back on four feet and into the trailer. The potentate jogged from the central bus station area up to the traditional site of Calvary, and it was all Buck could do to watch. He was grateful there was no mock crucifixion, but still it turned his stomach to see Carpathia stand at the edge of the Mount and again spread his arms as if embracing the world.

Suddenly Fortunato stepped beside his boss and tried to mimic his pose. He could hold it only so long before having to scratch his backside or his ankle. Some in the crowd seemed to develop sympathetic itches. "Behold the lamb who takes away the sins of the world!" Fortunato bellowed.

Buck gritted his teeth and looked away, noticing that Chaim's breath now came in short gasps.

The sky blackened, and people pulled their collars up and looked around for shelter. "You need not move if you are loyal to your risen ruler!" Fortunato said. "I have been imbued with power from on high to call down fire on the enemies of the king of this world. Let the loyalists declare themselves!"

Buck froze. While thousands jumped and screamed and waved, he stood stock-still, fearing that just about anyone would be able to tell he opposed Carpathia. Chaim crossed his arms and stared directly up at Fortunato, as if daring the man to strike him dead.

"Today you shall have opportunity to worship the image of your god!" Fortunato shouted, but he could be seen only when lightning flashed. Buck saw rapturous looks on the faces of the crowd. "But now you have opportunity to praise him in person! All glory to the lover of your souls!"

Thousands knelt and raised their arms to Nicolae, who remained with his hands outstretched, drinking in the worship.

"How many of you will receive the mark of loyalty even this day at the Temple Mount?" Fortunato implored, now scratching in three places, including his stomach.

Buck stared at the strobelike image of Carpathia's pitiful sycophant, wondering if he would be revealed and struck dead by the man whose power came from the pit of hell.

Thousands rose from their knees to wave, to assure the leader of Carpathianism that they would be there, taking the mark in the shadow of the image. That at least made Buck and Chaim less conspicuous.

"My lord, the very god of this world, has granted me the power to know your hearts!" Fortunato said. The people jumped and waved all the more.

"Not true," Chaim whispered. Buck leaned close. "Carpathia — Antichrist — Satan is not omniscient. He cannot tell his False Prophet what he himself cannot know."

Buck narrowed his eyes at Chaim. So this was it? This was the opposition? This was Moses standing against Pharaoh? Buck gestured as if Chaim should shout it out, make it clear. But Chaim looked away.

"I know if your heart is deceitful!" Fortunato said between claps of thunder, rubbing his body in the flashing light. "You shall not be able to stand against the all-seeing eye of your god or his servant!"

The hymn to Nicolae spontaneously erupted again, but Buck did not have the heart to sing even his own lyrics.

Suddenly the crowd fell deathly still, and the thunder diminished to low rolls that seemed to come from far away. Fortunato stood surveying the massive throng, still scratching, but his eyes piercing. Carpathia had somehow maintained his pose for several minutes. Heads and eyes turned toward a high, screeching voice from the base of Golgotha. The crowd evaporated from around a woman who stood pointing at Carpathia and Fortunato.

"Liars!" she railed. "Blasphemers! Antichrist! False Prophet! Woe unto you who would take the place of Jesus Christ of Nazareth, the Lamb of God who takes away the sin of the world! You shall not prevail against the God of heaven!"

Buck was stricken. It was Hattie! Chaim dropped to his knees, clasped his hands before his face, and prayed, "God, spare her!"

"I have spoken!" Fortunato shouted.

"Yours is the empty, vain tongue of the damned!" Hattie called out. She lifted her pointing finger from the two on the hill and raised it above her head. "As he is my witness, there is one God and one mediator between God and men, the man Christ Jesus!"

Fortunato pointed at her, and a ball of fire roared from the black sky, illuminating the whole area. Hattie burst into flames. The masses fell away, screaming in terror as she stood burning, mighty tongues of fire licking at her clothes, her hair, enveloping her body. As she seemed to melt in the consuming blaze, the clouds rolled back, the lightning and thunder ceased, and the sun reappeared.

A soft breeze made Hattie topple like a statue. People gaped as she was quickly reduced to ash, her silhouette branded onto the ground. As the fire died and the smoke wafted, Hattie's remains skittered about with the wind.

Fortunato drew the attention back to himself. "Marvel not that I say unto you, all power has been given to me in heaven and on the earth!" Carpathia carefully made his way down the Place of the Skull, and the silent crowds moved to follow. As people passed the smoldering ashes, some spit, and others kicked at the powdery stuff.

Buck was overwhelmed with memories of meeting Hattie, of introducing her to Carpathia. He turned and grabbed the praying Rosenzweig by the shoulder and yanked him to his feet. "That should have been you," he hissed. "Or me! We should not have left her with the responsibility!"

He let go of the man's robe and marched off toward the Garden Tomb, not caring whether Chaim kept up with him. If Rosenzweig would not accept the mantle, despite having been a believer even longer than Hattie, maybe Buck was being called to stand in the gap. He didn't know what Carpathia or Fortunato had in store for the tomb, but this time, if need be, he would be the one to oppose Antichrist.

Rayford hadn't felt as motivated or useful since he had first become a believer. Supervising the advance of his Operation Eagle troops, he had kept just an intermittent eye on what Carpathia was up to. It would be clear when Chaim revealed himself and sent the remnant toward refuge. That would be his cue to start watching for the return to

Mizpe Ramon and the airlift to safety.

But now his phone was alive with messages. He took Chloe's call first. "What was that?" she asked. "Clearly Fortunato zapped someone, but they didn't show who! Was it Chaim?"

"I don't know," Rayford said. "Let me call you back."

David reported the same thing just before Rayford heard from Mac and then Abdullah. "I'll call Buck," he told them.

But Buck wasn't answering.

David spent the next hour setting up near what he knew to be a "high place," a site used centuries before by pagans who believed they were sacrificing to their gods by being as close to heaven as possible. He was lonely already, Albie having headed back as soon as he was unloaded. David didn't know how long it would be before he was joined by as many as a million others. So far he had seen only from the air the stunning red-rock masterpiece of a city carved from stone. He couldn't imagine what it would look like from close-up when he had the time to explore.

No one seemed to know what happened with Fortunato and the crowd at Calvary, and David's occasional glances at the screen merely showed the crowds making their way to the Garden Tomb. Then he heard a tone and stood still in the lofty quiet of the high place. Someone was trying to reach him on his computer. David scrambled from a cave he had decided might be his first living quarters. He reached his computer and sat cross-legged before it. The play-by-play from Jerusalem droned on, commentators filling time before the next event, no one specific about what had gone on at the last site. He checked the encoded Operation Eagle site but found nothing new.

The tone sounded again, and he switched screens to receive a summons from Chang Wong in his apartment at the palace in New Babylon.

"I found the mother lode!" Chang had written. "Uploading so you can celebrate with me."

Supreme Commander Walter Moon was clearly not comfortable in front of a crowd, particularly the size of the one pressing around the Garden Tomb. A microphone and sound system had been hastily rigged up for him, and he read nervously from notes. Buck had been among the first to arrive, and he had lost Chaim.

The attitude of the crowd had changed.

The festive, eager anticipation had given way to dread, yet no one seemed to feel free to leave. They had seen the power delegated to Leon Fortunato, and surely no one wanted to give the impression they weren't following through on their commitment to taking the mark of loyalty.

"Thank you for being with us today," Moon began. "As you may know, I'm Global Community Supreme Commander Walter Moon, and I'm filling in temporarily for the Most High Reverend Father Fortunato as he goes on ahead to prepare for Potentate Nicolae Carpathia's address at the Temple Mount an hour from now."

"Is he all right?" someone called out.

"Oh, he's better than all right," Moon said, "judging by his performance at Golgotha." He apparently thought that would elicit a laugh, and when it didn't, he searched his notes again to find his place.

Buck called Chang. "We on secure phones, Mr. Wong?" he asked. "Be sure."

"Yes, sir, Mr. Williams, and I just communicated with Mr. Hassid by computer that —"

"Sorry, kid, no time. Check with Medical and see what's happening with Fortunato."

"I'm sorry?"

"What didn't you hear?"

"I heard you all right, sir, but I was under the impression you were with the pageant there in Jerusalem. That's where Carpathia and Fortunato are, along with —"

"Fortunato's disappeared and they're saying he's gone on ahead for preparations."

"I'm on it." Buck heard him tapping at a keyboard. "Good call, Mr. Williams," he said. Now reading, " 'Classified, top secret, director-level eyes only . . . Most High Reverend, blah, blah, blah, under care of palace surgeon in chief, mobile unit, Jerusalem, blah, blah.' Ah, here it is. 'Preliminary diagnosis rash, several boil-like epidermal eruptions, testing for carbuncles.' That's all that's here for now."

Four

Tsion worried about Chloe. She had a lot on her mind, sure, and the pressure had to be enormous. But she seemed so distracted. No doubt she dreaded Buck's being in yet another dangerous situation, but if Tsion had to guess, being so far from the action frustrated her. Everyone in the Trib Force had, at one time or another, tried to impress upon Chloe that she was among its most crucial members and that few people anywhere could do what she was doing. But she was a young woman of action. She wanted to be there in the thick of it. Tsion wished he could dissuade her.

He had enjoyed the respite from his uncomfortable cot, but while he and Chloe monitored the boring TV feed from Jerusalem, waiting for the fiasco to reach the Garden Tomb, Kenny had fallen asleep. Chloe looked at Tsion apologetically as she attempted to rise with the toddler in her arms. She poked out a free hand and he reached to pull her off the couch. As she made her way to Kenny's crib, Tsion thought he heard something from his study. Chang again?

He padded back and found a timed message composed two days before and sent automatically on a schedule determined by the sender. It read:

Dr. Ben-Judah,

Please pass this along to my brothers and sisters in Christ, old friends and new. I don't know what to make of it except that I believe I have been called of God to risk my life for the cause. It certainly was nothing I was seeking, and I hope you all know I have no grandiose view of myself.

I knelt to pray in my hotel room in Tel Aviv . . .

Tsion stood, his spirit recognizing that this was no frivolous imagining from a new believer. He bent over the screen and read, finally groaning and making his way back out to where Chloe was watching the end of a brief speech by Walter Moon. "I have forwarded a message to your computer that you need to read right away," he said, knowing his quavering voice scared her.

"Is it Buck?" she said. He shook his head. "Chaim?"

"No," he said. "Please wake the others. We will want to pray. And you will want to call Cameron."

David ignored the signal that he had a message from Tsion. That could wait as he checked the upload from Chang. Not only had the young man pieced together recordings from devices in the palace, starting in the Wongs' guest apartment the morning in question, but he had also taken the time to include a translation, where necessary, from Chinese to English. David would check the tape with Ming later to be sure the translation was accurate. Chang began with the news that he remembered "only snatches of this before the so-called anesthetic. You must have known they use no such thing."

David knew. But he hadn't known any more than Chang about what had really gone on. Chang's pieced-together production began with the audio of another loud

88

argument between him and his father. Mrs. Wong kept trying to pacify her husband and son, but she failed.

"You will be among the first to take the mark of loyalty!" the subtitles read, as David listened to Mr. Wong fiercely whisper to the boy in Chinese.

"I will not! You are loyal to Carpathia. I am not!"

"Do not speak such heresy to me, young man! My family is loyal to the international government as I have always been to my superiors. And now we know the potentate is the son of god!"

"He is not! I know no such thing! He could be the son of Satan for all I know!"

David heard a slap and someone crashing to the floor. "That was I," Chang wrote.

"You saw the man resurrected! You will worship him as I do!"

"Never!"

A door slammed. Then a phone call. "Missah Moon! Son talk crazy. Say he not want mark, but he just scared of needle. You got tranquilizer?"

"I can get a tranquilizer, Mr. Wong, but it comes in the form of an injection."

"Injection?"

"Shot. Hypodermic needle?"

"Yes! Yes! I can do."

"You can administer the injection?" Moon said.

"Pardon?"

"Give the shot?"

"Yes! You bring!"

They rang off, and Mr. Wong apparently returned to where Chang had locked himself in a room. "You be ready to go in ten minutes!"

"I'm not going!"

"You will go or answer to me!"

"I'm answering to you now. I'm telling you I'm not going. I don't want to work here. I want to go home."

"No!"

"I want to talk with Mother."

"Very well! Mother will talk some sense into you."

A few minutes later, a quiet knock. "Mother?"

"Yes." The door opened. "Son, you must do what your father says. We cannot survive in this new world without showing loyalty to the leader."

"But I don't believe in him, Mother. Neither does Ming."

A long silence.

"She doesn't, Mother."

"She told me. I fear for her life. I cannot tell your father."

"I agree with her, Mother."

90

"You are a Judah-ite too?"

"I am, and I will say so if he tries to make me take the mark."

"Oh, Chang, don't do this. I will lose both of my children!"

"Mother, you must read what Rabbi Ben-Judah writes too! At least look into it. Please!"

"Maybe, but you cannot cross your father today. You take the mark. If you are right, your God will forgive you."

"It doesn't work that way. I have already made my decision."

Mr. Wong returned. "Let's go. Mr. Moon is waiting."

"Not today," Mrs. Wong pleaded. "Let Chang think about it awhile."

"No more time for thinking. He will embarrass the family."

"No! I won't! You can't make me."

Silence. Mrs. Wong: "Please, Husband."

"Very well, then. I will tell Mr. Moon not today."

"Thank you, Father."

"But someday soon."

"Thank you for your patience, Husband."

It sounded as if both parents left. Then the door opened.

"Father?"

"You *will* think about it?"

"I have been thinking about it a lot."

The bed squeaked. "Father, I — ow! Don't! What are you doing? What's that?"

"Help you relax. You get some rest now."

"I don't need any rest! What did you do?"

"See? You are not so afraid of needles! That did not hurt."

"But what was it?"

"It will help you calm down."

"I'm calm."

"You rest now."

The door shut.

"How long take, Missah Moon?"

"Not long. Don't wait too long or he won't be able to walk by himself."

"Okay. You help."

They returned.

"Chang?"

"Mmm?"

"You come with us now?"

"*Who?*"

"Missah Moon and me."

"*Who?*"

"You know Missah Moon."

"No, I —"

"Come on now."

"I will not . . . take . . . the . . . mmm . . ."

"Yes, you will."

"No, I'm . . ."

The sound continued with the two men

encouraging Chang to walk with them and his mumbling in Chinese and English about not wanting to, refusing.

"Now, watch this," Chang wrote. "The surveillance camera from the hallway picks up that they're pretty much carrying me down the hall, and look what I'm doing! Crossing myself! I don't even know where I got that! And look! Here, I'm pointing toward heaven! I know it's impossible to prove what I was doing, since whatever they gave me made me forget even the conversation with my mother. And I can't tell what words I'm trying to form there, but I had to be trying to say I was a believer!"

The whole rest of the way, as Chang tied together the angles from various cameras all the way to the corridor leading to Building D, David watched as Walter Moon and Mr. Wong prodded Chang along. At some point a third man met them, carrying a camera. The boy wept, pointed, and tried to form words. Moon reassured the photographer and any onlookers that the boy was "all right. He's okay. Just a little reaction to medication."

Most shocking was that indeed there was a surveillance camera in Building D, and by the time they got Chang there, he was unconscious, eyes shut, drooling, moaning.

"Take cap off," his father said. "Smooth hair."

A woman technician who looked Filipino fired up the device. "This boy, he is all right?" she said.

"Fine," Moon said. "What's the region code for the United Asian States?"

"Thirty," the tech said, setting the implanter. "I worry that I might get into trouble for —"

"Do you know who I am?"

"Of course."

"I'm telling you to do your job."

"Yes, sir."

The woman swabbed Chang's lolling forehead with a tiny cloth and pressed the mechanism onto his skin, producing a loud click and whoosh. "Thank you," Moon said. "Now be sure this place is ready for the lines in about an hour."

The technician left, and Mr. Wong and Mr. Moon took turns keeping Chang sitting up. "Thing wears off almost as fast as it goes to work," Moon said.

"Fix hair more," Mr. Wong said, slapping Chang's cheeks. "We get picture."

The photographer shot Chang with a digital camera. The boy came to, and his father held the camera before his face. "There!" Mr. Wong said. "Look at new employee, one of first to take mark!"

Chang wobbled and pulled back, reaching for the camera and trying to focus on the picture. His shoulders drooped and he glared at his father, his face stony. When Mr. Wong and Mr. Moon stood him up, he said, "Where's my hat?"

He jammed it on and stood there until he regained his equilibrium. He said something to his father in Chinese. "I said, 'What have you done?' " he wrote.

"Someday you thank me," Mr. Wong said. "Now we go somewhere, relax till interview."

"I remember just snatches of the argument from the apartment and my father injecting me," Chang wrote. "I have a vague recollection of the flash of the camera and being angry at my father. After that, I only remember sitting awhile in a side room with Moon and my father and slowly realizing that I had been given the mark of loyalty. I wanted to kill them, but I was also embarrassed. I worried what you would think. I was still out of it for the first part of our meeting, but then I decided to play tough, try to make you see the benefits. You already know, though I didn't, that the meeting in your office was recorded too. I can send that if you need reminding, but that's the end of this upload."

David sat back and realized his legs had gone to sleep. He rolled his head to release tension in his neck. By now, Chang should be busy monitoring the Garden Tomb. David clicked on the message that had been forwarded from Tsion.

Buck's phone vibrated in his pocket, but he didn't look to see who it was. He was prepared if God was calling him to take Chaim's place, but that was foolish. Surely, the chosen one would be an Israeli believer. Maybe Chaim was calling, lost in the crowd. Buck reached in his pocket and shut off the phone. Let him find his own way. It was long past time for the man to accept his role. Nobody said it would be easy. Nothing was easy anymore. But God's call wasn't hard to recognize. It was clearly on Chaim. If Hattie had the courage to do what she had done, surely knowing she couldn't survive, how could any of them shirk their duties again?

Carpathia stepped from behind a draped curtain near the tomb, smiled, and opened his arms to the crowd. Less animated now, they merely applauded. The cheering, the kneeling, the waving were over. It seemed most just wanted to get on to the Temple Mount and get in line for their mark. That would insure them against the fiery fate of the crazy woman at Mount Calvary.

"I was never entombed!" Carpathia announced. "I lay in state for three days for the world to see. Someone was said to have risen from this spot, but where is he? Did you ever see him? If he was God, why is he not still here? Some would have you believe it was he behind the disappearances that so crippled our world. What kind of a God would do that? And the same people would have you believe I am the antithesis of this great One. Yet you *saw* me resurrect my*self!* I stand here among you, god on earth, having taken my rightful place. I accept your allegiance."

He bowed and the people clapped again.

Moon stepped back to the mike and read from his notes. "He is risen!"

The people murmured, "He is risen indeed."

"Come, come," Moon said, smiling nervously. "You can do better than that. He is risen!"

"He is risen indeed!" the crowd responded, and someone applauded. The ovation slowly built until Moon held up a hand to silence it. "We are providing you with the opportunity to worship your potentate and his image at the Temple Mount, and there you may express your eternal devotion by accepting the mark of loyalty. Do not delay. Do not put this off. Be able to tell your descendants that His Excellency personally was there the day you made your pledge concrete."

Speaking softly now and making it sound like an afterthought but still clearly reading, Moon added, "And please remember that neither the mark of loyalty nor the worshiping of the image is optional."

A helicopter nosed into place and descended to take Carpathia and the rest of the dignitaries to the Temple Mount. Buck still had not seen Chaim since he had left him near Golgotha. The crowd dispersed quickly, and many ran in the direction of the loyalty mark application site.

Unable to reach Buck, Rayford called Tsion. "Hattie was the victim, then, in whatever happened at Calvary?" he said.

"That is what we have pieced together, Rayford. We are grieving and praying, but we are also amazed at how God spoke to her."

Rayford had known Hattie for years, of course, and had once jeopardized his marriage over her. He asked to speak with Chloe. At first neither he nor his daughter could speak. Finally Rayford said, "It seems forever ago that you met her."

"Think she accomplished anything, Dad?"

"That's not for me to say. She obeyed God, though. That seems clear."

"What was he up to there?"

"I don't know. If someone in the crowd was wavering, who knows?"

"They would see what happens when you oppose Carpathia," Chloe said. "I don't see what it was all about. Everybody here is speechless."

Rayford tried to dismiss an intruding thought but couldn't. "Chloe, are you envious?"

"Of Hattie?"

"Yeah."

"Of course I am. More than I can say."

He paused. "Kenny okay?"

"Sleeping." She paused. "Dad, am I a scoundrel?"

"Nah. I know how you feel. At least I think I do. But most people see you as a hero, hon."

"That's not the point. That's not why I'm envious."

"What then?"

"She was there, Dad! Front lines. Doing the job."

"You're —"

"I know. Just put me out there next time, will ya?"

"We'll see. You heard from Buck?"

"Can't raise him," she said.

"Me neither. I imagine he and Chaim are treading carefully."

"I just wish he'd check in, Dad."

Buck waited at the Garden Tomb until the crowd was gone. He no longer cared how suspicious he looked. He scanned the horizon and worried how he would explain himself if he lost track of Chaim. Buck forgot what he had been trying to prove or elicit by leaving him. He was still frustrated with Chaim, of course, but what should he expect from an old man who had endured so much? Chaim had hardly sought this assignment.

Buck moseyed among the olive trees, drawing glances from guards. He recalled his first meeting with Dr. Rosenzweig. He had known of him years before that. It wasn't common to become friends with story subjects, especially Newsmakers of the Year, but it was fair to say the two had been close.

The afternoon sun was hot. The garden was still a beautiful spot, untouched by the earthquake. An armed guard, so still he could have been a mannequin, stood by the entrance to the tomb. "May I?" Buck said.

But the guard did not even look at him. "If I'm just a minute?" he tried again. Zero response.

Buck shook his head and ducked inside as if to say, "If you're going to stop me, stop me."

Still the guard did not move. Buck found himself in the surprising coolness of the sepulchre. The slanting light from the entrance cast a thin beam where Christ's burial cloth would have been left. Buck wondered why Carpathia and his people had left this place untouched.

He looked up quickly when Chaim shuffled in. Buck wanted to say something, to apologize, anything. But the man was weeping softly, and Buck didn't want to intrude. Chaim knelt at the slab of rock where the light shone, buried his face in his hands, and sobbed. Buck leaned against the far wall. He bowed his head, and a lump invaded his throat. Could it be that Chaim would claim here the final vestige of courage to follow through on his assignment? He looked so small and frail in the oversized robe. He seemed so overcome that he could hardly bear up under his grief.

Buck heard a sigh from outside, then the creak of leather, the crunch of footsteps. The entrance filled, the silhouette of the guard nearly blotting out the light.

"Just give us another minute, please," Buck said.

But the guard remained.

"If you don't mind, we'll leave in just a moment. Sir? Do you speak English? Excuse me . . ."

The guard whispered, "Why do you seek the living among the dead? Fear not, for I know that you seek Jesus, who was crucified. He is not here, for he is risen, as he said."

Chaim straightened and whirled to look at Buck, squinting at him in the low light.

"You," Buck said to the guard. "You're — you're a —"

But the guard spoke again. "And the Lord spoke to Moses, saying: 'This is the way you shall bless the children of Israel. Say to them: "The Lord bless you and keep you; the Lord make his face shine upon you, and be gracious to you; the Lord lift up his countenance upon you, and give you peace." '

" 'So they shall put my name on the children of Israel, and I will bless them.' "

"Thank you, Lord!" Chaim rasped.

Buck stared. "Sir? Are you a —"

"I am Anis."

"Anis!"

The guard stepped back outside. Buck followed, but the guard was gone. Chaim emerged, shielding his eyes from the light. He grabbed Buck's arm and pulled him to a souvenir shop, where a young woman looked as if she was about to close up. Buck found it hard to believe such a place remained open in the Global Community.

Chaim seemed to know exactly what he was looking for. He picked up a small, cheap replica of the container in which the Dead Sea Scrolls had been found in the caves of Qumran. He took it to the young woman and looked to Buck, who felt in his pockets for cash. "Two Nicks," she said.

He peeled off the bills, and Chaim opened the package on the way out. He discarded the box and the tiny printed scroll and put the palm-sized clay vessel and its miniature top in the pocket of his robe. Suddenly his gait was sure and quick, and he led Buck back the way the crowd had come. Golgotha was deserted now, but Chaim found his way to where Hattie had been immolated. He knelt by what was left of her ashes and carefully scooped a handful into the little pot and pressed the top down.

Chaim put the container of ashes back into his pocket and stood. "Come, Cameron," he said. "We must get to the Temple Mount."

Five

David Hassid sat stunned in the desolate aloneness of a "high place" in Petra. While the pagan religions of the ancient past had used such locations to sacrifice to their gods in a helpless, desperate attempt to gain favor, all he wanted was to express to God his thanks for grace. Nothing he could do or say or give or sacrifice could gain what God had offered him freely.

All he could see were sky, clouds, valleys, and the occasional bird of prey. It was clear this would be the ideal cradle of refuge for the remnant of Israel, for those who recognized that Jesus *was* the long-awaited, prophesied Messiah. It was he who would put the finishing touches on God's love affair with his chosen people.

But David's own field of expertise, the gadgets and marvels of technology, would not allow him the proper reprieve to exult in the holiness of God's plan. He had needed, desperately, to know the truth about Chang. But now the news of Hattie Durham had rocked him. And here was a brief message, laboriously pecked in from Buck's cell phone, that said David needed to monitor activities at the Temple Mount. Yet another message from Tsion announced a final teaching on the next event on the prophetic calendar, Antichrist's desecration of the Holy of Holies.

Well, that was not news, and Tsion had taught on it before. But if the rabbi felt the need to clarify and crystallize it for his billion constituents, who was David to argue? The teaching, according to the worldwide Net announcement, would be posted that evening. The very people who might most benefit from Tsion's teaching could be in flight for their lives the next day.

David tapped in the string that brought up the GCNN coverage of the Temple Mount activities and patched the other half of his screen to an ancient video monitor that kept a twenty-four-hour eye on the Wailing Wall. He was convinced the camera there had long been forgotten, and it was amazing it still functioned, though the fidelity of the picture had been compromised by the years.

David wanted to set his transceivers in strategic spots to maximize the wireless network he envisioned for Petra. But here came yet another urgent message from Chang:

I have been invigorated, encouraged, motivated. Dr. Ben-Judah concurs that the record vindicates me, though he fears Carpathia and his henchmen are devious enough to come up with the idea of doping *known* believers and forcing the mark on them, and that would be a catastrophe.

I know you're busy, but I thought you'd want to know: I intercepted a private transmission between Moon and the head of both Peacekeeping and Morale Monitor forces in Jerusalem. Apparently Walter was spooked by the change in the attitude of the crowd with the martyrdom of the dissident and the sudden mystery about Fortunato's health. Without informing Carpathia, he has directed that armed personnel lead the way in taking the mark of loyalty. If you haven't checked it out yet, connect with the Temple Mount and look at the chaos.

So that's what had Buck so exercised that he would use his phone to transmit a message to David's computer. The official GC broadcast feed showed news anchors nearly beside themselves with glee. "Look at the hundreds and hundreds of military vehicles lined up for miles outside the Old City. They would clog the narrow passageways leading to the Temple Mount anyway, but these are mostly unmanned. Only a skeleton crew of, we would estimate, perhaps one uniformed Peacekeeper maintains custody over every four or five vehicles. We've learned that the ones left to keep an eye on the rolling stock are personnel who have already received the mark of loyalty. The rest are leading the way today, becoming patriotic examples to civilian citizens. Indeed, by the time the massive crowd followed Potentate Carpathia's pageant through the Via Dolorosa and half of what is known as the Stations of the Cross from the now defunct Christian religion, the loyalty mark application site was already clogged with Peacekeepers and Morale Monitors.

"Many citizens are less than happy about the delay, but the response from Global Community brass, including His Excellency himself, appears to be one of delight. Here's the scene at the Temple Mount, where tens of thousands of GC personnel noisily jockey for position to receive the mark, and civilians, patient for the most part, are lined up all the way outside the city walls, awaiting their turn.

"Here's our reporter, Anika Janssen, with several civilians deep in the long lines."

The tall, blonde reporter exhibited mastery of at least the rudiments of several languages as she guessed nationalities and began the interviews in citizens' native languages. Mostly she asked in their tongue if they understood English so translators would not be forced to employ captioning on the screen.

"What do you make of this?" she asked a couple hailing from the United African States.

"It is exciting," the man said, "but I confess we expected to be among the first in line, rather than the last."

His wife stood nodding, appearing reluctant to speak. But when Ms. Janssen waved the microphone in her face, the woman proved opinionated. "Frankly, I believe someone in authority should insist that the soldiers make way. Those men and women are assigned here. Many of us are on pilgrimages. I do not mean to criticize the risen potentate, and I can hardly blame those who happened to have the privilege of transportation and could get here first, but this does not seem fair."

Other interviews unearthed the same attitudes, though most seemed almost bemused, or perhaps afraid, to complain publicly. "Oh, look at this special privilege," Anika Janssen said. "Here is Ms. Viv Ivins of the potentate's inner circle, working the lines, so to speak. She is greeting people, thanking them for their patience. Let's see if we can get a word with her."

To David it seemed that Ms. Ivins had been directed to a spot where a camera crew would notice her. She was certainly ready with the party line. "I'm so impressed with the loyal citizens and their patience," she said. "His Excellency was overwhelmed at the eagerness of his own personnel to become examples and role models of loyalty."

"Though there is, of course, a visible, prominent guillot—"

"Which we prefer to call a 'loyalty enforcement facilitator,' " Ms. Ivins said with an icy smile. "Of course it represents the gravity of such a decision. In all candor, Anika, our intelligence reports indicated that we might face more opposition here, in the traditional homeland of several obsolete religions. Yet I daresay that except for the lunatic fringe, such as the lone representative of the Judah-ites who recklessly challenged the power and authority of our Most High Reverend Father of Carpathianism, any such stubborn opponents have learned to keep silent."

"Speaking of Reverend Fortunato, ma'am, what can you tell us? We expected to see him here."

"Oh, he's fine, and thanks for asking. He's fallen a bit under the weather, but he passes along his greetings and best wishes and expects to be back at full strength tomorrow for the potentate's blessing of the temple."

"The blessing of it?"

"Oh, yes. We believe that the beautiful temple was constructed with the best intentions to honor god, even though the ancients were unaware that they had misplaced their devotion. They meant to serve the one true god but were misled by their own innocent ignorance and erred only in directing worship to their chosen deity. We now know, of course, that our risen potentate is clearly the god above all pretenders and that his rightful place is in a house built for the one who sits high above the heavens. By making this his own house of worship, he lends credibility and authenticity to it, and it becomes the true house of god."

"Besides the Judah-ites and their seemingly large Internet following —"

"Clearly inflated and exaggerated, of course."

"Of course. But besides that faction, might you expect opposition from holdout Jews who are neither Christ-followers nor Carpathianists?"

"An excellent question, Anika. You do your homework. This should give the lie to those who say that the Global Community News Network is merely a shill for the potentate."

"Thank you. So, opposition?"

"Well, that is what we were led to believe and what we have been prepared for. It is still possible, of course, but I am confident that the display of divine power exhibited a few hours ago, along with the overwhelming enthusiasm on the part of GC personnel and these thousands of civilian pilgrims, will far overshadow any pockets of resistance."

"But should either the Judah —"

"Have you seen the image of the potentate yet, Anika? The Reverend Fortunato judged the entries himself, and the winner is stunningly beautiful."

"I have not seen it yet, but I hope to — oh, I'm getting word that our cameras do have a shot of the image, so let's go there now."

Buck had found the area around the Temple Mount — now dominated by the gleaming new temple itself, of course — so congested that he and Chaim were able to just amble around and observe, drawing little attention despite Chaim's getup. Buck looked for other dissidents and was surprised to see that many Orthodox Jews were allowed at the Wailing Wall. He could not get close enough to see whether anyone in that area had the mark of the believer, but he suspected that these devout men of prayer were prepared to oppose the desecration in more overt ways than merely wearing their own religious garments and assembling to pray at the Wall.

The rest of the Mount had been entirely converted into a virtual factory of efficiency. Dozens and dozens of lines herded the Carpathian faithful, or at least the fearful, to stations where they were registered, processed, prepped, and finally marked. Most accepted the mark on their foreheads, but many took it on the backs of their right hands.

Unlike what Buck had seen in Greece, here it was not assumed that anyone in line would decide against taking the mark. In the middle of all the processing stations stood one gleaming guillotine with two operators sitting patiently beside it. Ten feet behind the contraption was a freestanding frame with a drape hung on it, apparently so that the disembodied could be discreetly hidden once the awful sound and severing had served their deterring purposes. No sense rubbing it in, apparently.

As the supplicants finished showing each other their marks and posing for pictures, they were funneled to the east-facing steps of the new temple, where the winning image of Carpathia stood at the second to the top level. The temple itself, a sparkling replica of Solomon's original house for God, was pristine but simple on the outside, as if modest about the extravagance of cedar and olive wood, laden with gold and silver and brass on the inside.

The image of Carpathia appeared bigger than life, but everything Buck had heard about it confirmed it was as exact a copy of Carpathia himself as it could be. Behind it were two freestanding pillars outside the entrance to the temple, and Buck could see what appeared to be a recently fabricated platform, made of wood but painted gold, in the porch area. "Carpathia leaves out nothing," Chaim told him. "That appears to

113

be a replica of where both Solomon and the evil Antiochus — a forerunner of Antichrist — stood to address the people in centuries past."

Many gasped and fell to their knees upon their first glimpse of the golden statue, the sun bouncing off its contours. Unlike the mark application lines, this one moved more quickly as dozens at a time rushed the steps and knelt — weeping, bowing, praying, singing, worshiping the very image of their god.

Chaim's revulsion mirrored Buck's own. The older man looked more resolute than before, but his carriage evidenced no more authority or promise. And still he limped. Buck wasn't sure how Chaim felt or how he would know when the time had come to reveal himself as the enemy of Carpathia, but the more he watched, the more Buck could barely contain himself. He realized that these people — all of them — were choosing Satan and hell before his very eyes, that he was powerless to dissuade them, and that their choice was once and for all.

Buck estimated it would be hours before the GC personnel made way for the average citizens. He found a ledge where Chaim could rest and asked if he wanted anything to eat. "Strangely, no," Rosenzweig said.

"You eat. I could not."

Buck pulled a meal bar from deep in his pocket and showed it to Chaim. "You're sure?"

Chaim nodded, and Buck ate. But he could enjoy nothing while thousands eagerly lined up to seal their doom. He swallowed his last bite and was scanning the area for a water vendor when a cloud shouldered in front of the sun and the temperature dipped. As if on cue, conversation stopped and the colossal crowd stared at the image, which seemed to rock forward and backward, but which Buck was convinced was an illusion.

The voice emanating from it was no illusion, however. Even the rabbis at the Wall stopped praying and moving, though Buck could see they were not in the line of sight of the statue.

"This assemblage is not unanimous in its dedication to me!" the image boomed, and grown men fell to their faces, weeping. "I am the maker of heaven and earth, the god of all creation. I was and was not and am again! Bow before your lord!" Even the workers in the mark application lines froze.

Buck worried that he and Chaim would be exposed. Though the old man had to be as frightened as he, neither, of course, knelt before the evil apparition. He forced himself to look away to see if he could find other believers, and he was amazed at what appeared to be row after row of them at the far edges of the crowd. Some were dressed in fatigues; many could have easily been mistaken for GC. They had to be part of Operation Eagle! They must have driven into Jerusalem, found the schedule delayed, and wandered to the Temple Mount, prepared to help with the evacuation.

Buck wanted to signal them, to wave, to approach, to embrace his brothers and sisters. But who knew how far God chose to extend his protection? The Trib Force believed Chaim would somehow be supernaturally insulated, but other brave believers had been martyred for their faith and courage.

"The choice you make this day," the golden image roared, "is between life and death! Beware, you who would resist the revelation of your true and living god, who resurrected himself from the dead! You who are foolish enough to cling to your outdated, impotent mythologies, cast off the chains of the past or you shall surely die! Your risen ruler and king has spoken!"

The sun reappeared, the people slowly rose, and more and more tourists and pilgrims joined the lines. Buck was jealous that those undecided should hear both sides, yet when he looked at Chaim, he saw passivity.

As if the man could read his mind, Rosenzweig said, "They know their options. No one alive could doubt that a great gulf is fixed between good and evil, life and death, truth and falsehood. This is the battle of the ages between heaven and hell. There is no other option, and no honest man or woman can claim otherwise."

Well, the old man knew how to summarize, but his was still the plaintive, weak voice with the thick Hebrew accent that reminded Buck of Jewish comedians or storytellers or timid scholars — the latter of which Dr. Rosenzweig certainly was. Buck wanted the faith to believe that somehow this modest specimen of a man — so endearing, so engaging — could capture the imaginations, the hearts, and the minds of people on the fence.

And yet that was not Chaim's calling. He was to stand against Antichrist — the evil one, the serpent, that old dragon, the devil. He was to go nose to nose with Carpathia himself, while instructing the remnant of Israel that it was time to flee unto the mountains. Different as Chaim appeared now, whom would he fool? He had been a close personal friend of Carpathia's long before Nicolae became head of the Global Community. Chaim had once murdered the man! Would Chaim not be immediately recognized from his voice alone?

Buck wondered if he himself had the faith to believe this was anything but folly. If there were really a million Messianic believers in Israel, surely they were unarmed. Carpathia was of no mind to let them go! He had more than one hundred thousand armed, plainclothes Morale Monitors and uniformed Peacekeepers. His arsenal of personnel carriers, tanks, missiles, rocket launchers, cannons, rifles, and side arms was on public display. Buck shrugged. Only God could do this, so that made the thought process simple: You either believed it or you didn't.

Buck had long since chosen to believe it and had to fight a grin. Resting apparently none too comfortably beside him was the most unlikely leader of a million people. He couldn't wait to see how God would manage this.

By now, thousands of GC personnel had received the mark of loyalty and clogged the area, celebrating. Their commanding officers urged them to return to their posts and vehicles, and suddenly the Temple Mount was alive and animated again. Men and women, clearly midlevel managers, stood in a ring near the front of the application centers, using bullhorns to remind the newly tattooed and chip-implanted novices that their spiritual obligation for the day was only half over.

"The worship of the image is not optional!" they shouted. "You are not finished here until you have knelt before the living, breathing, speaking image of your lord."

It wasn't as if they were trying to get out of it, Buck thought. But many of these were young people, excited, flushed with renewed enthusiasm for their work. They had seen the manifestations of power. They had seen the potentate himself. They knew that Nicolae's making the temple of Jerusalem his own was tantamount to setting up residence in the mosque of the Dome of the Rock or moving into what had once been St. Peter's Basilica in Rome. This would establish him once and for all the true god over all. And if the pathetic, weakened resistance had breath left, if they truly believed there was a higher being than His Excellency the potentate, where were they? Did they dare reveal their true loyalties in the face of such overwhelming evidence?

And now the revelers were still again. Those with the bullhorns clicked them off.

Activities in the line ceased. Carpathia himself appeared in his white robe and gold sandals and shiny rope belt, smiling, standing one step above his own image, arms outstretched. The silence gave way to a deafening roar. Would he speak? Would he touch the worshipers? Some must have wondered the same, for they slowly rose from their knees on the steps and moved as if to advance upon him. He stopped them with a gesture and nodded toward the center mark application line.

There came his top military brass in all their finery, dress uniforms with white gloves, broad epaulets, buttons with sheens as reflective as their patent-leather shoes, capturing and emitting every staggered ray from the sun. Two dozen men and women, heads high, bearings regal, marched to the front of the line, upon command stood at ease, and removed their uniform caps.

One by one they proudly submitted to the application of the mark of loyalty, each receiving it on the forehead, several asking for the largest, darkest tattoo so their homeland designations would be obvious from far away.

As the last of these were processed, the effusive crowd bubbled over again as the dozen members of the Supreme Cabinet marshaled themselves into the staging area. The last three in this contingent were Suhail Akbar, Walter Moon, and Viv Ivins. While the military brass knelt on the temple steps, worshiping Carpathia and his image, the cabinet waited until all were processed and then moved as one to the worship area.

All the while, Carpathia stood benevolently above and beside the gold statue, gesturing toward these humble shows of loyalty. The assembled masses cheered as Mr. Akbar turned to display the giant black *42* that dominated his olive forehead. Then Mr. Moon displayed his -6. Finally Viv Ivins chose to kneel on the pavement as she received the application, then slowly stood and turned. Buck could not make out her number, but he knew her native Romania was part of the United Carpathian States and that her discreet tattoo would read *216*.

The cabinet solemnly filed to the temple steps as the military brass moved away. One by one they ascended the steps on their knees, finishing by wrapping their arms around the statue's feet, their shoulders heaving with emotion. Carpathia watched each one and dismissed them by placing his open palm upon their heads.

Finally only Viv Ivins remained at the base of the steps. The crowd seemed to wait breathlessly as she delicately removed her shoes, tugged up the hem of her suit's smart skirt, and began the slow, awkward climb on her knees. Her hose ran with the first brush against the marble, but people seemed to moan in sympathy and in awe of her willingness to publicly humble herself.

When finally she reached the third step from the top, she only briefly embraced the statue, then detoured slightly and went up one more stair, where she prostrated herself and kissed Nicolae's feet. He raised his face to the sky as if he could imagine no greater tribute. After several minutes, he bent and reached for her, but instead of letting him help her up, she enveloped his hands and kissed them. Then she reached into a pocket and pulled out a vial — Buck assumed perfume — and poured it over Nicolae's shoes.

Again Carpathia feigned a humbly honored look and shrugged to the crowd. Finally, as he pulled Ms. Ivins to her feet, leaving her a step below him, he turned her to face the crowd and rested his hands upon her shoulders.

When the cheering died, Nicolae announced, "I personally will be watching from a secure vantage point, all night if need be, until the last devoted citizen of Jerusalem receives the mark of loyalty and worships my image. And tomorrow at noon, I will ascend to *my* throne in *my* new house. I shall initiate new ceremonies, and you will see again the 'friend' who accompanied me for as long as she could on the journey today. And you shall be led in worship by the Most High Reverend Father of Carpathianism."

Nicolae waved farewell to every side, and the application lines began moving again.

"I'm tired," Buck said. "Shall we head back to the hotel to rest and pray and prepare for tomorrow?"

Chaim shook his head. "You go, my friend. I feel the Lord would have me stay."

"Here?"

Chaim nodded.

"I'll stay with you," Buck said.

"No, you need your rest."

"How long will you be?"

"I will be here until the confrontation."

Buck shook his head and leaned close. "Will that be before or after the desecration?"

"God has not told me yet."

"Chaim, I cannot leave you. What if something happens?"

The old man waved him off.

"I can't, Chaim! Leave you here overnight? I would never forgive myself."

"If what?"

"If anything! You sit here until the last mark has been applied, and it will be obvious you have not taken it. I have reason to think Carpathia is watching, as he said. He doesn't sleep anymore, Chaim. He'll know."

"He will know soon enough anyway, Cameron. Now you go. I insist."

"I need to check with the others. This is lunacy."

"Excuse me? Cameron, you believe God has chosen me for this?"

"Of course, but —"

"He is leading me to stay and prepare. Alone."

Buck pulled out his phone. "Just let me —"

"I will take full responsibility for the consequences. I have my inspiration in my pocket. The young woman who modeled the ultimate obedience once personally encouraged me, though she was newer even than I to the things of God. You are to go back to the hotel to rest and pray for me."

"God told you that too?"

Chaim smiled sadly. "Not in so many words, but I am telling you that."

Buck was at a loss. Should he pretend to go but watch from somewhere? He'd done that before. It was near this very spot where he had seen the two witnesses resurrected and raised to heaven.

"I see your mind turning," Chaim said. "You do what I say. If it is true that I have been assigned this task, it must come with some leadership responsibility."

"Only for a million people."

"But not for you?"

"I am not a Messianic Jew, sir. I am not part of the remnant of Israel."

"But surely you must obey one who is to answer for so many."

"I don't follow your logic."

"Ah, Cameron! If this had to do with logic, what would I be doing here? Look at me! An old man, a scientist. I should be in an easy chair somewhere. But here I am, a stranger in my own mirror, trying to tell God he has made a mistake. But he will not listen. He is more stubborn than I. He uses the simple to confound the wise. His ways are not ours. The sheer illogic of his choice of me forces me to the reluctant acceptance that it must be true. Am I ready? No. Am I willing? Perhaps. After tonight, I must go forward, willing or not. Do I believe he will go before me? I must."

It seemed as if he and Chaim were alone in a sea of people. Buck pawed at the pavement with his foot. "Chaim, I —"

"Cameron, I would ask that you call me Micah."

"Micah?"

Chaim nodded.

"I don't get it."

"I am not foolhardy enough to call myself Moses, and I shall not reveal my real name to Nicolae unless God wills it."

"So you'll tell him you're Micah? Why not Tobias Rogoff? Zeke has provided identification for that and —"

"Think about it and you will understand."

"Should I bring *my* fake ID? You don't have a new name for me, do you?"

"You will not need a name."

"You know this for sure."

"As sure as I know anything."

"So I bring no ID."

"Your papers show you as Jack Jensen. Should that be checked, you would be traced to the ranks of the Peacekeeping forces. How would you explain a GC corporal assisting the leader of the opposition?"

"So I'll come without papers, and if they demand to know who I am, I'll be deemed a vagrant."

"I will identify you as my assistant, and that will satisfy them."

Buck looked away. "I liked you more

when you were *less* sure of yourself."

"And Cameron," Chaim said, "you *are* a vagrant. We all are. We are aliens in this world, homeless if anyone is."

Buck thrust his hands deep into his pockets. He couldn't believe it. The old man had persuaded him. He was going to leave his old friend alone overnight with the enemy. What was the matter with him? "Micah?" was all he could say.

"You go," Chaim said. "Check in with our comrades and your family. And think about my new name. It will come to you."

Six

The late-afternoon sun made beautifully interesting shadows on the stunning architecture at Petra. David found a sweater and pulled it over his shoulders as he descended from the pagan high place to one of the most remarkable cities ever built.

The various buildings, tombs, shrines, and meeting places had literally been carved out of the striking red sandstone millennia before, and though its early history was largely speculative, the place had become a tourist attraction in the 1800s. David wondered how the new inhabitants of such a surreal place would make comfortable quarters out of solid rock. Tsion taught that God had promised food from heaven and that clothes would not wear out, but what would substitute for insulation, inner walls, and anything resembling modern conveniences?

The place was spread out, many of its famous edifices — the treasury of the pharaoh, the five-thousand-seat amphitheater, the various tombs — connected by a system of gorges and channels dammed and rerouted by the various civilizations that had inhabited the area.

Because David had arrived by helicopter, he had to hike down to the main level to find the sole passageway leading in. With rock walls over three hundred feet high in places and a trail at points fewer than seven feet across, it was no wonder most visitors rode in on camel, donkey, or horseback. Operation Eagle would fly in the majority of the newcomers, because a million fleeing Israelis would be slaughtered if they had to traverse the roughly mile-long, narrow pass on foot.

David could see why the city had been a perfect defensive location thousands of years before. Tsion taught that the Edomites, who inhabited it at the time of Moses, had refused to let the Israelites pass through. But in this world of high-tech travel, only a miracle could protect unarmed innocents from aerial attack. Rather than a place of refuge, David decided, without the hand of God this place could just as easily be ideal for an ambush.

David's life was no longer about creature comforts. And he had forgotten what leisure time was. Until the Glorious Appearing, this would be where the action was, where miracles would be the order of every day. David's people would inhabit this city, and they would be preserved from illness and death, insulated against their enemies until Messiah liberated them. If witnessing that meant making his bed on a slab of stone, it was a small price to pay.

David made sure his laptop had stored enough solar energy to remain charged throughout his night in a cave. In the loneliness at the top of the only world he knew anymore, reading Tsion's post of what he believed Antichrist was up to, monitoring the Carpathian-fashioned news, and communicating with his confreres would serve as David's only links to humanity.

He expected, within twenty-four hours, the first of more company than he would know what to do with. How a million of them could be contained even in the vast area surrounding the great rock city was a problem only God could solve. David had learned not to wonder and question, but to watch and see.

After checking in with everybody and doing his best to explain how he could leave Dr. Rosenzweig unattended, Buck spent that evening at the King David Hotel, watching television with Chaim's Bible before him. He read through Micah, seeing parallels between the Jerusalem of then and now, and he noticed the reference to Moses. Clearly the book was a dire promise of God's judgment, but Buck was not enough of a theologian to decipher its significance to Chaim. The prophecies seemed to deal more with the first coming of Christ than with the Rapture or the Glorious Appearing, but perhaps Chaim planned to use some of the words and phrases when dealing with Carpathia.

The TV news carried mostly rehashes of the day's events, but at least Hattie's death was not glossed over as it had been during the live coverage. While she was not identified — the death of a woman they thought dead previously would have been a puzzler to the GC anyway — it was clear she had died for her courage to speak against the ruler of this earth. The GC did not spin it that way, of course, but boasted of the event, using it as an example of the veracity of Carpathia's claims of deity and confirmation of Fortunato's role as his designate of spiritual power and wonders.

Buck was exhausted, nearly too much so to sleep. But as he stared at the ceiling in the darkness, eager to get back to the Temple Mount at first light, he rehearsed Dr. Rosenzweig's insistence on being called Micah rather than Chaim. The names floated before his mind's eye. And he slept.

In the middle of the afternoon in Chicago, Dr. Tsion Ben-Judah printed out the message he planned to post on the most popular Web site in history. He asked Ming and Chloe to review it for him. They sat together and read.

TO MY DEAR TRIBULATION SAINTS, BELIEVERS IN JESUS THE CHRIST, THE MESSIAH AND OUR LORD AND SAVIOR, AND TO THE CURIOUS, THE UNDECIDED, AND THE ENEMIES OF OUR FAITH:

It has now become clear that Nicolae Carpathia, the one who calls himself the ruler of this world and whom I have identified (with the authority of the Holy Scriptures) as Antichrist, along with his False Prophet Leon Fortunato (upon whom has

132

been bestowed the audacious title of the Most High Reverend Father of Carpathianism), has scheduled what the Bible calls the desecration of the temple.

As with every other connivance and scheme Antichrist believes is the product of his own creative mind, this event too has been prophesied in the infallible Word of God. The Old Testament prophet Daniel wrote that during this time in history "the king shall do according to his own will: he shall exalt and magnify himself above every god" and "shall speak blasphemies against the God of gods."

The prophet also predicted that "many countries shall be overthrown," but one of those that "shall escape from his hand" is Edom. That, friends, is where Petra lies. Sadly, Egypt will not escape his hand. He will have "power over the treasures of gold and silver, and over all the precious things of Egypt; also the Libyans and Ethiopians shall follow at his heels."

Antichrist has already begun fulfilling the prophecy that "he shall go out with great fury to destroy and annihilate many." Fortunately, someday "he shall come to his end, and no one will help him."

It is also prophesied that the great archangel, Michael, shall "at that time" stand up. He is referred to as "the great prince who stands watch over the sons of your people," referring to the remnant of Israel, those Jews like myself who have come to believe that Jesus is the Messiah. Praise God, Daniel also foretells that "at that time your people shall be delivered, every one who is found written in the book."

You know from my previous teachings that the book referred to is the Lamb's Book of Life, in which are recorded those who have trusted in Christ for their salvation. While I cannot be more specific now, due to the divine experience of a beloved colleague just within the last few days, I believe that Michael the archangel is standing watch and that deliverance is nigh.

Jesus himself referred to the prophecies of Daniel when he warned of "the 'abomination of desolation' . . . standing in the holy place." I believe he was speaking of the very desecration planned by Antichrist.

Many were confused before the rapture of the church and believed that the apostle Paul's second letter to the Thessalonians referred to that event when he spoke of "the coming of our Lord Jesus Christ and our gathering together to him." We may rejoice, because it is now clear that Paul was speaking of the Glorious Appearing. Paul writes, "Let no one deceive you by any means; for that Day will not come unless the falling away comes first, and the man of sin is revealed, the son of perdition, who opposes and exalts himself above all that is called God or that is worshiped, so that he sits as God in the temple of God, showing himself that he is God."

Our hope is in the promise that "the lawless one will be revealed, whom the Lord will consume with the breath of his mouth and destroy with the brightness of his coming. The coming of the lawless one is according to the working of Satan, with all power, signs, and lying wonders, and with all unrighteous deception among those who perish, because they did not receive the love of the truth, that they might be saved."

We often wonder, when the truth is now so clear, why not everyone comes to Christ. It is because of that very deception! People did not, as Paul says above, "receive the love of the truth." He says it is "for this reason God will send them strong delusion, that they should believe the lie, that they all may be condemned who did not believe the truth but had pleasure in unrighteousness." Can you imagine it? There are people who know the truth, know their futures are doomed, and yet still they take pleasure in sin! A warning, if you are one of those: Due to your rebellion, God may have already hardened your heart so that you could not change your mind if you wanted to.

Now, if the following is not a description of the two who would steal the souls of every man and woman, I don't know what is: "So they worshiped the dragon who gave authority to the beast; and they worshiped the beast, saying, 'Who is like the beast? Who is able to make war with him?' And he was given a mouth speaking great things and blasphemies, and he was given authority to continue for forty-two months. Then he opened his mouth in blasphemy against God, to blaspheme his name, his tabernacle, and those who dwell in heaven. It was granted to him to make war with the saints and to overcome them. And authority was given him over every tribe, tongue, and nation.

"All who dwell on the earth will worship him, whose names have not been written in the Book of Life of the Lamb slain from the foundation of the world."

What could be clearer? If you are in Christ, you are eternally safe and secure, despite all that we will have to endure these next three and a half years. If you are undecided, I plead with you to make your choice while you are still able. That many have already had their hearts hardened by God — a truth that may go against what we once believed about him — is nonetheless clearly the danger of putting off receiving Christ.

One day I pray God will grant me the privilege of speaking in person to the Israeli believers who will soon be led to safety and out of the way of harm from Antichrist. Brothers and sisters in the Lord, pray as the final events of this halfway point of the Tribulation period unfold and usher in the rest of the time before the Glorious Appearing.

Your friend in Christ,
Tsion Ben-Judah

Tsion was intrigued that the young women were clearly finished reading, but rather than give him their assessment, they whispered among themselves. He cleared his throat and looked at his watch.

"Ming has a wonderful idea, Tsion," Chloe said. "She believes her brother could pirate his way into the Global Community News Network and counter Nicolae's next message to the world with your own teaching."

"What, put my message text on the screen?"

"No," Ming said. "You. Live. In essence you would debate his every point."

"But how?"

"I will check with Chang, but the little camera atop your monitor, the one you now use only to project your image to the Tribulation Force when they are away from Chicago, could be used to broadcast over television as well."

"But might we risk showing clues that would give away where we are?"

"We would have to work to preclude that, of course."

"But isn't this Dr. Rosenzweig's purview?" Tsion said. "Shouldn't he be the one to counteract Antichrist?"

"He probably will be," Chloe said. "Any showdown between those two will likely be on international television anyway."

"Then what would I be needed for?"

"Once the flight to Petra has commenced, Nicolae will be speaking out against you and us so-called Judah-ites. It would be like a tag-team wrestling match. When Chaim is no longer there to oppose him in person, you will debate him via his own television network," Ming said.

Tsion quietly accepted the manuscript

back and keyed in the transmission. "I like the way you think, Mrs. Toy," he said.

"So do I," Chloe said. "I only wish you could have mentioned Hattie by name or said that she was a Trib Force member."

"I did not want to give away that we even have people in the area, though I am certain the GC assumes we do."

"And yet, Tsion," Chloe said, "you mentioned Petra by name."

The rabbi covered his mouth with his hand. "I did, didn't I?"

"I meant to say something before you transmitted it," Chloe said.

"That is why I wanted you to review it."

"I'm sorry, Tsion. I assumed you had a reason."

"It is not your fault," he said, collapsing into a chair. "What was I thinking?"

Rayford's eyes popped open at dawn, and a decision he debated in the night had been made. Leah and Hannah had their mobile medical unit stocked and ready, so Leah could do double duty, also monitoring the incoming and outgoing Israelis. That meant Rayford didn't have to stay at Mizpe Ramon. Surely he would be of more use actually piloting a chopper.

He dressed quickly and found the airstrip

buzzing. The sun shimmered over the horizon, and Rayford realized it wouldn't be long until he and his comrades would begin counting the days to the end, the *real* end — the Glorious Appearing and the Millennial Kingdom. Much had to happen first, of course, but the head-spinning pace of the last several weeks would give way to precious lulls between the final judgments of God before the Battle of Armageddon. Then things would pick up again. How he looked forward to at least some rest between crises. Rayford pushed his hair back and put on his aviator's cap. The next few days would determine whether he or his loved ones would even survive to the end.

Buck stood under a shower as hot as he could stand it, but the King David must have installed some sort of a regulator. After a few minutes, the water went tepid, then cold. With personnel and energy decimated, there was only so much to go around.

Buck put only enough money in his pocket to be sure he could top off the tank of the car. Following Chaim's advice, he left his wallet and ID in the room. Finding a place to park was harder than the day before, and he had to walk a half mile farther, finally reaching the streets lined on each side with empty military personnel carriers.

Early as it was, the Temple Mount was already filling. Colossal TV monitors were visible from every vantage point, and people waiting for the noon festivities occupied themselves watching the GC network feed and waving when they saw themselves on-screen.

To Buck's great relief, Chaim was in plain sight, not far from where the two witnesses had traded off sitting while the other preached. Buck rushed to Dr. Rosenzweig, who sat with his knees up, staring into the sky. "Morning, Chaim," he said, but the man did not acknowledge him. "Sorry," Buck added quickly. *"Micah."*

Chaim smiled faintly and turned to him. "Cameron, my friend."

"Did you eat?"

"I remain sated," Chaim said.

"Remarkable."

"God is good."

"And has he encouraged you, strengthened you, empowered you?" Buck pressed.

"I am ready."

He didn't sound ready. In fact, he sounded and looked even wearier than he had the day before. "Did you sleep?" Buck said.

"No. But I rested."

"How does that work?"

"There is nothing like resting in the Lord," Chaim said, as if he'd been doing it all his life.

"So, what happens now?" Buck said. "What's the plan?"

"God will reveal it. He shows me only what I need to know, when I need to know it."

"Terrific."

"I detect sarcasm, Cameron."

"Guilty. I'm a plan-your-work-and-work-your-plan kind of a guy."

Chaim reached for Buck's hand and rose unsteadily. He groaned as joints cracked. "But this is neither my plan nor my work, you understand."

"I guess. So we just stand around waiting?"

"Oh no, Cameron. Even I do not have the patience to wait until high noon."

"And if Carpathia does not appear until then?"

"A ruckus will flush him out."

Buck found that intriguing, but again, this frail, little old man hardly looked up to causing anything. Was he expecting Buck to do something? Without papers? Without the mark? Buck was willing, but he didn't know yet what he thought of Chaim's judgment.

"When did they stop administering the mark?" Buck said.

"They have not stopped. See, two lines remain open over there, but it appears one is about to shut down, despite the number of those waiting. You have noticed nothing this morning, have you, Cameron?"

"Noticed?"

"The difference between today and yesterday."

Buck looked around. "Crowd's bigger, earlier. Military vehicles are still everywhere outside the Old City. But why are they closing a line with people still in it? And why didn't they finish last night? More people showed up?"

"And you a journalist!"

"I'll bite. What'd I miss?"

"You said it yourself. The vehicles are still there."

"So? A show of strength. Carpathia probably expects opposition today."

"But they would not leave and come back," Chaim said. "You think these soldiers slept in those trucks? They would not have to. They have accommodations, centers, places to muster."

"Okay . . ."

"How many soldiers did you see with the trucks today?"

"To be honest, Chaim, uh, Micah, I was focused on making sure you were still here and all right. I was in a hurry and not paying attention."

"You certainly weren't. Now look, they are herding what is left of that line into the only one still open."

"And I suppose you know why."

"Of course," Chaim said.

"And you're not even a journalist. But still, you'll tell me."

"They closed that line for the same reason the Temple Mount is filled with civilians rather than GC today."

Buck spun and took in the whole area. "Sure enough. Where are they?"

"They are suffering. Soon they will be as bad off as poor Mr. Fortunato, who must be miserable almost unto death by now. How utterly ingenious for our Lord to plant in someone's mind the brilliance of having the GC personnel go first yesterday. They received the mark of the beast; then they worshiped his image. And now they are victims of Revelation 16:1–2."

"The plague of boils!" Buck whispered.

Chaim looked at him meaningfully with a close-mouthed smile, then moved away from Buck and into an open area. Buck stumbled and nearly toppled, startled by the huge, deep sounds emitting from the little man's throat. Chaim's voice was so loud that everyone stopped and stared, and Buck had to cover his ears.

"I heard a great voice out of the temple!" Chaim shouted, "saying to the seven angels, 'Go your ways, and pour out the bowls of the wrath of God upon the earth.' And the first went, and poured out his bowl upon the earth; and there fell a noisome and grievous sore upon the men which had the mark of the beast, and upon them which worshiped his image."

The thousands who had been milling about fell back at the piercing voice, and Buck was astounded at Chaim's bearing. He stood straighter and looked taller, his chest puffed out as he inhaled between sentences. His eyes were ablaze, his jaw set, and he gestured with balled fists.

Now the curious began to gather round the old man in the brown robe. "What?" some said. "What are you saying?"

"Let him who has ears hear! Surely the God of heaven has judged the man of sin, and those who have taken his mark and worshiped his image have been stricken!"

"Crazy old fool!" someone called out. "You're going to get yourself killed!"

"We'll see your head rolling before you

know it, old man!"

If it was possible, Buck thought Chaim grew louder. He needed no amplification, for it was obvious that everyone within sight heard him. "None would dare come against the chosen one of God!"

The people laughed. "You're a chosen one? Where is your God? Can he do what our risen potentate can do? You want fire from heaven to leave you in a heap of ashes?"

"I demand audience with the evil one! He must answer to the one true God, the God of Abraham, Isaac, and Jacob! He dare not touch the remnant of Israel, believers in the Most High God and his Son, the Messiah, Jesus of Nazareth!"

"You'd better just —"

"Silence!" Chaim roared, and the echo reverberated off the walls and left the crowd speechless.

Three young armed and uniformed guards, including one female, jogged up. "Your papers, sir," she said.

"I neither have nor need any documentation. I am here under the authority of the Creator of heaven and earth."

"Your forehead is clear. Let me see your hand."

Chaim showed the back of his right hand.

"Behold the hand of the servant of God."

The woman raised her rifle and nudged Chaim's arm, trying to steer him to the mark application line. He would not budge. "Come, sir. You are either drunk or undernourished. Save yourself the grief and me the paperwork. Get your mark."

"And worship the image of Carpathia?"

She glared at him and pulled back the firing mechanism on her rifle. "You will refer to him as His Excellency or His Worship or as the risen potentate."

"I will refer to him as Satan incarnate!"

She pressed the barrel of her weapon upon Chaim's chest and appeared to squeeze the trigger. Buck stepped forward, fearing both the blast and seeing his dear friend hit the pavement. But the young woman did not move, did not so much as blink. Chaim looked at her male partners. "When did you receive your marks?"

They both cocked their weapons. "We were among the last," one said.

"And you worshiped the image?"

"Of course."

"You too will soon suffer. The sores have begun to rise on your bodies."

One looked at the other. "I do have something inside my forearm. Look."

The other said, "Will you stop? We have

cause to shoot this man, and I may just do it."

"Shoot him!" someone hollered from the crowd. "What is wrong with your supervisor?"

Both eyed her warily, then said to Chaim, "Sir, we're going to have to ask you to get in line to take the mark or bear the consequences."

"I have not been called to martyrdom just yet, young man. When my time comes, I will proudly bow before the blade, worshiping the God of heaven. But now, unless you too want to be stricken motionless, you will get word to the one you worship that I demand an audience."

One turned away and spoke into his walkie-talkie. Then, "I *know*, sir. But Corporal Riehl is incapacitated, and —"

"What?"

"He paralyzed her, sir, and —"

"How?"

"We don't know! He's demanding —"

"Shoot to kill!"

The young man shrugged, and both pointed their rifles at Chaim.

"Give me that!" Chaim said, grabbing the walkie-talkie. He depressed the button. "Whoever you are, tell your so-called potentate that Micah demands an audience with him."

"How did you get this radio?" the voice said.

"He will find me and my assistant in the center of the Temple Mount with three catatonic guards."

"I warn you —"

Chaim switched off the walkie-talkie. Within seconds, half a dozen more guards, two in plainclothes, advanced, weapons drawn. "You don't demand a meeting with Potentate Carpathia," one scolded.

"Yes, I do!" Chaim shouted, and the six studied their paralyzed compatriots.

"Well, sir, may I have your name?"

"You may call me Micah."

"Okay, Mr. Micah, sir. The potentate is at the Knesset, where his Jerusalem headquarters have been established. If you'd like to accompany us there and request —"

"I am demanding a meeting with him here. You may tell him that if he refuses, he will face more than a decimated, suffering staff. I am prepared to return to the plagues called down from heaven by the two witnesses! Ask him if he would like his medical staff to try to treat your boils and carbuncles with water that has turned to blood."

Seven

David was not sure what time the noise of heavy equipment woke him, but he knew immediately what it meant. He had been nonplussed by Dr. Ben-Judah's mentioning Petra in his worldwide post, and there was no question the enemy monitored the Web site.

David crept back to the high place in the blackness of the wee hours, the stars not providing enough illumination to keep him from skinning shins, stubbing toes, and falling several times, scraping hands and arms on the rocks. His eyes having adjusted to the darkness, far below he saw the semicircle of GC tanks and artillery forming at the perimeter. Though they kept few lights on, he was able to make out that they had closed the main foot-traffic entrance and were heavily stationed around the most likely airdrop zones as well.

David believed God had promised to protect the children of Israel who would flee the anger of Antichrist, but what of the volunteers who helped them? How were they to escape an enemy already a step ahead? How could Tsion have made such a blunder? David phoned Rayford but got no answer. He tried Albie.

Tsion could not be consoled. He paced, a hand over his mouth, praying silently. Ming and Chloe had tried to reason with him, reminding him that God was sovereign, but he could not make sense of what he had done. He kept the television on, dreading the news of a massacre once the flight from Jerusalem began.

Tsion finally sat on the arm of the couch in front of the television. The tall, fat young man they incongruously called Little Zeke — his recently martyred father had been Big Zeke — lumbered in with a sketchpad. "Wanna see what I'm thinkin' about doing with Ming? I mean, it's hard to disguise a, um, Asian woman, but I'm gonna try to make her look like a guy, I think. I've got a picture of her brother, and with the right haircut and clothes and, you know, wrappings and stuff —"

"Forgive me, Z, but —"

"Oh, I've already told her I don't mean to insult her or anything. I mean, she's thin and small, but I'm not saying she looks like a guy now. In fact, she's really quite pretty and attractive, and feminine."

"I'm preoccupied here, Z. I am sorry. I have made a terrible mistake and I'm praying that —"

"I know," Zeke said. "That's really why I came out here. I mean, I was working on Ming's identity for real, but I thought maybe talking about that would take your mind off —"

"Off tipping off the other side about where our brothers and sisters are headed? Thanks, but I do not see how the GC could do anything but beat them there and lie in wait for them."

Zeke set his pad on the couch and eased his bulk onto the floor. "You're the Bible guy," he said, "but something about this just seems sort of logical to me."

"Logical? Hardly."

"I mean, there must have been a reason, that's all."

"To humble me, perhaps, but this is quite a price. I never claimed to be perfect, but I pray so hard over my messages, and God knows I would never intentionally —"

"That's what I mean, Doc. God must have wanted this to happen somehow."

"Oh, I do not —"

"You said it yourself, you pray about this stuff. That doesn't make your messages like the Bible, I guess, but God's not gonna let a regular human like you mess up his plan with one mistake, is he?"

Tsion didn't know what to think. This uneducated young man often had fresh insight. "Maybe I have myself overrated."

"Maybe. You didn't seem to when you were just the guy who teaches a billion people. Why didn't you let that go to your head?"

"I do not think of it that way, Z. It's humbling, a privilege."

"See? You could get cocky about having this big Internet church, but you don't. So maybe you shouldn't start thinkin' you're important enough to get in God's way."

"Obviously I am not above mistakes," Tsion said.

"Yeah, but come on. You think God is gonna say, 'I had this deal all figured out till Ben-Judah went and messed it up'?"

Tsion had to chuckle. "I suppose he can overcome my blunders."

"I hope so. You always made him out to be big enough."

"Well, thank you, Z. That gives me something to —"

"But it goes past that, even," Zeke said. "I still think God might have had a reason for lettin' you do that."

"For now I am just trying to take in that God can overrule my error."

"You wait and see, Doc. I bet you're gonna find that either the GC doesn't buy it because it looks like such an obvious phony lead. Or they think they've found something juicy and they try to take advantage of it, only to see it blow up in their faces."

At dawn Rayford was alarmed to find Albie with Big George, uncrating several of each of the two kinds of weapons the latter had had shipped in. "What're we doing, Albie?"

"Your phone not working?"

Rayford patted his pocket and pulled it out. "Nuts!" he said. "Used it too much yesterday." He pulled the solar pack from it and clipped it to the outside of his shirt pocket, where the sun would rejuvenate it, and put a fresh pack in. He found he had missed several calls.

Albie said, "Let me save you checking all

those out and tell you what Hassid's and my calls were about."

"Everybody back off." The newest arrival to the Temple Mount was a tall, athletic-looking, dark-haired plainclothesman with the outline of a handgun under his jacket. "Who're you?" he said to Buck, as the rest of the Morale Monitors and Peacekeepers, including the three who had been paralyzed, stepped back.

Buck thought he had been prepared for everything, but he felt his pockets as if about to produce his ID, then pointed to Chaim. "I'm with him. Who are you?"

"Name's Loren Hut, and I'm chief of the Global Community Morale Monitors. I have the potentate on the phone for the troublemaker." He looked at Chaim, making the pressing crowd laugh. "For some reason my people can't seem to get through to a demented old man. That has to be you."

Chaim said, "Tell your boss I do not care to speak to him except in person."

"Not possible, Mr. —"

"Micah."

"Best you're going to get is this call, Mr. Micah. Now I'm not feeling well this morning, and you're already pressing your luck."

"Not feeling well how, Mr. Hut?"

"Do you want to talk to His Excellency or —"

Chaim looked away, shaking his head.

Hut scowled and put his phone to his ear. "False alarm. Apologize to the potentate for me. . . . Well, sure, I'll talk to him, but I don't want to waste his — good morning, sir. Yes . . . I don't know . . . I'll be sure to get full reports from everyb— well, yes, I can get it done. . . . You want me to do that? I — yes, I know, but it's not as if he poses a real threat . . . yes, sir. Nine in the clip . . . if that's what you want . . . I don't disagree, it's just that he's a frail . . . I could do that. . . . Affirmative, you can count on me."

Hut slapped his phone shut and swore. "You," he said to Buck, "keep your distance. Be glad for your sake I kept you out of this. And you people —" he gestured toward the crowd — "stay back!" Some moved; most didn't. "Don't say you weren't warned!"

"Sores starting to get to you, young man?" Chaim said.

"Shut up! You're about to die."

"That will not be up to you, son."

"Actually, yes it will. Now be quiet! Corporal Riehl, are you all right?"

"A little foggy," she said flatly. "What do you need?"

"Find a GCNN camera crew and get 'em over here. The potentate wants me to put nine in this guy, but he wants to see it."

"So do I," she said, trotting off.

"Mr. Hut," Chaim said, "will you be able to do your duty? You are getting worse by the second."

Hut bent over and vigorously scratched his abdomen and belly. "I don't have to be a hundred percent to kill a man at point-blank range."

"That will not happen."

"You think you can paralyze me?"

"I never know how God will act."

"Well, I know how *you* will act. You'll be squirming and screaming and pleading for your life."

"My life is not my own. If God wishes it, he may have it. But as I have further responsibilities, including talking in person to the coward who would ignore me, God will spare me."

Corporal Riehl returned with a turbaned man with a camera on his shoulder. With him was a short black woman carrying a microphone. "What are we doing?" she asked with a British accent.

"Just tell me when you're rolling," Hut said. "This is for His Excellency."

"Live or disc?"

"I don't care! Just cue me!"

"All right! Hang on!" She spoke into a small radio. "Yes!" she said. "Carpathia himself. Just a minute." She turned to Hut. "Central wants to know your authority."

Hut swore again and scratched himself from abdomen to shoulders. "Hut!" he said. "GCMM! Now let's go!"

"Okay," the woman said, stepping in front of the camera. "This is Bernadette Rice, live from the Temple Mount in Jerusalem, where we are about to witness an execution ordered personally by His Excellency Nicolae Carpathia. Behind me, Loren Hut, new chief of the Global Community Morale Monitors, will administer the sentence to a man known only as Micah, who has refused the mark of loyalty and resisted arrest."

When people from other areas of the Temple Mount saw on the giant TV monitors what was going on, they flooded the area around Chaim and Buck and Hut.

"Don't let Kenny see this!" Zeke called out. "But come quick, both of you!"

It was after midnight in Chicago, and Tsion had slipped off the arm of the couch to a cushion, where he sat hunched forward, peeking at the screen between his fingers. "God, please . . ."

"There's Buck!" Chloe said, pointing.

Tsion thought Cameron looked weird, standing casually, hands in his pockets.

The GCMM chief pulled his side arm from its holster, paused to scratch himself with his left hand and right elbow, then prepared the weapon. He spread his legs and held the gun in both hands, aiming at Chaim's hands, which were clasped in front of him. Hut's angle would make the bullet pass through them without hitting his body.

The explosion of the first shot made Buck skip out of the way and the crowd recoil, but Chaim didn't move, except to flinch at the sound. Hut stared in disbelief at Chaim's unmarred hands and moved to his opposite side, aiming the second shot at them again. The crowd scattered. *BLAM!* Another apparent miss from just inches away.

Hut, scratching himself all the way to the knees between shots now, aimed at Chaim's foot and fired. Nothing. Not even a hole in the robe. Hut lifted the hem with his left hand and fired at the other foot. Moaning in agony and apparently fear, Hut scratched with his free hand, pressed the muzzle onto one of Chaim's knees, then the other. The shots produced only noise.

The crowd laughed. "This is a joke!"

someone said. "A put-on! He's shooting blanks!"

"Blanks?" Hut screamed, whirling to face the heckler. "You'd bet your life on that?" He fired shot number seven into the man's sternum. The back of the victim's head hit the ground first, the sickening crush of his skull clear on the TV reporter's microphone.

With the crowd running for cover and Bernadette Rice falling out of the picture, Loren Hut fired at Chaim's left shoulder from six inches, then pressed the gun to the unharmed old man's forehead. Chaim looked sympathetically at the shaken, writhing Hut, and casually plugged his ears. The barrel of the gun left a small indentation on Chaim's skin. The bullet proved harmless.

Hut tossed the gun away and threw his arms around a tree, rubbing his body against it for relief. He cried out in agony, then turned and summoned Corporal Riehl. He reached for her rifle and pointed it under his own chin. Chaim approached calmly.

"No need for that, Mr. Hut," he said. "The death you have chosen will overtake you in due time. Put down the weapon and summon Carpathia for me."

★ ★ ★

Hut threw down the rifle and staggered away, but already Buck heard the thwocking of chopper blades. Two helicopters touched down, and the crowd — which had largely retreated — cautiously returned, avoiding the corpse that lay in a pool of blood.

Carpathia was the only civilian in either bird, and he wore his jet-black, pin-striped suit over a white shirt and brilliant red tie. He strode directly to Chaim and Buck while seven uniformed Peacekeepers formed a semicircle behind him, weapons trained on Chaim.

Nicolae smiled at the crowd and turned to locate the GCNN cameraman. Bernadette was still on the ground, trembling. "Keep rolling, son," he said. "What's your name?"

"R-R-Rashid."

"Well, stand right here, R-R-Rashid, so the world can see who dares mock my sovereignty."

Carpathia approached Chaim and faced him from three feet away, arms crossed. "You are too old to be Tsion Ben-Judah," he said. "And you call yourself Micah." He cocked his head and squinted at Buck, who feared that Nicolae recognized him. "And this is?"

"My assistant," Chaim said.

"Does he have a name?"

"He has a name."

"May I know it?"

"There is no need."

"You *are* an insulting dolt, are you not?" Carpathia spoke to a guard, nodding at Buck. "Get him out of here. The mark or the blade."

Buck set himself to resist, but the guard looked petrified. He cleared his throat. "Come with me, please, sir."

Buck shook his head. The guard looked helplessly back at Carpathia, who ignored him. Suddenly the guard dropped, wriggling on the ground, scratching himself all over.

"All right," Carpathia said. "I concede I have you to thank for the fact that nearly my entire workforce is suffering this morning."

"Probably all of them," Chaim said. "If they are not, you might want to check the authenticity of their marks."

"How did you do it?"

"Not I, but God."

"You are looking into the face of god," Carpathia said.

"On the contrary," Chaim said, "I fear God. I do not fear you."

Rayford spread a topographical map on

the hood of a truck. "Let's get Mac and Smitty in on this too," he said. Albie phoned them.

Big George leaned in. "Anywhere we could hunker down within a couple of miles of Petra?"

Rayford shook his head. "I don't know. Whole area looks a lot different on paper than from the air. I know you're gung ho ho and everything, but I'm not prepared to do any killing."

"All due respect, Cap," George said, "but they're going to be killing our people. You might change your mind when you see that."

"We're here to get people to safety, not to kill the enemy."

Albie slapped his phone shut. "What if killing the enemy is the only way to get the Israelis to safety?"

"That's God's job."

"I agree," Albie said, "at least from what Dr. Ben-Judah says. But I'd hate to see us lose one brother or sister, and if these weapons are what it takes, I say use 'em."

Buck would never forget a detail of this macabre meeting, and the entire world was watching.

"So, Micah," Carpathia said, shifting his

weight, "what will it take for you to lift this magic spell that has incapacitated my people?"

"There is no magic here," Chaim said, in a voice that sounded as far from his own as Buck could imagine. "This is the judgment of almighty God."

"All right," Nicolae said, smiling tolerantly. "What does *almighty God* want in exchange for lightening up —" and here he made quotation marks with his fingers — "on this *judgment?*"

Chaim shook his head.

"Come, Micah. If you would negotiate on behalf of *God,* surely you can think of something!"

"Those who have taken your mark and worship your image shall suffer."

Carpathia moved close, his smile gone. "Do not tell my beloved not to accept the mark of loyalty or worship me!"

"They know the consequence and can see it here."

Rashid began to pan the camera around to take in many agonized loyalists. "Do not!" Carpathia whispered to him, grabbing his shoulder and swinging him back. Then to Chaim, "If anyone refuses my mark, I will put him to death myself!"

"The choice then," Chaim said, "is life with

excruciating pain or death at your hand."

"*What* do you want?"

"You will carry out your plan for the temple," Chaim said, "but many will oppose you for it."

"At their peril."

"Many have already decided against you and have pledged themselves to the one true God and his Son, the Messiah."

"They will pay with their lives."

"You asked what I wanted."

"And you propose that people be allowed to shake their fists in my face? Never!"

Rashid dropped to one knee, trembling. Carpathia shot him a look. "Get up!"

"I can't!"

"I see the *42* on your forehead, Rashid! You need not fear!"

"I am not afraid, Excellency! I am in pain!"

"Agh! Set the camera on a tripod and tend to your sores!"

Chaim continued calmly. "A million of God's chosen people in this area alone have chosen to believe in Messiah. They would die before they would take your mark."

"Then they shall die!"

"You must let them flee this place before you pour out revenge on your enemies."

"Never!"

"The recompense for stubbornness is on your hands. The grievous sores on your followers shall be the least of your troubles."

Buck looked past Carpathia to where the mark application lines had been replaced by makeshift medical tents. Lines of people waited in misery for treatment. Some held their friends as they gingerly moved about, only to collapse under their own pain. Bernadette had crawled away. Rashid was headed toward the tents. Every guard who had accompanied Nicolae staggered away. One of the helicopters stopped idling and the pilot tumbled out, whimpering. The pilot of the other was slumped over the controls.

Civilians, many of whom had been among the last to take the mark and worship the image, tried to run from the Temple Mount, only to stumble with sores appearing all over their bodies.

Chaim said, "Your only hope to avoid the next terrible plague from heaven is to let Israelis who believe in Messiah go."

Finally Carpathia appeared shaken. "And what might that next plague entail?"

"You will know when you know," Chaim said. "But I can tell you this: It will be worse than the one that has brought your people low. I need a drink of water."

Carpathia caught the eye of a loyalist and told him to "fetch Micah a bottle of water." Chaim stared at the potentate as they waited.

"You are nothing but a thirsty old man in an outsized robe."

"I am not thirsty."

"Then why —"

"You shall see."

"I can hardly wait."

The man came running with the water. He gave it to Carpathia, who handed it to Chaim. The old man held it up and peered at it. "I could not drink this anyway," he said.

"What is wrong with it?" Nicolae said.

"See for yourself."

Chaim handed it back, and the bottle turned nearly black as the water turned to blood.

"Ach!" Carpathia said. "This again? Do you not know what happened to your two associates at the Wailing Wall?"

"Any advantages you gain are by God's hand, and they are temporary."

Nicolae turned to see the disaster at the Temple Mount, nearly everyone writhing. He turned back to Chaim. "I want my people healthy and my water pure."

"You know the price."

"Specifics."

"Israeli Jews who have chosen to believe Jesus the Christ is their Messiah must be allowed to leave before you punish anyone for not taking your mark. And devout Orthodox Jews must be allowed a place where they can worship after you have defiled their temple."

"The Orthodox Jews do not even agree with you, and yet you speak for them?"

"I reserve the right to continue to attempt to persuade them."

"Would you take them to Petra with the Judah-ites?"

"I would propose Masada as a site for them to gather. Any we are able to persuade would then join us."

"In Petra."

"I did not say where."

"We already know where, you fool, and it required no intelligence on our parts."

"You tread on dangerous ground when you call a fool one who has been granted the power to turn your water to blood."

Carpathia screamed into the air, "I need the assistance of loyalists who have not yet taken the mark or worshiped my image!" A few civilians came running. "Follow me to the Knesset Building. Obey me, and I will reward you."

David made his way from horizon to horizon, trying to gauge the extent of the GC presence at Petra. While there seemed to be countless vehicles and weapons, the personnel seemed to be in trouble. Most languished on the ground or on the beds of trucks, being ministered to by others thus far less affected. He called Albie to report.

Rayford headed east toward Petra in a vehicle carrying three each of the weapons George had brought to Mizpe Ramon. Albie and Mac followed in identical vehicles, similarly laden. George and Abdullah rode together in a vehicle carrying DEWs. Rayford hoped to find a spot to set up and, using David Hassid as their eyes, see how many vehicles he and Albie and Mac could destroy with the fifty-caliber rifles. There would be no need to kill any GC, if David's reports were accurate. As the enemy fled, George and Abdullah, from closer proximity, would try to overheat their skin, making their sores all the worse. Rayford's biggest concern, after avoiding any intentional killing, was the five of them getting back to Mizpe Ramon in time to ferry the first escapees from Israel into Petra.

Eight

Buck followed Chaim to the temple, where, within twenty minutes, civilians without the mark of the beast scurried to set up TV cameras and make arrangements, apparently following hastily written and reproduced instructions. From where he and Chaim sat, Buck saw others tidying up the Temple Mount, some carting off the slain heckler, some directing people either to spectator locations for what they called the "temple festivities" or to first-aid lines, and still others replacing in the medical tents GC doctors and nurses who had themselves fallen too ill to help out.

"Pray for me," Chaim said.

"Why? What? Carpathia is not even here yet."

Chaim stood and began to speak, again in a huge voice. "Citizens! Hear me! You who have not taken the mark of loyalty! There may still be time to choose to obey the one true and living God! While the evil ruler of this world promises peace, there is no peace! While he promises benevolence and prosperity, look at your world! Everyone who has preceded you in taking the mark and worshiping the image of the man of sin now suffers with grievous sores. That is your lot if you follow him.

"By now you must know that the world has been divided. Nicolae Carpathia is the opponent of God and wishes only your destruction, regardless of his lies. The God who created you loves you. His Son who died for your sins will return to set up his earthly kingdom in less than three and a half years, and if you have not already rejected him one time too many, you may receive him now.

"You were born in sin and separated from God, but the Bible says God is not willing that any should perish but that all should come to repentance. Ephesians 2:8–9 says that nothing we can do will earn our salvation but that it is the gift of God, not of works, lest anyone should boast. The only payment for our sins was Jesus Christ's

171

death on the cross. Because besides being fully man, he is fully God, and his one death had the power to cleanse all of us of our sin.

"John 1:12 says that to as many as received him, to them he gave the right to become children of God by believing on his name. How do you receive Christ? Merely tell God that you know you are a sinner and that you need him. Accept the gift of salvation, believe that Christ is risen, and say so. For many, it is already too late. I beg of you to receive Christ right now!"

David Hassid, hiding in the rocks atop Petra, tried to coordinate with Rayford and his cohorts two miles away. They were so well hidden that he couldn't see them, though he thought he had seen plumes of dust south of the village of Wadi Musa, immediately east of Petra. They conferenced up on their secure phones, and Rayford told him George and Abdullah were trying to get close enough to use the directed energy weapons. David couldn't spot them from his perch either.

"We can see the GC hardware from three different locations," Rayford reported. "Anybody manning those weapons?"

"Not that I can see," David said, whispering because he had no idea how his voice might carry down the mountainside.

"They're likely waiting for word from Jerusalem that the Israelis are on their way."

"It's hard to tell the location of personnel," Rayford said.

"To my right and your extreme left," David said, "the first six or so vehicles appear unmanned. Only a few of all the soldiers are still ambulatory, and they seem to be tending to the others either directly below me or to my left."

"Take cover," Mac said, cutting in. "These things take a while to aim. It's going to be hit-and-miss at first, and probably more miss than hit."

"Just don't overshoot," David said. "I've got a small cave staked out. When we're done, I'll be incommunicado for a while."

"We'll each fire two rounds from the big guns," Rayford said. "After you've heard six, come out and try to reconnect. We're trying to drive the personnel to your left so we can safely take out some of the vehicles. If we can get the soldiers on the run, George and Smitty will try to make 'em miserable."

"They're already miserable," David said. "But I hear you. If they think staying put is going to get 'em killed, they'll start walking back to Israel! Okay, I'm out."

He ducked into the cave and sat waiting for the first blast.

Rayford tried to remember everything George had told him about the fifty-calibers. He set up two in the truck bed, side by side and loaded. Fifty yards away, Albie had the same setup. And fifty yards farther, Mac was ready. They would fire once in that order, then start over for the second round. Each would watch through high-powered telescopes to try to gauge the adjustment for the second shot. Six rounds were perfect to start, Rayford thought, because at some point the miserable GC would wonder if the barrage would ever stop and whether they had a prayer of surviving. All he wanted was to destroy their weapons and their transportation, send them running, and discourage any hope of ambushing the Israelis.

George had told him it was impossible to judge the wind between weapon and target and so to aim high, accounting for the effect of gravity over two miles, and to not expect accuracy within more than twenty or thirty yards. Rayford worried that an errant shot would kill someone, including David. He lay on his stomach in the bed of the truck, made his final adjustments, and locked in on the left-most vehicle. If he missed left, the bullet would at least spook the soldiers. If he missed right, he had all kinds of vehicles he might hit, yet he should still avoid hitting personnel.

Rayford had his finger on the trigger and the stock pressed hard against his right shoulder. The scope showed him dialed up forty feet above the target. Just before he squeezed, he reminded himself to keep his eyes open — not that it would make any difference in trajectory. Only amateurs shut their eyes.

Thinking about his eyes reminded him of his ears and George's desperate admonition to plug them somehow. How close had he come to deafening himself? Rayford rolled to his side, ripped a strip from his shirttail, tore it in half, and forced a bunched-up wad of material into each ear. As he was settling in again, hoping he had not affected the aim, his phone chirped.

It was Albie. "You going first or what?"

"Yeah. Almost forgot my earplugs."

"Oh, man! Thanks for reminding me!"

"Ten seconds."

"Give me thirty," Albie said. "We want to fire in close succession, but I've got to get something in my ears too. Remind Mac, eh?"

Rayford dialed Mac. "Another half minute while we get earplugs in."

"Say again?"

"Did you remember earplugs?"

"Just a second. Let me get this out of my ear! Now, what?"

"A few more seconds. Ready?"

"Been ready, boss. Let's commence."

Rayford looked at his watch and settled back in. How loud could it be? How much recoil? The stories had become legends. People shot these all the time. Should be interesting, that's all. He would squeeze off the round and stay put, watching through the scope to see where it hit.

It was as if he had not protected his ears. If his eyes were open when he pulled the trigger, they were driven shut when the stock drove deep into his shoulder, sending him sliding on his belly until his boots slammed into the back of the cab. The explosion was so loud and the heat so intense from a six-inch burst of fire shooting out the side that Rayford found himself dazed, ears ringing, head buzzing, hands vibrating.

The weapon flew forward off the resistance from his shoulder until the legs of the bipod dropped off the edge of the truck. Rayford had meant to count one-thousand-one up to one-thousand-seven while looking through the scope, but all he could do was groan, hearing himself as if in an echo chamber, his ears not really working yet.

His other weapon had rattled off its bipod and lay on its side, and Rayford was glad it had not gone off. Albie was to wait three seconds from the sound of Rayford's shot, and Mac another three after that. Rayford heard the boom from Albie's rifle and figured he had four seconds to get the second weapon into place and still see where his first bullet hit.

He yanked it up, but the scope seemed cockeyed, and Mac's weapon sounded only a little farther away than Albie's. Rayford should be shooting again within a few seconds, but he was desperately searching with the scope for his first shot while trying to line up the second. He hurt all over, and his body resisted putting itself through that again.

He saw a huge cloud of pink smoke, assumed he had hit the rock face above the vehicles, quickly aimed lower and more to the right, and squeezed, the concussion driving him back yet again. Rayford knew he had closed his eyes with that shot, but a cloud of sand and a black plume told him their first three rounds were high, low, and luckily right on. His second shot sent a shower of sparks and more red dust, Albie's brought back the sound of twisted metal, and Mac's seemed to still be in the air.

By now, George and Abdullah should be shooting the directed energy weapons, but as DEWs had no projectiles, they emitted only a clicking sound Rayford was unable to hear. He pulled the cloth out of his ears, then crawled to the second weapon and removed the scope. He sat up and tried to survey the results. Without anything to support the powerful lens, it moved around too much. He went to his knees and lodged it against the side of the truck bed, then scanned slowly until he got his bearings. No GC personnel in sight.

Three vehicles from the left and about twenty feet up, a hole bigger than a truck had been blown deep into the rock wall. The fifth and sixth armored carriers appeared to have been blown away from the wall by a shot that may have gone between them. The next vehicle was aflame. There were two dug-up troughs of sand and another obvious hole in the face of the rock.

David called. "Whoa, ho!" he said. "Do that again and we're home free!"

"Don't count on it," Rayford said. "I don't *ever* want to do that again."

"It sounded like World War IV, man! The GC had to have started moving away with the first explosion, and by the time I looked over the edge, they were mostly at the other end. A lot of them were just pleading for their lives, but a few dozen lit out across the desert. The directed energy thingies must have worked, because it wasn't long before those guys were rolling around in the sand. Some are coming back to the trucks now, though, so you might want to think about a couple more rounds each."

Rayford slumped and groaned. And reloaded.

Tsion was still despairing at just before four o'clock in the morning in Chicago, so he was grateful for the report of the attack on the GC. "They knew where we would be, so we knew where they were," David wrote him. "The area will soon be secure for the fleeing remnant of Israel."

Tsion knew he should sleep, but he also knew the rest of the second half of the Tribulation would not all be this dense with activity. As he had often reminded an exhausted Rayford, there would be time to rest and breathe between Carpathia's breaking of the covenant and the Battle of Armageddon. If they could keep up their strength while trying to stay atop everything now, they could endure.

Tsion turned on the television to discover that the plague of sores had swept the world.

Even the reporters on TV were in pain, and one entire special channel was devoted to advice for the sufferers. While the potentate's visit to the temple at noon Carpathian Time was next on the network schedule, Tsion switched to the auxiliary channel to see what they were saying about something that was not of this world anyway. There was little relief for a plague sent by God, but the Global Community tried to put the best face on it.

In New Babylon, Chang worried he would be found out if people realized he was the one among them not afflicted with the sores. His boss had e-mailed him to see how he was, and Chang intimated that he had better stay in his room for several days. His boss granted that permission, provided Chang was sure to put in place what was necessary for the senior medical staff person in the palace to go live on the special channel with treatment advice.

Chang was able to do that without leaving his apartment. He watched a bit of the feed, reminding himself that at 1:00 Palace Time, Nicolae would enter the temple.

Dr. Consuela Conchita, with dark circles under her eyes and seeming to struggle to sit up straight, walked people through their own treatment. "The fact is that we have thus far been unable to specifically diagnose this pandemic affliction," she said. "It begins as an irritation of the skin, most often in areas normally covered by clothing, though it has been known to spread to the face and hands.

"In its initial stages it progresses to a serious itch, soon becoming a running sore that acts like a furuncle or a boil and sometimes even a carbuncle. But whereas the usual such maladies are caused by acute staph infections, these have not responded to conventional symptomatic treatment. While staphylococcal bacteria are naturally found in these sores, because such are found on our skin surfaces anyway, some as yet undetermined bacteria make this outbreak much more serious and difficult to treat.

"While these do not appear life threatening, they must be carefully managed to keep from becoming deeply infected abscesses. We have ruled out any causal relationship between the sores and the methods used to administer the mark of loyalty. So while the sores seem to affect only those who have the mark, the connection seems entirely coincidental.

"These types of skin problems can lead to permanent scarring, so it is important to keep the affected areas clean and use any anti-itching recipe you find helpful. Antibiotics have not yet proven effective at containing the infection, but are recommended nonetheless.

"Wear loose clothing to allow for good ventilation of the skin. Avoid intravenous drug use, and invest in a good antibacterial soap. Use hot or cold compresses, whichever best alleviates your discomfort. Fever and fatigue are common side effects."

Chang didn't know if it was the power of suggestion or just his own irrational fear. But he noticed an itch on his shin, leaped from his chair, and pulled up his pant leg. There was nothing visible, but he couldn't keep from scratching the spot. That made it redden, but was there something deeper? He told himself it couldn't be, that even if he *had* the mark of Carpathia, he had neither chosen it, nor had or would he ever worship the image of Nicolae, let alone Nicolae himself.

Buck could hardly believe it when dozens of unmarked civilians approached Chaim and asked to pray with him. "You realize you could pay with your life," Chaim told them. "This is no idle commitment."

People knelt before him, following him in

prayer. The mark of the seal of God appeared on their foreheads.

"Those of you who are Jews," Chaim said, "listen carefully. God has prepared a special place of refuge for you. When Carpathia's plans to retaliate reach their zenith, listen for my announcement and head south out of the city. Volunteers will drive you to Mizpe Ramon in the Negev. My assistant here will tell you how to recognize them by something we can see that our enemy cannot. If you cannot find transportation, get to the Mount of Olives where, just as from Mizpe Ramon, you will be airlifted by helicopter to Petra, the ancient Arabian city in southwestern Jordan. There God has promised to protect us until the Glorious Appearing of Jesus when he sets up his thousand-year reign on earth."

As noon approached, the men from the Wailing Wall made their way toward the temple. They were serious-looking, and clearly not happy. Many were in traditional Jewish garb and stood at the edges of the crowd that pressed in on Chaim. They listened, but none approached or spoke. Several glanced over their shoulders at the temple and at the monitors, apparently to be sure they missed nothing.

Chaim finished with the new believers,

and as they slowly dispersed, he gestured to those who had come from the Wailing Wall. "You holy men of Israel," he said, "I know who you are. You remain unpersuaded that Jesus bar Joseph of Nazareth is the foretold Messiah, yet neither do you accept that Nicolae Carpathia is of God. I urge you only to listen as a man enters your Holy of Holies and defiles it in his own name. I shall tell of Scriptures that foretold this very event. Then I will beg your indulgence yet again as I seek refuge for you at Masada, where I will present the evidence for Jesus the Christ as the Messiah of Judaism."

The holy men scowled and murmured.

"Gentlemen!" Chaim called out with authority. "I ask only for your attention. What you do with this information is entirely up to you. Without God's protection you run the risk of death opposing the ruler of this world, and yet his desecration of this holy site will enrage you."

Buck felt his phone vibrate and saw that Chang was calling. "Make it quick," Buck said.

"Are you aware of my sister's idea of my cutting in on Carpathia's broadcast and superseding it with Dr. Ben-Judah's?"

"Chloe told me. Can you do it for Chaim as well?"

"With your help."

"What do you need?"

"A camera and a microphone."

"Where do I get that?"

"You're there, Mr. Williams. I'm not. Obviously, Carpathia will have cameras in the temple and wants the world to see what he does there. My schedule says he's going to speak afterward, but I can't tell if that's inside or outside. If you can somehow commandeer a camera and mike while he's inside, I can put Rosenzweig on instead of Carpathia, and he won't know it until someone gets to him."

"I like that."

"I do too," Chang said, "but if he makes his speech outside, he'll see what we're doing."

"We've got to take that chance. And here he comes now. Chaim thinks he will speak outside on a replica of Solomon's scaffold. He's got an entourage of civilians around him carrying an extravagant throne, and some are dragging that pig from yesterday. Carpathia just told 'em, 'You will all be rewarded. Soon the world will know beyond doubt that I am god.' "

"No GC brass with him?"

"Yeah, I see Fortunato and Moon and a few others, but they look terrible. They're not going to be much help to him."

"There have to be unmanned GCNN cameras around, with all the technicians down with sores."

"I see a few on tripods, aimed at the temple."

"Can you grab one?"

"Who's going to stop me?"

"Go for it. I just need to know the number on the upper left in the back, and be sure a monitor and a mike are attached."

"Hang on."

Buck hesitated as Carpathia stopped near them, Fortunato, Moon, Ivins, and others mince-stepping behind, pale and haggard. The holy men turned and glared at them. Nicolae pointed at Chaim. "You I will deal with later," he said. "This spell of yours is temporary, and what happened to your two crazies at the Wailing Wall will befall you as well. And as for you," he added, gesturing to the angry men, "you will regret the day Israel turned her back on me. A covenant of peace is only as good as either side's keeping its word."

"Boo!" one shouted, and others hissed and clucked their tongues. "You would dare blaspheme our God?" Still more joined in, raising their fists.

Carpathia turned toward the temple, then

spun back. "Your God?" he said. "Where is he? Inside? Shall I go and see? If he is in there and does not welcome me, should I tremble? Might he strike me dead?"

"I pray he does!" a rabbi shouted.

Carpathia leveled his eyes at the men. "You will regret the day you opposed me. It shall not be long before you either submit to my mark or succumb to my blade."

He strode up the temple steps, but his suffering followers had to help each other ascend. The holy men followed several feet behind. When Carpathia and his people followed a contingent of his loyal civilians past the pillars and into the porch area, the men stood outside, rocking, bowing, crying out to God.

Buck jogged to an unmanned camera and mike, his phone to his ear. A small monitor and headphones dangled beneath the camera, fastened between two of the tripod legs. The monitor carried the network's global feed and just then showed Carpathia entering the temple. The camera operator must have been newly recruited, because he fumbled for the correct lens opening.

"Got it," Buck told Chang and read him the information.

"Good! Wireless. Get it as close to Rosenzweig as you can, and set the mike in the cradle beneath the lens."

Buck tried to wrestle the tripod, but the wheels were locked, and working with just one hand, he barely kept it from toppling. He told Chang he'd call him back and went to work on the wheels.

Meanwhile, Chaim unloaded on Carpathia again. "If you are God," he railed, "why can you not heal your own Most High Reverend Father or the woman closer to you than a relative? Where are all your military leaders and the other members of your cabinet?"

The attention of the crowds moved from Chaim to the temple entrance again. His ploy had worked. Carpathia had reappeared. Many of the holy men rushed down the steps, effectively blocking Nicolae's view of the camera now in front of Chaim, but Buck feared it appeared they were scared of the potentate.

"Where are your loyal followers," Chaim continued, "those who have taken your cursed mark and worshiped you and your image? A body covered with boils is the price one pays to worship you, and you claim to be God?"

To Buck it appeared Nicolae was merely trying to stare down the old man. The Rosenzweig Buck knew would not have been able to withstand that kind of psycho-logical warfare, but Micah — this new Moses — held Carpathia's gaze so long without even blinking that Nicolae finally turned away.

Buck studied the monitor. It looked like the last exchange had not been broadcast. The picture now showed someone in the studio in New Babylon announcing that GCNN was "returning to Jerusalem, where His Excellency will tour the famous temple. With the illness affecting much of our staff as it has so many around the world, we ask your indulgence, as many of the technicians helping bring you this special event are vol-unteers."

David worried when it took several rounds from the big guns and strategic use of the DEWs to finally dislodge from Petra the already boil-crippled GC forces. He was certain he had not been detected, and now he hoped the enemy's military brass would rule out reinforcements.

Rayford told him that he and Albie and Mac were okay except for sore shoulders and ringing ears, and that George and Abdullah had reported a few more hits with the flesh-heating weapons as the fleeing GC passed within a quarter mile of their blind.

"I wouldn't be surprised," Rayford added, "if you started getting a wave of new residents by late this afternoon."

That was as close as David had ever been to live combat, but it had almost not seemed fair. He couldn't imagine trying to stage an attack while most of your personnel were suffering from nasty sores.

Not knowing whether Chaim would lead or follow the escaping Israelis to Petra, David considered that he might be in charge until Dr. Rosenzweig arrived. He could think of no better plan than first come, first served, and he tried to scope out where the first quarter million would begin to settle. By the time he got back to his computer to see what was happening at the temple, a message was waiting from Hannah Palemoon.

David, there is a lull here, and of course we never know how long those last. We're praying that the small party that answered your call to thwart the GC there comes back healthy and successful.

This is not easy to write, but I feel I must get it off my chest. Besides that you are still grieving the love of your life, neither of us would likely have considered a relationship during this period of history anyway, and we barely know each other. So, please, please don't think I'm writing this in the context of any feelings I think either of us should have for the other.

We're friends, aren't we? That doesn't obligate us much, if at all. For both of our sakes, let me just say it. I was hurt at how cavalierly you treated me regarding your decision to not return to the United North American States at the end of Operation Eagle. It was a huge, complicated thing, a major crossroads in your life. I need to say too that it probably is the right decision.

But I learned about it along with everyone else. You apparently discussed it at length with Captain Steele, and next thing we know, it's announced, you're shaking hands and bidding farewells, and off you go. My friend, my buddy, the one I assumed I would lean on, is gone, just like that.

I'm sorry to lay this on you, but I just don't feel you have treated me like a friend. I would have felt honored to help you make the decision or at least have been informed of it privately, as if you cared what I thought. I could be making you glad you *didn't* see this neurotic nurse as a better friend. If this is crazy and you know without doubt that I will regret having sent it, pretend I didn't. And thanks, really, for some cherished memories.

Love in Christ,
Hannah

Nine

Buck focused on Chaim, framing him close to keep from giving clues to his whereabouts to anyone monitoring in New Babylon. If this worked the way Chang seemed to hope, the Global Community News Network people would try to pull Chaim off the air and, short of that, try to locate and reclaim the pirated camera.

Buck turned the monitor so both he and Chaim could keep track of Carpathia and also be able to tell when Chang switched to them. When GCNN moved to the camera inside the temple, they found a commotion. Nicolae barked at the volunteer cameraman's volunteer assistant, and the picture wobbled. Buck jammed on the headphones and heard the assistant. "I'm sorry, Excellency, but I don't want to do that."

"You would disobey me?" Nicolae whispered.

"I want to obey, sir, but —"

"Sir?!"

"Holiness! But I'm not supposed to even be in here, and they aren't going to listen to me."

"You are speaking for me, and if they are not out of here by the time I get to their stations, *their* blood will be used for the sacrifices."

"Oh, sir — Potentate!"

"Now, or you face the same fate."

GCNN in New Babylon broke in. "His Excellency's entourage has passed through the Court of Women, where Ms. Viv Ivins will wait. The rest have entered the Court of Men and apparently have come upon priests refusing to leave the temple for Potentate Carpathia's private tour, as was clearly stipulated.

"From the time he negotiated with the Muslims to move the Dome of the Rock mosque to New Babylon, the potentate made it clear that all activity in the rebuilt Jewish temple would be allowed only with his approval. It is no secret that Orthodox Jews have continued with the daily rituals and sacrifices of their own faith even after Enigma Babylon One World Faith was instituted as the only legal international religion, designed to incorporate the tenets of all faiths. After His Excellency resurrected himself from the dead, he became our object of worship, resulting in the dissolution of One World Faith and the establishing of Carpathianism. Still, the Jews and a faction of fundamentalist Christians known as Judah-ites — after their leader, self-proclaimed Messianic Jew, Dr. Tsion Ben-Judah — remain the last holdouts against our true and living god.

"His Excellency will eventually enter the Holy of Holies, but first he is insisting on the removal of the dissidents. Let's go back."

"Anyone not here in honor to me may be shot dead," Carpathia said. "Are you armed and prepared?"

"No!" the assistant cried.

"I am armed," Walter Moon said.

"You," Nicolae said, pointing to the assistant, "take Mr. Moon's weapon and do your duty."

Buck was riveted to the monitor as Nicolae stared not into the lens but past it to the volunteer. The camera turned jerkily to show the man refusing the gun. There was a rustle, a shot, a cry — and the man fell. The camera turned back to show Carpathia himself with the gun. "Show him," Nicolae said, and again the camera moved toward the body on the floor.

A change in ambient noise in Buck's headphones preceded Chang's voice. "Here we go," he said.

Chaim stepped back into position, and the red light shone on Buck's camera.

"Not only does the evil ruler of this world want to rid the priests of their rightful place in their own temple," Chaim said, "but it also appears he has personally committed murder at this holy site." What Buck heard did not match the movements of Chaim's mouth, and he realized the man was speaking in Hebrew and he was hearing in English.

The protesting holy men watching the monitors outside shouted and pumped their fists, bringing others crowding up the steps. Many of these, Buck noticed, had no marks of loyalty either, and their number was growing. He peeked at the small monitor beneath his camera. GCNN was broadcasting Chaim, though through his headset he could hear chatter about technical difficulties. Chang broke in again, assuring Buck, "I've got the New Babylon people muted off the air, but they're trying to get a bead on your camera. I'll switch back to Carpathia and let them wonder awhile."

"Hold till Chaim finishes this thought," Buck said.

"As Carpathia continues," Chaim said, "you should be able to see the laver where the priests wash their hands before they approach the main altar. The temple was creatively placed over a series of underground waterways where gravity allows constant water pressure for the various cleansings. Of course, he has no business in this place, and even a ceremonial washing of his hands will not exonerate him for defiling it."

"Switching," Chang said, and the monitor showed Carpathia signaling to his cameraman to follow.

"We were idle there for a moment," the man said.

"What did you miss?"

"I don't think we picked up the, you know . . ."

"My touching the blood?"

"No, Excellency. Shall we go back?"

"No!" Carpathia said, disgust in his voice. He held his black-red hands before the lens. "My faithful get the message." He raised his voice till it echoed and was distorted. "Any who dares interrupt my pilgrimage will find his blood on my fingers!"

Pounding footsteps made the cameraman whirl, and the screen filled with robed priests, charging Carpathia.

"See where this blood comes from!" Carpathia shouted, and the camera went to the faces of the priests, who stopped and paled.

Looking to where the body lay, they moaned and cried out, "Does your evil know no bounds?"

"Are you the god-haters," Nicolae raged, "who do not know me as a god, a god acknowledged by all others, but not named by you?"

One spoke up. "It should not surprise you that we showed our loyalty by offering daily sacrifices on your behalf."

"You have made offerings," Carpathia said, "but to another, even if it was for me. What good is it then, for you have not sacrificed to me? No sacrifice shall ever again be made in this temple except to me. Not *for* me, *to* me. Now leave or face the same fate as this unlucky one who was foolish enough not to believe that I have been allotted the nature of god!"

"God will judge you, evil one!"

"Give me your gun again, Supreme Commander!"

"We retreat not in fear but rather because

you have turned the house of God into a killing field!"

"Just go! I shall have my way in my home, and should you be found without proof of loyalty to me by week's end, you shall offer your heads as ransom."

The priests left with shouts and threats, and Buck saw their colleagues outside greet them with sympathy and encouragement. "Lovers of God, unite!" one shouted, and onlookers picked up the chant.

Buck's camera light went on, and Chaim began again. "The inner court inside the pillars has stairs that face east and lead to the main altar. Priests who revere God march around the Court of Priests and the Holy Place with their left hands closest to the altar. This one who would trample holy ground has already begun the opposite way, so his right hand will be closest to the altar. The Scriptures foretold that he would have no regard for the one true God. What plans he has for the beast with which he ridiculed the Via Dolorosa will be revealed only as he invades deeper into God's own territory.

"What a shameful contrast this is to the Shekinah glory of God, which has thrice appeared, the last time at this very temple. God appeared to Moses on Mount Sinai when the Ten Commandments were handed down. He appeared again when Moses dedicated the Tent of God. And finally he showed himself at the dedication of Solomon's Temple on this very site. Should God choose, he could reveal himself even today and crush under his foot this evil enemy. But he has an eternal plan, and Antichrist is merely a bit player. Though Antichrist has been granted power to work his horror throughout the world for a time, he shall come to a bitter end that has already been decided."

"We were off the air again, Excellency," the cameraman reported when they came back on.

"What are you doing wrong?"

"Nothing, Potentate! My red light merely goes off, and no matter what I do, it returns when it returns."

"Show that! Show the beauty of the construction that was for my benefit, even though the architect and the craftsmen did not know it at the time." The camera panned to the cypress, the cedar, the gold inlays and coverings, the silver and the brass. "No expense was spared in my house!" Nicolae exulted.

Leon Fortunato, apparently feeling left out, said something not picked up by the microphone. "Speak up, my friend!"

Carpathia said, removing his lapel mike and holding it to Fortunato's mouth.

"You, my lord," Fortunato rasped, obviously weak and wasted, "are the good spirit of the world and source of all good things."

David Hassid sat high above Petra, with the solar panel of his laptop facing the sun and the screen shadowed. Chang was amazing. But the drama being played out on international television and over the Internet made David wonder how Chaim was going to gain the ability to free the believing Jews. He wished he could somehow communicate with Chaim that the time was now to put out a call for everyone to flee before Carpathia finished the desecration and returned to retaliate.

But scheming was not his place, David knew. God had had this worked out since the beginning of time, and he alone could prompt Chaim.

The crowds outside the temple looked dangerous. Carpathia supporters tried to shout down the Orthodox Jews, but those who had received the mark and worshiped the image could barely stand. The growing opposition to Carpathia seemed to gain confidence with its numbers, especially considering that the potentate's inner circle and military personnel were so clearly incapacitated.

Still, David knew, Nicolae was a mortal incendiary, flaunting his temporary power. He instructed his ersatz camera bearer to set up behind him as he waited outside the veil hiding the Holy of Holies. David could only imagine the God of heaven watching with the rest of the world as, with a flourish, Nicolae removed a long knife from his belt and sliced the veil from as high as he could reach all the way to the floor, then pushed back each side. Over Carpathia's shoulder — already waiting near the brass altar — David could see Carpathia's own gaudy throne and the gigantic pig from the day before, now without a saddle and clearly no longer tranquilized. It fought two ropes around its neck, held by more Carpathia loyalists who had not yet received his mark. Fortunato and Moon shuffled into position behind the pig, as if only to be sure to be in the picture.

Suddenly the feed switched to the camera outside, and David knew Chang had to have tipped off Buck. He had turned his lens on the opposition watching the monitors. Many fell to their knees and tore their robes.

The scene switched back inside, where the pig squealed and strained and Carpathia laughed, approaching with the knife. He lunged at the animal and it dodged, making him slip. "Want to play?" Nicolae roared and leaped aboard, knocking the pig to its knees. It quickly righted itself, and the potentate nearly slid off. He caught himself on one of the ropes, pulled himself back up, and reached with the knife, slashing the animal's throat.

The pig went wild and dumped Carpathia to the floor. The animal thrashed as Carpathia struggled to his feet, his clothes covered in blood. The handlers held on, and the pig soon slowed and lost its footing.

Nicolae, abandoning any semblance of ritual, resheathed his knife and cupped both hands under the blood pouring from the dying pig's neck. Before he was even upright again, he flung blood toward the altar and splattered the pig handlers, who ducked and howled in hysterics. Fortunato and Moon were caught in the melee and appeared to force smiles, though they also looked as if they were about to collapse.

David sat with his mouth open, wondering how anyone could take seriously a man who not only thumbed his nose at God, but who also acted like a drunken reveler at a frat party.

When the pig finally stopped moving,

Nicolae attempted to butcher it with the knife and found neither himself nor the blade equal to the task. "Pity!" he cried, to the laughter of his people, and plopped himself down in his throne. "I wanted roast pork!"

Carpathia seemed to quickly tire of the silliness. "Get the pig out of here," he said, "and bring in my image." He stood and hurried to a spigot of rushing water. The camera stayed on his face, but it was clear he disrobed under the spray. "Cold!" he shouted, finally reaching for a towel provided by yet another lackey. Someone handed him the robe, sash, and sandals from the day before, and he looked directly into the lens. "Now, once my image is in place," he said, "we are out to Solomon's scaffold."

Chang patched in Chaim. "Is this not the most vile man who ever lived?" Rosenzweig said. "Is he not the antithesis of whom he claims to be? I call on all who have resisted or delayed in accepting his mark and plead with you to refuse it. Avoid the sentence of grievous sores and certain death."

David shifted and stretched his legs, eager to interact with someone about what everyone had seen. The most logical person he could think of was Hannah.

Buck feared his appropriated TV camera would be revealed when the small contingent of Orthodox Jews who had unintentionally worked together to shield it from Carpathia and his minions suddenly bolted away. The Temple Mount had become a roiling stew of angry citizens, and not just those without the mark of the beast. Loyalists had apparently come to the end of their patience with the loathsome sores all over their bodies. And the fiasco Carpathia had just perpetrated in the temple could not have amused more than his basest, most rabid supporters.

Messianic believers, new Christ-followers, the Orthodox Jews, and seemingly even thousands of undecided among the general populace had seen the new Carpathia. It was as if he had abandoned any attempt to persuade or convince anyone. He was to be revered and worshiped and followed because he was god, and anyone who didn't agree would suffer. But those who agreed most wholeheartedly were suffering the most.

But to have murdered a man in cold blood on international television, to literally drench his hands with the man's blood, to have announced the end of ceremonial sacrifices — except to himself — and then to not just claim the temple as his own house but to also defile it in such a graphic, disgusting way was more than the natural mind could comprehend.

Men in flowing beards cried out, "He would sacrifice a *pig* in the Holy of Holies and cavort in its blood?" They fell to their knees, weeping and moaning. But even more people crowded the pillars at the top of the steps, calling for Carpathia's own blood.

It became clear to Buck when Carpathia finally irrevocably tipped the scale against himself. The holy men shushed the crowd when Nicolae's small contingent of healthy men fetched the golden statue. A low rumble of dissent grew as thousands seemed unable to control themselves, while trying to hear what dastardly thing he would do next.

"Why worship at an altar of brass?" he said, his sneer filling the monitors. "If this is indeed the holiest of holy places, every supplicant should enjoy the privilege of bowing to my image, which our Most High Reverend Father has imbued with the power to speak when I am not present!"

Carpathia waited inside the temple for delivery of his statue, but when the assignees appeared to carefully tip it horizontally and bear it inside, they were surrounded by the mob. "Even GC personnel are fighting this, Chaim," Buck said, and the old man nodded. Buck shot him a double take. Chaim seemed more than solemn. He appeared distracted, probably running over in his mind his next step. This situation had turned uglier than anyone in the Tribulation Force had expected, from what Buck remembered of all their discussions and planning sessions. Something had to give — and soon.

When the protestors rushed the men carrying the statue, other loyalists from inside rushed out, brandishing weapons. A few fired into the air and the crowd backed off, waving their fists and cursing. When the monitors showed the men transporting the life-size image to the west end of the temple and up the steps to the Holy of Holies, the crowd had had enough and began rioting. If a person wore a GC uniform and was not part of the melee, he or she was a target of it.

Most uniformed personnel were too weak even to fire their weapons, but when some did and a few fell under their bullets, the throng erupted and attacked. The medical tents toppled, benches and chairs were upended, the guillotine was knocked over and stomped into pieces. Morale Monitors and Peacekeepers were trampled, their weapons yanked from their hands, and soon the TV monitors came crashing down. All over the Temple Mount people raged, screeching, "Down with Carpathia! Death to the monster! May he die and stay dead!"

Buck pulled Chaim to a safe spot and tried to shield the contraband camera. His monitor showed that the cacophony had reached Carpathia, and he appeared pale and shaken. "I am coming out to calm my people," he said into the lens. "They need only be reminded that I am their risen lord and god."

Few heard that over the din, but those who did must have spread the word quickly, because as Buck followed Carpathia's march back to the entrance of the temple, he looked up to see the Orthodox Jews leading the way to the fake Solomon's scaffold, which was quickly reduced to splinters.

A band of zealots spotted Buck's camera, and before he could convince them he was on their side, they grabbed it and smashed it to the ground. Desperate to see what would happen in front of the temple, Buck scampered up a tree and saw Viv Ivins meet Carpathia near the entrance. Something kept the rioters outside, and Buck guessed it could be only their reluctance to assassinate a man in the temple, despite what he had done there.

Nicolae looked petrified while trying to appear otherwise and kept looking back to find the rest of his entourage. They finally caught up, but simply remaining upright seemed to take the last vestiges of strength from Fortunato and Moon and many others. Carpathia pointed and shouted, and someone found him a microphone that was connected to loudspeakers in the outer court.

Like a madman choosing the wholly wrong approach to winning back the crowd, Carpathia held the mike in one hand and raised his other for attention, crying out, "You have breached the covenant! My pledge of seven years of peace for Israel is rescinded! Now you must allow me and my —"

But the rest was drowned out by the mutinous multitude. While they would not cross the threshold of the temple, they pressed right up to it, creating a human barrier between Carpathia and his freedom to step out. Suddenly they quieted and began to chuckle, then laugh, then roar with pleasure at what they had accomplished. It was as if they had cornered a helpless pest and now didn't know what to do with him.

"My brothers and sisters of the Global Community," Carpathia began again, "I will see that you are healed of your sores, and you will again see that it is I who love you and bring you peace!"

"You'll not leave here alive, pretender!" someone shouted, and others took up the cause.

Then, crystal clear in the early afternoon air, came the piercing voice of the little man in the brown robe, and all eyes and ears turned toward him. "It is not the due time for the man of sin to face judgment, though it is clear he has been revealed!"

The crowd murmured, not wanting to be dissuaded from killing Carpathia.

Chaim strode slowly toward the bulk of the group, and they respectfully, silently parted. "As was foretold centuries ago," Chaim continued as he angled toward the temple steps, "God has chosen to allow this evil for a time, and impotent as this enemy of your souls may be today, much more evil will be perpetrated upon you under his hand. When he once again gains advantage, he will retaliate against this presumption on his authority, and you would do well to not be here when his anger is poured out."

"That is right!" Carpathia hollered, his

voice sounding tinny compared to Chaim's authoritative tone. "You will rue the day when you dared —"

"You!" Chaim roared, pointing at Nicolae. "You shall let God's chosen ones depart before his curse is lifted, lest you face a worse plague in its place."

Buck, still wedged in the tree, phoned Chang. "Camera's trashed," he said.

"So I gathered."

"You getting this?"

"The GC's trying to talk over it. It's as if they can't decide whether Carpathia would want it on the air. Heads are going to roll."

"What'd Carpathia just say?" Buck said. "I missed it."

"Something about his being at the Knesset, available to negotiate or to answer honest inquiries from his subjects."

"They'll never let him get out of the —"

But they did. The crowd backed away for Nicolae and his people as they had for Chaim.

"Any chance of tapping into the Knesset?" Buck said.

"Not that I know of," Chang said. "Are you going?"

"If Chaim goes, I go."

"Leave your phone open. I'll patch it to everybody else."

But before Buck could get down from the

tree, Chaim raised his arms and gained the attention of the angry mob. "Let those who are in Judea flee to the mountains. Let him who is on the housetop not go down to take anything out of his house. And let him who is in the field not go back to get his clothes."

"Why should we flee?" someone yelled. "We have exposed the potentate as an impotent pretender!"

"Because God has spoken!"

"Now we're to believe *you* are God?"

"The great I Am has told me. Whatsoever he even thinks comes to pass, and as he purposes, so shall it stand."

Buck was sure the people would have none of it, but Chaim had apparently spoken with such authority that they were instantly calmed. "Where shall we go?" someone asked.

"If you are a believer in Jesus Christ as Messiah," Chaim said, "leave now for Petra by way of Mizpe Ramon. If you have transportation, take as many with you as you can. Volunteers from around the globe are also here to transport you, and from Mizpe Ramon you will be helicoptered in to Petra. The weak, the elderly, the infirm, find your way to the Mount of Olives, and you will be flown in from there."

"And if we do not believe?"

"If you have an ear ɔ hear, make your way to Masada, where you will be free to worship God as you once did here at his temple. There I will present the case for Jesus as Messiah. Do not wait! Do not hesitate! Go now, everyone!"

Buck was stunned to see many with Carpathia's mark stagger into the throng that was quickly forming to depart the Temple Mount. He knew they could not change their minds, that they had once and for all turned their backs on God. But they were now in no-man's-land. They were without the protection of God, and yet they had publicly crossed Antichrist. Should the plague of boils be lifted, surely GC forces would cut them down. The Orthodox Jews and the undecided were allowed at Masada, but no one who had taken the mark of the beast could enter.

David had been unable to raise Hannah on his computer, so he wrote his response to her E-mail and transmitted it just before watching the goings-on at the Temple Mount. Excitement coursed through him as he anticipated the first arrivals. He had spent hours setting up the basic framework of the wireless computer system, and now all he could do was wait.

Buck didn't want to lose Chaim, but he needn't have worried. The Temple Mount was soon empty and left a mess. Chaim descended the temple steps and motioned to Buck to follow. As they walked in the direction of the Knesset, Jerusalem seemed to explode around them. Looters smashed windows and knocked over merchandise kiosks in the streets. Drunken revelers sang and danced and sloshed drinks as they cavorted outside bars and clubs. Those suffering with boils wailed, and many tried to kill themselves in broad daylight.

Meanwhile, the Jewish believers, the undecideds, and the Orthodox Jews hurried along, seeking rides to the Mount of Olives, Masada, or Mizpe Ramon. Operation Eagle vehicles abounded, unidentified other than by eager drivers encouraging others with the mark of God on their foreheads to quickly get aboard. Drivers who saw Buck and Chaim either saluted or pointed to heaven. Everywhere people called out, "He is risen," and were answered by, "Christ is risen indeed!" Many were singing.

Buck suffered from sensory overload. He mourned Hattie. He missed Chloe and Kenny and feared for their safety. He was both horrified and thrilled by what he had seen, and he was also puzzled yet hopeful. He had not expected Chaim to have to persuade people to flee Carpathia while they believed they had already gained the upper hand. And of course he had no idea what to expect at the Knesset.

As a commercial pilot Rayford had thrived on the schedule, the predictability of his days. But on this mission he had had to adapt at a moment's notice, depending upon how God led Chaim. This could have been as simple as driving people from Jerusalem to Mizpe Ramon — roughly a hundred miles — then airlifting them about fifty miles southeast to Petra. But somewhere along the line both Masada and the Mount of Olives had been added to the itinerary, and it was Rayford's job to stretch his personnel to fit the task. One responsibility he carved out for himself was picking up Chaim and Buck once everyone else was safe. Dr. Rosenzweig insisted on their being among the last to arrive at Petra, akin to a captain and his first mate's being the last ones off a ship, but Rayford wouldn't know until the last minute where to pick them up.

"Binoculars?" Z said. "I can do ya one better'n that, Chloe. You lookin' up or out?"

"Mostly out," Chloe said, yawning. "Nothing specific." She didn't want Zeke to know what was on her mind. It wasn't that she didn't trust him. She simply didn't want any input. The adults had sat watching the temple debacle, and the flight to Petra was underway. Once she was satisfied that Buck was safe, she would be able to sit idle no more.

Zeke had come up with an interesting idea weeks before. Like everyone else, she liked the way he thought, though his way of expressing himself might fool a stranger into thinking he was less than bright. He had encouraged Chloe to clone herself via the Internet. "You know, recruit other people like you. There have to be lots of young moms who are feeling left out of the action. Teach 'em what you do, get 'em to do it in their areas and regions. You can't do it all yourself anyway."

The concept had ignited like a gaslit fire. Chloe uploaded manuals and lists of duties, procedures, cross-referenced contact databases — everything a regional director of the International Commodity Co-op would need. She was virtually working herself out of a job.

Now she had gone to the jack-of-all-trades and the one man besides her father who had inventoried the entire Strong Building. Zeke had gone further than Rayford, however. He had computerized a list of everything he had found. A tower that huge bore a mother lode of treasures. "I mean, there *are* binocs," he said. "Some really super-powerful, top-of-the-line types too. But knowin' you, you want the most powerful eyes I can find ya, am I right?"

"As usual."

"It'll be dawn soon. You want it like right now?"

"If possible."

"Be right back."

Zeke took several minutes. His computer told him where this item was, and he headed for the elevators.

Ming headed back to bed while Tsion reported that Chang had informed him he would try to patch Chicago in to the Knesset meeting of Chaim and Buck with Carpathia. "I need to sleep," Tsion told Chloe, "but I will keep an ear open for that . . . unless you want to."

"I've had enough of St. Nick for one night," she said. "Why don't you just record it and get some rest?"

Tsion nodded with a look that said her idea had scored with him. "That way I can listen if I want and not worry if I nod off."

Zeke returned, looking as if he couldn't wait to see Chloe's reaction. He handed her a plain white box that surprised her with its weight. She sat and opened it, producing a huge, squatty telescope about a foot long that took two hands to pull from the wrapping. "Wow," she said. "Will this need a tripod?"

"Not supposed to," Zeke said. "But you gotta brace it on somethin'. The window ledge will do. Want any help?"

"No thanks, Z. I appreciate it. Let me figure it out for myself. It's way past your bedtime too, isn't it?"

"Way past."

Ten

The sores had so decimated Carpathia's staff that Buck thought anyone could walk right past security at the Knesset and take him out. The weak, scratching, wincing crew looked up wearily at Buck and Chaim but barely acknowledged their presence. Not only was Buck not searched, but he was also not even asked his name. He and Chaim were ushered into a small conference room, where Nicolae sat with Fortunato on his right and Moon on his left. They looked like refugees from a quarantine camp, both hunched over the table, heads in their hands, barely able to keep their eyes open.

As the door shut behind Buck, Carpathia said sarcastically, "Forgive me for not standing." He pointed to two chairs. Buck sat quickly, then felt conspicuous when Chaim remained standing.

"I represent the one true God and his Son, Jesus, the Christ," the old man said. "I prefer to stand."

Carpathia appeared so angry he couldn't speak. His jaw muscles protruded as he ground his teeth, glaring. Chaim merely met his gaze.

"All right," Nicolae said, "I am letting these people run off to the hills. When do the sores go away? I upheld my end of the bargain."

"We had a bargain?" Chaim said.

"Come, come! We are wasting time! You said you would lift this spell if I —"

"That is not my recollection," Chaim said. "I said that if you did *not* let them go, you would suffer yet a worse plague."

"So I let them go. Now you —"

"It is not as if you had a choice."

Carpathia slammed an open palm on the table, making his cohorts jump. "Are we here to play word games? I want the sores on my people healed! What do I have to do?"

"Make no attempt to stop Israeli Messianic believers from getting to Petra."

Carpathia stood. "Have you not noticed?

I am the only full-time employee of the Global Community not suffering from the plague!"

Chaim remained calm. "And that only because you have not taken your own mark, though I daresay you worship yourself."

Nicolae rushed around the table and bent to face Chaim from just inches away. "Our medical experts have determined there is no connection between the application of the mark of loyalty and —"

"Why does your bad breath not surprise me?"

"You do not dare to lift the curse for fear your fate will be the same as that of your two associates at the Wall."

"If your medical experts know so much," Chaim said, "how is it that they have been able to offer no relief?"

Carpathia sighed and sat on the table, his back to Fortunato and Moon. "So you are not here to negotiate? You are here to tell me I am at your mercy and that there is nothing I can do to ease the pain of my people?"

"I am here to remind you that this script has already been written. I have read it. You lose."

Carpathia stood again. "If I am not god," he said, "I challenge yours to slay me now. I spit in his face and call him a weakling. If I remain alive for ten more seconds, he, and you, are frauds."

Chaim smiled. "What kind of a God would he be if he felt compelled to act on your timetable?"

Buck loved seeing Carpathia speechless. He seemed to tremble with rage, staring and shaking his head. Behind him, Moon tapped Fortunato's shoulder, making the reverend recoil. "Sorry," Moon whispered and leaned close to his ear.

"Excellency," Fortunato rasped, "a word, please."

"What? What is it?"

Fortunato struggled to his feet, clasped his hands before him, and bowed. "Please, Your Worship. A moment."

Nicolae looked as if he were about to detonate. He moved back behind the table, making Moon stand too. Fortunato pleaded with him in a voice too faint for Buck to hear.

"I suppose you concur, Moon," Nicolae said.

Moon nodded and Fortunato added, "It was *his* idea," which made Moon's face drop, and he shot Leon a look.

"You two get out of here. I want a meeting, you know where, with the full cabinet."

"Not here?"

"No! I said you know where! These walls have ears!"

The two gingerly made their way out. Carpathia looked down at Buck. "This one makes me nervous," he said. "Does he have to be here?"

"He does."

"My people are pleading for respite," Nicolae said. "I recognize that I am forced to concede something."

"And that would be?"

Carpathia's eyes danced, as if he hated with his entire being what he had to say. "That . . . I . . . must . . . submit to you in this. I am prepared to do what I have to do to enable a lifting of the plague." He lowered his head as if pushing against an invisible force.

"You are under the authority of the God of Abraham, Isaac, and Jacob, maker of heaven and earth. You will allow this exodus, and when I am satisfied that the people under my charge are safe, I will pray God to lift the affliction."

Buck wouldn't have been surprised to see smoke rise from Carpathia's ears. "How long?" Nicolae said.

"This is a huge undertaking," Chaim said. "Six hours should be telling."

Carpathia looked up hopefully.

"But should you attempt to lay a hand on

one of the chosen," Chaim warned, "the second judgment will rain down."

"Understood," Carpathia said, a little too quickly. He thrust out his hand.

Chaim ignored it, glanced at Buck, and left.

Buck rose to follow and wondered if Carpathia recognized either of them. He avoided eye contact, but as Buck slipped past Antichrist, Nicolae growled, "Your days are numbered."

Buck nodded, still looking away. "That's for sure."

Chloe scraped a three-inch hole in the black paint at the bottom of a window. Then she placed a cushion from the couch on the marble floor and set the telescope lens against the glass, bracing it on the frame. Several minutes of trial and error finally resulted in her discovering an image in the predawn haze. She thought she had seen something in the middle of the night several days before, but she had not been able to locate it again and thus told no one. Now she slowly scanned the horizon, trying to keep the hugely powerful apparatus steady and the image in front of her eye. The image was so magnified that she guessed she was viewing just a few feet square from more than half a mile away.

The problem was, of course, that such a lens required as much light as she could find. It was designed to bring stars into focus on clear nights. All she saw were the dark silhouettes of a ravaged skyline, and no light anywhere. Frustrated, she set the scope down and refocused with the naked eye, trying to get a bead on what she had seen faintly once. At about two o'clock in her field of vision and maybe three-quarters of a mile away, a speck of light stopped her. So it wasn't her imagination. The question was, what light would be on in a city the world thought was radiation contaminated? Was it possible Tribulation Force members were not the only intelligent life-forms in this alien universe?

She shook her head. Probably just a streetlight that somehow was still hooked up to power. Still, the scope might offer more clues. Keeping the speck in sight, she raised the instrument to the window and carefully studied the area. After a minute or two she realized she had aimed too high and was taking in the foreboding waters of Lake Michigan. Keeping the apparatus in place, she looked past it again and adjusted, then peeked through the eyepiece again.

The image jumped and moved, appeared

and disappeared. It was more than a street-light, but the harder she tried to focus on it, the more elusive it became. Her neck stiffened, her wrists cramped, her eye wearied. She realized she'd been holding her breath to minimize her movement, but that just caused her heart to beat harder. Finally she had to put the telescope down and move. But when she was ready to try again, the sun teased the eastern horizon. Chloe would have to try again another night.

"Mount of Olives?" Buck said, as he caught up to Chaim.

"Of course. Then to Masada to see what kind of a crowd we have attracted."

"Question. Why six hours? You trust him?"

Chaim shot Buck a look. "Trust him? Of course! He was willing to shake on it."

"Okay, dumb question. But there's no way everybody will be safe by nightfall."

"We already know he will break the agreement, Cameron. Revelation 12 is clear that Israel is given two wings of a great eagle, that she might fly into the wilderness to her place, but that the serpent spews water out of his mouth like a flood after her. No question he will attack somehow, plague or not. Tsion believes the 'flood' is Antichrist's army. That same chapter says the earth helps the woman by opening its mouth and swallowing up the flood. May the Lord forgive me, but I want to see that. Don't you?"

Buck nodded, finally grabbing his phone and listening to see if Chang was still monitoring. "You there?" he said.

"Working on the Phoenix connection," Chang said. "Thanks. That was spooky."

"You're the best."

"I'll call you when I'm ready to patch you in."

Chaim waited till Buck was finished, then asked, "You know what happens after God thwarts Antichrist's armies, do you not?"

"You mean before or after you drop the second judgment on him?"

"Before *I* drop it? I am merely the messenger, my friend."

"I know," Buck said.

"The Bible says the dragon becomes enraged with the woman and goes to make war with the rest of her offspring, 'who keep the commandments of God and have the testimony of Jesus Christ.' To me that sounds like the other believing Jews around the world."

"And what do we do about that?"

"I have no idea," Chaim said. "We obey, that is all."

Rayford was too antsy to sit at Mizpe Ramon waiting for the first arrivals. He set a course for the Mount of Olives and phoned Tsion in Chicago on the way. Rayford felt bad when it was obvious from Dr. Ben-Judah's voice that he had been sleeping. But he said, "You are never an intrusion, Captain Steele."

"I confess I'm troubled, Dr. Ben-Judah. My military training was during peacetime, so this is the first time I've been responsible for so many people in a dangerous situation."

"But you have been through so much with the Tribulation Force!"

"I know, but I just wish I could be assured I will see no casualties."

"We certainly have had no such guarantees in our inner circle," Tsion said, "have we?"

"That's not reassuring."

"I just want to be honest, Captain. I assume that is what you want."

"What I want is what I asked for, I'm afraid — the knowledge that I will lose no one."

"I believe we will lose none of the 144,000, but most of those are scattered throughout the world. I am also fairly certain that the prophecies indicate that God will protect the Messianic believers who are fleeing Jerusalem. But you are asking about your operation personnel."

"Right."

"I can only pray and hope."

"I'm committed to not engaging the enemy in kill strikes."

"I am sympathetic to that, and yet you wish for no deaths on your side either. I do not know how realistic that is. Would you not feel justified in an all-or-nothing situation?"

"You mean if it's my guy or theirs? I guess I would permit firing."

"You know, Captain, the enemy will most certainly suffer losses. The way the verses read, many will perish in the calamities God puts in their paths."

"I prefer leaving that work to him."

David checked for a response from Hannah, and seeing none, keyed in a connect to Chang, who had the bugged Phoenix 216 on-line for the Trib Force.

The first voice was Walter Moon's. "I should be in bed, Excellency. I hate to complain, but I might have wished this meeting had been held at the Knesset. The incessant moving about —"

"Oh, stop your blubbering, Walter. I am not discounting your discomfort, but you make it sound as if you are at death's door."

"It feels like we are, Lordship," Leon said. "I am not one to —"

"Of course you are! Now I laid down the law to this Micah character and got him to guarantee a lifting of this disease by nine tonight or there would be consequences."

"You did? Well, how —"

"He had better tread lightly with me."

"But I thought —"

"That is your problem, gentlemen. Sometimes you must act viscerally and do what needs to be done. Is everyone here?"

"Many are being pulled from sickbeds," Walter said. "Which is where —"

"You should be, yes, I know. Here are Viv and Suhail. Let me know when we are all here."

"How long will it take to recover, once the affliction has been lifted?" Viv asked.

"I do not know," Carpathia said. "But even if there is residual fatigue or pain, you must all fight through it and encourage your people to do the same."

"Mr. Hut completes the contingent, Potentate."

"You look terrible, son," Nicolae said.

"I feel worse," Hut said.

"I cannot imagine. So how is my inaccurate-shooting friend?"

"Very funny."

"Excuse me," Nicolae said, "but was that two times consecutively you addressed me without title?"

"Well, pardon me, your highness."

David heard movement and assumed Carpathia had stood. "You would employ sarcasm with me?"

"I shot that man eight times at point-blank range, *worshipfulness!* The heckler I killed from two feet away. You couldn't have killed Micah yourself."

"Mr. Akbar, your side arm, please."

"Oh, Excellency, is this nec—"

"Is *everyone* planning to disrespect me? I have death pills enough for the lot of you, and I deliver them through the barrel of this gun."

"If you could have killed Mr. Micah," Hut said, "why didn't you?"

"Oh, you honor him with a title, but not me — no, not your risen lord."

"You are nothing to me, Carpathia."

"On your feet, boy."

"I wouldn't give you the satisfaction."

BOOM!

Cries and gasps followed the sound of the body's tumbling. "Walter, have the stewards get him out of here. Now who is next?"

Silence.

"Is there then someone here who would care to fire upon me?"

"No!"

"No, Excellency!"

"Please, Potentate!"

"No!"

"Is there another among you who retains some notion that this is not serious business? I remind you that I was dead three days and raised myself! I have demanded your freedom from these sores, and though we cannot be certain until the time comes, I believe you will enjoy immediate healing. Regardless, you and yours will be ambulatory and able enough again to carry out my battle plan."

"Wouldn't an attack bring back the plague, Excellency?" Moon asked.

"Viv, do you see what I have to work with here? Mr. Moon is my supreme commander, my executive vice president, if you will, yet he wants to know if—" and here he mimicked Moon with a ridiculous plaintive whine— "an attack wouldn't bring back the plague! Honestly, Walter, do you think I am new to the negotiating game?"

"No, sir, I—"

"Spare me! The curse will be lifted at

2100 hours, and the hundreds of thousands of cowards will be in one of four places. Anyone? Come on! Someone?"

Suhail Akbar said, "The Mount of Olives, en route to Mizpe Ramon, Masada, or Petra."

"Excellent! Someone is thinking! And what is unique about so many people in so few places? Suhail?"

"They are together, and they are vulnerable."

"Precisely. I want the whole of Israel declared a no-fly zone for all but Global Community aircraft at 2115 hours."

David heard Suhail calling his people.

"And while you are at it, Director," Carpathia said, "establish a curfew at the same time in all of the United Carpathian States for civilian vehicular traffic. Prepare a retaliatory strike for the damage we suffered at Petra earlier today, assuming until further knowledge that that wanton ambush was initiated by the Judah-ites."

"Where will we attack, Potentate?" Akbar said.

"Masada at 2130 hours. Did you not predict attendance of more than one hundred thousand?"

"But those are not Judah-ites, Excellency."

"They are potential converts, man! And this Micah himself will address them! He will surely have followers with him, but he has unwittingly put them all in one box for us and tied a ribbon around it. What would it take to ensure annihilation?"

"We have the firepower, sir."

"No arrests on the road. No warnings in the air. Illegal vehicles will be destroyed on sight and invading planes shot from the sky. This Mizpe Ramon site was camouflaged to somehow make it appear a GC operation. Let us make use of it then. And if anyone remains on the Mount of Olives after 2100, they are fair game."

"Sir?" Moon said. "What if Mr. Micah does call down the plague of sores again?"

"He will know the consequences if we act with dispatch."

"But what if he follows through on his threat to turn the water —"

"The what-ifs will do you in one day, Walter. You serve the ruler of the universe, and we shall prevail. I have tricked this wizard into breaking his spell, and before he realizes his mistake, we will have regained the advantage. We can virtually eliminate the Jerusalem Orthodox Jewish population and cripple the Judah-ites to the point of extinction. Ideally, we will flush out Ben-

Judah himself, and this time he will not find me so hospitable."

"What about those who reach Petra?"

Carpathia laughed. "Petra as a place of refuge is ludicrous! It is as defenseless as Masada. They will be on foot, stuffed into a bowl of rock. An air attack should be over in minutes, but for that we shall wait until the last of them are there."

"The Judah-ites did display heavy fire-power today," Akbar said.

"That merely justifies whatever level of retribution we deem appropriate. Any casualties?"

"No reports of anyone actually hit. Two unaccounted for."

"Missing in action?"

"If you wish."

A long pause. Then Carpathia: "Two MIAs."

Buck and Chaim sat under an ancient tree on the Mount of Olives and watched thousands find their way in. Within an hour the Operation Eagle choppers began floating into position, Rayford himself among the first. The birds were loaded to capacity but were in no way keeping up with the growing crowd.

Buck had relayed the Carpathia meeting

word for word to Chaim as he listened by phone, but Dr. Rosenzweig had remained expressionless. In the end he said, "I am not surprised. I will pray that God will lift the plague of boils completely and restore everyone to full strength. I want them overconfident, full of themselves when they try to take vengeance. And when the second plague rains down, I pray it will carry God's full potency."

"Doctor, do we risk catastrophe at Masada?"

The old man shook his head. "I do not know, but I do not feel we should back down. We will finish before nine o'clock and warn the Jews of Carpathia's plan. They may leave or stay and fight, but I hope they will feel even more urgency to make their decisions for Christ too. As people are sealed by God, we will rush them to Petra."

Rayford felt alone in the packed chopper. Listening in on the Carpathia meeting had confirmed his worst fears. The only location he was confident of was Petra, and even there, he had to wonder if it was the place or the people who would be protected. He used his secure radio to reroute all air traffic directly to Petra. "No stops, repeat, no stops at Mizpe Ramon. Ground vehicles will deliver their charges to the foot passage into

Petra. Those who can walk in, will. Those who cannot — or when the passageway is too crowded, those who are left exposed — will need to be air-hopped inside. Continue the routes to and from the Mount of Olives. And ignore an expected air curfew. Take evasive and defensive action as necessary, but do not fail these people."

Rayford conference-called Albie, Mac, and Abdullah. "Wish we could get our heads together," he said. But each was either flying a load to Petra or returning to pick up another.

"Rethinkin' your no-shootin' policy there, Chief?" Mac said.

"I hope so," Albie said.

Rayford let out a heavy sigh. "I just don't want to lead anyone to slaughter."

"Arm us, Ray," Albie said. "George has enough weapons for —"

"Tell me George was not privy to the Phoenix patch-in," Rayford said. It wasn't that he didn't trust the man, but keeping need-to-know circles close was important and had been made clear.

Silence.

"Tell me, Albie!"

"Ray, you know me better than that. You said nobody but Trib Force, and that's the way we played it."

"How many of our pilots would know how to handle a fifty-caliber?"

"None of 'em, Ray," Mac said. "You issue those to drivers. Too erratic and dangerous from the air. Give us the DEWs. Somebody stops us on the ground, we heat 'em up."

"They're planning to shoot us out of the air, gentlemen!"

"Only way to prevent that with the fifties is to shoot first," Mac said. "It means a change of policy. Is that where you're goin', Ray?"

Rayford stalled. "Haven't heard from you, Abdullah. You there?"

"Here, boss."

"Well?"

"Not bad, thank you, sir."

"I mean, well, what do you think?"

"About what?"

"Smitty! Come on! I need some counsel here."

"We cannot shoot the big guns and fly too, Captain. That would take two pilots to a chopper. And out of what hole do we shoot such a weapon?"

"He's right," Mac said. "As usual."

"I am willing to trust God with my life," Abdullah said. "And if he would allow me, I would happily use a DEW to make toast of the enemy."

Rayford peeked over his shoulder at the

believers huddled behind him, fear and hope etched on their faces. They could not hear him over the noise of the engine and the whirring blades.

"All right, gentlemen," he hollered into the phone, "after you unload your passengers, swing by Mizpe Ramon and pick up a third of the DEWs each and distribute them to your respective squadrons. Albie, get George involved too. And the first one there, get Ms. Rose and Ms. Palemoon evacuated if they're ready. You'll need room for all their supplies too."

"You think the GC is going to waste the landing strip and our quarters?" Albie said.

"Likely."

"Where are we EVACing these women?"

"Masada for now."

"You gonna distribute fifties to ground drivers, Chief?"

"Still noodling that one, Mac," Rayford said.

David guessed it would be two hours from Chaim's speech at the Temple Mount until he saw his first arrivals. He called Rayford. "What gives with our nurses? Hannah owes me an E-mail response. They okay?"

"No reason to believe otherwise. Did you try calling them?"

"No response."

"I'll check in on them." He told David what was happening with the weapons and the med center.

"Need my help on that?" David said.

"You've got to hang in there and coordinate until Chaim arrives, and that could be a couple of days."

"I could appoint one of the first to get here. There's no science to this. How are you going to handle those big guns by yourself?"

"I'll get Leah and Hannah to help."

"They done tearing down and packing up?"

"Should be."

"You regret having the airstrip built and then having to abandon it?"

"Sure, but we needed it on the front end anyway. Where else were all our birds going to land?"

"Got any prospects on board?"

"For your job? I don't know, David. Why don't you stay put?"

"If they speak Hebrew and can elicit trust, that'll free me up to hop back to the strip with you and load the guns."

"I'm not even sure I'll issue the fifties," Rayford said.

"Well, I'm willing if you need me."

Late in the afternoon David climbed to the

high place and scanned the horizon. Nothing yet, but he heard movement in the rocks below. No way anyone on foot could have arrived before the choppers. He knelt and crept to the edge, holding his breath to listen. His heart banged against his ribs. He guessed two sets of footsteps, slowly moving.

David pulled out the only weapon he could think of, his phone, and readied himself to speed-dial Rayford. He rose to where he could peer over the side. Resolutely and gingerly picking their way through loose rock not fifty feet below him were two sickly, stumbling GC Peacekeepers, uniforms drenched in sweat. Each carried a high-powered rifle. David punched the speed-dial button for Rayford, and the Peacekeepers both looked directly up at him at the same time. Before he could get the phone to his ear, they dropped to their knees and angled their weapons at him.

David dropped the phone and dove for cover, sharp rocks digging deep into his knees and hands. The soldiers, obviously left for dead by their compatriots, must have felt a surge of adrenaline. They couldn't have expected to find anyone here after surviving the fifty-caliber assault from the other direction, but now they advanced with vigor.

David scrambled to his feet, only to discover something seriously wrong with his ankle. He tried hopping toward a cave, but unarmed he would be easy prey there. He heard his pursuers separate just below the ridge, the sounds of their boots in the rocks coming from about twenty feet apart. If they rushed him, David had nowhere to go.

He was no match for them, but retreat wasn't an option. He hopped toward the edge, bent to scoop a handful of jagged rocks, and reared back to fire at the first head that popped up.

Rayford glanced at his ringing phone and saw who was calling. Again. So soon. David had never proven to be a pest. "Steele here," he said.

All he heard were sounds of boots on rocks.

"David? You there?"

From a distance, "God, help me!"

"David?"

A desperate cry, a shout in Hebrew, burps of gunfire from at least two weapons, a fall, a grunt. David's hoarse whisper, "God, please!" Liquid splashing.

David lay on his back, his body numb, no pain even in his ankle. The cloudless blue sky filled his entire field of vision. His heart galloped and his panicked lungs made his chest rise and fall in waves. Though he could feel nothing, he heard blood gushing from his head.

The soldiers leaned over him, but he could not move his eyes to focus on either of them. If only he could appear already dead . . . but he couldn't stop his heaving chest. David could pray only silently now. He pleaded with God to let him neither hear nor feel the kill shots as the two pointed their muzzles at his heart and pulled the triggers.

Rayford's phone was still open, but all he heard after more deafening rifle shots were expressions of effort and what he could only imagine was the lifting of a body and the flinging of it over the side of a mountain. Then footsteps away from the phone, until they faded out of range.

Besides dreading what he would find at Petra, Rayford couldn't deliver a chopper full of believers to a spot that could be teeming with the enemy lying in wait. Hating himself for already thinking past what sounded for all the world like David Hassid's death, Rayford knew he had to keep that phone from falling into the wrong hands.

Eleven

Leah didn't understand Hannah, but that was okay. She didn't always understand herself either. They had secured the last of the medical supplies into hard-sided boxes that would fit into a cargo hold and were now monitoring Hannah's computer.

"You know for sure it was Hassid who called?"

Hannah nodded.

"And you want to talk to him, so why didn't you —"

"I'm not sure I want to talk to him until I know how he's going to respond to my E-mail. He should have written me back. Then I'd know and I could take his call. Maybe."

244

Leah shook her head. "Even if we didn't have only three and a half years, I'd tell you life's too short and you ought to call him. He's a busy guy. When would he have had time to write you back?"

"I found time to write."

"Hannah! We're not building a computer system here that has to serve a million people."

Hannah was staring at the screen. The news was nothing but Carpathia propaganda, pundits trying to spin his temple folly into something that made sense. Leah leaned in to look at the scroll across the bottom of the screen. "His Excellency the potentate guarantees healing from the affliction of sores by 2100 hours Carpathian Time."

"I'm stupid," Hannah said.

"I know."

"Stop it! We hardly know each other."

"Sorry. Why are you stupid?"

Hannah pointed to the computer's status bar below the scrolling message. It showed she had mail. "Bet that's from David," she said.

"Let's find out," Leah said, but before either could switch screens, their phones rang simultaneously. "Rayford," Leah told Hannah.

"Mine too," Hannah said.

Leah held up a hand. "Let me," she said. "Med center."

"Leah, Rayford. You two okay?"

"Yeah, except it looks like you called us both at the same time."

"I did. Hannah there?" Leah nodded at her and Hannah answered too. "You packed up and ready to go?"

"Yes," Leah said. "But where —"

"Just listen. I'm short on time. You know George?"

"Big guy? Calif—"

"That's him. I just pulled him off another assignment. He's gonna land there within three or four minutes and he's going to need help setting up a nest of fifty-caliber rifles. Smitty will join him soon."

"Don't they each have a load of passengers?"

"Yes, and we need to get them as far from the airstrip and the buildings as we can."

"They're not going to Petra?"

"Eventually. Just listen. By the time it's dark, those people need to be isolated and invisible from the air. After I land there briefly and take off again, any other aircraft over Mizpe Ramon will be GC, and George and Smitty will be defending the airstrip."

"And we'll be baby-sitting two loads of

passengers until someone comes for them?"

"Three. I've got a load too, and I need to pick up a fifty myself."

"Where are you going?"

"I've got a situation at Petra, and I'm going to need one of you to go with me. Leah, that would be you."

"Hold on!" Hannah said. "Who's at Petra besides David?"

"We've delivered no one yet. I want to be sure the area is secure before we —"

"Why wouldn't it be? What's the problem?"

"I don't know yet, but —"

"But there's a problem or David could tell you."

"I just can't reach him right now is all," Rayford said. "Let's not jump to any —"

"Then I'm coming. Leah can help George and Abdullah and herd these people somewhere."

"Hannah," Rayford said, "I —"

"Don't try to talk me out of this, Captain Steele. I —"

"Hannah! This is a military operation and I am your superior officer. I decide who will do what, and I've told you who is going and who is staying. Do you understand?"

"Yes, but —"

"Any questions?"

247

"No, but, well, I think I just heard from David."

"Either you did or you didn't. Did he call?"

"He e-mailed."

"You're sure?"

"Not entirely," Leah said. "Check it, Hannah."

She switched screens. "Yes, it's from him!"

"When was it sent?"

"Just a sec— oh!"

"Just now or . . . ?"

"No. Some time ago."

"Anything pertinent? Problems? He need help?"

"No," Hannah said, scanning it quickly. "Just personal stuff."

Leah put a hand on Hannah's shoulder and raised her chin at Hannah in encouragement. The younger woman looked terrified.

"Okay, Hannah? We clear?"

"Yes, sir."

"Let me talk with just Leah now, all right?"

Hannah slapped her phone shut while reading David's message.

"Leah," Rayford said, "I don't know what we're going to find at Petra, but David tried to call me and all I heard sounded like him being shot."

"Oh, no!"

"Bring heavy-duty, first-aid stuff and a stretcher."

"Got it."

"If we have to load him on the chopper, can you and I do that?"

"Worry about your end, Captain," she said. Then, whispering and turning away from Hannah, "And you'd better start worrying about that phone and those computers."

"Way ahead of you," Rayford said. "Be there in a few minutes."

Chang was studying the itchy spot on his leg under a light in his New Babylon palace apartment when Rayford called. After a fast briefing, Chang said, "Don't worry about the phone. I can neutralize that from here."

"What do you mean?"

Chang began tapping keys as they spoke. "I can nuke the innards, erase the mother chip. In fact, I just did."

"Now let's hope they haven't found it yet."

"When you connect with David," Chang said, "I need to talk with him."

"I didn't like what I heard, Chang."

"I know, but you can't be sure what you were hearing."

"I know David was unarmed."

"I'm checking on those computers."

"Right now? You can do that?"

"Thanks to David, we can do just about anything from here. Luckily, there's no way they can break into the software. That's on a revolving encoder that can only unravel itself, and it's programmed not to."

"Well, I don't understand all that, but I'm more worried we've got a bunch of crazed GCers up there who think they'd be helping their cause by just destroying all the hardware."

"They *would* be helping their cause. And they would set us way back. But there wouldn't be a bunch of them, would there?"

"How would we know?"

"These have to be leftovers from your attack, right?"

"Probably."

"You heard the Phoenix meeting," Chang said. "There were two unaccounted for."

Rayford put down well off the south end of the airstrip at Mizpe Ramon and sat talking with Mac and Albie by radio as Hannah and Leah met the chopper with medical supplies and a stretcher. As

Hannah led the escapees away from the craft, first finding out who understood English and Hebrew and using them to interpret for her, Leah tossed the supplies aboard and waited outside. "Mr. Smith is bringing your weapons," she mouthed.

Rayford nodded and told Mac and Albie to fly their charges to Wadi Musa, near Petra, and to assume they would be both seen and heard by the two GC suspected at Petra. "Tell your people to stay with the choppers until you come back for them, and then get to the footpath entrance as soon as you can. Don't go in until I get there with weapons for you."

"Question," Albie said.

"Make it quick."

"Have we been all wrong about this being a place of refuge?"

"Albie, all I know to do is to clear it for the people, get 'em in there, and trust God to take care of them."

"And if you find Hassid's body?"

Rayford hesitated. "Then I'm gonna assume it's them or us, and let me tell both you guys something: It's going to be them."

When Rayford leaped from the chopper, Abdullah was already hurrying across the sand from the munitions storage unit. He was bent under the weight of three fifty-caliber rifles on his shoulder with a huge belt of ammunition draped over them. His other arm pointed straight out from his body for balance. Rayford and Leah ran to him and helped carry the weapons to the helicopter.

"You all right, Smitty? You ready?"

"George is giving me a course crash," he said, "whatever that means."

"Crash course. Quick, fast."

Abdullah nodded. "I liked the DEWs, but I will shoot these too. George is setting up at a steep angle to take the enemy planes out of the sky, but I worry about accuracy."

"All you'll have to hit is one and the rest will run."

"I hope you are right, Captain. I will be praying for you, and I am hoping you are wrong about Mr. Hassid. He is a wonderful man."

Rayford hoped so too. He and Leah boarded, and as he guided the chopper up and away, he gazed at the Jordanian sprinting back to where George was setting up to defend the airstrip. Rayford was in the middle of exactly what he had hoped to avoid. People were going to die. One may already have. Knowing he would again see these beloved martyrs, along with all the others he had lost in so short a time, did little to console him. There had to be a limit to the trauma a man could endure. He should have long since blown past his.

Buck had helped Chaim board one of the choppers bound for Masada, and they arrived to find tens of thousands of curious Israelis streaming up the steps into the fabled fortress. Buck had been getting sketchy reports that the airlift had hit a few snags and that the return runs from Petra to the Mount of Olives would be delayed. Rayford was undoubtedly busy and in contact with his people, because he was not answering his phone or returning Buck's calls. Chang reported that he would rather Buck wait and talk with Rayford personally.

It was around nine in the morning in Chicago, so Buck called Chloe while Chaim was pacing behind him. Just before Chloe answered, Chaim bent and whispered, "I shall speak when this place is full."

Rayford could not think of a way to avoid detection by whatever GC might be waiting at Petra. Three choppers would land close by inside several minutes of each other, and it wouldn't be long before dozens more showed up. He considered rerouting the others to Mizpe Ramon, but he feared

Carpathia might order an attack there even before the lifting of the plague, in retaliation for the firing upon his forces. Fearing the airstrip was targeted made him wary to risk more than the three chopper loads already waiting near there. Who knew? Maybe Carpathia or Akbar were smart enough to delay their attack until dark.

With just himself and Leah to worry about, Rayford decided to set the helicopter down on the narrow Siq that led pedestrian and hooved traffic into Petra. He carefully positioned the craft close enough to the outside walls that even if they had been seen, it would be impossible to be fired upon from inside the city.

Unless the enemy was asleep or deep in a cave, they had to be aware that outsiders were coming. Mac and Albie jogged up, the latter gasping for air. "He is so much older and yet in such better shape," Albie said.

"I jog every day," Mac said. " 'Sides, I got about a foot on you."

"Catch your breath," Rayford said. "We've got about another mile to go on foot, and that just gets us into the city. Unless we want to be just targets, we're going to have to climb, and you remember how heavy these babies are."

He handed fifties and ammo to each man

while Leah dragged out her box of supplies. "The stretcher," she said. "Bring it or leave it?"

"We can always come back for it," he said, reminding Mac and Albie to carry the weapons vertically to focus the center of gravity. "When we get inside, we're going to split up. If there are only two of them, we'll even the odds a little. I'm assuming they'll be above us, which gives them the first advantage. Resist the urge to call out for David."

"That's your urge?" Mac said.

Rayford nodded. "I want to know what happened to him, even if it's what I fear."

"Let me look for him," Leah said. "I'll leave my stuff at the other end of the gorge. I don't know why you couldn't have spared another of those rifles."

"Too much to carry," Rayford said. "Anyway, I hope you're busy with a patient."

"I won't be much good to him if I'm dead," she said.

Mac handed her his side arm. "It's only a .45," he said.

"I'll take it."

"You know how to use it?"

"Safety on the left?"

Mac nodded.

"I know more than Captain Steele thinks I do," she said.

"We're only as good as the slowest man," Rayford said. "Albie, lead the way. We need to hurry, but don't waste all your energy."

Albie pulled up his trousers, tightened his belt, and retied his boots. Hoisting the weapon, he swung it vertically and leaned it back into one shoulder. He started off at a fast walking pace, frustrating Rayford, but soon enough he seemed to catch a second wind and began to trot. Mac dropped in behind, loping easily. Rayford let Leah slide in front of him and had to admit he was amazed that she could lug the medical box in one hand, keep her other arm out for balance, and still trot along apace. Rayford himself had little trouble keeping up, but he felt every one of his years — and every joint as well.

A little more than ten minutes later, the narrow, high-walled gorge opened into the stunning sight of Al-Khasneh — the Treasury, once purported to hold the riches of the pharaoh at the time of the Exodus. Under different circumstances, Rayford would love to have gawked at the towering façade cut out of solid rock, but he and his people — not to mention the million that were to follow — were at a point of no return.

Albie stopped and bent over, sucking for air. The rest quietly set down their loads. Rayford moved ahead of them and squatted, peeking out into the vast opening. It was then that he realized that either by dumb luck or the subtle leading of God, he had done something right. He heard the thwocking of at least one more helicopter and knew that more could not be far behind. All those birds had to give the GC, if that's who was here, pause. Where would *they* hide but in a cave? Unless they went on an immediate offensive, they would be quickly outnumbered and had to assume they would be easily overrun.

Rayford turned and whispered, "Leah, leave the med box here, take a hard right, stay low and out of sight as much as you can. Circle around as far as you can go before having to ascend. If that gives you too much exposure, find a place to stay hidden. Our main objective is to find David and get him out of here. He usually called me from one of the high places for best reception."

"Have you tried calling him again?" Leah said.

"Chang already nuked his phone to be safe."

"Safe for whom? What if he's trying to contact us?"

"We couldn't risk it, Leah," Rayford said. "Albie's going to be going left. Mac and I will cover each other and try to see what's straight ahead past the main monuments. We're all trying to get as high as we can without becoming targets. If you find David, click your radio twice and we'll find you. If you encounter the enemy, keep clicking till you see us. Questions?"

They looked at each other in the cool dimness of the gorge and shook their heads. As they moved out into the brighter but fading sun before twilight, Rayford was overwhelmed with the feeling he was in someone's crosshairs. It was nothing unique. He had felt the same way years before in weekend paintball games. There was just something about knowing you were likely beneath your enemy that made you feel you could be seen without being able to see.

Rayford must have seemed as slow to Mac as Albie had to Rayford, because as soon as they reached a clearing wide enough for him to get by, Mac easily moved on ahead. He was headed for the shadow of an outcropping of rock, and Rayford accelerated to stay with him. They knelt there, panting, and Mac squinted across the high horizon behind them. Two more choppers flew over, and almost immediately, Rayford heard two clicks on his radio. He and Mac caught each other's eye. "Who?" Mac mouthed, leaning out and looking to his left, where Albie would have gone.

Rayford leaned the other way and saw Leah behind a rock maybe a hundred yards away and thirty or forty yards up a rocky path. He elbowed Mac and they stared at her as she held up an open palm to them and kept her eyes in the direction of whatever she had seen. She pulled the .45 from her belt with her free hand, but her open palm and her gaze did not stray.

Finally she turned and looked directly at Rayford and Mac. She pointed two fingers at her eyes, then her index finger above her and to the left, which would put the target almost directly above the men. She held up two fingers. "Two directly above us?" Rayford whispered.

Mac nodded. "I'm guessin' she's lookin' a couple hundred yards up."

Rayford kept his eyes on Leah as he started to scoot out from under the rock overhang, but she held up her palm again, stopping him as she continued to watch. Suddenly she showed him the back of her hand and beckoned him out with her fingers. He hesitated, and she looked at him and nodded, then looked back up.

Rayford duck-walked out and turned to look. He stared at the sheer face of a rock wall and looked back at Leah to see if he could keep coming out. She nodded, and he heard two more clicks on his radio. That made him and Mac and Leah look to where Albie was climbing. He signaled the same as Leah from his vantage point. Rayford backed away from Mac, who stayed in position, until he saw the two GC with their backs to him on a high ridge. Both were uniformed and armed, but they looked lethargic, following the helicopters and checking the valleys below too.

Rayford signaled to both Leah and Albie to keep moving, then nodded to Mac to follow him. They hurried out and between building walls to a small gorge that led to a path toward higher ground. They waited at a bend where they were out of the line of vision of the two on the ridge far above. "They're too far from Leah and Albie to hear their radios," Mac whispered.

Rayford mashed the button and said, "How sure are we there are only two?"

"No idea," Leah said.

"They're not on assignment," Albie said. "They're hurting, and they don't seem to be answering to anyone. They're not doing anything specific. Just hanging around, waiting."

"You'd bet there are no others?"

"Not sure I'd stake my life on it," Albie said.

Mac clicked in. "That's exactly what we're doing," he said. "Make the call."

"If we had to decide, I'd say it's worth the chance. But what's the rush?"

"Hundreds of people starting to line up outside," Rayford said. "And they've got to be an hour above us."

Two clicks interrupted and Leah came on. "I see about a hundred yards I can advance without their seeing me. Shall I go for it?"

Rayford glanced at Mac, who nodded. "Affirmative. Three clicks when you're in place, but don't speak unless you know they're far enough away."

As soon as he said that, Leah began a long but smooth ascent, the side arm in her hand. The two GC abruptly turned and walked the other way. "They're headed your way, Albie," Rayford said.

"I hope they keep coming," he said, and he lay on his stomach, unfolding the built-in bipod and loading his weapon.

"That's not a bad idea," Mac said. "We can set up right here."

"We've got Leah up there without us then, Mac. We using her for bait?"

Mac shook his head. "Not unless they turn back toward her." He nodded at her. "She'll reach a flat area up there in thirty minutes." Mac thrust a round into the chamber of the big gun and stretched out on his belly.

A little more than twenty minutes later a chopper approached, and the GC stopped and stared at it, not even attempting to hide. Like mirror images, they raised their weapons and followed the trajectory of the craft. "Don't even think about it, scumbags," Rayford muttered.

Mac scooted to his left and sighed. "I've got a bad angle here. You still got a bead on 'em?"

Rayford sat up and peered through his scope. "Yeah." He punched the radio. "See 'em, Albie?"

"Do I ever! They've both got that big old mark with Carpathia's mug on it, about two inches high over their right eyes."

"Hold," Rayford said. "Maybe they've got David somewhere."

"I lost 'em," Albie said.

"Me too," Mac said.

"I've still got 'em," Rayford said.

Click.

"Go, Leah."

She clicked again.

"They're far enough away," Rayford told her. "What've you got?"

But Mac grabbed his arm. "Maybe she can't talk. Maybe she's got more company."

"Did I give her away by talking to her?" Rayford felt sick.

"Let me check," Mac said. "You got another weapon?"

"Nine millimeter is all."

Mac reached for it. "I got no angle anyway, and Big Bertha will slow me down."

Rayford dug the weapon from his belt in the back and handed it to Mac, who quickly rose and hurried off.

Another twenty minutes and Leah came back on. "You don't want to know what I found," she said.

Rayford almost collapsed from relief. "You're okay there?"

Mac heard the exchange and stopped on the path, his back to a wall.

"I'm okay," Leah said, her voice quavery. "Found David's phone."

"Good."

"Not so good. Lots of blood here, and it leads over the side of a ridge."

Rayford let his eyes shut for several seconds. "Better stay put."

"I've got to know, Ray. Permission to proceed."

"Denied. Those two come any farther around a crag and they'd be able to see you."

"Thought you said they were closer to Albie."

"They are, but there's a clear visual line if they come around."

"I'll risk it."

"Negative."

"C'mon, Rayford! They couldn't hit me from there anyway."

"Leah! Stay . . . put."

From as far away as she was, Rayford felt her glare. He wanted as badly as she did to know just whether the trail of blood led to David's body, especially if there was a chance he might still be alive.

"Where are they now?" she asked.

"I'll let you know if and when you may proceed. Any hope he's alive?"

"Not if this is his blood."

"How can you know that?"

"You sure you want to know?"

"Give me your professional opinion."

"There's an awful lot of blood here, Ray. If it's all one person's . . ."

"And you think it is?"

"One pattern shows a pulsating spray.

You want me to go on?"

"Yes."

"Another shows exit wound drainage and no pulse. And the blood leading to the edge looks like a drain too."

"So whoever it was, was dead before he went over the side."

"Affirmative."

"I want to know if it was David, Leah."

"So do I. Say when."

"Hold."

Twelve

Hannah found the Israeli believers remarkably low maintenance. Many had brought food, which they shared with others. All they wanted was to know when they might be transported to Petra, and the best Hannah could tell them was that she believed it would be that very evening. The people paced or sat and talked about Carpathia, what had gone on at the temple and the Temple Mount that day, and how excited they were about this new adventure. They wanted to meet Micah.

Big George, who proved shy around Hannah, and Abdullah, who was shy around everyone, busied themselves setting up their weapons nest where they could be seen neither from the sky nor by the Israelis, who did not need to be unduly troubled.

Hannah found herself praying for David, for Leah, for Rayford, and for the entire operation. When she had a moment, she stole back into the medical quarters and reread David's E-mail.

Hannah, forgive me. What can I say? You are right. I was insensitive. And don't give a second thought to your worry that I might misinterpret your feelings. The truth is, if there was one thing that niggled at the back of my mind in this whole decision, it was that I was going to miss you. I didn't know how to express it because I didn't want to be misunderstood either.

I don't know why we feel we have to tiptoe around these issues, especially now. No, we didn't know each other well enough to be thinking about anything but a friendship, and I am still in deep pain over Annie, of course. I would not likely have even wanted to consider a new romance with such a short time left.

On the other hand, I suppose it's understandable that we were awkward about this because we were, suddenly in my case, "available." It was stupid of me to fear you would misunderstand. We had become such good friends so quickly that, who knows, maybe I feared something deeper would develop just as quickly. Naturally, I was wary of that, and you should have been too.

We should have been able to simply let our bond of friendship grow and prosper, assuming nothing would have come of it. What I especially appreciate about you, Hannah, is how much you love God. It seems everything you do — how nice you are to people, what a servant attitude you have, your cheerfulness and encouragement during such dark, dark times — well, that is clear evidence of the work of Christ in you. You are an example to me and to anyone else who pays attention.

You're also right that there is likely no need for medical personnel here, and you're certainly not an Israeli. :-) You know, despite being ethnically Jewish, I am not purely an Israeli either, though I have distant roots here. Regardless, it's almost certain we won't see each other again until heaven or the Millennial Kingdom. That alone should have made me invest the time in a proper farewell, and if you would allow it, I'd like to try to make up for that by phone.

Because of what we have been able to put together using satellite and solar technology, it is just as easy — not to mention free — for me to call you in the States as it is to call you here, from about fifty miles away. When we have worked through the mess I caused by leaving without so much as a heart-to-heart talk, would you let me call now and then? I know the time difference is significant and we would have to pick our spots. We'll both be busy, but I'd like that if you would.

Speaking of busy, I recognize that by taking so long to deal with this, I may be getting back to you so close to the time when our real labor-intensive duties kick in that you'll barely have time to read this, let alone respond to it. It's kind of lonely here, no surprise, so if I find my-self doing nothing but waiting for the choppers to start arriving, maybe I'll call to make sure you got this and to save you the time of having to keyboard a re-sponse.

Anyway, because of who you are, I know you'll understand and forgive me, and I look forward to starting over again.

Your friend,
David

Rayford felt a fool. He was no military strategist. While his preys were clearly weak and bumbling, he had allowed all three of his people to move into untenable positions. Albie had no line of fire and dared not move. Mac was out of position with only a handgun. Leah had to substitute obedience for patience or she might get herself killed. Rayford himself was the only one with the angle and a shot at the two GCs, but the fifty-caliber he cradled was a one-shot wonder. And besides, he had only reluctantly concluded he would actually kill someone if it came to that. Nothing said he had the nerve or the ability.

The weapon, however, brought to the table everything he needed. He lay over it, delicately framing through the powerful scope a spot on the rock face his targets would pass if they continued on course. His right hand brushed the trigger while his left palm lay atop the scope, steadying the piece. And now Leah was on the squawker again, pushing to be allowed to approach the edge of the ridge.

Rayford didn't want to risk losing his aim, so he slowly reached for the radio with his left hand and drew it to his lips. "Negative. Don't call me; I'll call you."

He dropped the radio and cupped the

stock of the rifle in his left hand . . . waiting . . . waiting. The GC had stopped and sat together on a rock. Rayford carefully pivoted the rifle until he had them both in his sights. He turned his head slightly and saw Leah waiting. Their backs were to her. There was no reason she couldn't take her look, if she hurried. He picked up the radio, while focusing on the targets again. They looked up and a second later he heard what drew their eyes. Yet another chopper.

"Leah, go and return quickly. Don't reconfirm, just move."

Rayford gently set down the radio and tried to regulate his breathing. The two logy GCs filled the lens, and he believed he saw sores on their sweaty necks from two hundred yards. He aimed inches above the head of the one on the right. They both slid off the rock and knelt on one knee, aiming their weapons at the bird about to fly directly over them. It was an oversized job, a personnel transporter from United North American States Army surplus — a multimillion-Nick machine that no doubt carried at least two dozen fleeing Israeli believers. Well-placed projectiles from as high as the GCs knelt could conceivably bring it down. The mere sound and fury of Rayford's weapon putting a hole in the rock above them should save the helicopter, but he needed more incentive to take the risk.

It came from the radio and Leah's flat, halting news. "It's David . . . they butchered him . . . the birds are already upon him."

The GC tensed as if ready to fire, and Rayford slightly dropped his sight just as the soldier on the left leaned in front of the other. If he had only let David come back to Mizpe Ramon when he wanted to, Rayford wouldn't be in this mess. He remembered to roll up onto his toes and bend his knees, so when he squeezed the trigger the recoil merely sent him sliding back a yard or so. He had forgotten to plug his ears, however, so the explosion tearing against his shoulder was the least of his worries.

The blast stunned and deafened him. Without even the sensation of sound now, he slowly rolled his head, retrieved the toppled rifle, and looked through the lens. He feared he had permanently damaged his eardrums, but his vision had not been affected. In his periphery the big chopper continued past, and across the way both soldiers slumped, motionless, a cloud of rock dust rising behind them.

Rayford picked up his radio. "Be alert for others," he said, aware he was speaking too loudly. His words reverberated inside, but he heard none of them. "Let's see what we've got," he said.

Albie was the first to the targets. Then Leah, Mac, and finally Rayford. He expected Leah to turn away from the carnage, but she didn't. She said something and he asked her to repeat it. She took him by the shoulders and turned him to face her. "David looks worse than they do," she shouted, and he read her lips.

If that was true, he didn't want to see Hassid. But he knew they should bury the body. "Can we get him out?"

She shook her head. "Impossible."

"That's where these two should go too," Mac said, or at least that's what Rayford thought he said.

The bullet had ripped through the spine and heart of one soldier and the neck of the other before blowing a two-foot-diameter hole in the rock face. Rayford spun and caught himself, afraid he would be sick. Isolated by his deafness, he was overcome with remorse. He had done this. He had killed these two. He had lost a man in a place that was supposed to be a refuge. Now his airstrip was vulnerable, and the entrance to Petra swarmed with chopper loads of people waiting to be let in.

Rayford's knees buckled, but he was

borne up by Mac, who held him and pulled his face close. "This is war!" Mac said. "These men murdered our unarmed guy, and they would have killed any one of us. They were drawin' a bead on that packed chopper. You saved us all, Ray!"

Rayford felt his face twist into a grimace, and he tried to form words to express that he couldn't allow these mutilated bodies here when the place began to fill. But he could not speak, and Mac was already ahead of him. He said something to Albie, and the wiry little man stepped forward without hesitation. He stretched, then squatted to pick up the first victim. Bouncing once to settle the corpse in his arms, he moved ten feet toward the ledge and launched him into the unknown. He returned to do the same with the other.

"Get on the horn, Ray!" Mac said. "Let's get these people in here!"

Rayford shook his head and handed the radio to Mac, pointing at him. "With pleasure," Mac said. "Let's gather up and get out."

Rushing down and out was sure easier than coming in had been. Leah stayed close to Rayford, and he believed she looked the way he felt. Before they even reached the passageway, choppers were popping over the ridge and setting down to disgorge passengers. By the time they had traversed the mile through the narrow Siq back to Rayford's craft, a huge crowd had formed at the entrance. Mac had spent much of his time on the radio on the way out, and now he and Albie were urging people not to walk but to accept the helicopter lift into Petra.

Leah helped heft the fifty-caliber, her medical box, and the stretcher into the chopper, then pulled Rayford off to the side. "You can't fly until you can hear," she said.

"Yes I can," he said.

"You can hear again already?"

"You can hear for me."

She shrugged. "Well, I sure can't fly," she said.

Despite his youth and his grief, Chang had the maturity and presence of mind to carefully dole out the awful news about David Hassid. The Tribulation Force agreed that neither Chaim nor Buck need know until Chaim finished his work and was safe at Petra. Chloe said she would inform Buck at the appropriate time.

For the next several hours Chang monitored the Trib Force activities. Leah treated Rayford's ears back at Mizpe Ramon, informing everyone that time would be the best healer. The Israelis left there by George and Abdullah and Rayford were worked into later runs, and Rayford settled in with the other two in their fifty-caliber lair. They had seen nothing of the GC.

Leah reported that Hannah had taken the news of David's death so hard that she was unable to speak. Apparently she had steeled herself to join Leah on a flight to Masada with Mac, where they would reassemble the medical center in a tent. Meanwhile, it seemed to Chang one of God's clear miracles that not one mechanical failure was reported on the ground or in the air during the massive relocation effort.

When night fell in Jerusalem and the world seemed to wait for the nine o'clock reprieve from the plague of boils, Chang finally stood and stretched. He stared at himself in the mirror and thanked God for clear skin all over his body. Even the itch on his leg had disappeared, and he attributed it to either an insect bite or something psychosomatic.

He returned to his computer to check his E-mail, idly wishing the Masada event had not been an afterthought. There had not been time even to arrange for a speaker system, let alone anything Chang could tap into besides Buck's phone.

Chang was taken aback to discover a message from his mother. He quickly accessed it. It was filled with mistakes and retries, but plainly she had painstakingly taught herself how to compose and send the message, and from what she had to say, she had learned how to access Tsion Ben-Judah's Web site too.

Father upset over Carpathia's shameful exhibition in Jerusalem. Not know what to think. Wants me to ask what you think. What do you think? I will send this before he sees and will erase from storage. You answer careful in case he see. Carpathia seem bad, bad, bad. Ben-Judah very interesting, a prophet. How does he know in advance? I need to know how to send to Ming. Tell her I will.

Mother

Not long after dark and still an hour before 2100 hours, Chaim surveyed the packed fortress of Masada, and Buck looked out over the overflow crowd below. He agreed with the old man that almost everyone who was to come was likely there. Buck put an arm on Dr. Rosenzweig's shoulder and bowed his head.

"God, grant me the wisdom to say what

you want me to say," Chaim said, "and may these dear ones hear what you want them to hear."

"And God," Buck added, "anoint his voice."

There was neither a stage nor special lighting. Chaim merely stood on high ground at one end and raised his arms. The place immediately fell silent, and it seemed all movement stopped. Buck whispered into the phone to Chang, "At least record this. We can worry about enhancing fidelity later. The whole Trib Force will want to hear it."

"How are you on power?"

"One and a half packs left. Should be okay."

Chaim spoke in Hebrew, but again, Buck understood him perfectly. "My friends," he began in a voice of vigor and authority but, Buck feared, not enough volume, "I cannot guarantee your safety here tonight. Your very presence makes you an enemy and a threat to the ruler of this world, and when the plague of sores upon his people is lifted at nine o'clock tonight, they may target you with a vengeance."

Buck stood and looked to the far reaches of the fortress and outside below. No one seemed to have to strain to hear. No one moved or emitted a sound except Leah and

Hannah, quietly arranging the small, make-shift medical center. So far no one seemed to need their services.

"I will keep my remarks brief," Chaim said, "but I will be asking you to make a decision that will change your destiny. If you agree with me and make this commitment, cars, trucks, and helicopters will ferry you to a place of refuge. If you do not, you may return to your homes and face the gruesome choice between the guillotine or the mark of loyalty to the man who sat in your temple this very day and proclaimed himself god. He is the man who defiled God's house with murder and with the blood of swine, who installed his own throne and the very image of himself in the Holy of Holies, who put an end to all sacrifices to the true and living God, and who withdrew his promise of peace for Israel.

"I must tell you sadly that many of you will make that choice. You will choose sin over God. You will choose pride and selfishness and life over the threat of death. Some of you have already rejected God's gift so many times that your heart has been hardened. And though your risky sojourn to this meeting may indicate a change of mind on your part, it is too late for a change of heart. Only God knows.

"Because of who you are and where you come from, and because of who I am and where I come from, we can stipulate that we agree on many things. We believe there is one God, creator of the universe and sustainer of life, that all good and perfect things come from him alone. But I tell you that the disappearances that ravaged our world three and a half years ago were the work of his Son, the Messiah, who was foretold in the Scriptures and whose prophecies did Jesus of Nazareth, the Christ, fulfill."

Not a murmur or a word of dissent from all these Jewish people, Buck thought. Could this be Chaim Rosenzweig, the diminutive, soft-spoken scientist, commanding an audience of tens of thousands with the mere power of his unamplified voice and the authority of his message?

It was darker than dark at Mizpe Ramon, so Rayford couldn't even read lips. Fortunately, if George or Abdullah spoke directly at him, he was starting to be able to make out their words.

"I realize I'm the new guy and everything, Captain," George said, "but I been wonderin'. Is there anything here worth protectin' from the GC? I mean, let 'em concentrate their efforts on tearin' up the dirt we worked so hard to smooth out. And these temporary quarters aren't worth a nickel either. What say we get back where the action is and start flyin' some more people to safety instead of lyin' here waitin' for an enemy that might not show?"

Rayford rolled onto his back and stared at the star-filled sky. Abdullah waded in with his opinion, and Rayford had to push up on one elbow and get him to start over louder.

"I was just saying, boss, that I agree. As much as I would enjoy shooting the big guns and maybe knocking someone out of the sky who deserves it anyway, why waste ammunition? We might need it to protect ground troops or flights later."

Rayford's chopper was the only one left. George's and Abdullah's had been pressed into service. The captain rolled onto his back again and ran it all through his mind. The truth was, he didn't care if the GC attacked here. Let them waste their time. He was burned out, desolate, and needed the break. If someone else would fly his craft, and if perhaps Mac would take over running the operation, at least for a while, he could hang on till daybreak. Mac was temporarily in charge anyway, with Rayford's temporary — he hoped — handicap.

"Let's break camp," he said finally, and

the other two quickly broke down the weapons and loaded them. Rayford asked George to fly and Abdullah to tell Mac what was going on. He lay on the floor of the chopper and covered his face with his hands. The problem, Rayford told himself, was that he had a hero complex. He knew anything good that happened in a time such as this was God's doing and not his. But running out of gas before a mission was over was not his idea of what a leader would or should do.

Was it possible that God had allowed him to forget something so simple as earplugs just to put him out of commission long enough to restore his strength? He despaired over losing David and having to kill two men. But it all worked together to drain him. He was not even aware of dozing, but a moment later Abdullah woke him with a yank on the arm.

"Please to forgive me, but we are needed at Masada. Mr. McCullum believes that many, many more will need rides to Petra."

Buck found himself thrilled to the point of bursting. Much as Tsion Ben-Judah had done on international television years before, Chaim made the case for Jesus as the Messiah the Jews had sought for so long. As he ticked off the 109 prophecies fulfilled by Jesus alone, first one, then another in the crowd stood. Soon the entire crowd was on its feet. Still they were silent and no one moved around. A holy hush filled the place.

"He is the only One who could be Messiah," Chaim proclaimed. "He also died unlike anyone else in history. He gave himself willingly as a sacrifice and then proved himself worthy when God raised him from the dead. Even skeptics and unbelievers have called Jesus the most influential person in history.

"Of the billions and billions of people who have ever lived, One stands head and shoulders above the rest in terms of influence. More schools, colleges, hospitals, and orphanages have been started because of him than because of anyone else. More art was created, more music written, and more humanitarian acts performed due to him and his influence than anyone else ever. Great international encyclopedias devote twenty thousand words to describing him and his influence on the world. Even our calendar is based on his birth. And all this he accomplished in a public ministry that lasted just three and a half years!

"Jesus of Nazareth, Son of God, Savior of the world, and Messiah, predicted that he would build his church and the gates of hell would not prevail against it. Centuries after his public unmerciful mocking, his persecution and martyrdom, billions claimed membership in his church, making it by far the largest religion in the world. And when he returned, as he said he would, to take his faithful to heaven, the disappearance of so many had the most profound impact on this globe that man has ever seen.

"Messiah was to be born in Bethlehem to a virgin, to live a sinless life, to serve as God's spotless Lamb of sacrifice, to give himself willingly to die on a cross for the sins of the world, to rise again three days later, and to sit at the right hand of God the Father Almighty. Jesus fulfilled these and all the other 109 prophecies, proving he is the Son of God.

"Tonight, Messiah calls to you from down through the ages. He is the answer to your condition. He offers forgiveness for your sins. He paid the penalty for you. As the most prolific writer of Scripture, a Jew himself, wrote, 'If you confess with your mouth the Lord Jesus and believe in your heart that God has raised him from the dead, you will be saved. For with the heart one believes unto righteousness, and with the mouth confession is made unto salvation. For the

Scripture says, "Whoever believes on him will not be put to shame." For there is no distinction between Jew and Greek, for the same Lord over all is rich to all who call upon him. For whoever calls on the name of the Lord shall be saved.'

"For years skeptics have made fun of the evangelist's plea, 'Do you want to be saved tonight?' and yet that is what I ask you right now. Do not expect God to be fooled. Be not deceived. God will not be mocked. Do not do this to avoid a confrontation with Antichrist. You need to be saved because you cannot save yourself.

"The cost is great but the reward greater. This may cost you your freedom, your family, your very head. You may not survive the journey to safety. But you will spend eternity with God, worshiping the Lord Christ, Messiah, Jesus.

"If you choose Christ, pray this prayer with me: Dear God, I am a sinner and separated from you. I believe Jesus is the Messiah and that he died on the cross to pay for my sins. I believe he rose again the third day and that by receiving his gift of love I will have the power to become a son of God because I believe on his name. Thank you for hearing me and saving me, and I pledge the rest of my life to you."

All over the vast historic fortress — where legend said Jewish parents chose to slay their own children and themselves rather than fall into the hands of the Romans — men and women prayed that prayer aloud. The mark of the seal of God on the believer appeared on their foreheads, and thousands and thousands of them followed Chaim as he strode through the crowd and down the steps to where hundreds of vehicles and helicopters waited in long lines. Hannah and Leah and their equipment were among the first to go. Buck saw Mac assign his chopper to another flyer and help load the medical stuff into an idling truck. He got behind the wheel as Hannah and Leah herded about a dozen new believers in.

Thousands of others, despair on their faces, ran from the scene and looked for rides back to Jerusalem.

Buck caught up to Chaim and stood next to him, watching as the cars and trucks and choppers filled and took off. The old man breathed heavily and leaned over on Buck as if his last ounce of strength had been sapped. "Praise God," he whispered. "Praise God, praise God, praise God."

Buck looked at his watch. It was minutes before nine, and already the loudspeakers on GC vehicles began spreading the news that was being broadcast on television and over the Internet. "The entire state of Israel has been declared a no-fly zone by the Global Community Security and Intelligence director. All civilian aircraft, take fair warning: Any non-GC craft determined to be over Israeli airspace runs the risk of destruction.

"The potentate himself has also decreed martial law and has instituted a curfew on civilian vehicular traffic in Israel. Violators are subject to arrest.

"Due to the severity of the affliction that has befallen GC personnel, these curfews are required. Only a skeleton crew of workers is available to maintain order.

"His Excellency reminds citizens that he has effected a relief from the plague as of 2100 hours, and the populace should plan to celebrate with him at daybreak."

Abdullah woke Rayford again. He sat up, his hearing still gone. "Your son-in-law has requested transportation for Dr. Rosenzweig and himself from Masada to Petra, and he says you personally requested permission to convey them. Is that still your wish?"

Rayford nodded, wiped his face, and climbed into a seat. George descended to the staging area outside Masada, and they sat waiting until nearly everyone was gone save Chaim and Buck and a man standing behind them in a robe similar to Chaim's.

"Who is that?" Rayford asked, pointing.

"Dr. Rosenzweig and Mr. Williams," Abdullah said.

"No, the other," Rayford said.

"I do not understand."

"Who is with them?"

Rayford saw Abdullah glance at George, and George meet his gaze. "I see no one," Abdullah said, but Rayford assumed he meant he didn't know either.

Later, when GC vehicles began arriving at the site and finally only Buck, Chaim, and the other man remained outside, Abdullah stepped out of the chopper and held the door open. Chaim walked wearily, Buck with a hand on his arm. The third stayed a pace behind. As they boarded, it seemed to Rayford that Abdullah very nearly slammed the door on the unknown man.

They sat as George turned in his seat and Rayford introduced Chaim and Buck to him. "And introduce your friend," Rayford said.

Buck smiled. "I'm sorry?"

"Your friend. Introduce your friend. Who is this?" Rayford gestured toward the third man, who merely looked at him. Chaim and Buck looked to where he had gestured and then back to Rayford. "Well?" he said.

"What are we missing?" Buck said.

Rayford wondered if he was dreaming. He leaned toward the man as the man leaned toward him. "So, who are you?" Rayford said.

"I am Michael," he said. "I am here to restore and heal you."

Rayford stiffened as Michael cupped Rayford's head in his hands, his palms over the ears. Rayford's hearing was restored, and he felt a surge of life and energy that made him sit up straight. "You mean Michael the . . . I mean, *the* Michael?"

But the man was gone.

Thirteen

Rayford felt twenty years younger and wished he were piloting his own chopper. But George was doing fine. Abdullah sat next to him, scanning the sky and the ground with a serious, worried look. Buck sat next to Chaim on the long side bench, his head back, mouth open, sound asleep.

"You must be exhausted too, Dr. Rosenzweig," Rayford said.

"For the first time today, yes, and you know I was up most of last night."

"I heard. God has stood by you, hasn't he?"

"Captain, I confess I am famished! It is as if I have been fueled by the energy of the angels to whom God gave charge over me."

"Did you see them, sir?"

"Me? No. But you know Miss Durham saw Michael the archangel."

Rayford nodded. There would be time to tell his own story. "Abdullah?" he said, and the Jordanian turned. "Were there any foodstuffs in what we loaded?" He had been heating something over a flameless stove just before they left Mizpe Ramon.

"There were! Yes!" Abdullah was shouting and enunciating.

"I can hear, Smitty. I've been healed."

"Really!?" He leaned back and quit shouting, but still talked loudly enough to be heard above the din of the craft. "I have pita bread warm in an insulated box, along with sauce for the dipping."

"You sound like a waiter in a swanky restaurant."

"How would I know?"

Chaim leaned in. "That sounds like milk and honey to me."

Abdullah unbuckled himself and squeezed back between them, kneeling to retrieve the box. He pivoted and opened the lid, revealing a stack of nearly twenty round pitas about ten inches in diameter, steam rising.

The aroma permeated the helicopter and woke Buck. Big George even reached back without looking. Rayford slapped a couple of pitas into his open palm. "That's what I'm talkin' about!" the pilot said, though he hadn't said a word for an hour. All dug in, tearing at the chewy bread with their teeth.

"Lord, you know we are grateful!" Chaim said, his mouth full, and the others *amen*ed.

Abdullah was still kneeling by the box when he nudged Rayford and nodded outside. The sky was full of Operation Eagle choppers and GC craft, both fixed-wings and whirlybirds. Below, the streets were jammed with fleeing vehicles, careening around corners, bouncing over curbs and torn-up streets, pursued by GC vehicles with flashing lights.

The others turned to peer out. "How are we doing on fuel?" Chaim asked.

"Several hours' worth," George reported.

"Captain Steele," Chaim said, "could we remain in this area and monitor this?"

Rayford told George to find a friendly altitude, and they hovered in a wide-box pattern. A GC chopper moved in behind them at one point and summoned them with an all-frequency transmission. "Civilian chopper, you are advised to leave Israel airspace immediately."

"Captain," George said, "what frequency can they hear me on?"

Rayford told him and asked what he had in mind.

"I just think I should be courteous, don't you?"

"Don't antagonize them."

Everybody in the chopper laughed at that, and Rayford realized how absurd it was. The GC couldn't be any more antagonized.

George switched to the frequency Rayford suggested. "GC chopper, this is the civilian bird. Over which part of your populated city did you plan to send our flaming wreckage?"

"Civilian, you are violating a curfew established by Potentate Carpathia himself."

"I don't recognize the authority."

"Repeat, Carpathia! His Excellency himself!"

"I recognize the name, GC. I repeat, I don't recognize the authority."

Abdullah's eyes were alive. "You Americans are crazy brave!"

The radio crackled again. "By authority of the Global Community and its risen potentate and lord, His Excellency Nicolae Carpathia, you are commanded to land at once in the first available area and surrender yourself, your passengers, your cargo, and your craft."

"No thanks," George said.

"That is not a request, civilian. That is an order sanctioned by the potentate."

"Sorry, GC, but we're on a mission from the real risen Lord, and we have both human and edible cargo we don't wish to surrender."

"Repeat?"

"The part about the people or the pita bread?"

"Be forewarned, civilian chopper, we are fully armed and prepared to destroy your craft if you do not comply immediately."

"Right now?"

"Affirmative."

"Just a minute."

"You request time to comply?"

"No, I just need a minute."

"You have sixty seconds."

"I can't have a minute?"

"Fifty-five seconds, civilian."

"Let me make sure I get over the busiest streets here, GC, in case I'm not as invulnerable as I think I am."

"Coming up on forty-five seconds. Put that chopper down."

"We're eating and we have no airsick bags. If we have to use evasive measures, we could make a mess."

"Final warning. Thirty seconds."

"We won't be hearing from you again, then?"

"Negative."

"Not at all?"

"Correct."

"Not one word?"

"Twenty seconds."

"That's two words."

Rayford had to wonder if George was as scared as he was. The big man obviously believed they were safe because Chaim was aboard, and Rayford had more than enough reason to trust God. But when he saw the GC chopper back off to where a missile explosion would not damage the shooting craft, he believed they were about to be fired upon. "Buckle in, Smitty," he shouted.

Abdullah leaped into his seat while Rayford secured the food box. Buck looked as focused as Rayford, but Chaim seemed bemused. "We belong to God," the old man said. "His will be done."

Mac hadn't had this much fun since he was a schoolkid and his pet snake found his sister's room. He bounced along Jerusalem streets with a truckload of Israeli believers and two nurses from America. The scene reminded him of the Keystone Kops. Operation Eagle drivers simply would not be stopped. They swung around barricades, over boulders, through earthquake residue, and past GC Peacekeeper vehicles.

Back in Texas when Mac was a kid, you could drive a farm vehicle at twelve. By the sixth grade, he was driving tractors and combines, pickups and dump trucks. And now he had drawn a new personnel transport from France, driven in by an International Commodity Co-op volunteer who had ridden back to get another.

This was a fancy rig with power and the ability to be driven in automatic or manual. The former would come in handy on the open road, once they got south of the city, but in the chaos in which he now found himself, Mac enjoyed the six-speed stick. Even more, he was entertained — though that seemed too light a word for it under the circumstances — by the spectacle of the freshly healed GC personnel thumbing their noses at the Micah-Nicolae agreement and trying to get in the way of the exodus of a million people.

Nearly all the Operation Eagle vehicles were four-wheel drive and could pick their way around any obstacle. When the road filled with stopped cars and trucks, those in the back just swung out and around and made their own routes and paths. GC

Peacekeepers and Morale Monitors — the former in uniform, the latter wearing their badges and bright orange sashes — tried to direct traffic, stop civilian cars, check papers, and inform everyone they were violating the martial-law curfew. They were ignored, and Mac wondered how God was doing it. He saw a lot of weapons but heard little gunfire. No one allowed himself to be pulled over, and when GC vehicles blocked the path of a civilian car or truck, the latter just backed up and went around.

Mac wondered why the GC didn't shoot or ram these vehicles, but he figured he'd learn when he was singled out. For now, Leah was asking an Israeli in the passenger seat if she could switch places with him so she could talk to Mac.

"We going to make it?" she asked.

He shot her a glance. She was pale and her eyes darted about the scene around them. "Looks like it," he said. "You see any of ours who are *not* making it?"

She shook her head and fastened her seat belt, then sat with her hands balled into fists in her lap. "Uh, Mr. McCullum, Hannah is wondering why we're going to Petra, she and I, I mean. Obviously there's no need for medical personnel there, and neither of us is an Israeli."

"Me either," Mac said. "Obviously we're takin' these people to their new home. Chloe's got shipments of building materials and such that will need to be processed. Maybe you can help coordinate that while we're gettin' the last of the refugees delivered. That's gonna take a while."

"Okay."

"That a problem?"

"No, it's just that —"

"You're not gonna tell me it's not what you signed up for. I mean, we all do what we gotta d—"

"No, I know, it's fine. It's just that being at Petra is going to be real hard on Hannah with what happened, you know."

"I was there."

"So you see."

"Have her join me up here, would ya?"

"She can hardly talk, Mr. McCullum."

"I don't need her to talk. I need her to listen."

Rayford leaned as far to his right as he could and kept an eye on the GC chopper behind them. They apparently cared not a whit about who or what was below.

"Everybody secure?" he said. "Prepare for incoming." The pursuing craft was directly in line with them in a can't-miss situation. Rayford considered barking evasive maneuvers at George, but it would be futile. The GC flew a smaller, more agile bird. Even if George eluded the first fusillade, it would be only a matter of time.

"They're firing!" Rayford hollered, and buried his face between his knees. He had seen the orange bursts and the white tracers and expected the instantaneous ravaging of metal and Plexiglas and fuel tanks, the gush of cold air, the ball of flame, and the free fall.

He felt the blazing, screaming bullet tips shoot past between him and Buck and Chaim, and the white-hot streaks made him look up. The ammunition flashed through the bird, and the force of the air pushed George's head to the left and Abdullah's to the right as both involuntarily ducked and covered their ears. But there had been no damage to the back or front of the chopper.

Rayford stared as the shots found the tail rotors of a GC craft ahead of them and sent it spinning to the ground. He shuddered and realized he was gripping the seat so tightly his fingers had locked into position.

"Why are you so fearful? How is it that you have no faith? Be of good cheer! Do not be afraid."

Rayford turned slowly to see Michael next

to him again. "You all see him this time, don't you?" he said.

"We saw him," Chaim said. "Praise God."

"I heard him," Abdullah said, turning. But again, Michael was already gone.

Mac saw the flashing lights in his side rearview mirrors. "You're not going to stop, are you?" Hannah asked quietly.

"Take more'n that to stop me now." The GC behind him started in on their PA system. "I don't want to talk to them," he said. "I want to talk to you. Did you lose a loved one today?"

"Of course. Didn't you?"

"Yes, I did."

"Then you should understand."

"That's why I don't, Hannah. I'm not sayin' this is easy. But did you see David fold up and hibernate when he lost his fiancée? No, ma'am. I know you and David were close, but what do you think he'd want? Do I hafta remind you that Rayford lost two wives and a son? That Tsion lost his whole family? I'm not discountin' it, and I'm not sayin' you don't have a reason for wanting to stay away from Petra. But David was my boss and my friend, and this is no picnic for me either."

"I know."

"We're all going to need some grieving time, and we won't likely get it until we head back to the States. Meanwhile, we need you, Hannah. We don't have the luxury of grieving the way we used to. Too many people countin' on us. Now there may be nothin' for you and Leah to do inside Petra, but you know well as I do that none of us helpers are guaranteed safety. Who knows what kinda walkin' wounded we might have showin' up to drop people off?"

She nodded. "Mac, um, you'd better pull over."

"Ma'am?"

She pointed past him, out his window. A guard hung out the passenger side of a GC vehicle with a submachine gun pointed at Mac.

"Well," George said, "that was just about the most amazing thing I've ever seen. Do we keep testing our luck or do we get on to Petra?"

"If you think that was luck," Rayford said, "maybe —"

"Just an expression, Cap. I know good and well what that was."

"Let's stay here and watch," Abdullah said, craning his neck to see the chopper that had fired on them.

"No need to be in the middle of every-thing," Rayford said. "Get someplace where we can observe without unduly drawing more fire."

Chang phoned Tsion early in the after-noon Chicago time and walked him through how to broadcast live over international television from right where he was. "Is your monitor somewhere that you can stand be-hind it and survey the room?"

"Yes."

"Have someone sit where you're going to sit, and see what you can see past them. Anything that would be a clue to your whereabouts, get rid of it."

Tsion asked Ming to sit in his chair at the keyboard, and he squeezed between the back of the monitor and the wall. On the op-posite wall a clock would give away what time zone they were in. "Chang," Tsion said, "let me get rid of the clock, and then the background will be a blank wall."

"Good. And then, can you tell me how long your message — wait, sir?"

"Go ahead."

"Why not just change that clock to Carpathian Time and let people wonder where you are?"

"Interesting."

Ming broke in. "Won't they see it as an obvious trick, Chang?"

"They might if we made it prominent," he said. "Put it in the corner of the shot, and I'll make sure it's out of focus. People will think they have discovered something unintended."

"My message will be short, Chang," Tsion said. "Just enough to encourage the believers before you transmit Chaim's salvation message audio."

"Excuse me, Dr. Ben-Judah, but I'm getting something on my Phoenix 216 bug. Stand by."

"You go and get back to me later."

Mac held up a finger to the GC as if requesting a moment before he pulled over. He had speed-dialed Rayford. "Permission to fire upon the GC before they shoot out our tires."

"Denied, Mac. Just elude. Let God work."

"He can work through your nine millimeter, can't he?"

"You still have that?"

"Sorry."

"Just don't stop," Rayford said.

"Even with a flat?"

"Call back if they flatten your tire."

303

Mac stopped in the middle of the road with the GC next to him, but he refused to roll down his window. The GC pulled in front of Mac. When the passenger got out, Mac backed up and pulled around the vehicle, and the pursuit began again. When the GC got close, Mac slammed on the brakes. "Sorry, friends!" he yelled. "Shoulda told y'all to buckle up!"

The GC stopped within inches of Mac's bumper and they both jumped out, shouting and waving weapons. Mac took off again, and as soon as they jumped back in and accelerated, he swung left, popped a U-turn, and swung in behind them.

Apparently Carpathia still suspected the Knesset Building and thought his own plane was most secure. Chang followed an indication on the audiometer from the patch to the bugs there, and sure enough, it sounded as if workers were setting up for yet another meeting in the first-class cabin.

A couple of stewards were speaking in an Indian dialect, so Chang quickly fed it through a filter David had recommended and an immediate interpretation came up as captions.

"They will not destroy the rebel airstrip, then?"

"It appears the GC will use it for its own purposes. They will take out the buildings and clear it of the enemy, of course, but then they will fly in their own troops, who will be trucked to Petra to head off the fleeing insurgents. They will try to — shh, they are coming."

"Mr. Akbar, sir."

"Pakistani?"

"No, apologies, Director."

"Speak English?"

"Yes, English."

"This will be a small gathering, just the potentate, Reverend Fortunato, Mr. Moon, Ms. Ivins, and myself."

"Oh, thank you, sir. We had already made room for too many, had we not?"

"No problem. You know what everybody likes. Have it out and available. And don't forget Ms. Ivins's fondness for ice."

"A thousand thank-yous for reminding me, sir. 'More ice, please,' she says constantly. Water for you and Mr. Moon, juice for Mr. Fortunato, and —"

"*Reverend* Fortunato."

"Oh yes, humble apologies."

"I do not care. But you do not want to make that mistake in front of His Excellency."

"Or the Most High Reverend Father, ha!"

Chang heard Suhail Akbar chuckle. "Make yourselves scarce once everything is in place."

Chang formatted the program to record and then switched back to Chicago. "Ready?" he said.

"I am," Tsion said. "How do I look?"

"Scared."

"I do not wish to look scared."

"Can't help you there, Doctor. We're pirating the only show in town all over the world. If anyone is watching TV, listening to radio, or surfing the Net, you're what they're going to get."

"*That* sets my mind at ease!"

"Just trying to explain your nerves, sir."

"Say when."

"Now."

"I am on?" Tsion said. "Seriously?"

But Chang didn't dare answer for fear of his voice being traced. He held his breath, grateful Tsion had not used his name.

"Greetings," Tsion said. "It is a privilege for me to address the world through the miracle of technology. But as I am an unwelcome guest here, forgive me for being brief, and please lend me your attention . . ."

Chang checked in on the Phoenix. It sounded as if everyone was there and settling in. "Commander Moon, get someone to turn off that television. Wait! Who is that?"

"You know who that is, Excellency," Leon said. "That's the heretic, Tsion Ben-Judah."

"More than a heretic," Carpathia said. "He is behind this Micah, thus the plague of sores. So now he consolidates the Orthodox Jews with him. How did he get a television network?"

"That is GCNN, Potentate."

"Well, get him off there!" Carpathia raged. "Walter!"

The TV in the Phoenix went silent, and Carpathia exploded. "I mean get him off the air, you imbecile. Call whom you have to call, do what you have to do! We have overcome the plague and now we will look like buffoons, allowing the enemy on our own network!"

Moon was on the phone, his voice shaky, sounding to Chang as if he feared Carpathia would put him to death if Tsion was aired a minute longer. Moon swore and demanded to be put through to the head of broadcasting. "No excuses!" he cried. "Pull the plug! Now!"

"Give me that phone!" Carpathia said. "Cut the feed! Cut the signal!" It sounded as if the phone was flung across the cabin. "Turn it on! Let me see!"

Moon: "I'm sure they've at least gone to black, Excellen—"

"Turn it on! Ach! Still there! What is it with you people? Suhail, come here. Right here!"

"Excellency."

"No restrictions on curfew enforcement." Carpathia spoke so quickly that his words ran together and Chang had to strain to understand. "Shoot to kill at the Mount of Olives, at Masada, on —"

"Those locations have been cleared, Highn—"

"Do *not* interrupt, Suhail! Every civilian plane destroyed and —"

"We have suffered casualties on the ground from crashing planes, sir —"

"Do you *hear* me? Do you understand what I am saying? Do I need to have you executed the way I will execute Walter if this Ben-Judah *is not off the air when again I look at the screen!?*"

Moon wailed, "What more can I do, Excellency?"

"You can die!"

"No!"

"Suhail, a weapon."

"Please, sir!"

"Now, Suhail!"

Scuffling. *BLAM!* A scream.

"Hold out your other hand, Walter!"

"Please!"

BLAM! More screaming. More shots, fresh cries with each. The banging of shoes against seats and tables as Moon, Chang assumed, frantically tried to crawl to safety. More rapid shots in succession, wailing like a terrified baby, finally a last shot, and silence.

"You're doing the right thing, Nicolae," Viv Ivins said. "You should kill them all and start over."

"Thank you, Viv."

Fortunato: "I worship you, risen master."

"Shut up, Leon. Suhail, put a fresh clip in this."

Sounds of the snapping in of more ammunition.

Fortunato: "I bow in respectful silence to your glory. Oh, for the privilege of kissing your ring."

"Now give it to me, Suhail."

"As you wish, Excellency, but I will execute anyone you wish. I have always carried out your directives."

"Then do what I say!"

"Anything, Potentate."

"I want dead insurrectionists! Run them down. Crash their vehicles. Blow their heads off. As for Petra, wait until we know for certain Micah is there, then level it. Do we have what we need to do that?"

"We do, sir."

"In the meantime, someone, anyone, get — Ben-Judah — off — the — air!"

"I will pray him off, Your Worship," Fortunato said.

"I will kill you if you do not shut up."

"Quieting now, Highness. Oh!"

"What!?"

"The water! The ice!"

Chang jumped up and turned on the faucet over his sink.

Blood.

Fourteen

The taillights ahead went bright red, so Mac slammed on his brakes. But suddenly the GC vehicle disappeared from his vision. In the distance, Operation Eagle cars and trucks roared on, but behind them a great cavern opened and the pursuing GC dropped into it.

Mac jumped out and realized his front tires were on the edge of the gigantic crevasse. Amazingly, the lights of the GC cars grew smaller as they continued to fall. The cavity in the earth was hundreds of feet deep, and his idea to sneak behind the GC had almost been fatal. His knees rubbery, he climbed back into the truck and carefully backed away, looking for a way around.

Roaring up past him came yet another

GC car, but as it neared the drop-off, its two occupants leaped out and rolled, their weapons clattering onto the pavement. Their car hurtled into the great beyond. The Peacekeepers slowly rose, retrieved their rifles, and took aim at Mac's truck. "Duck!" he shouted, and his head banged Hannah's shoulder as they both leaned toward the middle of the front seat. In the back, the Israelis tussled for position.

The bracketing of gunfire made Mac shut his eyes and cover his head, but it stopped almost as soon as it had started, and he rose and stepped out to see the Peacekeepers sprawled dead. No one else was around. He could only surmise that their own bullets had somehow killed them. Mac's Operation Eagle truck stood unscathed. His phone rang.

It was Rayford. "Tsion's on the air right now," he reported.

"Well, that's good, Cap. Nothin' I could use more right now than a little broadcast entertainment."

"Say again?"

"Nothin'."

"What's your location?"

"The Grand Canyon."

"I don't follow."

"Good idea not to."

"Mac, you all right?"

"Yeah. 'Cept for almost drivin' my people into the netherworld, I'll make it."

"Sounds like you'll have a story, as usual. Can you see what's happening in the air over Jerusalem?"

"Guess I been lookin' the other direction, Ray."

"Well, look up and listen."

The air battle had moved away from Mac, but in the distance he could see it, and its low rumbling echoes came rolling back. "They hittin' anybody?"

"Only each other," Rayford said. "Look out below."

"I heard *that!*"

Chang was overcome by a feeling so delicious it made him tingle to the top of his head. All over his computer were frantic codes and messages and attempts by the broadcasting division in the next building to yank GCNN off the air. But nothing they did worked. He hoped Tsion would finish soon so he could go to the Chaim audio. That would drive them crazy. With no visual to worry about, they would catch each other coming and going trying to mute the sound.

With one ear monitoring Tsion to know when to make the switch, Chang was also still listening to the cockpit of the Phoenix.

Carpathia had turned his verbal guns on Fortunato.

"What good is a religion if you cannot come up with some miracles, Leon?"

"Holiness! I called down fire on your enemy just yesterday!"

"You cooked a harmless woman with a big mouth."

"But you are the object of our worship, Excellency! I pray to *you* for signs and wonders!"

"Well, I need a miracle, *Reverend*."

"Excellency," Akbar interrupted, "you might consider this phone call miraculous."

"While that infernal Ben-Judah remains on the air, the only miracle is that either of you remains alive. So, thrill me."

"You recall we lost two prisoners in Greece recently?"

"Young people, yes. A boy and a girl. You have found them?"

"No, but as time and manpower allowed only a cursory investigation, the best we came up with were witnesses who said a Peacekeeper named Jensen may have been involved in both disappearances."

"Yes, yes, and though he was our man, you lost track of him. So you have found him now?"

"Maybe."

"I hate answers like that!"

"Forgive me, Excellency. You know how this Micah and his sidekick seemed to appear out of nowhere."

"Get to the point. Please! You are making me crazy!"

"We got a tip that the two were seen at the King David Hotel, but when everyone fell ill, we didn't have time to pursue it. Now we have, and we even know what rooms they occupied."

"And this is a miracle?"

"We have combed both rooms. One contained a wallet that appears to belong to Jensen. The photo, however, does not match the photo in our personnel files."

"Why would he be foolish enough to leave his identification behind? It is clearly an attempt to mislead."

"We're comparing with our international database fingerprints lifted from each room."

Chang's fingers flew. He was into the GC Peacekeeper personnel file in seconds and eradicated all vestiges of Jack Jensen.

"Suhail, there must be dozens of different people's fingerprints in a hotel room, from every recent guest to the staff to —"

"The predominant prints in the one room trace to Chaim Rosenzweig."

Carpathia laughed. "The man who murdered me."

"One and the same."

He laughed again. "Well, which do you think is Rosenzweig? The one in the robe or the one with the scarred face?"

"Excellency, the prints from the scarred man's room do not lead to Peacekeeper Jensen, interestingly enough. They match the prints of a former employee in your inner circle."

Back Chang went into the system, and seconds later Cameron "Buck" Williams, former media czar for the Global Community, was gone as if he had never been there.

"I did not study the sidekick," Carpathia said, "but he did not remind me of anyone."

"He was your first media guy."

"Plank? Nonsense. Confirmed dead."

"My mistake. Your second media guy but first choice."

"Williams?"

"That's the man."

"Micah's assistant is not Cameron Williams, Suhail. I would know. And let me tell you something else — Micah is *not* Dr. Rosenzweig."

"All due respect, Excellency, but miracles of disguise can be wrought today."

"He may be approximately the same

height, but that voice? That look? That bearing? No. That could not be playacting." There was a long pause. "Anyway," Carpathia said quietly, "I pardoned my attacker publicly."

"And that protects him from whom?"

"Everyone."

"Including yourself?"

"Excellent point, Suhail."

"Anyway, you yourself installed Walter Moon as supreme commander. That apparently didn't give *him* tenure."

Chang heard the men laugh, while in the background Viv Ivins supervised the removal of Moon's body and the cleanup of the area.

Chang switched to Tsion's broadcast, which closed with Dr. Ben-Judah's promise to travel to Petra to personally address his million strong "brothers and sisters in Messiah."

Someone called Suhail. Chang heard him ask Carpathia's permission to take it, then: "Ben-Judah is coming to Petra, Excellency."

"Delay its destruction until his arrival."

"And the blood problem is international."

"Meaning?"

"Intelligence is telling me the waters of the sea are 100 percent blood."

"What sea?"

"Every one. It's crippling us. And we have a mole."

"Where?"

"At the palace. And connected here somehow."

"How can you know that?"

"Jensen and Williams? Their files have disappeared from our central database since you and I began discussing them."

"Quarantine this plane, Suhail."

"Sir?"

"We will kill the mole, of course, but we must find the leak first. Lie detector tests for everyone. How many is that?"

"Fortunately, not many. Two stewards, myself, and Leon."

"You were wise to leave me out and diplomatic to leave Viv Ivins out. Do not be diplomatic."

"You want her polygraphed, Excellency?"

"Absolutely."

"Perhaps I'll conduct it myself," Suhail said.

"And who will conduct yours, Mr. Akbar?"

"Actually, Excellency, lie detecting has become quite streamlined. We now merely use a computer program that detects changes in the FM frequency of the voice. A person has no control over it. He or she can speak at a different pace or even volume, but the FM frequency will change only under stress."

"*Real*-ly."

"It's gold, sir."

"Do include me in the testing."

Chang hacked into the personnel files and created a record showing him in the infirmary and treated symptomatically for boils for the last two days. He saved everything from his computer to the secure minidisk in the bowels of the palace, then purposely crashed the hard drive on his laptop, erasing everything in it. He created a phantom auxiliary hard drive buried under such massive encoding that only another computer working twenty-four hours a day for years could even hope to crack it. He accessed the miniature archive and downloaded everything he needed, then pulled the cords and packed up the machine, putting it deep in a closet. David — the only other person on the planet who could have detected a thing on his hard drive — was actually no longer on the planet.

Chang would be at his desk in his department the next morning, right on time and ready for work. Not only would they not find the mole, but they would also strike out in their search for a contact person in the executive cabinet.

★ ★ ★

George put down well outside the growing throngs at Petra, opened the door for ventilation, and Buck and the others dozed as load after load of more escapees was delivered. Rayford and Chaim had decided to keep Chaim's presence a secret for as long as possible so as not to interfere with the massive move into the safe place. Though some had begun walking in and others were airlifted, by daybreak, hundreds of thousands clogged the Siq, awaiting their helicopter hop inside. They sang and rejoiced and prayed.

Buck left the chopper and walked among the people, keeping an eye on the skies and the western horizon as he listened to the radio. Global Community forces had been decimated, nearly half lost in firefights in the sky that never touched Operation Eagle or during ground pursuits that left GC vehicles and bodies buried so deep that rescue operations were abandoned.

The GCNN radio network had switched back to Carpathia's auspices sometime in the night, after Chaim's case for Jesus as the Messiah had been broadcast around the world, followed by his prayer of allegiance to Christ. Buck believed Tsion's prediction that a worldwide revival would break out in the midst of the worst terror of the Tribulation. Reports from around the globe revealed tragedy and death related to the seas having turned to blood.

Ships that counted on processes that made the waters of the ocean drinkable found it impossible to convert the blood. Rotting carcasses of all species of aquatic life rose to the surface, and crews of ships fell deathly ill as many boats radioed their inability to get back to land.

Carpathia announced that his Security and Intelligence forces already had determined the true identities of the impostors who claimed to represent the rebels and that it had been their trickery that resulted in the great seawater catastrophe.

Night had fallen in Chicago, and Chloe found a way to excuse herself during a lull in the news. She took her new telescope and set up at a window far from curious eyes. Waiting until the sky was black, she first scanned the city with the naked eye. The tiny beacon she had noticed some time before still shined from about three-quarters of a mile away.

Chloe carefully settled and steadied herself, bracing the instrument and aligning it with what she had seen. At long last she was able to bring the illusive beam into focus and calm the jumpy lens. To her astonishment, the source of light was at ground level. She sat and sat, cramping again but forcing herself to stay still so she could study the image until it made sense to her overtaxed brain.

She ran the various shapes and images through the grid of her life's memory, and gradually Chloe thought she came to understand what she was looking at. One window on the ground or basement floor of a big building, maybe ten or twelve stories, emitted light from inside. And the more she sat staring, the more convinced she was that there was activity inside. Human activity.

At eight in the morning Palace Time, Chang was assigned by his supervisor to help monitor reports of deaths and casualties attributed to the oceanic disaster. To the wonder of everyone involved, lakes and rivers had not been affected.

In the large office where Chang and some thirty others sat at desktop computers, he made it a point to only occasionally grunt a response to coworkers who tried to draw him out. He neither looked anyone in the eye nor smiled. His boss, a tall, bony Mexican named Aurelio S. Figueroa, proved an officious loner who treated his superiors like kings and queens and treated his subordinates like servants.

"How are we today, Wong?" Mr. Figueroa said, his Adam's apple protruding.

"Okay, sir."

"Happy in your work?"

"Happy enough."

"Have you heard the news?"

"About?"

"Supreme Commander Moon."

"I saw nothing on the news about him."

"Come, Master Wong, I know you are a Carpathia pet. Surely you have inside knowledge."

Chang shook his head.

"Moon is dead."

"Dead? How?"

"Shot to death outside the potentate's plane."

Chang tried to appear stunned and curious, but he hated being drawn in as Figueroa's confidant. "The enemy?"

"No! Don't be naïve! Our people at that level are surrounded by security."

"Who then?"

"They suspect the stewards." Figueroa leaned close. "Both Indians."

"But why?"

"No one else would have done it."

"Why would *they*?"

"Why not? You know the Indians."

"No, I do not."

"They have a contact on the inside."

"On the inside of what?"

"Here."

"Why?"

"You *are* naïve, aren't you?"

Chang bit his tongue. He hated stupid people, especially ones twice his age. "Not too naïve to guess your middle name."

Figueroa's eyes turned dark. "What does that have to do with anything, Wong?"

Chang shrugged. "Forget it."

"You couldn't know it anyway."

"Of course I couldn't."

"Unless you saw my personnel file."

"How would I do that?"

"You couldn't. Not without my knowing. Everything done on these computers is recorded, you know."

"Of course."

"I could see if you have been snooping."

"Feel free."

Figueroa broke into a wide grin. "But I trust you, Wong! You are a friend of His Excellency."

"Well, my Father is."

"I suppose you have heard they have asked for lie-detecting software. I uploaded it this morning."

"How would I know that?"

Figueroa clutched Chang's shoulder, and it was all Chang could do to keep from recoiling. "Because you are connected, my friend!"

"I'm not."

"We are all going to be subjected to searches, you know. Interrogations."

"Why?"

"I told you! The Indians, the stewards, have a connection here, a leak."

Chang shrugged.

"You want to be first or last?"

"To what?"

"To be interrogated."

"I have nothing to hide. They can interrogate me anytime they want."

"They will search your apartment, want to see your personal computer."

"They may feel free. The hard drive has been worthless for some time."

"Then you have nothing to worry about."

"I was not worried."

Figueroa looked around, as if realizing he might be criticized for paying too much attention to one worker. "Of course, you weren't, Wong. You're connected."

Chang shook his head. "Who will replace Moon?"

"Akbar is too important where he is.

Fortunato has already had that job. Maybe Ms. Ivins, who knows? Maybe no one. Maybe Nicolae himself. One thing is certain, Wong," Figueroa added, turning to leave, "it won't be you or me."

"Don't be so sure," Chang said, hating himself for playing these games.

As Chang expected, Figueroa stopped. "What are you saying? What do you know?"

"Nothing to speak of, sir," Chang said. "Have to protect my connection, you know."

"You're putting me on. You know nothing."

"Of course."

"Seriously, now. I mean it."

"Me too, sir."

Five minutes later, as Chang was collating reports from around the world and assembling them for a briefing, Figueroa called from his office. "You swear you've never tapped in to see my personnel files?"

"I swear."

"If I ran a review on your computer, the one here and your own, it would bear that out?"

"This one would."

"But your personal computer?"

"I told you. The hard drive crashed."

"Then this about knowing my full name . . ."

"Would be guessing, sir."

"Want to guess?"

"I'm busy, sir."

"I'll give you one guess."

"I was just talking. I don't know."

"Come now, Wong. Take a shot. Tell you what — you get it right, I'll leave your name off the interrogation list."

"How could you do that?"

"I have my ways."

"Why would I care about being interrogated?"

"It's a waste of time, a nuisance, stressful."

"Not if you're innocent. I never even heard of the Indian stewards."

"The offer stands."

Chang sighed. Why had he started this? And who would believe Figueroa gave a rip anyway? "I know it starts with an *S*."

"Everybody knows that. It's on my nameplate. But maybe it's like the *S* in Harry S Truman and stands for nothing."

"You use the period after it, so it stands for something. I'd just be guessing."

"Unless you're lying about hacking into my file, a hundred Nicks says you couldn't guess in ten tries."

"I have only one guess."

"Let's hear it."

"Sequoia."

A long silence. Figueroa swore. "You couldn't know that!"

"I'm right?"

"You are and you know it, but how did you know? It's not even a Mexican name. Not even Spanish."

"I'm guessing Indian. American Indian, I mean."

"Tell me how you knew that."

"Guessing, sir. I thought it made sense."

Why would a light be on in Chicago? Was it possible, Chloe wondered, that someone else had somehow discovered that David Hassid had planted the radiation readings in the Global Community database computer? That reminded her she had not yet told Buck the horrible news.

Chloe tried to plot where she would find the lighted window, then put up the telescope and phoned Buck. It broke her heart to hear that he was at Petra and as excited as she remembered him being in a long time. She let him go on and on about what had happened, how Rayford had seen and been healed by the angel, and how he and the others in the chopper had eventually seen him as well when he protected them from gunfire.

Chloe could only agree with Buck about the signs and wonders, the confrontations with Carpathia, the supernatural change in Chaim, the thrill of pirating the network for the spreading of the truth. Finally he must have noticed her enthusiasm did not match his. "You okay, babe?"

"I have bad news for you, Buck. Two GC MIAs murdered David Hassid, and we all agreed not to tell you and Chaim until your work was almost finished. . . . Buck? Are you there?"

"Give me a minute," he said finally.

"I don't know when Daddy was going to tell Chaim. It ought to be soon if he's right there on-site."

"Yeah," Buck managed. "He'll probably somehow get everybody else out of the chopper first. We don't want the people to see Chaim yet."

"Of course."

"Chloe, what're we going to do?"

"I don't know. The most awful part is, it's only going to get worse. Before I fall asleep I run over in my mind everybody we've got left and I can't help but wonder . . ."

"Who'll be next, I know. I didn't know David as well as some of the others did, but just from a practical, logistical stand-point . . ."

"He was so crucial," Chloe said. "And how much do we know about Ming's brother?"

"David was high on him, but he is still a teenager. And he'll never be in the same position, have the same access David had. I hate to talk about it only in terms of what it means to the Trib Force, but —"

"The mourning process has to be so blunted, Buck. Everything's life and death now. Each loss makes it harder for the rest of us to survive, and it's only natural that we look at it that way. I just want you all back here and safe one more time."

"Soon," Buck said. "Your dad wants to use Abdullah's underground contacts to get use of a supersonic plane that will hold eight or so. Albie's credentials are still intact, so he would fly us all back to the States and pick up Tsion for a personal visit to Petra."

"I want to go," she said.

"You just said you wanted us back in one piece."

"I need baby-sitters."

"Be serious. We all need some R and R before Armageddon."

"I don't."

"What're you talking about?"

"Dad promised I could go on the next mission if all the bases were covered. I took that to mean if there were enough people here to watch Kenny."

Buck was silent.

"You don't approve."

"No," he said. "Kenny could stand losing me more than you."

"Don't be silly."

"*I'm* being silly? Listen to yourself. You're his mother."

"So I get the whole responsibility."

"That's not what I'm —"

"And you're so crucial to the frontline work of the Trib Force that we can't risk losing me and leaving you to be Kenny's primary caregiver."

She could tell Buck was angry. "I can't believe I'm standing here in the middle of the desert, arguing with my wife about who's going to watch the baby. Listen, you can't come back with Tsion, because the GC is waiting till he returns before they make an air strike here."

"Yet you send Tsion into that, and a billion people a day are dependent on him."

"We believe he'll be protected here."

"And I won't?"

"We don't know. David wasn't."

"I don't want to fight about this on the phone, Buck. Please don't be closed to it until we get a chance to talk it through. And be careful. I love you and I couldn't live without you."

With her phone in her pocket, Chloe nonchalantly chatted with Zeke out of the hearing of the others. "If I were to go out for a walk, would you keep an ear out for Kenny and not feel obligated to mention to anyone else that I'm gone?"

"This time of night? Ma'am, it's —"

"Z, please. I'm a grown woman and I need to get out of here. I'll have my phone with me."

"I couldn't lie for you."

"I didn't ask you to. Just don't volunteer anything. I don't want anyone to worry."

Buck headed back to the helicopter. The transfer of people into Petra was slow but steady. He wanted to let Rayford know he knew about David and give him a chance to tell Chaim. But as he worked his way through the enthusiastic crowd, beautifully bronzed children, exhausted by the flight and sleeping on parents' shoulders, distracted him. How he missed Kenny!

The crowd suddenly shifted and smiles froze. Their attention turned to the east, and Buck jogged to where he could see. Billowing across the desert came three huge clouds of dust that threatened to blot out the diminished sun. The two on the left continued to separate themselves from the one on the right. Buck dialed Chang, only to find out he was temporarily incommunicado. He dialed Rayford.

"Chloe told me about David. Get rid of the others for a minute and tell Chaim. And what do you make of what's coming?"

"Abdullah's figured it out," Rayford reported. "GC ground forces. They're going to separate until they can come at the people simultaneously from three different directions, forcing them into the Siq, which will hold only so many."

Buck began sprinting toward the chopper. "The news of David can wait. Are the rest of us safe, or just Chaim? And are the people safe outside the entrance?"

"I'm going to switch places with George and get up where I can get a look at these troops," Rayford said. "When I come back down, be close by. We may have to take up arms."

"Arms?" Buck said. "I heard about those. Count me out."

"You may change your mind if the GC opens fire."

I just might, Buck thought.

Fifteen

Chloe slipped out in dark slacks and a black jacket. Besides her phone, she carried an ancient Luger she found among Rayford's keepsakes. She had experimented with it until she figured out how to load it and work the safety. She only guessed how it might fire, but it gave her a measure of security she hadn't known was available.

She walked five blocks in the pitch-blackness of unlighted streets and heard nary a sound. Chloe looked to her left at every cross street now, imagining she was close to her target. How far off could she be? Maybe a quarter of a mile, she decided. So she went left two blocks and started looking both ways at each corner.

Rayford ascended and hovered at less than a thousand feet, just high enough to allow himself a sense of what the Global Community Security and Intelligence forces were sending their way. "George," he said, "switch seats with Dr. Rosenzweig, please."

"What are we looking at?" Chaim said as he settled in. Rayford told him and pointed to where the two other columns of tanks, armored trucks, personnel carriers, and rocket launchers peeled off to circle around the massive crowd of Israelis.

"I worry that only you Israeli believers are safe," Rayford said. "But are even you safe outside the walls of Petra?"

"Captain, the question must be academic. Without a miracle of God, we are still hours from having more than half our people inside. How long before these attackers reach us?"

"They're probably within firing range right now," Rayford said. "In twenty more minutes they will all be in position. If they advance as soon as they are mustered, they would be able to fight hand to hand within ten more minutes of that."

"So half an hour . . ."

"Maximum."

"My people are neither armed nor prepared to defend themselves. We are at the mercy of God."

"I'm tempted to have you urge all believers who are not Israelis to get into Petra as quickly as they can," Rayford said. "Do you think your people would defer to them, allowing them to get to the front of the helicopter lines and make way for those who would walk in?"

"Not without understanding, and how would there be time to explain?"

"The alternative is that Operation Eagle suspend the airlift and every able-bodied believer, except those from Israel, be armed and prepared to stand against this attack."

"You will be hopelessly outnumbered, Captain."

"But we would inflict damage, and we would not go down without a fight."

"I would not begin to try to advise you," Chaim said. "You must do what you must do. What is God telling you?"

"He's telling me I am as afraid as I have ever been, but I cannot stand by and allow a massacre. Are you able to operate a weapon, Doctor?"

"Forgive me, but I am not here to resist with arms. I am to take charge of these people in Petra and prepare the way for a visit from Tsion. And when he again leaves, I will remain."

Rayford looked over his shoulder and shouted, "George, Abdullah, find out where Albie and Mac are. Tell them our situation and to connect with us as soon as we're on the ground, if they can. Stand by to load weapons and set up a perimeter a hundred yards in front of the Israelis."

"I am only guessing, Captain," Abdullah said, "but if we are to surround them up to the walls on either side of the Siq, we will likely stand more than fifty yards apart each."

"I didn't say this would be easy or even successful, Smitty. I'm open to suggestions."

"I have none."

"Then round up our guys and tell the rest that all Operation Eagle personnel are on combat duty effective immediately." He turned back to Chaim and motioned him to lean close. "Doctor, I need to tell you what happened here yesterday. . . ."

Chang had been the fastest keyboarder in his Chinese high school, regardless of whether they were inputting in Chinese or English. Now he sat speed-typing code into a secondary window every chance he got.

He maneuvered his monitor in such a way that it faced neither the surveillance camera in the corner nor his coworkers if they remained at their stations. He also forced himself to look not at the characters he was typing but at the reflection off the screen, which told him when Figueroa or anyone else happened to stroll within view.

The secondary window, as he designed it, would show up on any check of the machine as a local notepad, but he programmed his codes so they would appear as random keys rather than any sensible strings. If questioned, he could attribute the gibberish to residue in translating from Chinese to English or even a computer language. He was building and formatting an independent drive he could access from anywhere and which would duplicate the capability of his laptop.

Chloe kept peeking at her watch and asking herself if she was a fool. What did she expect to find? Was she just satisfying her curiosity? Being out by herself, especially in the dark, gave her a wholly satisfying sense of freedom, which in turn made her wonder if she was too young for the responsibilities she bore. She was a wife and mother, head of an international co-op that meant the difference between health and starvation for its millions of members. And yet she needed this kind of an escape? One with perhaps more danger than she knew?

Finally she reached a corner, where she looked right to no avail and then left, which made her stop. Could that be her source of light, that faint strip of a lighter shade that seemed to color the darkness four or five blocks away? Did she have the time or energy to see if she had been that far off in her calculation? Of course. What else was she out here for? It was clear Buck and probably her dad were not really going to let her journey to Petra with Tsion when an air attack was certain. This might be her only mission, and of course, the odds were it would prove to be nothing. But even if it was folly and turned out to be nothing but a game of hide-and-seek in the dark, it was better than nothing.

She turned left.

Rayford banked and circled to drop back down, and as the craft leveled and settled, he saw Buck hurrying toward him, motioning with a finger across his neck to cut the engines as soon as possible. From all over the area, other drivers and chopper pilots emerged from vehicles and aircraft and headed his way, awaiting instructions and weaponry for the stand against the GC.

The crowd, however, seemed to ignore both the Operation Eagle personnel and the GC, though the clouds of dust and the sounds of engines drew closer. Rather, the people all seemed riveted to where the Siq led into the high-walled path into Petra. Rayford had dropped too quickly to see what they could be looking at.

Buck reached the chopper, more frantically signaling the cut-engine message, and Rayford quickly shut down and reached past Chaim to push open the door. "Everybody out," Buck said. "You've got to see this!"

"Do we need weapons?" Rayford called, and they tumbled out.

"Doesn't look like it. Follow me. Chaim, you all right?"

"Call me Micah, but yes. Lead the way."

"Aren't we afraid of people recognizing him?" Rayford said.

"No one's looking," Buck said.

"So I noticed," Rayford said, sprinting behind Buck and realizing that Chaim had hiked up his robe and was somehow keeping pace. George and Abdullah pounded along behind.

Buck led them to an incline, then bent and

charged up to where a giant boulder offered a flat surface from where they could overlook the hundreds of thousands. "There," Buck said, "near the entrance. See?"

Chloe grew more excited the farther she walked. The contrast between the light and the darkness grew stronger, and she knew she had found what she had seen from the safe house in the Strong Building. The possibility that it represented anything more than a rogue light left on by some quirk of the power grid was, she knew, likely only in her head. But as she came within a block and a half of the window, which was barred and indeed at street level, she saw the camera. It sat directly above the window, hooded by a thick metal box that she would not be surprised to learn was covered with graffiti. A tiny dot of red light glowed from it, and the lens, though she could barely make it out, swiveled in a 180-degree arc.

Chloe was certain she was too far from any light source to have been picked up by what appeared to be an old camera, but she slowed and stayed close to buildings and the rubble of buildings, stopping whenever she detected the lens pointing in her direction. When it swung away, she hurried to get closer.

Finally she crossed the street away from the camera and pressed her back up against a wall. Again she stopped when the camera seemed to find her, and when it swung the other way, she edged closer. Eventually she was within three feet of where the light from the window reached the wall next to her across the street. Inside the window she saw only a fluorescent ceiling unit with three of its four tubes illuminated. When next the camera scanned her way, she realized the light barely touched her left sleeve. She stood stock-still, wondering if the camera had any kind of a motion sensor.

Here came the rotation of the lens again. Chloe remained where she was but moved her arm slightly in the edge of the light. The camera stopped rotating and the light in the window went out. Now all she could see was the dot of red, and it remained stationary. She imagined the lens opening to try to decipher what stood across the street there in the darkness.

Should she run? Was it possible that whoever or whatever controlled the camera and the light was as scared as she was? Did it or they want to catch her or scare her off? or simply be aware of what was out there? Chloe took a deep breath and, trying to relax, worked to regulate the rise and fall of her diaphragm. One thing she was sure of, if she could trust David and Chang, this was not GC.

Chloe tiptoed halfway across the street and noticed a faded sign on the wall, but still it was too dark to make out. She stood there, the camera seeming to study her. Finally the fluorescent light came back on. She did not move, except to raise her eyes and read the sign. It was some sort of currency exchange. That meant that behind the bars was a window likely made of bulletproof glass.

She put her hands in her pockets, the handgrip of the Luger nestled in her right palm. The camera stayed on her as she moved closer to the window, and the lens moved only enough to keep her centered, the faint whine telling her it was also adjusting constantly to keep her in focus. At long last, throwing caution to the wind, she bent at the waist and peered inside the window.

A squawk box crackled to life. "Identify yourself and explain your mark."

There, just above the heads of the people at the front of the crowd, stood the man Rayford knew to be Michael. He was dressed similarly to Chaim, though he was taller. He held both hands aloft, and such a hush fell over the Israelis that everyone could hear him, though he spoke in normal, conversational tones. Rayford stood far beyond the edge of the throng, yet it sounded as if Michael spoke directly into his ear.

If the effect on the crowd was the same as on Rayford, they were filled with a sacred peace.

Michael began, "Fear not, children of Abraham. I am your shield. Fear not, for God has heard your voice. He says to you, 'I am the God of Abraham your father: fear not, for I am with you, and will bless you.'

"Behold, the Lord your God has set the land before you: go up and possess it, as the Lord God of your fathers has said unto you; fear not, neither be discouraged. Hear, O Israel, you approach this day unto battle against your enemies: let not your hearts faint, fear not, and do not tremble, neither be terrified because of them; be strong and of a good courage, fear not, nor be afraid of them: for the Lord your God, he it is that goes with you; he will not fail you, nor forsake you.

"Peace be unto you; fear not: you shall not die. Turn not aside from following the Lord, but serve the Lord with all your heart. God your Father says, 'You shall eat bread at my table continually. Be courageous, and be valiant.' Fear not: for they that be with us are more than they that be with them.

"You shall not need to fight in this battle: set yourselves, stand still, and see the salvation of the Lord with you, O Judah and Jerusalem, for the Lord will be with you. God shall hear you, and afflict them because therefore they fear not his name. Say to them that are of a fearful heart, 'Be strong, fear not: behold, your God will come with vengeance, even God with a recompense; he will come and save you.' "

Michael stepped down and began walking through the masses, who backed away and followed with their eyes. As he strode past, he continued to encourage. "For the Lord your God will hold your right hand, saying unto you, 'Fear not; I will help you, people of Israel.' So says the Lord, and your redeemer, the Holy One of Israel.

"Thus says the Lord that created you, O Israel, 'Fear not: for I have redeemed you, I have called you by your name; you are mine.' It shall be well with you. Be glad and rejoice: for the Lord will do great things. The very hairs of your head are all numbered. Fear not therefore: you are of more value than many sparrows.

"The Lord God says, 'Fear not, for I am the first and the last.' Stand firm then, remnant of Israel. Fear not! Fear not! Fear not! Fear not!"

The crowd began to take up the chant, louder and louder, as Michael found his way to the edge of the people, facing what was now the middle column of desert dust, fast approaching. He stood grasping his robe at the chest, chin raised toward the advancing armies of the evil one, and behind him the teeming thousands matched his pose.

Rayford and Buck and Abdullah and Chaim hurried down and fell into the crowd behind Michael. Rayford couldn't know how the others felt. As for him, fear was gone and he had never rested more surely in God.

Chloe found her throat constricted, but they could see her mark! She was able to croak, "If you can see it, it does not need to be explained."

"Identify yourself."

"What more do you need to know than that I am a sister in Christ?"

"How are you able to survive the radiation? Are you supernaturally protected?"

"I will answer only when I know whether you are all brothers and sisters."

"Persuade us you are not radioactive and we will welcome you inside."

"I must know if any enemy is among you."

"We are all believers. No Carpathianists, no GC."

"The radiation is a ruse perpetrated by the Judah-ites." Chloe had crossed a line she could not retreat from. Any more information that might be secreted to the enemy, and she would be giving away the safe house and her comrades.

"To what purpose?"

"You should be able to surmise."

"Are you alone, sister?"

"You mean —"

"Is anyone with you now?"

"No."

There was a long silence. The camera remained on her, the light on in the empty room. It had a ratty, gray, short-nap industrial carpet, a green countertop built into a wall, and three Plexiglas-windowed transaction stations, all long since retired from use.

A door in the far corner opened slowly, and a black man in bare feet, beltless suit pants, and a white, sleeveless T-shirt emerged. Maybe in his late twenties and muscular, he moved cautiously across the carpet, standing directly under the light, looking out, not smiling but not scowling either. Chloe detected hope, curiosity, perhaps bemusement in his eyes. He invited her closer to the window with a wave, and she lowered her face to within inches of it. He broke into a huge grin. "Greetings, sister!" he called out, and she saw the mark of God on his forehead.

He hurried back to the door and called to others. A black girl came out, about Chloe's age, wearing shorts and socks and an oversized man's white shirt. Chloe felt on display, as if at the zoo. And here came two middle-aged Latino women — one big boned but gaunt, the other thin and short.

"You're okay?" the young black woman called out. "How long you been outside?"

"Almost an hour. But I've been out before. Lots of times."

"And you're okay?"

Chloe smiled. "I'm okay! Not contagious!"

"Let her in!"

"Yeah, let her in!"

"Get Enoch! He'll decide."

First in line, Rayford noticed, in each of the three massive divisions of GC battalions, were full-track tanks, chewing up rocks and dirt and sand, bouncing and rolling over the uneven ground. Behind them, beyond the clouds of dust, from what he had seen from the air, were missile launchers.

348

Then came cannons, then armored personnel carriers, trucks, jeep-type vehicles with gun-toting soldiers, then smaller cars.

Rayford judged their speed at about thirty-five miles an hour, and he assumed they would soon synchronize a stopping point where every weapon in their arsenals would have maximum kill power. But there seemed no slowing as they drew within half a mile, then a quarter mile. They bore down on the unarmed civilians.

Rayford suddenly had a sinking feeling. He had only assumed the rest of the Operation Eagle forces would merely stand in confidence behind Michael. But what if they acted on old information? What if Albie or Mac or someone else had provided them weapons and they returned fire, or worse, initiated it?

He wanted to grab his phone and his walkie-talkie and confirm with his people that they were to stand down, to remain unarmed. But the GC were nearly upon them now. The noise reverberated off the rock walls and the dust blew all around them. Still, neither side opened fire. Rayford finally ducked and turned, covering his eyes against the dust and peeking back to be sure none of his people took overt action. As far as he could see, the Israelis and the Operation Eagle forces remained calm, standing firm, trusting in God's protection.

Rayford had to fight a smile. In his humanness he allowed that he could be in heaven within seconds, and his survival instinct wanted him to defend himself. But the promises of God also rang in his ears. He shook his head at the lunacy of Carpathia's ego. Clearly this three-pronged army had been instructed not to fire unless fired upon, and they intended to run over the Israelis and grind them into the ground!

They were within a hundred feet now, yet Rayford heard not a sound from behind, not a cry from anyone's lips. This flood from the serpent's mouth was going to hit an invisible wall or be swept away by some wall of water from nowhere, or the Israelis and their helpers would prove so ethereal that the weapons of destruction would pass harmlessly through them.

Ten feet and ground zero, and suddenly the entire mass of God's people fell to their knees and covered their ears at the thunderous peals that resounded like mountains falling. All around the sea of people, right at the feet of those in the front on every side, the earth split and ripped open for a mile in every direction away from Petra.

The echoes from the shattering of the

earth were as loud as the actual cleaving, and as the tanks and missiles and cannons and personnel armaments were fired in panic or from being shaken to their core, the projectiles rose vertically and eventually dropped back down onto the plunging armies. Smoke and fire rose in great belches from the colossal gorge that appeared to reach the bowels of hell. The roar of racing engines, whose drivetrains propelled steel tracks or wheels that merely spun in thin air, could not cover the screams of troops who had been just seconds from squashing their prey and now found themselves hurtling to their deaths.

Rayford and all those around him pulled their hands from their ears and thrust them out wide to keep their balance as, still on their knees, they were rocked by aftershocks. It was as if they surfed on unsolid ground as the earth slowly healed itself. The walls of the chasm came back together as the Red Sea must have millennia before, and the loose, rocky topsoil was suddenly new. The dust settled, and quietness wafted over the assembled.

Michael was gone. Chaim slowly rose and addressed the people. "As long as you are on your knees, what better time to thank the God of creation, the God of Abraham,

Isaac, and Jacob? Thank him who sits high above the heavens, above whom there is no other. Thank the One in whom there is no change, neither shadow of turning. Praise the holy One of Israel. Praise Father, Son, and Holy Ghost!"

Enoch turned out to be an incongruously named Spaniard who carried, of all things, a cheap, hardbound Bible, the kind you would find in a hotel or a pew. He too was strangely dressed, wearing expensive shoes with missing laces and no socks, khaki pants, and a tank top–type shirt. These people, Chloe decided, looked like they had raided a Salvation Army barrel.

Enoch conferred with the others, then motioned Chloe around the corner to the main entrance, where she waited while he released lock after lock. Finally the inner door was open, and Enoch crossed the shallow lobby to push open the outer door. "We have limited food supplies," he said, as he held the door for her.

"I'm not looking for food," she said. "I was just curious about the light."

"We thought we were the only ones left in the city," he said. "We run the camera just in case but are just days from shutting it down to conserve energy."

"I have so many questions," Chloe said.

"So do we."

"I'm afraid I can't say much," she said. "I'll understand if you choose not to, either."

"We have nothing to hide," Enoch said.

"What is this place?"

"It was once a currency exchange. But it adjoins the basement of an old office building that was abandoned. Since they were connected, we thought it would be safer for us to stay largely underground, especially since there was a safe standing open. We never found the combination, so we do not close it all the way, but some prefer to sleep in it."

Enoch led Chloe through the old exchange lobby, where the curious who had eyed her through the window now shyly greeted her and stared. Just past the door and down the hall stood the huge, walk-in vault, and she had to assume this was a bank in one of its first manifestations. No currency exchange, even in Chicago, would need a vault that large.

"How many of you are there?" Chloe asked.

"As of last night, thirty-one."

"You're not serious."

Enoch cocked his head and smiled. "Why would I not be?"

"What are you doing here? How did you get here?"

"Well," he said, pushing open a door that led to a large-pillared basement room, "I'm sure that's what my friends and I want to know from you." She stepped in to meet everyone's curious and wary eyes.

Rayford was on his walkie-talkie to Operation Eagle personnel. "Let's step it up, people. I want constant rounds of chopper hops to get these people inside Petra. Building materials and miscellaneous stuff flown or carried in. We believe Carpathia made a major blunder and used our Mizpe Ramon airstrip rather than destroying it, so we can use it to take off and get back to our homelands before he finds out what happened here. No one is left to tell him, so for now he has to assume he has simply lost radio contact.

"When Micah is inside, our mission is accomplished. Good-bye and Godspeed."

Rayford clicked off the walkie-talkie and conference-phoned Trib Force members, old and new, among the crowd. "Let's be ready to get home and get Tsion. He's got a speaking engagement scheduled here."

Sixteen

Chloe sat in a cheap metal folding chair surrounded by a wide-eyed mix of cross-cultural people in their twenties and thirties. She had many questions, but they insisted on asking theirs first. Clearly they were true believers, but still she prayed silently, pleading with God for peace about telling them of the Tribulation Force.

"None of you have been outside since the bombing of the city?" she said.

They shook their heads. Enoch carried the conversation. "If we come to believe it is safe, all of us will take a walk before dawn. Now tell us more."

Chloe took a deep breath. "You vouch for everyone in here, Enoch?"

"Check our marks," he said.

Chloe knew that was unnecessary. And she saved her two biggest revelations till last. "The spiritual mentor I have told you about is Jewish. He was a rabbi. He is Dr. Tsion Ben-Judah."

The group sat, obviously stunned, many smiling, others shaking their heads. Finally a Latino said, "Ben-Judah lives in Chicago?"

She nodded. "And I am Chloe Steele Williams."

Enoch leaned toward her, trembling. "And we are hungry," he said, making the others laugh.

"You look it," she said. "What have you been living on?"

"Canned goods and dry goods. We've been slowly rationing them, but they're fast running out. If Dr. Ben-Judah is right and we have three and a half years to go, we're not going to make it. Do you think the co-op might —"

"Send a couple back with me and I'll load them up with enough to feed you for a month. Then we'll figure a way you can contribute to the co-op and start trading for food and supplies."

Several stood to volunteer. "We also want to travel," Enoch said, "to help other people, to tell them the truth. We're desperate for a chance to do that."

"We ought to be able to manage it, in time," she said. "Now tell me your story."

Laslos Miklos had been used to an affluent lifestyle, owning a lucrative lignite-mining business in Ptolemaïs, Greece, before the disappearances. But when he and his wife became believers in Christ, his hundreds of trucks and dozens of buildings became fronts for the efforts of the Greek underground church, which became the largest in the United Carpathian States.

The Greek Jesus-followers lived on the edge of danger, but for a time it seemed Nicolae Carpathia was more interested in projecting an image of tranquillity in the region named for him than in rooting out dissidents. Laslos did not think he and his fellow believers became overconfident, but somehow one of their secret meeting places had been discovered, someone caved, and the largest assembly had been raided. Many were martyred, the rest scattered.

Laslos lost his wife to the guillotine — also his pastor and his pastor's wife, plus dozens more adults and many teenagers. He had not been at the meeting the night of the raid and now lived with guilt. Was there something he could have done? Though he still felt the hand of God on his life, the Lord was strangely silent about his blame. Laslos was the most prominent among those who had escaped and immediately went into hiding, north of the city.

He feared that a hideout connected in any way to his business would easily be discovered. But he knew of a long-abandoned dump surrounded by mountains of debris, including soil and gravel and chunks of concrete. With the help of trusted friends, he dug himself a dirt-walled chamber where he slept during the day, far below ground and with just enough room for plumbing, a cot, and a small television. In the dead of night, when the walls seemed to close in on him, he would steal away to connect with other believing desperadoes, who then hooked up with clandestine members of the International Commodity Co-op, where they were supplied with food and other necessities.

From those brief, terror-filled meetings grew tiny replicas of the former underground church that had been so vibrant. Laslos and his friends shared with each other what they knew of the rest of the surviving church and passed precious messages back and forth. The few who had wireless computers and enough power downloaded and printed Tsion Ben-Judah's daily messages and Buck Williams's *The Truth* cyberzine. To Laslos these were more priceless than food and water.

The squat, heavyset, fifty-six-year-old widower retained huge, rocklike muscles from his early days of manual labor in the mines. Now he stayed out in the night for as long as he dared, keeping to side and back streets. Sleeping during the day helped keep his claustrophobia in check. More than once he found himself praying that he would wake up in heaven, reunited with his wife and other loved ones.

Late one morning he was awakened by footsteps in the gravel above his hideaway. As quietly as a man of his girth and age could manage, Laslos moved to the edge of his bed and slipped onto all fours on the wood floor. He painfully crept a few feet to where he could reach his handgun, a classic revolver he had never fired, not even on a practice range. It was, however, loaded and — he believed — in working order. A man of peace all his life, he no longer wondered whether he would shoot to kill a Global Community Peacekeeper or Morale Monitor who threatened him or any believer.

The sun cast dusty beams between the cracks of the door over the top of the chamber and the rickety wood planks leading down into the space. The door was level with the ground, and its topside had been inlaid with gravel to blend in. As Laslos stood near the bottom plank, his neck awkwardly craned, staring at the underside of the door, he cocked the revolver and held his breath. The footsteps were atop the door now, tentative, as if aware of the subtle difference between a metal surface with rigid, glued-on stones and the hard-packed but loose gravel of the real ground.

Laslos used his free hand to guide himself and started slowly up the planks, listening over the thud of his pulse for any clue to whether his intruder was alone. When he drew within inches of the door, he leaned to peer through a peephole undetectable from the other side and found himself looking from the boots to the head of a teenage boy, bare armed and wearing neither uniform nor badge nor gun.

Suddenly the boy squatted, as if studying the door. "Mr. Miklos?" he whispered.

Laslos had to calculate countless options at once. If this boy was undercover GC, Laslos had been found out. He could pretend to be fooled, open his door to the boy, and surprise him with a bullet between the eyes. But if the boy was a believer and had been directed there by one of Laslos's friends, he should threaten the comrade with a bullet for stupidity. Either way, for some reason this lad believed Laslos was there, and he was.

He couldn't risk slaughtering his visitor without cause. "Who goes there?" Laslos said quietly in Greek.

The boy dropped to all fours, as if overcome. "Oh, Mr. Miklos!" he rasped desperately. "I am Marcel Papadopoulos! My parents —"

"Shh!" Laslos interrupted, uncocking the weapon and tossing it down onto his bed. He unbolted the locks and grunted as he pushed up the door. "Are you alone?"

"Yes!"

"Hurry!"

The boy turned and nimbly backed down the steps. Laslos returned to refasten the locks. When he came back down, the boy was sitting in a corner on the floor, his knees pulled up. Even in the low light of the underground, the boy's mark was plain on his forehead.

Laslos sat on the bed, realizing the gun was gone. How could he have been such a fool? "I knew your parents, of course," he began carefully. "I knew you too, did I not?"

"Not really," Marcel said. "I was in a different house church from my parents."

Laslos *had* seen this boy with his parents occasionally, he was sure of it. "Did you not think I'd notice you took my fake pistol?"

"Oh, sir! I was just looking at it!" He held it out and Laslos wrenched it away. "It looks and feels so real, Mr. Miklos! Is it really fake?"

"Hardly. How can you be so stupid and survive on the street? What made you think I would not just grab another weapon and shoot you dead?"

"I don't know, sir. I wasn't thinking."

"Who sent you?"

"The old toothless one with the car. He calls himself K."

"I should wring his neck."

"Don't blame him, please, sir. He warned me not to come during the day, but I have run out of places to go. The GC is thin here with so many assigned to Israel, but they are on their way back, and there is no more grace period for taking Carpathia's mark. I have seen people dragged off the street."

"Your parents, weren't they with Pastor Demetrius and — ?"

"They were. And so was I. But a believer who had infiltrated the GC accused me of being an American and dragged me out, then let me go. I gave him my parents' names, and I have been praying ever since that he got them out too. But I know they would have found me if he had."

"He did not. We know who he is, Marcel. He also was able to get a young woman out."

"I have met her! Tall, brown hair. Georgiana something. But she was not from our church. She found her way to one of the co-op stations. Her story was just like mine. How did this man do it?"

Laslos sighed heavily. "Frankly, he blundered with you. He used another boy's name for you. . . ."

"Yes, I told him the only other name I knew from in there. Paulo Ganter."

"Well, this fake GC told authorities at the prison that you were Paulo and that he was deporting you back to the United North American States. But when Ganter took the mark of loyalty, his ID checked out, and they quickly realized someone else was gone. By process of elimination, they know your name. He must have done the same with the girl. You may not have marks they can see, but you are marked young people. Fortunately your liberator was gone before they realized what he had done."

"How I would love to thank that man. He's American."

"I know," Laslos said. "I know him."

"Could I get a message to him?"

"It could be done."

The boy sighed and his shoulders sagged. "What am I going to do now, Mr. Miklos? I am out of options."

"You can see there is no room for you here."

"We could expand."

"*We?* Let's not get ahead of ourselves, son. This is no way to live. You need a new look, a new identity, and you must continue to keep from being seen by the GC at all costs."

Rayford assigned Leah and Hannah to search out the computer savvy among the Israelis. "Tell them that once they have located the computers in Petra, our man in New Babylon will contact them on-line and provide information on how to get the network up and running."

Rayford, Albie, Mac, and George joined dozens of others to resume chopper duty, making run after run to get Israeli believers inside. Chaim was in seclusion, preparing to address the entire populace when they were settled. Buck had temporarily taken the duties David would have had: getting building and miscellaneous supplies in and organized so builders and finishers could get started. Already volunteers were passing out blankets and helping people get settled.

Rayford was nearly overwhelmed with the attitude of the Israelis. Maybe because of their faith, maybe because of the miracles, maybe because of the novelty of what they were about, they displayed cooperation and a camaraderie Rayford found unique. Considering they were uprooted from their homeland and targeted by the entire evil world system, he would not have been surprised to see manifestations of impatience and anger.

Rayford sent Abdullah bouncing over the desert in one of the most able four-wheel-drive vehicles they could recruit to rendezvous with his co-op contact from Jordan. The contact was bringing in a long-range jet with room for everybody heading back to Chicago. All the co-op guy wanted in exchange for the loan of his plane was to be delivered to Crete on the Trib Force's way to the States and to be brought back from there on their way back.

That gave Rayford the idea that they should stop in Greece to check on their brothers and sisters. Trouble was, Albie was the only one left with other-than-suspect papers. During one of his hops into

Petra, Rayford phoned Lukas Miklos.

Chang noticed on his monitor evidence that his bug of the Phoenix 216 had kicked in. He couldn't wait till the end of the workday to get back to his apartment and see what had been recorded. He switched to the GCNN feed and learned that Carpathia was already on his way back to New Babylon. Hiding his trail, Chang hacked into the encoded schedule for surprise inspections of GC personnel's private computer systems. The encoding was so elementary he nearly laughed aloud. He discovered he was third on the list and could expect a "random" visit that evening at around 2000 hours.

His screen suddenly came alive with a flash from Figueroa's office, and for an instant Chang thought he might have allowed himself to be caught using the office desktop for unapproved purposes. He covered his tracks with a burst of keystrokes and informed Figueroa he was coming.

Chang hurried to the office that had been David Hassid's. Figueroa had rearranged the furniture and redecorated it within hours of moving in, and now he glided about in it as if he were the Global Community potentate himself.

"Have a seat, Wong," he said. "Cigar?"

"Cigar? Do I look like a smoker to you? Anyway, isn't the whole complex smoke free?"

"A director's office is his domain," Figueroa said, lighting up. Tiffany, who had also been Hassid's assistant, looked up quickly from just outside the office window and scowled. Shaking her head, she left her desk and loudly slapped a switch on the wall between her office and Figueroa's. A ventilation fan came on, sucking the blue smoke into the ceiling. "I love when she does that," the director said, but Chang thought he looked embarrassed.

Figueroa leaned back in his chair and put his feet up on the corner of his desk. Apparently he miscalculated, because as he pulled the huge cigar from his lips, his heel slipped off the desk and his center of gravity shifted. His boots slammed the floor and he nearly flew out of his chair. He dropped the cigar in the process and leaped from his chair to keep from burning himself.

He picked it up and brushed off the seat, quickly licking a finger that had found a hot ash. It was all Chang could do to keep a straight face when Figueroa smoothed himself, put the wet end of the cigar back in his mouth, and sat again. He leaned back but thought twice about putting his feet up and merely crossed his legs. This shifted his weight back more than he expected, and he had evidently not yet learned how to tighten the chair's tilt, for he was suddenly leaning back, legs still crossed, but with both feet in the air.

Figueroa seemed to try to subtly lean forward, but failing that, tried to appear that this was the way he wanted to sit. He pulled the cigar out again and rested an elbow on the arm of the chair, blowing smoke toward the ceiling while trying to maintain eye contact with Chang. "So," he began, the effort to keep his head erect clearly straining his neck. He let his head fall back as if searching the ceiling for what he wanted to say, and suddenly he was inches from toppling over backward. He quickly reinserted the cigar, gripped both arms of the chair until his knuckles were white, and pulled himself up again. He leaned forward, careful to keep his weight centered.

"I, uh, spoke too soon when I exempted you from being interrogated," he said.

Chang made a teenager's face at him. "What? I thought you were in charge here."

"Oh, I am. Make no mistake. But I would have to answer for it, probably to the potentate himself — we talk, you know — if I made an exception for anyone, especially in my own department."

"So you're going back on your word."

"I didn't exactly give my word."

"No, you just said it, and apparently that doesn't mean anything."

"Of course it does, but you're going to have to roll with me on this one. I'll owe you."

"It's not that big a deal. Forget it."

"No, now I want to be known as a man of his word. Tell you what — I'll conduct the polygraph myself."

"Now it's a polygraph?"

"Well, not really. The type I told you about is all."

"Fine."

"You're a good man, Wong."

"Yeah, I'm great."

"No, really, you are."

Chang pressed his lips together and looked away, shaking his head.

"I'm trying to be friends here," Figueroa said.

Chang looked back at him. "You are? Why would you do that?"

"You intrigue me, that's all."

"Oh, no. You're not —"

"Wong! I'm a married man!"

"Thank goodness."

"No, like most everybody else around here, I'm intrigued with your gifts and skills."

"Which I'm not using as long as I'm sitting here."

"Don't be a hard guy, Wong. I'm in a position to do you some good."

"You're not even in a position to keep your word."

"Hey, that was uncalled for."

"Come on," Chang said. "What's this about? That would have been uncalled for only if it weren't true."

"Okay, fair enough. It's just that you're bordering on insubordination, and you don't seem to care that as your boss, I hold your destiny."

"What, you're going to fire me if I don't make nice?"

Figueroa took three short puffs and studied him. "No. But I might fire you if you don't tell me how you knew my name."

"I told you, I guessed."

"Because to tell you the truth," Figueroa continued, as if not listening, "I can't think of a way in the world you would know that."

"Me either. You could have denied it and I wouldn't have known the difference."

"Now see? That's a level of thinking I have to admire. That's intuitive."

"Whatever."

"No, because you know what? I started thinking about my personnel file, and I had to wonder if I ever gave *them* my full name. So, know what I did? Huh? I checked it myself. Not there."

"What do you know."

"So you really did guess."

"Wow. I'm something."

"You are."

"Can I get back to work now?"

"One condition."

"I'm listening."

"Promise you won't say anything about my telling you I've got your destiny in my hands or that I could fire you, any of that."

"Already forgot it."

"Good man. Because I know your dad and you-know-who are tight, and . . ."

"Already forgot it."

"You want to be a project leader, a group head, anything?"

"Just want to get back to work."

"Fair enough."

"Three and a half years ago there was, like, a church in here," Enoch said. "Some of us —" he turned to the group — "how many went to the church thing at least once?" About half a dozen raised their hands. "The rest of us had just seen a flyer, a brochure, about the place. We still have those, don't we?" Someone went to get one.

"It's kinda simple, just a regular piece of paper folded in half and then printed on the four pages in black and white."

Someone handed Chloe one. On the front it read "The Place." Inside, it said "Jesus loves pimps, whores, crack heads, drunks, players, hustlers, mothers with no husbands, and children with no fathers."

On the next page it told who made up the people of The Place, mostly people who had once been like those listed on the previous page. "We talk about Jesus and what the Bible says about him and you. Come as you are. Address and time on the back."

Chloe looked at the back, where, besides the address and times, the brochure also said "Food, clothes, shelter, work, counseling." She looked up at Enoch and realized she was blushing. Everybody in the room seemed amused.

Enoch reached for the brochure and faced his people. He read off the list of who Jesus loves, one by one, pausing after each for a show of hands. Everyone raised a hand at least once, and several did many times, always with huge smiles. Enoch carefully set down the brochure, looked meaningfully at Chloe, and rose. With lips trembling and tears streaming, he gestured to the assembled and whispered, "And such were some of you."

They nodded and *amen*ed.

"But you were washed . . ."

"*Amen, hallelujah!*"

"But you were sanctified . . ."

"*Praise Jesus!*"

"But you were justified in the name of the Lord Jesus and by the Spirit of our God."

And they stood with hands raised, humming and singing,

> "*Amazing grace, how sweet the sound,*
> *that saved a wretch like me;*
> *I once was lost but now am found,*
> *was blind but now I see.*"

"Rayford, my friend, how are you?" Laslos exulted. "You will not believe who is here with me. Is Cameron there?"

"Unavailable just now. So who is with you?"

When Laslos told him, Rayford said, "I'll have Buck call. He wondered what happened with those kids."

"Marcel tells me Georgiana remains on the run too. It is as if God himself told you to call. You must come get these children and get them out of here."

"Nowhere is safe, Laslos."

"But your safe house! Your man with the disguises and the papers! We are literally one wrong look from death here."

Rayford hesitated. "We're stopping on Crete. If you could somehow get them there . . ."

"Captain Steele, you have not seen the oceans! There is no water travel. None. Could we not somehow try to get them to the airport your people flew into last time? It would be risky, but we could —"

"It would be a death trap for us, Laslos. We will have virtually everyone with us."

"There must be some way. Someone."

"Let me noodle that," Rayford said.

"I don't understand 'noodle.'"

"I'll think about it."

"Almost every one of us has the same story," Enoch explained to Chloe. "The streets, these neighborhoods, were our lives. A lot of us had some kind of religious background as kids, but obviously we moved a long way from that. More than half of us served time, and almost all of us should have. The line between legal and illegal didn't exist for us. We called everything we did a matter of survival.

"Most of us had seen this place and knew

something churchy went on here. What surprised us were the people who came and went. All colors and nationalities and people we'd known. We all saw the brochure and, though we didn't admit it then, it enticed us, you know? Something that straightforward, that in-your-face, calling things what they are. When you're at the end of yourself, wondering in the night what's to become of you in the morning, you start wondering if there's hope anywhere or if you are too far gone. You remember yourself as a kid and recall that there was something still innocent about you, and you wonder what happened to that person.

"Any of these people will tell you that they either came here once or twice to try to work the system and get something free, or they even came sincerely and sat through a meeting or two. But all of us, even those who never came once — me, for one — were fixin' to get around to it. One of these days, we were going to check out The Place.

"You know the rest. End of the world. People disappearing. We all lost somebody, and this place just about lost everybody. Well, where did we run to first? Right here. Empty clothes all over the place and nobody to tell us what was what. But this poor little church must have had some money from somewhere because they thought to record everything they did. Audio and video. Here we are — two, three dozen no-account street people, some of us women who lost babies — and somebody finds those discs, man, and the players. It didn't take us long to learn the truth. It was all there.

"Most of us stayed, sleeping in here, watching, listening, studying, praying to get Jesus, and all of a sudden, World War III. Chicago's toast. We've got one TV and one computer hooked up. First we hear it was not nuclear; then the next wave is, and we expect to die of radiation poisoning. It doesn't happen, but we don't dare test the atmosphere outside. We knew if it was full-blown radiation, we were not protected just because we were inside some basement, but we figured we were safer in than out. Till now."

Rayford called George and asked if he wanted a mission on his way back to San Diego. "I thought you'd never ask," he said.

Rayford gave him the gist of the assignment and said, "I can't give you papers on short notice, but if I can reach our guy in New Babylon, you can bluff your way around in Greece. If they check on you,

you'll appear to be in the system."

"I can come up with some reason why I don't have papers. And you want these kids delivered to Chicago?"

"Unless you're prepared for them in California."

Knowing what was coming that evening, Chang felt out of touch with the Trib Force. Not until after his "surprise" visit at about eight o'clock could he key in the stuff Rayford wanted for this George Sebastian, nor could he find out what had happened on the Phoenix 216. He made sure he was watching GCNN and reading a book at the time, but even he was surprised at the nature of the drop-in.

Chang thought Figueroa's assignee — a cocky, condescending Scandinavian named Lars — would have at least knocked. But at a few minutes after eight, as Chang watched coverage of Carpathia and his senior cabinet being enthusiastically welcomed back to New Babylon, he heard a key in his door. It was just as well. He quickly turned up the TV and pretended he didn't hear a thing until they burst in. This was the best cover. He was relaxing, watching TV, reading, not even thinking about his worthless laptop.

The door swung open and two uniformed

Peacekeepers marched in. "Mr. Chang Wong?" one said.

"That's me," he said, rising. "Did I forget to lock my door?"

"Turn off the television, please, sir, and join us over here, if you would."

"What if I wouldn't?"

"Now, sir."

"Thanks for making me feel welcome in my own place."

"This is not your place, Mr. Wong. This is the property of His Excellency, the potentate, and you serve here at his behest."

Chang made a show of turning off the TV and dropping his book onto a chair. As he approached, the Peacekeepers moved aside and one of them announced, "This, sir, is Mr. L—"

"Lars!" Chang said, smiling, though he had barely done anything more than greet the guy. "How are you, man? I know him! We're in the same department."

"We need your cooperation and silence, Mr. Wong," the Peacekeeper said.

"Ooh, okay! What's up?"

Seventeen

The Peacekeepers asked if they could search Chang's apartment. "For what?" he said.

"Routine," they told him.

"You won't find any routine here. I am studying English words new to me and my current favorite is *serendipity*. That's what you'll find here, the opposite of *routine*."

"Funny. We don't need your permission. We were just being polite."

"Of course. My clue was your use of a master key to get me to answer the door."

While they searched the apartment, Lars set up a high-powered laptop on Chang's small kitchen table. "I'll be asking a few questions," he said.

"No, you won't."

"Stop being a smart-aleck," Lars said. "This is my assignment."

"Do the questions relate to finding a leak from the palace to the suspected mole?"

Lars turned ashen. "You've already been interrogated?"

"No, but I have my reservation in with another *interlocutor* — another new word. You like?"

"Computer!" the other Peacekeeper called out. "Looks like his personal laptop."

"If you had told me what you were looking for, I could have directed you to it."

"This your only one?"

Chang was tempted to pretend there was another, but the fun of watching them try to locate it wouldn't be worth their leaving the place in more of a shambles. He nodded.

"Over here with that," Lars said.

"I'm so glad you're here, Lars," Chang said. "I had everything on that hard drive, and I mean *everything*. Maybe you won't feel so bad about losing the interviewing assignment to our boss if you have this project to work on."

"Project?"

"I crashed the hard drive, and I've tried everything."

"Everything *you* know."

"That's right! That's why I'm so glad

you're here. I must be missing something, and even if it's something complex, I know you can solve it."

"You bet your life I can."

Chang, of course, was betting his life Lars couldn't. "I don't want to be up late, Lars."

"Oh, this shouldn't take long."

"I'm just saying maybe you want to call Mr. Figueroa so he can do whatever he has to do with me while you're retrieving my information."

"What're you, serious?"

"He promised."

"Why?"

"You'll have to ask him that."

"He'll ask you the same questions I would, and you'll answer into the same mike."

"Only with him, I'll answer. With you I won't."

"Then you'll be suspected as the leak, and you don't want that, guilty or not. You hear what happened to the stewards today?"

Chang didn't like it when he was asked a question to which he didn't know the answer. "Shock me."

"Sentenced to death."

That did shock Chang. "For what?"

"Subversion. Treason. They flunked the lie detector test. They were feeding information to a mole here. Conversations between the potentate and his people were acted upon before they were through talking." Lars handed him a lapel microphone. "Put this on."

"Not for you," Chang said.

"For Figueroa then."

Chang applied it to his shirt, praying silently. The key, he knew, was how the questions were worded. In his mind, a mole was an animal; he was a human being. If the questions were too specific and unequivocal, he'd be in trouble. "Start with my computer, will you? I'd really love to see all that stuff I had stored."

"You don't back up your stuff?"

Chang shook his head. "Nah. Do you?"

"Not as much as I should, but you gotta know you're going to fry something — hard drive, motherboard, whatever — every few years."

"Guess I've been lucky."

Lars dialed, tucked his phone between his cheek and neck, and started pecking furiously at Chang's laptop. "Yes, Mr. Figueroa, sir. I'm at Chang Wong's apartment and he says — oh, you did. Well, yes, right now. I'm helping him with a computer problem, so we'll be here. Thank you, sir."

Slapping his phone shut, eyes still on

Chang's computer, Lars mumbled, "On his way. My, you *have* fried this thing."

"Really, Lars? You can tell already? Wow."

"Yeah, it won't let me in at all. Let me try this." He appeared to try everything. "Nothing. Believe me, Wong, if anything was here, I could get it for you."

"No doubt."

"But this acts like it's been exposed to some super electromagnet."

"Haven't heard that term in a while."

"You know the drive is all about electricity and that a magnet can wreak serious havoc."

"Really?"

"Oh yeah, it's quite simple."

"For a brain like yours, maybe," Chang said. "I just know what buttons to push."

"Well, there's a lot more to it than that."

"I suppose. It's Greek to me."

"Thought you were supposed to be some kind of a genius," Lars said.

"Live and learn. Look what I did to my own laptop. Ten gigs somewhere in the ether."

"Should have called me at the first sign of trouble. There had to be warnings."

"Yeah, I saw a lot of strange stuff, but you know, laptops are temperamental."

"Not if they're treated right. Did you

defrag and run ScanDisk and all that?"

"Not often."

"Obviously not. I don't think there's anything here."

"You can't help me?"

"If anyone could, I could. But there's either something on the drive or there isn't, and in this case, there clearly isn't."

"What if it was on a different drive, named something else?"

"You couldn't do that by accident," Lars said. "I could do it, but you have to know what you're doing."

"Which I don't."

"Obviously. Here's what I *can* do for you. While you're being interviewed, I can format your whole drive for you so you can start rebuilding."

"That's got to be hard. Complicated."

"Nah. Won't take much."

"You'd do that for me?"

"What are friends for?"

Chloe had sneaked two of her new friends into the Strong Building in the wee hours of the morning. Only Zeke was stirring, and he blanched at the new faces. Chloe introduced the young man and woman with such enthusiasm that she knew he'd understand they were okay, without wondering if she was covering and he should go find a weapon.

Once he heard the story, Zeke offered to help them transfer a serious amount of foodstuffs to their place. Chloe wrote every detail she could remember and e-mailed it to the rest of the Trib Force before collapsing just before dawn and sleeping till almost noon. She assumed she would be scolded for taking such a risk, but she was so excited she was amazed she was able to sleep at all.

No surprise to Chang, Figueroa arrived looking all business and gave him a stare that communicated he should avoid any familiarity in front of Lars.

"Ignore me," Lars said, taking Chang's laptop to a couch and settling in with it. "Just making sure this is ready for a whole new protocol." Chang wondered if Lars *could* affect his encoded drive with his clumsy efforts.

Figueroa pointed to a chair and sat across from Chang. He dismissed the other Peacekeeper, then whispered, "I didn't think you were going to hold me to this."

"I could have let it slide," Chang said. "Proved you were completely untrustworthy. Mind if I take a peek at that software?"

Looking bored, Figueroa pivoted the machine to face Chang. He sighed. "Newfangled stuff. Supposed to be better than the bulky old hardware."

Chang knew it wasn't all that new. He had seen it in China and even played with it. He made a show of tilting the screen so the light was just right. "Interesting," he said, and as Figueroa leaned closer, Chang added, "Sequoia, ah, I mean, Aurelio."

Figueroa sat back, obviously peeved. "I'd appreciate your addressing me by my last name."

"Excuse me, of course," Chang said.

Figueroa grabbed the laptop and pulled a small notebook from his pocket. "State your name," he began, then walked Chang through a series of banal, obvious questions. "Is today Sunday?"

"No."

"Is the sky blue?"

"Yes."

"Are you a male?"

"Yes."

"Do you work for the Global Community?"

"I am employed by them, yes."

Figueroa looked up at Chang. "That's the answer you want to give?"

"Yes."

"Are you loyal to the supreme potentate?"

Chang closed his eyes and reminded himself that Jesus Christ was the only person who fit that definition. "Yes," he said.

"Have you ever done anything that would be considered disloyal to the supreme potentate?"

"Not intentionally, no."

"Stick to yes or no answers."

"No."

"Do you get confidential information from someone who leaks it to you from the inner circle around the supreme potentate?"

"No."

"Is the supreme potentate risen from the dead and the living lord?"

"Yes."

"Can His Excellency Nicolae Carpathia personally count on your continuing loyalty for as long as you serve as an employee of the Global Community?"

Chang hesitated, making Figueroa look up again. "Understand the question?"

"Of course."

"Then your answer is yes?"

"No."

"Don't start playing games now, Chang, or we'll have to do this all over again."

"Well, Mr. Figueroa, I can certainly say in all sincerity that I will continue to show the same level of loyalty to the Global Community leader that I have shown him since the beginning."

"So that's a yes?"

"It merely is what it is."

"What would he think of this?"

"Probably that you're wasting your time, and mine."

"You don't want to just say yes and be done with it?"

"That's the last question?"

"Yes."

"How'm I doing so far?"

"It looks fine," Figueroa said.

"Then let it ride."

"That last answer could look evasive."

"To whom?"

"To anybody who's got a question."

"Do *you* have a question, Mr. Fig—"

"Man, do you ever just give a straight answer?"

"Should I?"

"Agh!" Figueroa swept up the equipment. "Let's go, Lars."

"Yes, sir. Laptop's ready to go, Chang."

"Find any of my stuff on it?"

"No, but you can rebuild from here with a clean slate."

"You have no idea how I feel about what you've done for me here, Lars."

"Well, you're welcome."

It was time for the Trib Force assignees to Operation Eagle to head for Mizpe Ramon and the flight home. The overflow crowd of Israelis was bivouacking outside Petra, and Chaim was about to be airlifted to a spot where all could see and hear him, from both inside and outside. Rayford, Buck, Mac, Leah, Hannah, and Albie stood in a circle with Chaim, holding hands. Big George from San Diego sat in an idling chopper fifty yards away, waiting to lift Chaim into Petra, then transport the Trib Force to Mizpe Ramon, from where he would also fly his own plane to Greece, then to Chicago, then to San Diego. "Let's get George in on this," Rayford said, beckoning him with a wave. "I have a feeling we're going to be seeing more of him."

George jumped out and jogged over. "Micah ready?" he said.

"In a minute, George," Rayford said. "Get in here with us." As they bowed their heads, Rayford told everyone of George's assignment in Greece later that night.

"Wish I could go too," Buck said. "But I'm too hot right now. You'll love those kids, George."

"We should pray," Rayford said.

"One moment, please," Chaim said, letting go of Rayford's hand on one side and Hannah's on the other. He pulled from his robe the miniature urn containing Hattie's ashes. "We do not worship the remains of those who go to God before us, and my wish is to one day toss what is left of these to the winds from a high place of worship to the one true God here at Petra. I believe that is what our impetuous but sincere young sister would have wanted. But first I want to entrust these to you, Captain Steele, to take back to her new brothers and sisters in the safe house, back to some who knew her and loved her even long before she gave herself to the Christ. Then bring them back with Tsion Ben-Judah, and we will remember her one last time before he addresses the remnant of Israel. And as we think of David Hassid, we wish only that we also had a token by which to remember our courageous brother, who knew so few of us personally but who contributed so much to the cause."

"I have a token," Leah said, producing David's phone.

"Would you take that, too, to our comrades in Chicago for a moment of remembrance, looking forward to the day when we shall see this dear one again?" Chaim said.

Leah handed it to Hannah. "I would like

his friend to take it," she said. Hannah thanked her with a hug.

"And now," Chaim said as they joined hands again, "to those who are called, sanctified by God the Father, and preserved in Jesus Christ: mercy, peace, and love be multiplied to you, beloved, building yourselves up on your most holy faith, praying in the Holy Spirit, keep yourselves in the love of God, looking for the mercy of our Lord Jesus Christ unto eternal life.

"Now to him who is able to keep you from stumbling, and to present you faultless before the presence of his glory with exceeding joy, to God our Savior, who alone is wise, be glory and majesty, dominion and power, both now and forever. Amen."

Finally alone again, Chang waited a few minutes, then moved a chair to his door, stood on it, and secured a latch he had built in along the top that would keep out even those with a master key. He dropped into his chair with his laptop and typed in "Christ alone." That brought up a screen with a grid of two hundred dots square. He counted in eighteen rows from the bottom and thirty-seven from the right and clicked on it. A fifteen-digit counter appeared, the numbers ascending at a rate of several hundred a second. Chang keyed in a multiplier, factored in the current date and time, and sent the product hurtling toward a synchronous number ninety seconds away. Four more minutes and three complex, moving targets later, Chang was back in business. He was connected to every Tribulation Force computer, including those at Petra, and anything he wanted at the palace and on the Phoenix 216.

Chang transmitted hundreds of pages of instructions encoded for the Petra machines, checked the locations of reporting gadgets from phones to computers to handhelds, and let everyone know he was up and running. Then he checked Rayford's specifications for the man he called Big George and planted GC credentials in the main palace database. They had decided to use his real name in case his prints or other details were cross-checked. George Sebastian of San Diego, California, in the United North American States, would be transporting a teen male prisoner and a teen female prisoner from Greece to the States. He would fly a high-speed, transatlantic, four-seat Rooster Tail and would be traveling WOP — without papers — due to a recent undercover mission, but for identification purposes he was six feet four and weighed two hundred forty pounds, dark complexion, blue eyes, and blonde hair. He had level–A-minus clearance and reported directly to Deputy Commander Marcus Elbaz. Chang entered a six-digit code that George was to memorize and recite if asked.

Chang understood that Rayford had planned all this with Lukas Miklos, who would inform Mr. Papadopoulos, who would inform Georgiana Stavros. Lukas was to use his own contacts and resources and be responsible for making sure that the two young people rendezvoused with George.

Chang then located the newest Phoenix 216 recording since last he had listened in. He put on his headset.

The bug first picked up Akbar. "I assume you are pleased with the new pilot, Excellency."

"All I care about is getting out of this godforsaken country, Suhail. Can he accomplish that?"

"Oh, Supreme Potentate," Fortunato sang out, "Israel is no longer godforsaken. It is now *truly* the Holy Land, because you have been installed as the true and —"

"Leon, please! You have conferred upon your underlings the power I have imbued you with, have you not?"

"I have, Your Worship, but I prefer not to refer to them as underl—"

"Have any of them, one of them — you, for instance — come up with a thing to match the oceans-to-blood trick?"

"Well, sir, besides the calling down of fire from heaven and the, uh . . . I'd like to think I played some small role — whether just the influence of my presence in part of the meeting with Mr. Micah or . . . anyway — in the healing of the sores."

"I do not believe you realize, Leon, the scope of the tragedy on the high seas. Do you?"

"Enough to hope it's not a permanent thing, Excellency."

"You hope? Think, man! Suhail, does the right-reverend-whatever get the cabinet briefings? Does he read the —"

"Yes, sir, he's on the list."

"Leon, read the reports! Our ships are dead in the water! Our marine biologists tell us every creature in the water is surely dead by now! If this *is* temporary and the water turns pristine tomorrow morning, do you think all the fishies will come flopping back to life too?"

"I certainly hope so!"

"Imbecile," Carpathia muttered, and Chang assumed Fortunato didn't hear him.

The potentate tended to murder people he referred to that way, and Leon would have been pleading for his life. "Suhail, can we not get this plane off the ground?"

"We're waiting for Ms. Ivins, sir."

"Where is she?"

"If I may speak to that, Potentate," Leon said.

"Of course, if you know where she is."

"She wanted one last visit to the temple. She wants to be the first woman to go into the main part and see where you went, worship your image in the Holy of Holies, sit on the, uh, in the —"

"What?! You are not saying she would dare sit on the throne of god!"

"No, sir, I misspoke there, sir. I'm certain she wanted only to see it, to perhaps touch it, take a photograph."

"Why are you not there with her?"

"She wanted only security. She plans to walk in alone and, I believe, just violate a few traditions."

"I like that."

"I thought you might. She thought you might too."

"Find out if she is en route."

"In the meantime, Potentate," Akbar said, "we have received the software for lie detection."

"Yes, get that started now and begin with the stewards."

Chang heard dread in the voices of the Indians. They answered with conviction and earnestness. "You both test entirely truthful," Akbar concluded. They wept, expressing their gratitude.

"Been tested, have you?" Carpathia said, as the sounds of their bustling about and serving came through the system.

"Yes, sir. Thank you, sir."

"Indeed." Carpathia sounded skeptical and dismissive. "Test the pilot, Suhail."

"Ms. Ivins is on the tarmac, sir."

"There is time. First him, then Leon, then her. And here is a question I want added to her session."

The pilot sounded unconcerned, almost bored, answering quickly and matter-of-factly. "He's clean," Akbar reported. "Reverend Fortunato, are you ready?"

"I have nothing whatever to hide," Leon said. But when he was asked the day of the week, he asked if it was a trick question. His answers became more whiny and pensive, but of course, he was cleared too.

The plane took off; then Suhail could be heard talking with Ms. Ivins. "I'm assuming, ma'am, that you are willing, just as a matter of procedure, to submit to the truth test."

She chuckled. "And what do we do if I am revealed as the leak to the mole?"

"Please clip this on, ma'am."

"Ready."

"State your name."

"Ms. Vivian Ivins."

"Is today Sunday?"

"No, but I would like to know if I got the first question right."

Akbar laughed. "Is the sky blue?"

"Yes."

"Are you a male?"

"No."

"Do you work for the Global Community?"

She hesitated. "Yes."

"It showed okay, ma'am, but just out of curiosity, why the hesitation?"

"I have never really considered myself an employee of the Global Community. I serve Supreme Potentate Nicolae Carpathia, and I have most of my adult life. I would, even if I were not compensated, but yes, I also actually am part of the personnel of the Global Community."

"Are you loyal to the supreme potentate?"

"Yes."

"Have you ever done anything that could be considered disloyal to the supreme potentate?"

"No."

"Do you leak confidential information from the supreme potentate to anyone at GC headquarters?"

"No."

"Is the supreme potentate risen from the dead and the living lord?"

"Yes."

"Can His Excellency Nicolae Carpathia personally count on your continuing loyalty for as long as you serve as an employee of the Global Community?"

"Yes, and beyond."

"Did you sit on his throne in his temple in Jerusalem today?"

"I — no."

"Thank you, Ms. Ivins."

Chang heard Akbar unbuckle and leave, but it was clear Viv Ivins immediately followed. "Director Akbar, wait, please. Before you share the results with His Excellency, let me have a word with him."

"Certainly."

"My lord," she said quietly.

"Yes, dear one," Carpathia said.

"May I kneel and kiss your hand?"

"That depends. How did you do on the little test?"

"I don't know, but regardless of the results, I answered truthfully until the very end."

"You were deceitful in your answer to *my* question?"

"I was, sir, but I immediately regretted it and have come to beg your forgiveness."

If Carpathia responded, Chang couldn't hear it.

"I told Reverend Fortunato what I intended to do," she said, "and he advised me against it."

"Did he? Did you, Leon?"

"I did, sir."

"Good for you! But it should not be only the Most High Reverend Father of Carpathianism who knows what a defilement it would be to presume to sit on the throne of god!"

"I am so sorry, Nicolae," and Chang got the impression she said his name the way she had when Carpathia was a small boy. Nicolae again fell silent.

"I did not do it as an act of insubordination, I swear. I merely envied your moment and felt a deep need to share it. I would like to think I earned the right with —"

"*Earned the right?* To sit on *my* throne? To take *my* place?"

"— with my years of service, with my uncompromising devotion, with my love for you. Oh, don't dismiss me, Your Worship. Forgive me. Please! Nicolae!"

Chang heard her weeping. Then Nicolae: "Suhail, let's administer the test to each other." Ms. Ivins's crying faded as she must have moved back to her seat.

Akbar was brief and confident, and when it was Carpathia's turn, of course the questions were slightly revised. But Carpathia was in a testy mood.

"State your name," Akbar began.

"God."

"Is today Sunday?"

"Yes."

"Is the sky blue?"

"No."

"Are you a male?"

"No."

"Do you serve the Global Community?"

"No."

"Are you loyal to the citizens under your authority?"

"No."

"Have you ever done anything disloyal to the Global Community?"

"Yes."

"Do you leak confidential information to someone inside GC headquarters that undermines the effectiveness of your cabinet?"

"No. And I would personally kill anyone who did."

"Did you rise from the dead and are you the living lord?"

"Yes."

"Can the Global Community count on your continuing loyalty for as long as you serve as supreme potentate?"

"No."

"You astound me, Excellency."

"Well?"

"I don't know how you do that."

"Tell me!" Carpathia said.

"Your answers all proved truthful, even where you were obviously sporting with me and saying the opposite of the truth."

"The truth is what I say it is, Suhail. I am the father of truth."

Eighteen

On the flight home, Buck called Lukas Miklos.

"I imagine you want to talk to the young man whose life you saved, eh, Cameron?"

"I do, Laslos. And I'm sorry all my other messages to you about what happened that night had to come electronically and not even by phone. I wish I could have given you your wife's message in person, but —"

"I understand, my friend," Laslos said, his voice quavery. "I remember every detail of it. I wish only that I could have gone to heaven with her."

"I can't imagine how hard it is," Buck said. "But the church needs you there, and —"

"Oh, Cameron, I am useless. I am not free to help in any real ways anymore. Sometimes I wish they would just find me so I could testify for God before they kill me."

Buck wanted to counter him, but what could he say? "We sure appreciate your help in getting those kids out of the country."

"I'll do what I can. I look forward to getting them connected with your pilot, but it's unlikely I can risk coming out of the shadows to meet him. I will get them as close to the airport as I dare. Here, let me have you talk to the boy."

"Hello, sir?" Marcel said, and Buck remembered the voice from their only encounter.

"I'm so glad to talk to you again, son. I didn't expect I ever would."

"I can't thank you enough, Mr. Williams. I know you got in trouble for that. Will I meet you in Chicago?"

"You sure will."

"Mr. Miklos has told me so much about you and your family and friends. I hope I will be safe there."

"Safer than where you are, I guess. And the girl?"

"Georgiana, um, Stavros," Marcel said. "I was so surprised when I heard she had the same story as mine. We finally were introduced at a co-op center."

"And you have been able to communicate with her?"

"It's all set. We will meet her on the road. Mr. Miklos will stay with us for as far as he can."

"That's quite a journey on foot."

"He has arranged for someone to drive us, at least until we are a couple of miles from the airport. Then the pilot, Mr. Sebastian, is it — ?"

"Yes."

"— will come find us and walk us in as prisoners."

"We'll be praying for you all."

Chang listened to several minutes' worth of small talk, then a pitiful effort by Viv Ivins to again reconnect with Nicolae and get his forgiveness. Finally Nicolae summoned Akbar. "Suhail," he said, "I am not going to replace Mr. Moon as supreme commander."

"I see."

"The job and the title are redundant."

"Whatever you say, Excellency."

"I will count on you more and more, and you may inherit duties that might otherwise have been carried out by a supreme commander."

"As you wish."

"First assignment: Take action on our security leak."

"I'm, we're — sir, we are already conducting a full investigation at the palace, but as you know, we turned up nothing on the plane. . . ."

"How does that make sense? You told me it was as if someone were relaying our very conversations to someone with access to the central database."

"That's what it seemed. We are scouring headquarters for weaknesses in our fire walls, but the late Mr. Hassid put the system in place, and there was not a better person in the world for that job."

"His replacement, the South American —"

"Mexican, sir. Figueroa."

"You have confidence in him?"

"A stellar record. Not the technician Hassid was, but capable. He is overseeing the testing, and he himself will also be tested, of course."

"I want to send a message to whoever is subverting us from inside. Get them to panic, put them on the defensive."

"I'm open to any suggestion, Potentate."

"Charge the Indians."

"Sir?"

"The stewards. Convict them of treason."

"Uh, on what evidence?"

"They are the only logical ones, Suhail. The pilot was not even on board during most of our meetings. They were."

"But they tested clean."

"Who knows that but you and I?"

"Um-hm."

"No one, am I correct?"

"You are."

"Whisper it to Leon. And to Viv. Then release it to the media. They should disembark in New Babylon in handcuffs. Do you have two pair on board?"

"I do, but —"

"A problem?"

"I'm at your service, sir, but I'm missing something. The mole will see we fingered the wrong perpetrators. Rather than put him or her on the defensive, it may make us look like soft opponents."

"So much the better. Let him grow overconfident. Still, he will see what we do with people we believe are insurrectionists."

"If convicted, the penalty is death."

"Oh, Suhail! If they get off this plane in shackles, consider them convicted. The executions should follow within forty-eight hours."

"Done."

"And your conscience, Director?"

"My conscience?"

"Knowing the truth, does this give you pause?"

"No, sir. You are the father of truth. My conscience is at your service."

There was a long pause. "They do good work, though, do they not?" Carpathia said at last. "The stewards?"

"Quite."

"No need to inform them or cuff them until we touch down. But do get the information trail started. And then we need to discuss the final solution for the Israeli dissidents and the Judah-ites. Let me know as soon as you have casualty statistics on Operation Petra."

Laslos wished he could go with the two young people all the way to the safe house in America. What an adventure! But how could he justify abandoning his brothers and sisters in Greece? The net was tightening and few of them would survive until the Glorious Appearing, but no one would question giving the teenagers a better chance.

Being involved in getting them connected with this pilot made Laslos feel alive again. He dreaded the end of the caper when his friend K would drive him back to Ptolemaïs. He would then walk the last mile and a half to his secret place and settle into his awful routine.

The plan was for K to pick up the boy and him in the country at the north edge of town. They would stay on the outskirts, getting Marcel close enough to the co-op to where he could walk there and get his meager bag of belongings. Georgiana Stavros would wait for them on the southern end of town, off the road that led to the airport. Cameron Williams and Marcel had told him she was a tall brunette, fair-skinned for a Greek, and pretty. Laslos liked to imagine that she looked like his wife when first he met her more than forty years before.

Chang noticed that Carpathia's plane sounded as if it was descending when Suhail Akbar returned to talk with the potentate. "Ah, Director," Nicolae began, "we are planning something very special for Petra when Ben-Judah is confirmed present, no?"

"Sir, we need to talk."

"Answer my question, Suhail."

"Yes, of course, but I have bad news."

"I do not want bad news! Everybody was healthy! We had plenty of equipment for the Petra offensive. You were going to ignore the city — waiting to destroy it when Micah and

Ben-Judah were both there — and overtake those not yet inside. What could be bad news? What do we hear from them?"

"Nothing. Our —"

"Nonsense! They were to report as soon as they had overtaken the insurgents. The world was to marvel at our complete success without firing a shot, no casualties for us versus total destruction of those who oppose me. What happened?"

"We're not sure yet."

"You must have had two hundred commanding officers alone!"

"More than that."

"And not a word from one of them?"

"Our stratospheric photo planes show our forces advancing to within feet of overrunning approximately five hundred thousand outside Petra."

"A cloud of dust and the enemy, in essence, plowed under."

"That was the plan, Excellency."

"And what? The old men in robes and long beards fought back with hidden daggers?"

"Our planes waited until the dust cloud settled and now find no evidence of our troops."

Carpathia laughed.

"I wish I were teasing you, Potentate.

High-altitude photographs ten minutes after the offensive show the same crowd outside Petra, and yet —"

"None of our troops, yes, you said that. And our armaments? One of the largest conglomerations of firepower ever assembled, you told me, split into three divisions. Invincible, you said."

"Disappeared."

"Can those photographs be transmitted here?"

"They're waiting in your office, sir. But people I trust verify what we're going to see . . . or not see, I should say."

Carpathia's voice sounded constricted, as if he'd rather explode than speak. "I want the potentate of each of the world regions on his way to New Babylon within the hour. Any who are not en route sixty minutes from now will be replaced. See to that immediately, and when you determine when the one from the farthest distance will arrive, set a meeting for the senior cabinet and me with the ten of them for an hour later. And these Jews," he said slowly, "we expect them all to be in Petra as soon as they can be transported there?"

"Actually, they will not all fit. We expect Petra itself to be full and the rest to camp nearby."

"What is required to level Petra and the surrounding area?"

"Two planes, two crews, two annihilation devices. We could launch a subsequent missile to ensure thorough devastation, though that might be overkill."

"Ah, Suhail. You will one day come to realize that there is no such thing as overkill. Let the Jews and the Judah-ites think they have had their little victory. And keep the failed operation quiet. We never launched it. Our missing troops and vehicles and armaments never existed."

"And what of the questions from their families?"

"The questions should go *to* the families. We demand to know where these soldiers are and what they have done with our equipment."

"Tens of thousands AWOL? That's what we will contend?"

"No, Suhail. Rather, I suggest you go on international television and tell the GCNN audience that the greatest military effort ever carried out was met by half a million unarmed Jews who made it disappear! Perhaps you could use a flip chart! Now you see us; now you do not!"

"I'm scared," Marcel told Laslos as they

stole out of the hideaway at nightfall.

"There is no need to be, son. You are just excited. You have endured tragedy, as we all have, but you are being given a second chance. If you are not safe with the Tribulation Force, you will never be."

They walked the mile and a half in the dark on dirt paths Laslos had come to know well. Though he walked more than he rode and never drove anymore, he still felt the pain and weariness of his age. Marcel seemed to have to wait for him, and Laslos wished he could tell him to go on. But he wanted to feel useful. He was part of the escapade, part of the plan. These precious young people would be in his charge until he sent them off with Godspeed to rendezvous with George Sebastian.

Half a mile outside Ptolemaïs, Laslos spotted K's tiny white car well off a rarely used road. Laslos stopped Marcel with a touch, then made a birdcall. K tapped the brake and the taillights went on briefly. "That means no one is around," Laslos said. "Run to the car. I will be there."

He knew Marcel wanted to stretch those lanky legs, and as Laslos shuffled along as quickly as he could, he enjoyed watching the boy lope to the car. K had long since removed the inside light, so when the door opened, the car still looked dark. When Laslos arrived, K was behind the wheel, Marcel next to him.

Laslos squeezed into the minuscule backseat, directly behind Marcel. K, older than Laslos, bald and bony, wore a small black stocking cap and spoke with difficulty because most of his front teeth were missing. He said, "He ith rithen," and the boy and Laslos — though wheezing — said, "Christ is risen indeed."

K drove carefully to the edge of the city and parked on a dark street. "You know where you are?" Laslos asked the boy.

"I think so," Marcel said. "The co-op is in the cellar under the pub a block and a half that way?"

"And you know the password?"

"Of course. They have my stuff."

"And they will confirm that the girl —"

"Georgiana."

"— yes, is waiting."

Marcel nodded and jumped out of the car. Laslos quickly cranked down his window. "Psst! Do not run," he whispered. And the boy slowed.

K turned and grinned at him. "Young people," he said.

"How long until our luck runs out, K?"

K shook his head and his smile faded.

"We are already living on next month'th time, Lathloth."

"What happens if you ever get stopped?"

"Thath the end of it," K said. "They'll take me to get the mark but I'll tell them to jutht kill me, becauth I'm through fighting."

Laslos clapped his friend on the shoulder. "But you're doing damage until the time comes, eh?"

"Muth ath I can."

Marcel returned, a canvas bag over his shoulder. "Any problem?" Laslos said.

He shook his head, tossing the bag in the back, leaving just enough room for the girl. "She's supposed to be there, and nobody followed me. Look for one small stone on top of two others, eight kilometers from the airport. She'll be in the underbrush near there. Just pull over and she'll find us."

K stayed outside the city and headed toward the airport road. They saw no GC Peacekeepers or vehicles, but still Laslos found his right leg bouncing, his hands clasped tightly in his lap. When they passed the 10K sign, Laslos leaned forward and helped K watch the odometer. A few minutes later Marcel said, "There!"

K's headlights showed two small stones on the left side of the road with another laid casually atop them. No one would have noticed if they hadn't been looking for them. K checked his mirrors, and Laslos shifted so he could look out the back too. "Nobody," he said.

K pulled off to the side, his right front tire crunching the three stones. He sat with the engine idling and the lights on, squinting into the rearview mirror. "Let's go, young lady," Laslos muttered. "We don't want to be seen."

"Want me to call for her?" Marcel said.

"She was supposed to find us, right?"

"Right."

"Always stick to the plan. If the plan changes, you don't improvise. You leave."

K nodded. "Ten thecondth," he said. "I won't thtay here longer."

"There she is!" Marcel said.

Georgiana ran up to the car, and Laslos leaned across Marcel's bag to open her door. She was shivering in jeans and a white, short-sleeve shirt, and a ratty, red baseball cap hooding her eyes. She carried a small, dark green satchel, barely a foot long. "Marcel," she said. "Good to see you again."

"Yeah, hi! Let's go!"

She jumped in and put her bag between her feet. "You must be Laslos," she said. "I'm Georgiana." She squeezed his arm. Her dark fingers were cold. She put her hands on K's shoulders. "And this must be K."

Marcel raised a hand, and she gripped it. "This is exciting," she said, then rubbed her palms together.

"He ith rithen," K said.

"Amen!" she said, nearly squealing. "He is risen indeed!"

"Is that all you brought?" Laslos said.

"It's all I have, sir," she said, smiling. "And all I need."

"Venturing out into the new world with hardly a thing to your name."

"God is able," she said. "Marcel tells me you have a gun."

"Marcel has the mouth of a young man," Laslos said. "You must both learn to say little and listen much."

"I'm sorry," she said. "Am I talking too much? Just excited, that's all. I haven't felt this way since the day Mr. Williams let me go."

Marcel nodded.

"So I can't see your gun, Mr. Laslos?"

"Miklos. I do not bring my gun out of my home. I am not looking to hurt anyone. It is for my safety, that's all."

"But K has a gun," she said, squeezing his shoulders again. "Don't you, young man?"

K smiled shyly and shook his head as he

416

pulled the car back onto the road.

"You watch too much television," Laslos said. "American TV, am I right?"

"Not for a long time. When I do see it, it's all Carpathia, Carpathia, Carpathia."

Laslos's leg was still bouncing, his hands still pressed together. "You're both clear on the plan, then?" he said.

"If Marcel is, I am," Georgiana said. "He's the one who told me. We're meeting this George guy off the road up from the airport. He'll take us in like we're his prisoners, and the computer will show that's what he's there for."

"Yes, and you must avoid eye contact, look sullen, and just go directly to the plane with him. Maybe you could let Marcel wear your hat low enough to cover his eyes and you could let your hair hang in your face."

She was still rubbing her hands together. "This thing wouldn't fit him. Anyway, we'll recognize the pilot how again?"

"He should be the only man on the road looking for you," Laslos said.

"But he's a big man, right? An American?"

"Way over six feet tall and almost two hundred and fifty pounds," Marcel said. "Light hair, blue eyes, and —"

"You'll know him," Laslos said. "We should pray."

"Yes," Georgiana said. "Please."

"Why don't you pray?" Laslos said.

"I'm too nervous," she said.

"All right," Laslos said. "Lord, we thank you for these young people and ask you to go before them and protect them. We —"

"There he is!" Georgiana said. "Is that him?"

A big, young man strode purposefully up the right side of the road. He wore big boots, khaki pants, and a light, zippered jacket. His hair looked almost white, his face dark. Laslos couldn't make out the eye color, but the man stopped and looked directly into the car as K slowed and passed, pulling over fifty yards beyond him.

Marcel reached for his door handle, and Georgiana reached for her bag.

"Wait!" Laslos said. "He's early." He rolled down his window and leaned to stick his head out, aware that Georgiana was digging in her bag and ready to go.

"Mr. Miklos?" the man called out, but Laslos thought he detected a European accent.

"Hey, Mr. Sebastian!" Marcel shouted before Laslos could shush him.

Now jogging and having cut the distance between him and the car, the man hollered, "Marcel? Georgiana?"

"Keep rolling, K," Laslos said. "This isn't right."

"Why?" Georgiana said. "What's wrong?"

"If that's Sebastian," Laslos said as K slowly pulled back onto the road, "he'll find us."

"No!" Georgiana whined. "Stop!"

"We'll not make this transfer in the middle of the road," Laslos said.

"K, pull over," Georgiana said with sudden authority. She pulled a huge handgun with a silencer from her bag and pressed it against Laslos's temple. "I'll kill him if you don't stop."

"Don't stop, K!" Laslos cried. "Marcel is for real! I know him!"

K stopped accelerating but coasted. "Stop now," she said. "I mean it."

Marcel whipped around, kneeling on the seat to face her. He yanked her cap off, and as the silencer pulled away from Laslos's head, he turned to see Georgiana's forehead and the mark of the beast. The whistling, abbreviated punch of the shot filled the car with the acrid smell of gunpowder, and Marcel was driven back with such force that he folded under the dashboard. The windshield was covered with gore, and Laslos grimaced at the gaping hole in the back of the boy's head.

"Stop now, K!" she wailed, pointing the gun at the back of his head. The older man wrenched the wheel back and forth, pushing the accelerator to the floor. The little car rocked violently, and Laslos felt himself bang into his door handle before his bulk went flying back over Marcel's bag toward the girl.

She fired through K's neck and he went limp, the car losing speed and angling toward the gravel. Laslos wrapped his massive arms around the girl and pressed the bottoms of his feet against the door on his side, trying to smash her against her own door. He could only hope the gun was buried somewhere in the crush, but the sounds of more than one set of running footsteps told him that unless he wrestled it away from her, he would soon join his wife in heaven.

The car thudded to a stop, and they both rolled forward into the back of K's seat. Two other men had joined the Sebastian impostor, and all carried weapons. One jerked the girl's door open and dragged her out with one hand. Laslos tried to hang on, but he had no leverage. He lay on Marcel's bag across the backseat, his arms leaden, gasping.

"You all right, Elena?" one of the men said.

Laslos saw her nod with disgust. "He's the only one left," she said, pressing the gun to his forehead. He turned his hands over, opening his palms toward heaven, and closed his eyes.

"We're short-staffed tonight, sir. Hard copy is quicker than the computer, if you don't mind."

"I hear you," George said. "But I told you, Old Man Elbaz had me on recon runs over rebel territory in the Negev, and we were all required to leave our IDs at the field HQ. It's all in the computer."

The airport GC clerk swore. "They never think about what those decisions mean to us little guys."

"They never think at all," George said. "Sorry."

"What're ya gonna do?" the clerk said, sighing as he tapped his fingers atop the monitor, waiting for the info. "Hey, what about all the guys goin' AWOL in Jordan?"

"Don't think I wasn't tempted," George said. "Strangest deal I've ever seen."

"You get the boils?"

"Who didn't?"

"Here it is. You're good. You got a number for me? Six digits."

"Zero-four-zero-three-zero-one."

"That's it. And where're your prisoners?"

"Being held up the road."

"Need a vehicle?"

"That would be great."

"You're coming right back?"

"Right back. I'll secure 'em in the plane and bring the wheels directly to you."

The clerk tossed him a set of keys and pointed to a Jeep. George decided he could get used to Trib Force work, if it was all this easy. Couldn't be.

He sped a mile and a half up the road and pulled over. What was that in the distance? The girl? Alone? He turned on his brights. She was running toward him. Screaming.

He stepped out. "Georgiana?"

"George?"

"Yes!"

"We were ambushed!"

As she got closer he saw she was covered in blood. He reached for her. "What happened? Where are the oth—"

But as the girl slumped against him, wrapping her arms around his waist, she called out, "Unarmed!" Two men, one about his size, rushed from the bushes with weapons trained on him. Another pulled a Jeep into view, doors standing open.

The big man jumped into the car George had borrowed at the airport. The other kept a weapon on him as the girl handcuffed and blindfolded him. He was tempted to drive his bulk into her, make her pay for whatever she was involved in. But he wanted to conserve his strength for any real chance to escape. They pushed him into the Jeep, and as it took off, he heard the other vehicle behind.

"We're going to have fun with you, Yank," the driver said. "By the time we're through, we'll know everything you know."

Fat chance, George thought — and wanted to say. But he had already blundered enough, leaving his plane and his weapons unprotected and venturing unarmed into enemy territory, trusting a risky plan devised by well-intentioned brothers, but civilians after all. Maybe the proverbial horse had already escaped the open barn, but too late or not, his training kicked in. Not only would he not say, "Fat chance," but he would also not say anything. The only way these people would know he was capable of uttering a word was if they remembered he had spoken to the girl. Unless he somehow escaped, his next word would be spoken in heaven.

He bounced and lost his balance as the Jeep accelerated, and he kept bouncing off the door, then almost into the lap of the captor to his left. The man kept pushing George back upright. He could have planted his feet more firmly and kept from jostling so much, but he didn't mind being a two-hundred-forty-pound irritant to the enemy.

"So, George Sebastian of San Diego," the driver said, "and a newly recruited Judahite. A little information will buy you some dinner, and a lot will have you on your way back to the wife and little one before you know it. Hungry?"

George did not respond, not even with a nod or shake of the head.

"Lonely then, perhaps?"

The man next to George, less fluent in English, said, "Do you know who is really Elbaz? Because we think we do."

"We *do!*" the girl said.

George let the next curve throw him into the man, who pushed him back. "Sit up, you big stupid person!"

Nineteen

Sound asleep over the Atlantic and never so happy to be heading home, Rayford at first thought the incoming call was a dream. Then he wished it were.

The caller ID showed it originating in Colorado. Before Rayford could speak, a weird, nasal voice said, "I believe I followed your instructions on how to call you securely, but could you confirm that before I proceed?"

Rayford sat straight up. "Stand by," he said, believing he knew whom he was talking to. He checked the tiny LCD readout as David Hassid had instructed him. "You're secure," he said.

"You've got trouble," the voice said. "Do

you have anybody inside at New Babylon to replace your guy that died?"

Rayford hesitated.

"Hey, it's me."

"Who?"

"Ah, you may know me as Pinkerton Stephens. GC stationed in Colorado."

"I need to be dead sure, Mr. Stephens."

"Aka Steve Plank."

"A little more, please."

"Your grandson's name is Kenny Bruce."

"How did you know our guy died?"

"Everybody knows, man. Didn't he go down with three others right in front of Carpathia?"

"Not really, Steve."

"Not bad, Captain. But anyway, New Babylon thinks he's dead, so he's clearly not inside."

"We're covered inside."

"Good. Then maybe you know this."

"What?"

"About your trouble. Where are you?"

Rayford told him.

"And you have not been brought up to speed by the palace?"

"I thought I had."

"You've been compromised."

"Me personally?" Rayford said.

"Actually, no. Depending on what alias

you're using, I think you're okay. But I just got a high-level, for-your-eyes-only briefing from Intelligence, and for the first time I thought I'd better take you up on your request to be informed."

"I'm listening."

"The alias your friend, the one I met, is using has been exposed. I and S is speculating that Deputy Commander Marcus Elbaz is actually a former black marketer out of Al Basrah."

"How?"

"This is mostly coming out of Greece, Rayford."

"Oh no. Tell me we weren't wrong about the guy we sent in there."

"Sebastian? No, he's solid. But they've got him."

"Oh no. Start from the top."

"First, you've got your Elbaz character flying your plane right now, right? And the craft is ostensibly a GC issue."

"Right."

"His name and that bird are on everybody's screens, so don't —"

"Got it. Don't land as GC or as Elbaz."

"You're scheduled into Kankakee, right?"

"You got it. What happened in Greece, Steve?"

"Stay with me. First, I think I've found a

way to get you close to where you want to go. Back to Chicago, correct?"

"Affirmative."

"Okay, listen up. I put in a request for cargo out of Maryland with a stop at the auxiliary field near where Midway used to be. That's as close to Chicago as they'll let anybody land, due to the radiation, you know."

"Right."

"You know as well as I do that you could put down at Meigs."

"On the lake?"

"Sure."

"We're not going to draw any suspicion from heat-seeking stratospheric GC recon planes?"

"Not if your guy keeps the phony radiation levels up to speed on the database."

"This is a pretty big jet to land at Meigs, the way I remember it."

"You've got reverse thrusters, don't you?"

"Of course."

"It can be done. But there's nobody on the ground there, of course. But listen, Ray, if your guy is still keeping track of Chicago and what the GC thinks about it, he'd better get in there and tinker."

"What're you saying?"

"I doubt anybody else has checked lately,

but just to be sure I wasn't leading you into a trap, I looked up that area, and something was giving off moving heat signals down there within the last several hours."

"We always tell him before we go out, walking, driving, or with the chopper. That way he can head off any readings we emit."

"Well, somebody's on the move down there. Not much, but it'll arouse suspicion like it did with me."

"So back to Greece, Steve. We know Buck's Jack Jensen ID is history."

"That's not the worst of it. He cut loose a couple of kids from a detention center and one of 'em — the girl, Stavros — got herself caught. You can't blame her; she's just a teenager, but apparently she cracked and gave up a lot. Story she told matched up with what they figure happened with the boy, who had used the name Paulo Ganter. 'Course Ganter was still in there, so they figured out by process of elimination who got sprung. Kid named Papadopoulos. His parents both refused to take the mark. GC in Greece plants a young woman with similar looks to this Stavros in the underground. She starts askin' around about the boy, somebody gets 'em connected, and she tells him her story — which is just like his. Badabing, she had to be freed by the same guy, nobody checks her out, she stays away from people who would know she wasn't who she claimed to be, and —"

"— she walks our people into an ambush."

"Yeah, and it's bad, Rayford."

"Just tell me."

"GC says the ruse went squirrelly at the end and their operatives wind up having to kill an old man named Kronos, a big fish — name of Miklos — and the boy."

Rayford sat in the screaming jet with the phone to his ear, head in his hand, eyes shut. "And Sebastian?"

"Alive and well, but they're confident they can get what they need from him to lead them to Ben-Judah. He's former military, so he might be tougher than they think."

"Plus he doesn't know that much."

"He was supposed to bring the kids to you, though, right? He's got to know enough to hurt you."

"He does. Any idea about the disposition of the real Stavros?"

"I think that goes without saying, now that they have a connection to you guys. She's served her purpose."

"We don't have to assume the worst."

"Oh, sure we do, Rayford. Of course we do. I always do."

Plank asked if Rayford had anybody on board whose face was not known to the GC. "Well, I've got three people aboard who are thought dead."

"Can any of 'em look like a Middle Easterner?"

"One's a Jordanian."

"Perfect. Does he have a turban?"

Rayford leaned over and woke Abdullah. "Do you have a turban, or can you make yourself one?" Abdullah gave him a thumbs-up and went back to sleep. "That's affirmative, Steve."

"Can you put him on the radio and pretend he's your pilot?"

"He flies."

"Perfect. Here's his new name and a refueling docket number for Maryland. Your next stop after that should be Resurrection Field here, south of Colorado Springs. I won't expect you."

"No, but you'll log us in as if we made it."

"Of course."

"Words aren't adequate, Steve. . . ."

"Hey, one of these days I'm gonna need a place to hole up . . . if I survive that long."

With Buck, Hannah, Leah, and Mac also asleep, Rayford chose to tell only Albie what was going on. There would be plenty of time for Abdullah and Albie to switch seats. Rayford called Chang.

Twelve hours later Chang sat at his terminal in the office, grateful he'd been able to sleep after a flurry of emergency activity in the night. He wondered how David had managed this on his own and prayed that God would either deliver him or send someone to help him. Chang was unaware of any other believers in New Babylon, but still he held out hope. While he sat monitoring the overwhelming reports of death and ruin on the bloody high seas, he was recording the meeting of the ten regional potentates with Carpathia, Akbar, Fortunato, and Viv Ivins.

The workday was interminable, but Chang walked a fine line. He had to appear above reproach while maintaining a typically irreverent attitude. David had warned him that if he appeared too good to be true, someone would assume he was. And new as he was in assisting the Tribulation Force, he feared he would be unable to keep pace emotionally. Losing David had rocked him. He couldn't imagine how the others dealt with the loss of Miss Durham, then their main contact in Greece. Things were supposed to get worse and worse. Fear and loneliness didn't begin to describe his feelings. He prayed that until he was rescued from this assignment, God would somehow allow him to stay rested, stay strong, and be able to carry on despite the danger and tragedy.

In Petra Chaim felt as if he were already in heaven. How was it that God could make it so that a million believers could live together in harmony? Chaim reminded the people that Tsion Ben-Judah had promised to come and address them in person, and they lifted such a roar that he himself could barely wait for that day.

"You know, do you not," he said, unamplified yet miraculously able to be heard by all under his charge, "that the Word of God tells us we will live here unmolested, our clothes not wearing out, and we will be fed and quenched until the wrath of God against his enemies is complete. John the Revelator said he saw 'something like a sea of glass mingled with fire, and those who have the victory over the beast, over his image and over his mark and over the number of his name, standing on the sea of glass, having harps of God.' Beloved, those John would have seen in his revelation of heaven and who had victory over the beast are those who had been martyred by the beast. Death is considered victory because of the resurrection of the saints!

"Sing with me the song of Moses, the servant of God, and the song of the Lamb, saying: 'Great and marvelous are your works, Lord God Almighty! Just and true are your ways, O King of the saints! Who shall not fear you, O Lord, and glorify your name? For you alone are holy. For all nations shall come and worship before you, for your judgments have been manifested.'

"John said he heard the angel of the waters saying, 'You are righteous, O Lord, the One who is and who was and who is to be, because you have judged these things.'

"And what," Chaim continued, "of our enemies who have shed the blood of saints and prophets? God has turned the oceans into blood, and one day soon he will turn the rivers and lakes to blood as well, giving them blood to drink. For it is their just due.

"But what shall we his people eat and drink, here in this place of refuge? Some would look upon it and say it is desolate and barren. Yet God says that at twilight we shall eat meat, and in the morning we shall be filled with bread. In this way we shall know that he is the Lord our God."

That evening a great flock of quails invaded and a million saints enjoyed roasting them over open fires. In the morning, when the dew lifted, there on the rocky ground were small, round flakes as fine as frost. "We need not ask ourselves, as the children of Israel did, 'What is it?' " Chaim said. "For we know God has provided it as bread. Take, eat, and see that it is filling and sweet, like wafers made with honey. As Moses said to them, 'This is the bread the Lord has given you to eat.'

"And what shall we drink? Again, God Almighty himself has provided." Chaim raised both arms, and springs of fresh, cool water flowed from rocks in every quarter of Petra, enough for everyone.

The refueling had gone without incident in Maryland, but Rayford wondered when their supply of impostors would run dry. A couple of hours later, Rayford took the controls for the landing at the tiny airstrip by Lake Michigan near what was left of downtown Chicago. His passengers were rested but stunned by the news related in his call from Steve Plank.

The news had also proved devastating at the safe house. Chang reported from New Babylon that he had been able to cover in the computer for the motion and heat activity of Chloe's movements that might otherwise have raised a red flag, and Tsion told Rayford by phone that Chloe was sick about having been responsible. "But she has exciting news," Dr. Ben-Judah said. "She is insisting on being the one to pick you up. And yes, we have the young Mr. Wong covering for your landing and your transport here."

The landing was a test of Rayford's skills, and as he touched down as close to the water as possible, he wondered if he would have been smart to let Mac handle it. But the reverse thrusters left him with room to spare, and he maneuvered the jet between two abandoned buildings, where it could be recognized from the stratosphere only from an angle available just a few seconds a day.

The others allowed Buck out first to greet Chloe. She drove a Humvee from beneath the Strong Building and had brought Ming to hold Kenny. Rayford stretched and watched the reunion as the other five clambered out and unloaded luggage. Finally safe again in the building, introductions were made all around before they knelt and prayed and wept over lost and endangered loved ones. Rayford showed them the urn of Hattie's ashes, and Hannah passed around David's phone.

" 'Course we ain't leavin' this George guy by himself in Greece, right?"

"Exactly, Zeke," Mac said. "But we've got a lot of planning to do in a short time, and you're gonna be as busy as any of us."

"I know some people I'll bet would want to help," Chloe said.

Chang's day had been filled with co-workers' rumors and gossip. Two Indian stewards from Carpathia's plane were to be put to death for leaking secrets to a mole in New Babylon. Everyone was under suspicion and tested. The general invitation for all employees to visit the spectacular new office of the supreme potentate had been suspended with his earlier-than-expected return from Israel. But those who saw it gushed about the ceiling that rose to the now transparent roof, so it was as if the office itself looked into heaven. It had been widened, the walls of adjoining offices and conference rooms demolished to make one gargantuan space in which the king of the world could relax or conduct business or hold meetings. Which he had done all day with the potentates of the ten world regions.

Chang hurried to his apartment to hear the recording of that meeting, but first he checked copies of what the assembled computer whizzes had sent around the world from their secure system in Petra. What a thrill to see Chaim's pronouncements and accounts of the miracles retold and broadcast to the globe. Reports had come back immediately of people on every continent printing these out or passing them on electronically. Secret house churches were encouraged, and many people were becoming new believers. People undecided and disillusioned with Carpathia sought out the believers, and international revival was happening right before Chang's eyes.

And it was none too soon, considering Carpathia's high-level meeting. He had quickly quelled the cooing over his new digs and gotten down to business. "The world has changed, gentlemen," he said, "as much in the last several days as in the last three and a half years. Please, no hands. I know all your problems and want to talk about mine today. Without some miraculous intervention, the oceanic catastrophe will not soon be remedied. We must be creative in our approaches to it. But have you noticed something, my friends? Is it as obvious to you as it is to me? We have the Jews to thank for our current predicament.

"Yes, the Jews. Who have been among the last to embrace Carpathianism? The Jews.

Who is their new Moses? A man who calls himself Micah but whom we believe to be none other than the Jew who vainly assassinated me, Dr. Chaim Rosenzweig.

"Who are the Judah-ites? They claim to be Jesus-followers, but they follow Ben-Judah, a Jew. Jesus himself was a Jew. They are fond of referring to me as Antichrist. Well, I will embrace Anti-Jew. And so will you. This is war, gentlemen, and I want it waged in all ten regions of the world.

"For my part, we are planning to stagger and ultimately eradicate the so-called Jesus-believers who are nothing but Judah cultists. Tsion Ben-Judah himself, who claims a billion adherents, has publicly announced what will prove to be his fatal blunder. He has accepted an invitation from the brash Micah you-know-who — whom we have to thank for the plague of sores and the seas of blood — to personally speak at Petra to the million cowards who refused to express loyalty to me and yet ran like children when they had the chance."

"Excellency," someone said, "could you not have stopped them before they reached Petra?"

"Please do not interrupt! Of course we could have easily overrun them, but they have made it much easier and more economical for us. They are now all in one location, and as soon as Ben-Judah makes good on his promise, we will welcome him with a surprise. Or two. Or three. Security and Intelligence Director Suhail Akbar . . ."

"Thank you, Your Worship," Akbar said. "We are carefully monitoring the activities of the Judah-ites, and while we have not infiltrated the Jews at Petra, they have confined themselves to that area, saving us the work. We are prepared to rally two fighter-bombers when we know Ben-Judah is en route — we believe him to be only one or two hours from Petra anyway — and we should be able to drop one annihilation device from each craft directly onto Petra, literally within minutes of his arrival. We will follow with the launch of a missile that will ensure total destruction. That was scheduled to be launched from an oceangoing vessel but will now be launched from land."

Chang had to chuckle at the Intelligence area's falling for the clock ruse from Tsion's pirated TV appearance.

Carpathia took over again. "The Judah-ites have proven to be such hero worshipers and so dependent on the daily Internet babblings of Ben-Judah that his death alone may mean the end of that nuisance. While we are aware of other pockets and strongholds of Judah-iteism, we do not believe any other leader has the charisma or leadership required to withstand our unlimited resources.

"But make no mistake, my loyal friends. The Jew is everywhere. Is there one potentate here who would aver that you do not have a significant Jewish population somewhere in your region? No one, of course. Here is the good news, something to make you forget the inconvenience of this journey I required on short notice. I am opening the treasury for this project, and no reasonable request will be denied. This is a war I will win at all costs.

"Maintain your loyalty mark application sites and make use of the enforcement facilitators. But, effective immediately, do not execute Jews discovered without the mark. I want them imprisoned and suffering. Use existing facilities now but build new centers as soon as possible. They need not be fancy or have any amenities. Just make them secure. Be creative, and share with each other your ideas. Ideally, these people should either long to change their minds or long to die. Do not allow that luxury.

"They will find few remaining Judah-ites to sympathize with them. They will be alone and as lonely as they have ever been, even though their cell mates will be fellow Jews. There are no limits on the degradation I am asking, requiring, you to inflict. No clothes, no heat, no cooling, no medicine. Just enough food to keep them alive for another day of suffering.

"I want reports, gentlemen. Pictures, accounts, descriptions, recordings. These people will wish they had opted for the guillotine. We will televise your best, most inventive ideas. From time immemorial these dogs have claimed the title 'God's chosen people.' Well, they have met their god now. I have chosen them, all right. And they will not find even death a place they can hide.

"Apply for all the funds, equipment, rolling stock, and weapons you need to ferret out these weasels. The potentate who demonstrates the ability to keep them alive the longest, despite their torment, will be awarded a double portion in next year's budget.

"Questions?"

Twenty

George Sebastian had planned to wait to eat until he had his charges on board and was free in the air again, leaving Greece. Now, of course, hunger was the least of his problems, but weakness wouldn't help either. The Greeks, particularly the thugs who had ambushed him and — he assumed — the people with whom he had been expected to connect, hoarded their water supply. The news from the high seas had everyone rushing to lakes and rivers to stock up on freshwater fish. Water would soon be more valuable than gold.

His captors were well connected, he could tell that. After they drove more than forty minutes north, then about twenty east, if he still had his bearings, they plowed through softer soil, and he heard leaves and branches brush heavily against the Jeep. It sounded as if the vehicle he had appropriated was still behind them. George was grateful for his training, which had included blindfolding and mock torture. He had been astounded at how helpless he felt, even when he knew his own people were in charge. To be bound and blind, even knowing you weren't going to die, was a dreadful, sickening, fearful thing. He had been allowed to get hungry and thirsty, and the most harrowing part was being left alone long enough for his mind to play tricks on him. Back then he knew he was still in California, not far from San Diego, not far from home. But his timekeeping techniques, his mind games to keep himself calm and sane, quickly dissipated with the passing of the minutes, and the young, strong, healthy recruit began imagining it had been hours.

He wanted to take what he had learned from that trauma and use it in this one, but he hated to even recall it. Having no resources had been the worst. George had been considered one of the most creative and innovative soldiers in his platoon. When they were dropped into the middle of the woods thirty miles from base, wearing only shorts and boots, he was always the first one back. He could improvise, find his way based on shadows, foliage, intuition. He knew how to protect himself from the sun, to keep from walking in circles — somehow a common malady for people who had lost any sense of direction.

But being left in a dark room without so much as the sound of one other person breathing, no muffled sounds outside of officers or fellow recruits gossiping about how long he'd been there, that had been true torture. Though he had quickly freed himself from the bindings, he could not free his hands from each other. But he was able to stand and walk, getting a measure of the room, helping time pass by remembering songs and poems and birth dates and special occasions.

But when he ran out of all that and began losing count after two hours, he had been tempted to call out, to tell his fellow GIs that he had had enough, that he got the point, that it was time to return him to normal. But who did that, other than the weaklings, the washouts? He had to face that he too wanted to cry, to scream, to beg and plead, to kick at the wall, to ask if they hadn't forgotten him. He had succumbed to the temptation at long last to make noise so at least if he *had* been forgotten, they would be reminded and could save face by pretending it was all part of the drill.

He remembered what it was like to be hungry and thirsty and desperate, but there had always been that fail-safe. Deep in the recesses of his fast-unraveling mind had been the knowledge that this *was* training, this *wasn't* real, there was no real threat to his life and health and mind. No one was going to inflict permanent injury, no one would threaten his new bride, nothing would happen to his parents.

His superiors had trained the men in basic transcendental meditation, which most of them passed off as something for weirdos, druggies, and holy men from the East. Yet George had seen some benefit to thinking beyond his consciousness, or at least trying to. Even back then, even before becoming a believer in Christ, he didn't want anything to do with any religious aspects of meditation. But he did long to transcend this life, to reach a point beyond himself, to be able to park his senses and emotions on a plane where they would be safe from the threat of mere mortals.

It hadn't worked long then, and that was what he feared now. This was the real thing. While he regulated his breathing and told himself not to think about his hunger and thirst, they were things he could not blot from his mind. The more he tried, the worse they invaded.

He was nudged along in the night — no light whatever peeked through his blindfold — by the butt of a rifle, and as much as he tried to catalog all the information he could remember since the girl had clumsily frisked him and he had been jumped, his overriding emotion was shame.

No, he had not been the one who got the teenagers caught — along with anyone helping them. But while the assignment excited him, he had not treated it like a military operation. Back in the Negev, that was war, pure and simple — except when they had been surrounded by superior firepower and it went from armed conflict to no fair. It had done his soul good to see what happened to anyone who thumbed his nose at God. *Our general is better than your general,* he thought, *so game over.*

That almost made him smile. Why should he worry about the people who held him now when Michael the archangel could step in and make them faint dead away — if they were lucky?

He was held up briefly, then heard two doors open. He was nudged inside and sensed a light come on. A few more steps, another door, a musty smell, a shove from behind, steps leading down, but how many? He started carefully, feeling with his foot, but he was bumped again, rushed his feet hoping he would come to the bottom before he lost balance, and failed.

George didn't know how far he might tumble down these wood stairs. The best he could do was tuck his chin to his chest, clamp his eyes shut as tightly as possible, and draw his knees up to his chest. He counted two, three, four stairs, then hard-packed dirt. His momentum carried him a couple of rolls, and the whole way down, he expected to hit a wall or who-knows-what with some part of his body.

When he finally came to rest on his right side, he could hear from their footsteps that his feet faced his captors. He kept his knees drawn up and feigned more pain than he had. He groaned slightly and did not move. He waited until steps drew close to him, then thrust out both feet with all that was in him.

No one on his base could do squats with more weight, and no one could touch him in leg presses. Had he been able to see the man before him, he could have broken both his legs. But his thrust had found purchase on only one of the man's legs. The man cried out, something giving way in the knee, it seemed to George. The man went flying and rolled, his weapon clattering.

"Idiot!" the other man said, and George heard the girl stifle a laugh.

"I'll kill him!" the one on the floor said, grunting and whimpering in pain as he struggled to his feet and cocked his weapon.

"Stop it!" the other said. "He's our only link."

"Well, she didn't have to drop all three of them."

"What's done is done. He's it, so don't do anything stupid again."

"Again?"

"You don't think that was stupid? What are you doing over there?"

A muzzle at his neck. "Keep still there, big boy. Up we go." A hand on the cuffs, pulling until he had to get up or injure his arms. He was led to a chair and pushed back onto it. He had the impression only two of the men and the girl were downstairs with him. Footsteps upstairs. He tried to slow his breathing so he could hear. The one upstairs was talking, but no one was responding. He was on the phone, talking about the car — probably to the clerk who had lent it. Then he said something about the plane. George decided it would serve him right if they shot him right there. He had treated this assignment like a game and now had exposed the entire Tribulation Force. And, if these men had any credibility, the others in Greece had been killed.

Cigarette smoke. Blown in his face. *Please,* he thought. These people had seen too many movies. Maybe cataloging their gaffes would help. Someone squatted next to him, he assumed the second one down the stairs. The other would be wary for a while.

"We can make this hard or make this easy," the man whispered, and George couldn't help himself. He pressed his lips together hard, but he couldn't keep from giggling. He wanted to ask if they were going to try good-cop, bad-cop too, but he had resolved to say nothing.

"We know who you are, Mr. Sebastian," and George lost it. He laughed aloud, knowing what the next line had to be. "We know who you work for."

Trying to keep from laughing only made it worse, and he sat there, shoulders heaving, squealing to keep from guffawing. He took a backhand directly on the mouth, splitting his upper lip against his teeth.

George was almost relieved when that sobered him. He wiped his mouth on his shoulder, tasted blood, and spat. At least he wouldn't get himself killed for being unable to stop laughing. When the man said he would cut to the chase, trying to make it sound normal with his thick accent, George almost laughed again. But his stinging lips were swelling, and he had a hunch that would be the least of his pain by the time this was over.

"All we need to know is where we can find your people. Your information proves correct; you are free to go." As if they wouldn't kill him for not having the mark of loyalty. "We have them narrowed to the United Carpathian States."

George cocked his head ever so slightly. That had surprised him, and he didn't mind it showing, because he knew they would think he was shocked that they knew. It was no secret Tsion Ben-Judah would soon be on his way to Petra, so why did they care about anyone else?

"You might be more surprised by how much we know. Rosenzweig is no threat as long as he stays in the mountains. His assistant we know to be Cameron Williams, who illegally transmits over the Internet material subversive to the Global Community, a crime punishable by death. We know there is a mole connected to the Judah-ites some-

451

where within the GC. And the pilot who has disguised himself as a GC officer has pushed his luck too far. He has been linked with another Williams identity, who also passed himself off as GC and temporarily freed two rebel prisoners. We have reason to believe a former guard at the Buffer, now AWOL, may be connected with these people."

George wondered if they had made the connection between Ming Toy and Chang Wong. Maybe the fact that she had been married and now had a different last name would delay that realization. It would be only a matter of time, of course. Chang had to get out of New Babylon.

George's captor sounded as if he believed George was surprised by how much they knew. In fact, the opposite was true. Apparently they had never connected the crash of the Quasi Two with the Trib Force, and no one even knew it had been empty.

More smoke in his face. "So, you just tell us where to look, and when you are proved trustworthy, you go home to your family."

Most ironic of all, George would not have been able to give away the Trib Force if he'd wanted to. For his own safety, Rayford had told him only to fly Marcel and Georgiana to a Kankakee, Illinois, airstrip and that he would meet George there. Whether George accompanied them to the safe house, wherever it was, or flew on home to San Diego, would have depended on timing, weather, and any suspicion that might have arisen over whether the GC were onto him.

The man near him tried the next strategy in the hostage-taker's guidebook. He laid a hand gently on George's shoulder and whispered, "All we need is a specific location. No one knows where we got it, you go free, and everybody's happy."

The man had been so full of clichés that George was tempted to answer with one of his own: a bloody spit to the face. But if there was one thing he knew well, it was that apathy was more offensive than resistance. As long as he resisted, his captors knew they were getting to him. When he ignored them, they had nothing to grab on to, and the insult of not being taken seriously had to drive them crazy.

Ironically, George had learned that from his wife. He didn't mind when she argued with him. But when she gave up and said she didn't care, *that* got to him. Disengaging, he knew, was a cruel strategy. And he employed it now with a vengeance. He didn't shake his head. He didn't try to kick. Since he had shown a modicum of surprise over the man's asserting that he knew the Trib Force was in the local region, George had barely moved a muscle. The man had to wonder if he was even listening. In fact, he wasn't.

To keep from even the temptation of responding nonverbally, George began reciting silently the books of the Bible. Then his favorite verses. Then his favorite songs.

The Greek nudged him with his weapon, and George didn't want him to think he had dozed off. He raised his chin.

"Well, what will it be, Sebastian? You're refusing? At least say so. No? Tell me you've chosen not to say anything. You just want to give me rank and serial number? We already know your name. Come on. Not even that?"

Chang monitored all the various feeds and sites as he continued to listen to the Carpathia meeting recording. Most alarming was a list directed to Suhail Akbar that informed him of all the AWOL GC employees his department was aware of. Chang found his sister's name and deleted it, but he knew he might have been too late. How many knew that she was his sister? Perhaps not even Akbar. Moon had known. And Carpathia himself had known. Chang could only hope that such detail stayed below the potentate's radar level. Who knew what could come of it? Yes, he appeared to be loyal, even to the point of the mark. But if investigated, how long could he keep his parents and his sister out of it? Now wasn't the time, but one day soon he would have to raise the issue with Rayford Steele. He believed he could monitor the palace and GC headquarters from the safe house.

In the Carpathia meeting, someone responded to Nicolae's new emphasis on the Jewish question with a question of his own. "Does this mean you no longer want video-disc records of our beheadings?"

"Oh, no! That remains a more than enjoyable pastime. As you know, I no longer require sustenance or rest. I am able to take advantage of unlimited time while others eat and sleep. One of the benefits of godhood is the time to revel in the folly of my opponents. Sometimes I sit for hours in the night, watching head after head drop into the baskets. These people are so smug, so stubborn, so pious. They sing. They *testify*. Do you not just *love* that word? They testify to their god and against me. Ooh, that makes me feel so bad, so jealous. But then what happens? From fifteen feet above, that heavy, gleaming, razor-sharp blade is released. It takes one-seventieth of a second to reach the bottom of the shaft — did you know that? And the last two-hundredths of one second is all it takes to slice through the neck as if it were not there.

"I love it! The only problem, dear friends, is that if anything, the guillotine is too humane! For certain it is far too quick and deadly for the Jew. How far can you go in inflicting pain upon a man or woman before he or she dies? I want to know! I want you to report it to me with all the visual and audio evidence you can. And you know whom I want you to use as test subjects.

"For a special treat today, during our break we will witness the execution of the two insurgents we discovered serving on my own plane. We still search for the mole here at headquarters, but perhaps he or she will also see the beheadings today and will be flushed from hiding to plead for his or her life."

"The guillotine then, for these two?" someone asked.

"I know," Nicolae said. "Pedestrian. But we do not have a lot of time, and it will be a nice respite from the meeting."

Many of the others expressed agreement and excitement. Chang was sickened. He was tempted to download some of this bile for his mother, but it was too risky with his father still being such a Carpathia loyalist.

He held out a modicum of hope for them both, having not heard whether his father had followed through yet on their taking the mark in their own region. Until he was able to convince his mother and get to his father with hard evidence, he was persuaded that his father would turn him in in a heartbeat if he thought Chang was subversive.

Rayford called a meeting of the three remaining original members of the Trib Force, plus Tsion, in Tsion's study. "I hope we're talking about who's going to Petra with Dr. Ben-Judah," Chloe said.

"We are," Rayford said, "among other things." Tsion looked deep in thought as they settled in. "You all right, Doctor?"

"Troubled, I confess," the rabbi said. "I should not be surprised, but it seems we have come to a crossroads. I know we will lose more and more as we head toward the end, but it seems as if our tenuous bit of safety is unraveling fast."

"It is," Rayford said. "We know George can't give us up beyond pointing them in the direction of Illinois, but I don't think he'll do even that."

"Neither do I," Buck said. "They're not going to get a thing out of him."

"Except perhaps his life," Tsion said, sighing.

"What are we going to do about our new friends?" Chloe said.

"That's one of the reasons we're here," Rayford said. "It seems to me, as exciting and encouraging as it is to discover these wonderful new brothers and sisters, your escapade was reckless and could have cost us everything."

Chloe shot him a double take and looked as if she'd rather argue with him as her father than have to respond to him as head of the Trib Force. "All due respect, but I didn't know what stratospheric detection could tell the GC. Shouldn't we all be told that kind of stuff?"

"How were we to know you would venture out on your own?"

"Last time, I discovered the new safe house. And look what has come of this foray."

"You're lucky what came of it," Rayford said. "What if they had been GC or just lowlifes? We'd have lost you, probably the safe house, and thus our whole reason for being."

"I'm sorry, but now we have people we can help and who can help us."

"Did you think about sensitivities, Chloe,

such as maybe they don't want to move to our building, even though it would provide infinitely more safety and advantages? Maybe they don't want to become part of the Tribulation Force. They have been self-governing and self-sufficient up to now. Maybe they don't want to be used for dangerous missions, using aliases and all that."

"They *do* want to move here," Chloe said. "They *do* want to help with travel and assignments. But you're right. They want to maintain their own organization. They're comfortable with each other, and while they would like to have Dr. Ben-Judah's involvement, Enoch is their pastor and they want it to remain that way."

"So," Rayford said, "all the benefits of the Trib Force, but none of the responsibilities."

"Oh, they'll pay," Chloe said. "They'll work. They'll travel. They'll exchange all kinds of things for food and necessities, just like any other co-op members. It's not like they should owe us rent on a building we don't own."

"They've made a point about not answering to us?"

"No, I'm making that point. Is it a requirement that they be subordinate to you?"

"That's not it at all, Chloe. We just don't

have time for squabbles, lack of organization, confusion about responsibility."

Tsion held up a hand. "These are wonderful brothers and sisters, Captain Steele. I believe they will be a vibrant addition to the building and that we should take it a step at a time. See how it works while you and I are gone. I would not recommend using anyone new on this trip."

Chloe shook her head. "It's already been decided that it's you and Tsion?"

"No —"

"What's the point of a meeting about it if —"

"I said no, Chloe. Yes, Tsion and I are going. But others will go."

"Me included, I hope."

Rayford stared at her. "I might have hoped the same before you risked exposing us."

Chloe stood. "I don't believe this," she said. "The co-op can't go on without me? Buck can't watch Kenny?"

Rayford looked to Buck, not wanting to be parental when Chloe's husband was right there. "Careful, Chloe," he said. "Daughter or not, there's protocol."

Buck reached up and took her hand. "Don't talk yourself out of an interesting assignment," he said.

"I'm not looking for interesting," she said. "I'm looking for crucial."

"How does Greece sound?" Rayford said, and she sat. "I'm going to Petra with Tsion. I'll have a new look and a new name. As soon as the GC recognizes that I'm not Buck, we're guessing their attention will be on Tsion anyway. We need another flyer for insurance over there, so Abdullah will go. I wanted you and Hannah to go to Greece. You're the least exposed people we have, at least until we know for sure whether the GC still suspects Hannah and the others from the plane crash being at large. You would be less suspicious and threatening, being women."

"Who would fly us?"

"If we can get the logistics done, Chang will have a GC plane delivered to Crete. You two and Mac would split off there and head into Greece while Tsion and Smitty and I go on to Petra. You'll be posing as GC, and it'll be dicey without the mark. Mac will trail you and keep an eye on you, also posing as GC. Ideally we want at least one of you to talk your way into overseeing the Sebastian situation for the senior cabinet."

"How long will it take them to catch on to that?" Chloe said.

"It would work only as long as you made it

work. We all need to get with Zeke for new identities, papers, looks. All but you anyway. I don't think anybody knows what you look like. But how do I explain giving such an assignment to someone who pulled —"

"Captain," Chloe said, "let me do it to prove myself."

On instructions from the safe house in Chicago, Chang began building dossiers on everyone traveling to Crete, then to Greece or Petra. Rayford's height and weight and a close enough birth date were entered, along with identification that showed him to be a brother to Abdullah Smith's phony persona. Both would pose as Egyptians in full regalia. Fortunately, Abdullah had not shaved for nearly two weeks, and he would craft his long stubble into a goatee, which Zeke would tinge gray. Rayford would have his skin chemically darkened, allow a mustache to grow thick and dark, and wear glasses with small, round lenses.

Taking advantage of Hannah's dark coloring, Zeke was transforming her into a New Delhi Indian, rather than a Native American. Chloe could go as she was, but with a new name and Canadian roots.

Mac was the challenge. He would be

easily recognized as Carpathia's former pilot, so his coloring was altered to eliminate his freckles and the hint of red in his hair. He would also be issued glasses but would have to rely on bluster as a GC commander with a new name to throw off overzealous clerks.

"The biggest advantage you all have," Chang wrote Rayford, "is the decimated state of the GC around the world. 'We' are so understaffed, ill, and dying that maintaining strict security has become virtually impossible. Fortunately, in many areas, there are surplus vehicles, except in Israel, of course."

Once everything was in place in the computer, Chang listened to more of Carpathia's meeting while composing a nuanced — he hoped — message to his mother. The trouble was, she was not normally a woman attuned to nuances.

"We have our engineers working around the clock," Carpathia was saying, "on the water issue. All saltwater marine industries are dead, of course. We have lost hundreds of thousands of citizens, who may never be retrieved off the high seas. Vessels can go only so far through a liquid with such a thick, sticky consistency, and the diseases brought by the rotting carcasses of sea creatures may be our most serious health issue ever. Yes, worse than the boils and sores. People only wished they could die from those. The water crisis is again decimating our citizenry."

"Holiness," someone said, "in our region we have seen an alarming trend. Even those with your mark of loyalty are beginning to speak out in protest against you. We counter with the fact that this is not your doing, but you know people. They want to blame someone, and you become the target."

Before Carpathia could answer, Fortunato jumped in, and Chang thought he sounded like his old self. "This shall not be tolerated," he said. "I hereby decree and shall pass this word along to the priests of Carpathianism in all ten regions of the world that from this day forward, every citizen of the world shall be required to worship the image of their supreme potentate, their true and risen lord, when they rise in the morning, after they eat their midday meal, and before they retire at night."

"How shall we enforce such an order?" someone said.

"See to it," Carpathia said. "This, from the Most High Reverend Father, is inspired!"

"But, sir, there are still many who have

not yet even received the mark of loyalty!"

Fortunato again: "They shall surely die!"

"Reverend!" Carpathia said, admiration clear in his tone.

"I have spoken," Leon said, warming to his point. "The time is long past for delays and excuses. Take the mark of loyalty to the god of this world or die! Anyone found without the mark on his or her forehead or right hand shall be given immediate opportunity to receive it, and upon their rejection, shall be put to death by guillotine."

There was silence as Chang sensed the regional potentates were considering the ramifications.

Finally Carpathia spoke. "With one notable exception," he said.

"Well, of course, Excellency," Leon said. "You need not take your own mark of loyalty!"

"Oh, Reverend!" Carpathia said, clearly disappointed. "You were doing so well!"

"Forgive me, Your Worship. The exception?"

"The Jew! The Jew, Reverend Fortunato!"

"Of course!" Leon said. "As the potentate himself has clarified, the blade is too good for the Jew."

Chang finished his letter to his mother with the following:

Assuming that you and Father have yet to take the mark of loyalty, ask Father how he would feel about a ruling that said he must take it immediately or die. What does that do in the heart and mind of someone who would otherwise be a loyalist? Does it rob him of any satisfaction he might get out of pledging allegiance to a leader?

That is what is coming, Mother, and you and he may hear it soon after receiving this. As soon as the regional potentate for the United Asian States returns from New Babylon, you may expect just that ruling. The time has never been riper for seeking another object of one's devotion. It may seem riskier at present, but in the end it will make the difference between eternal life and death.

Twenty-one

Rayford had never doubted Zeke's brilliance or artistry, but the young man outdid himself over the next several days. Around the Strong Building, various members of the Tribulation Force and members of The Place shot double takes at the soon-to-leave crew as their looks changed daily. Rayford caught himself studying his own visage in the mirror, wondering how such a transformation was possible.

"Your young brother keeps going with this, Captain Steele," Enoch said, "and you'll find out what it's like to be a black man."

As the people from The Place moved in on another floor in stages, the two groups began to share meals and prayer times. Enoch promised that his people would pray for the Trib Force entourage every minute they were gone. "And then some of us want in on one of your trips. We wouldn't even have to be disguised. Nobody's expecting to see us."

The day before the flight overseas, the Global Community News Network announced a special appearance of Carpathianism's Most High Reverend Father Leon Fortunato. He had a message for the entire world, and it would be broadcast live over television, radio, and the Internet at noon Palace Time and every hour on the hour for twenty-four hours so all the peoples of the world would be able to see it.

At three in the morning in Chicago, per Rayford's invitation, everyone in the Strong Building, except the babies, padded out and gathered in the commons near the elevator, where they watched television. The announcement would have proved anticlimactic, because it only reiterated what had been announced regionally anyway, save for what happened — which would be blamed, unfairly in this case, on the ubiquitous but elusive palace mole.

"We go live now to the sanctuary of the beautiful Church of Carpathia off the palace court here in New Babylon and the Reverend Fortunato."

Leon had assembled a massive choir behind him, and as he stepped into the pulpit, clearly standing on a small riser to make himself look taller, he was in his finery. He had added to the purple and gray and gold busyness of the robe and tassels. On his pate perched an Islamic-looking, flattopped, head-hugging cap. It seemed to try to incorporate the sacred symbol of every historical religion Leon could remember, but the effect made him look like an exploding ringmaster.

He stood there feigning solemnity and dignity while the choir sang "Hail Carpathia"; then he spread his notes before him.

"Fellow citizens of the Global Community and parishioners of the worldwide church of our risen lord, His Excellency, Supreme Potentate Nicolae Carpathia . . . I come to you this hour under the authority of our object of worship and with power imbued directly from him to bring to you a sacred proclamation.

"The time has expired on any grace period related to every citizen receiving and displaying the mark of loyalty to Nicolae Carpathia. Loyalty mark application centers remain open twenty-four hours a day for anyone who for any reason has not had the opportunity to get this accomplished. Effective immediately, anyone seen without the mark will be taken directly to a center for application or the alternative, the enforcement facilitator.

"Furthermore, all citizens are required to worship the image of Carpathia three times a day, as outlined by your regional potentate, also under threat of capital punishment for failing to do so.

"I know you share my love for and dedication to our deity and will enthusiastically participate in every opportunity to bring him praise. Thank you for your cooperation and attention, and may Lord Nicolae Carpathia bless you and bless the Global Community."

Fortunato tried to finish with a half wave, half salute, but suddenly the lights went out in the church. They came back on just in time for everyone to see the choir stumbling over each other to flee and Fortunato falling off his little platform, trying to get up, and having to billow out the skirt of his robe to do it. All eyes seemed to be on something in the ceiling, but as the camera panned that way, something happened to the camera operator, and the picture shook and wobbled.

Text rolled across the bottom of the screen: "Please stand by. We have temporarily lost picture and sound." Yet the interior of the church was in plain sight. And while the camera seemed to be at a cockeyed angle, showing only the empty platform and choir loft, the sound of people stampeding out the doors was clear as well.

Suddenly superimposed over the screen was a face so bright it lit the room from the television. The voice was so loud that a woman sitting near Enoch reached up and turned the volume off. Yet the voice could still be heard.

"If anyone worships the beast and his image and receives his mark on his forehead or on his hand, he himself shall also drink of the wine of the wrath of God, which is poured out full strength into the cup of his indignation. He shall be tormented with fire and brimstone in the presence of the holy angels and in the presence of the Lamb.

"And the smoke of their torment ascends forever and ever; and they have no rest day or night, who worship the beast and his image, and whoever receives the mark of his name.

"Here is the patience of the saints; here are those who keep the commandments of God and the faith of Jesus.

"Blessed are the dead who die in the Lord."

The scene changed to the GCNN anchor desk in New Babylon, where a woman said, "We apologize for that malfunction, which should be ignored. We will now show again Reverend Fortunato's message in its entirety."

This time, as soon as the video rolled, the message from the bright visage overwhelmed it. Again the error message flashed but could not overcome the angelic announcement. Back at the GCNN desk the anchorwoman said the network would be off the air until further notice. But the instant the screen went dark, it came back on again with the message. Script from the network announced technical difficulties, but nothing could eradicate the shining face and the loud pronouncement.

Chang checked his computer, and there too the message played and played. He went outside into the hot sun, and there in the sky was the overpowering image of the angel of God. Chang dropped hard to his knees, panting, astounded that anyone anywhere in the world could doubt that Carpathia was the enemy of the one true God, and after this, they could doubt it only out of stubborn rebellion. He ran back in to e-mail his parents, only to discover they had already written him.

Your father says we will risk our lives, live in hiding, or face the death machines before we will take the mark. He is nearly suicidal over forcing you. I tell him you already sealed by God, and so is Ming. I will connect to Ben-Judah Web site. We will be worshipers of God and fugitives. Pray.

Rayford knew it was folly to expect his people to rest during the day in anticipation of an early-evening flight from Chicago to Cyprus, then to Jordan. But they tried. Having their new friends from The Place in and out all day — singing, praying, and having church — was like a prelude to heaven. Before they piled into the Humvee, in which Buck would deliver them to the aircraft, the whole group huddled in a huge circle on their knees, praying.

George Sebastian's training was out the window by now. The resolve, the meditation techniques, the strength of character had been scraped away, replaced by hunger, thirst, loneliness, and, yes, fear. His silence had brought blows, none enough to do permanent damage, he knew, at least not yet. But his forehead and the back of his head had been butted enough times by the stock of a rifle that pain echoed through his skull.

George had been laced across the shoulders and shoulder blades repeatedly by what felt to him like the chain off a bicycle or motorcycle. Finally a fist struck him in the cheek and the jaw so many times that he knew he would never look the same. He tried and tried to time the swings and punches from his captors so that he could move with the blow. Finally he got the idea to do the opposite. When he sensed a fist was coming, heard the inhale of the assailant, felt the air movement, he lifted his chin and took it square. Just before he hit the floor and lost consciousness, he knew he had succeeded. Sleep, in any form, had to cover his body's ravaging need for food and water.

They had not been able to get to him with talk of his family. He knew better than to think his family would be any safer if he talked. If they really knew where his wife and child were, they could easily already be dead. He had despaired of his own life by now too. As long as he would wake up in heaven, there was no sense in giving up a thing.

The power to maintain silence had not come from within, but from without. He had, at long last, surrendered to God even whatever resources he thought he had. He came to on the cold floor in a corner with no idea of the passage of time, only that his middle was racked with hunger, his throat desiccated.

His captors argued. "Do you want him dead? You get us killed if we lose him. Give him some water. Enough to keep him alive anyway."

A few drops on his lips felt like a fresh spring, but he forced himself not to drink it in for fear they would think it was enough to satisfy him. He let most of it dribble until they quit being stingy with the bottle. He grasped the neck of it with his teeth and sucked as hard as he could, filling himself with enough to refresh him before they twisted it away. Then they pulled him back to the chair and resumed.

Abdullah landed at what was left of the airport at Larnaca on Cyprus midmorning. Albie's contact had recommended it as one of the least patrolled airstrips in the United Carpathian States. He proved dead-on. And he was waiting with a craft, appropriated by Chang's computer magic, that Mac would fly to Greece and land at an abandoned strip Chang had located some eighty miles west of Ptolemaïs. He had forged an order to a local GC operative, requiring him to deliver six Peacekeeper vehicles to an earthquake-damaged vacant lot a half mile from there. The memo came back to the bogus New Babylon commander: "You're out of your mind. Best I can do is one."

"Watch your tone," Chang's imaginary brass had answered. "One will do for now."

Rayford had not begun to seriously worry until he saw the stress on Chloe's face as they parted in Cyprus. Of course, it wouldn't have been natural if she wasn't scared. He wanted her on edge. But the open-endedness of their mission concerned him most. She and Hannah and Mac would fly in there, drive toward Ptolemaïs, and what? Start asking around and trust their GC identities? It sounded like suicide, but there was no way they would abandon George Sebastian as long as there was a chance he was still alive.

Rayford embraced her fiercely before she disembarked, wondering, his throat constricted, whether he would see her again. Chloe held on the way she had with Buck and Kenny in Chicago, and when finally she turned to go, Rayford feared he had not said enough. In fact, he had said nothing.

Toward Amman, Albie's friend took over the flying. As far as anyone knew, he was alone. Once he was in and down and hangared, Tsion, Rayford, and Abdullah would emerge from the plane and walk across the runway to the tarmac, as if appearing from nowhere. When accosted, as they would surely be, Tsion would ask to talk directly with Carpathia, offering hope for an end to the blood in the oceans if he and his two anonymous companions could borrow a helicopter for the trip to Petra.

All Rayford could think of was that the last non-Israeli he had sent into Petra had not come out. And yet he and his Operation Eagle forces had proved invulnerable to the attack of Carpathia's army. Whether it had to do with timing or location, he could not know. He just didn't want to jeopardize Abdullah's life, or his own, if he could help it. But he couldn't. The risk was there, and they were going.

Chang furtively monitored Suhail Akbar's and Nicolae's offices as he sat at his terminal. With the heat turned up and security forces combing the place for a mole, he had to be more careful than ever. He kept an eye on Figueroa's office and constantly covered his tracks. Finally pay dirt.

Director Akbar's secretary informed him that GC Security in Amman was calling, ostensibly with Tsion Ben-Judah on the line for Carpathia. "Put them on," Suhail said. When they were patched through, he insisted on talking with Ben-Judah personally. "How do I know it's really you?"

"You do not, sir," Tsion said. "Except that your own people are telling you it is I. I have a request of Carpathia and will ask it only of him."

"You would be wise to address him appropriately and formally, Dr. Ben-Judah."

"And then he will overlook the fact that I refer to him daily to a billion people as Antichrist, the enemy of God, and to Fortunato as his False Prophet?"

"Hold on."

Suhail told his secretary to give him time to get to Carpathia's office and to then transfer the call there. Two minutes later, Akbar sat panting in Nicolae's office when he hit the speaker button.

"Dr. Ben-Judah!" Nicolae began, as if to an old friend.

"I am requesting helicopter transport to Petra for myself and two associates without interference, in exchange for considering asking God to withdraw the plague of the seas having turned to blood."

"And why should I contemplate this?"

"You do not need me to tell you that. Surely your people are telling you that there has never been a time of greater resistance to you around the world. Renaming all of the oceans the Red Sea could not be in your best interest."

"If I have someone ferry you to Petra, the seas will return to water?"

"I do not speak on God's behalf. I said I would consider asking him."

"You would only consider it?"

"I will ask. He will consider it."

"Granted."

"But we need only the aircraft. Not a pilot."

"*Real*-ly. Granted."

Tsion hung up. Carpathia said, "You are welcome. Suhail, how long to Petra from Amman by helicopter?"

"I will see to it that they are issued one that will get them there in no more than an hour."

"And everything else is in place?"

"Of course."

"I want the area leveled within minutes after his arrival and the missile to make sure within moments after that."

"I will merely give my fighter-bombers

time to get out of the way. They will make visual confirmation that he is there, drop their payloads, clear the area, and we will launch."

"From?"

"Ironically enough, Amman."

"Excellent. And the planes are equipped with videodisc recording devices?"

"Of course, but not only that."

"Something more?"

"We have arranged for you to watch live."

"Do not tease."

"A monitor will be in your office."

"Ooh! Oh, Suhail! Something to enjoy."

Had Rayford not been petrified, he might have enjoyed that Tsion looked the same in the Jordan sun as he did around the Strong Building. It was Abdullah and Rayford who looked like Middle Easterners in their robes. Tsion looked more like a rumpled professor.

"Who is your pilot?" a GC guard asked.

Tsion nodded to Abdullah, and they were led to a chopper. Once in the air, Rayford called Chloe. "Where are you?" he said.

"We're on the road, Dad, but something's not right. Mac had to hot-wire this vehicle."

"Chang didn't tell the guy to leave the keys?"

"Apparently not. And of course you know Mac. He's going to hop out and thumb a ride with some other GC while we drive merrily into town, trying to pass ourselves off as assignees from New Babylon to check on the Judah-ite raids."

"You ready?"

"Am I ready? Why didn't you make me stay in Chicago with my family? What kind of a father are you?"

He knew she was kidding, but he couldn't muster a chuckle. "Don't make me wish I had."

"Don't worry, Dad. We're not coming out of here without Sebastian."

When Abdullah came within sight of Petra, Chaim was in the high place with a quarter million people inside and another three-quarter million round about the place, waving to the helicopter. A large flat spot had been prepared, but the people covered their faces when the craft kicked up a cloud of dust. The shutting down of the engine and the dissipating of the dust were met with applause and a cheer as Tsion stepped out and waved shyly.

Chaim announced, "Dr. Tsion Ben-Judah, our teacher and mentor and man of God!"

Rayford and Abdullah climbed down unnoticed and sat on a nearby ledge. Tsion quieted the crowd and began: "My dear brothers and sisters in Christ, our Messiah and Savior and Lord. Allow me to first fulfill a promise made to friends and scatter here the ashes of a martyr for the faith."

He pulled from his pocket the tiny urn and removed the lid, shaking the contents into the wind. "She defeated him by the blood of the Lamb and by her testimony, for she did not love her life but laid it down for him."

Abdullah nudged Rayford and looked up. In the distance came a screaming pair of fighter-bombers. Within seconds the people noticed them too and began to murmur.

In New Babylon Chang hunched over his computer, watching what Carpathia saw transmitted from the cockpit of one of the bombers. Chang layered the audio from the plane with the bug in Carpathia's office. It became clear that Leon, Viv, Suhail, and Carpathia's secretary had gathered around the monitor in the potentate's office.

"Target locked, armed," one pilot said. The other repeated him.

"Here we go!" Nicolae said, his voice high-pitched. "Here we go!"

★ ★ ★

Tsion held out his hands. "Do not be distracted, beloved, for we rest in the sure promises of the God of Abraham, Isaac, and Jacob that we have been delivered to this place of refuge that cannot be penetrated by the enemy of his Son." He had to wait out the roar of the jets as they passed over them and banked in the distance.

"Yes!" Nicolae squealed. "Show yourselves; then launch upon your return!"

As the machines of war returned, Tsion said, "Please join me on your knees, heads bowed, hearts in tune with God, secure in his promise that the kingdom and dominion, and the greatness of the kingdom under the whole heaven, shall be given to the people of the saints of the Most High, whose kingdom is an everlasting kingdom, and all dominions shall serve and obey him."

Rayford knelt but kept his eyes on the bombers. As they screamed into range again, they simultaneously dropped payloads headed directly for the high place, epicenter of a million kneeling souls.

"Yessss!" Carpathia howled. "Yes! Yes! Yes! Yes!"

Epilogue

Rejoice, O Heavens! You citizens of heaven, rejoice! Be glad! But woe to you people of the world, for the devil has come down to you in great anger, knowing that he has little time.

Revelation 12:12, TLB

About the Authors

Jerry B. Jenkins (www.jerryjenkins.com) is the writer of the Left Behind series. He is author of more than one hundred books, of which eleven have reached the *New York Times* best-seller list. Former vice president for publishing for the Moody Bible Institute of Chicago, he also served many years as editor of *Moody* magazine and is now Moody's writer-at-large.

His writing has appeared in publications as varied as *Reader's Digest*, *Parade*, in-flight magazines, and many Christian periodicals. He has written books in four genres: biography, marriage and family, fiction for children, and fiction for adults.

Jenkins's biographies include books with

Hank Aaron, Bill Gaither, Luis Palau, Walter Payton, Orel Hershiser, Nolan Ryan, Brett Butler, and Billy Graham, among many others.

Eight of his apocalyptic novels — *Left Behind*, *Tribulation Force*, *Nicolae*, *Soul Harvest*, *Apollyon*, *Assassins*, *The Indwelling*, and *The Mark* — have appeared on the Christian Booksellers Association's best-selling fiction list and the *Publishers Weekly* religion best-seller list. *Left Behind* was nominated for Book of the Year by the Evangelical Christian Publishers Association in 1997, 1998, 1999, and 2000. *The Indwelling* was number one on the *New York Times* best-seller list for four consecutive weeks.

As a marriage and family author and speaker, Jenkins has been a frequent guest on Dr. James Dobson's *Focus on the Family* radio program.

Jerry is also the writer of the nationally syndicated sports story comic strip *Gil Thorp*, distributed to newspapers across the United States by Tribune Media Services.

Jerry and his wife, Dianna, live in Colorado.

Dr. Tim LaHaye (www.timlahaye.com), who conceived the idea of fictionalizing an account of the Rapture and the Tribulation, is a noted author, minister, and nationally recognized speaker on Bible prophecy. He is the founder of both Tim LaHaye Ministries and The Pre-Trib Research Center. Presently Dr. LaHaye speaks at many of the major Bible prophecy conferences in the U.S. and Canada, where his nine current prophecy books are very popular.

Dr. LaHaye holds a doctor of ministry degree from Western Theological Seminary and a doctor of literature degree from Liberty University. For twenty-five years he pastored one of the nation's outstanding churches in San Diego, which grew to three locations. It was during that time that he founded two accredited Christian high schools, a Christian school system of ten schools, and Christian Heritage College.

Dr. LaHaye has written over forty books, with over 30 million copies in print in thirty-three languages. He has written books on a wide variety of subjects, such as family life, temperaments, and Bible prophecy. His current fiction works, written with Jerry B. Jenkins — *Left Behind*, *Tribulation Force*, *Nicolae*, *Soul Harvest*, *Apollyon*, *Assassins*, *The Indwelling*, and *The Mark* — have all reached number one on the Christian bestseller charts. Other works by Dr. LaHaye are *Perhaps Today*; *Spirit-Controlled Temperament*; *How to Be Happy Though Married*; *Revelation Unveiled*; *Understanding the Last Days*; *Rapture under Attack*; *Are We Living in the End Times?*; and the youth fiction series Left Behind: The Kids.

He is the father of four grown children and grandfather of nine. Snow skiing, waterskiing, motorcycling, golfing, vacationing with family, and jogging are among his leisure activities.